Antonio's new plan had revolved around courting Liliana, breaking down her resistance in stages.

And with a single "okay," she'd thrown everything out of whack. He felt like he'd been pushing with all his strength against an immovable object when suddenly all resistance was removed.

Then she'd thrown him for a loop again by whisking off his tie. As the silk had hissed as if relieved to part with his shirt, her eyes had been turbid with so many emotions. He thought he'd seen shyness, uncertainty, resignation, recklessness… and hunger.

Then, she touched him.

She slipped that small, delicate hand beneath the shirt that suddenly felt on fire and slid her burning palm over his flesh. Dipping low, as if she was searching out his heart.

* * *

Billionaire Boss, M.D.
is part of
The Billionaires of Black Castle series:
Only their dark pasts could lead
these men to the light of true love.

BILLIONAIRE BOSS, M.D.

BY
OLIVIA GATES

First Published in Great Britain 2016
By Mills & Boon, an imprint of HarperCollins*Publishers*
1 London Bridge Street, London, SE1 9GF

© 2016 Olivia Gates

ISBN: 978-0-263-91877-9

51-0916

Our policy is to use papers that are natural, renewable and recyclable products and made from wood grown in sustainable forests. The logging and manufacturing processes conform to the legal environmental regulations of the country of origin.

Printed and bound in Spain
by CPI, Barcelona

USA TODAY bestselling author **Olivia Gates** has written over forty books in action/adventure, thriller, medical, paranormal and contemporary romance. Her signature is her über-alpha male heroes. Whether they're gods, black-ops agents, virtuoso surgeons or ruthless billionaires, they all fall in love once and for life with the only women who can match them and bring them to their knees. She loves to hear from readers always, so don't hesitate to email her at oliviagates@gmail.com.

One

"Lili...look alive! The boss man himself is about to arrive."

Liliana Accardi swung away from the microscope to impale her coworker with a glare, his rhyming—whether he meant it or not—annoying her.

But it was just as well he'd interrupted her. Instead of the gray-scaled cells she was supposed to be studying, she'd been seeing only red. Ever since she'd heard the news that would end all her professional and scientific dreams. No way was she rushing off to go stand in line while said new "boss man" inspected them like a shepherd inspected his newly acquired flock.

Brian Saunders raised his hands in a "don't kill the messenger" gesture. "I just think you should come, if only to get firsthand word on the direction of his management. Maybe he'll allow you to carry on with your work, after all."

"Yeah, sure. From what I've read about him since I

started my morning with the delightful news of his take-over, Antonio Balducci rules his empire with a steel fist. He'll never allow me independence."

Brian spread his arms. "You know me, I never say never." At her hardening glare, he grinned. "I'm in the same hijacked boat as you. I just decided to deal with my captivity and go on the journey with a different attitude."

She huffed, deflating in her chair.

Brian was right. He was just another victim of the tsunami takeover. She should save her wrath for their new boss.

But Balducci wouldn't be *her* boss for long. Not if he insisted on sweeping years' worth of work and results under the rug and forcing them to dance to his profit-hungry tune.

Despite a medical degree, two master's degrees and lucrative offers, she'd spent years at Biomedical Innovation Lab with a salary that barely paid the bills. All to do marginalized but necessary research.

Until Balducci Research and Development opened its bottomless maw and swallowed them whole. They now sloshed deep in its belly among other chomped-off acquisitions.

What most galled her was the humiliating speed with which everything had been initiated and finalized. The commercialized global whale, a major tentacle of the Black Castle Enterprises leviathan, had assimilated them in mere hours.

Antonio Balducci, the billionaire celebrity surgeon, had tossed a hundred million dollars their way—chump change for him—and once again proved that money was the most powerful incentive on earth.

"Uh-oh." Brian took a step back as he spoke. "You've got that look on your face."

She frowned. "What look?"

"The one you get when you've decided to go to war."

She huffed a chuckle, half amused, half embarrassed. "I didn't realize I was *that* easy to read. After all the years I spent battling my verbal incontinence, thanks for letting me know I've only developed the mental and emotional variety."

An indulgent smile lit up Brian's genial face. "You're just straightforward and spontaneous."

She rolled her eyes. "Which are the PC words for unrestrained and blunt."

"And it's something everyone is thankful for."

She groaned. "You mean it's not only you as my best friend who can see through me? Everyone else can read me like a ten-foot neon sign?"

Brian's grin was appeasement itself. "And they love you for it. In a world full of pretense and games, you're a rarity and an incredible relief. Not to mention extremely cute."

"An outspoken five-year-old is cute. A transparent thirty-one-year-old is not."

Brian wrapped an arm around her shoulder and gave her an affectionate squeeze. "You'll be cute when you're a hundred and thirty-one." He pulled her up. "Now let's go meet our new boss. I have a feeling this won't be as bad as you think."

Taking off her lab coat, she tossed him a challenging glance. "I bet you it's worse."

"You're on." He never could resist a challenge. "If I'm right, you go on a date with one of the restless bachelors that plague my serenely married existence."

Unable to resist Brian's infectious good cheer any longer, a smile spread Lili's lips. All nine of Brian's brothers and brothers-in-law were either single or divorced. He and his wife, Darla, were always trying to set them up.

"But if I'm right," Lili said, "you strike me off your list

of possible bachelordom cures. I'm the last woman on earth you should consider for such a task, anyway."

"I know, because you'll never get married. You've told me a hundred times." He grinned knowingly. "All the women who turn out to be the best wives say that. Including Darla."

Lili stifled a scoff. "You're comparing me to Darla, the paragon of domesticity and motherhood, and a savvy businesswoman to boot, when I can barely manage a single life that consists of work, exercise, sleep, study, rinse and repeat?"

"Details, details." Brian winked as he held the door open for her. "You could well be twins where it counts."

She shook her head, but let him have the last word. She was nothing like Darla or any other woman born with the ability to conduct intimate relationships or nurture families. Like her mother. And she'd long been at peace with that.

So she was confident she'd win their bet, and at least one good thing would come out of their current mess. Brian would finally stop trying to shove her into his version of a fulfilling existence.

As she passed him on her way out of the lab, she swept it in one last regretful look.

If things went according to her projections, as she was certain they would, this would be the last time she saw it.

Their new boss was late.

As she sat in her usual seat halfway down the conference table, Lili fumed.

Either Balducci had met his demise—and they couldn't possibly be that lucky—or he didn't consider them worthy of his legendary punctuality. And that boded even worse for them than she'd expected.

Her bleary gaze scanned the room. All thirty of the BIL

employees were there and unlike her, they'd all clearly run back home to dress for the occasion, leaving only her in an appropriately drab-as-her-mood outfit. Also unlike her, they seemed relieved, even excited at the takeover. Even hating this as much as she did, Lili realized why. She had been feeling the toll of the obstacles they'd had to tackle continuously to do what other better-funded labs did in a fraction of the time. But to her, setbacks, false starts and near misses were an expected part of scientific endeavor. It seemed her attitude hadn't been shared by the others as she'd thought, and she was the only one with a purely negative stance on the takeover. And a hostile one toward the man behind it.

Everyone else was awed by the very mention of the legendary Dr. Antonio Balducci. The buzz she was sensing wasn't only over any favorable expectations with him at the helm, but also over the opportunity of meeting him in the flesh. The ladies especially looked aflutter at the prospect. From her online research of him, she grudgingly conceded their reaction was the normal one, not hers.

Since she reserved her curiosity for scientific matters, she'd barely known a thing about him before she'd heard the news. After she had, she'd gone through the stages of shock, denial and fury, and through everything she could find on him on the net.

To her surprise, she found three parallels with him from the first thing she read. Like her, he was a doctor, and he'd been born to an Italian father and was an only child. But that was where their similarities ended.

He was an American now, naturalized three years ago, while she was an American through her mother. Both his parents were long dead, while her own mother had died only a year ago, and her father who had never existed in her life, had recently—and to her continuing surprise, very enthusiastically—reentered it.

Pulling her thoughts away from that development, she turned them to the man at hand.

Not much was known about Antonio Balducci's early life. He was raised in Austria, his mother's homeland, where he became fluent in six languages and where he lived until he graduated from medical school. It was only about eight years ago that information about him, staggering in quantity and quality, had started pouring in.

That was when he'd shot onto the world scene, an awe-inspiring figure whose success in every field he entered was phenomenal. Being a founding member of the global juggernaut Black Castle Enterprises was meticulously documented, as well as his founding of the conglomerate's medical R & D business—the arm of his empire that had taken over her beloved lab.

Adding to his lure for the media was his effect on the females of the species. Women went nuts over him like they did over music and soccer legends like Presley and Beckham. If she'd thought his effect a media exaggeration, she was seeing empirical evidence of his irresistibility to women right before her eyes. And that was before he actually arrived.

But all that wasn't what he was best known for. Most of his fame stemmed from being sought after by the world's elite to perform or even consult on their rejuvenations. But his *biggest* achievement was being hailed as a trauma and reconstructive surgical god whose work bordered on magic.

She ground her teeth together. The only magic she thought Balducci practiced was the black kind. To her, he was the capricious force who was pulverizing everything she'd worked for, just because he could.

And the damned man dared be late for her destruction! Suddenly conversation was cut off as if someone had hit Stop. She looked up and saw all eyes glued to the doorway behind her. That meant...

She swung around to catch the moment when the man who'd quashed her ambitions bulldozed into her territory. And it was her turn to feel she'd been caught in a stasis field.

As everything decelerated to a standstill, a mental protest went off inside her mind.

No one should be all that, and look like that, too. Is there no fairness in this world?

Gaping and unable to do anything about it, she stared at the figure in the doorway. In a slate-gray suit that molded to a body that belonged to a world-class athlete, not a surgeon and entrepreneur, Antonio Balducci dwarfed the room with his physical and personal presence.

While viewing his photos online, she'd dismissed the possibility that he looked that good in real life, believing he'd had his photos touched up or he'd achieved his perfection surgically.

But even across a packed room, she knew neither of that was true. If anything, the photos had downplayed his looks. And she could discern surgical interventions from a mile away and she had no doubt whatsoever that every one of Antonio Balducci's jaw-dropping assets was authentic.

At forty, the man had skin that looked like an alloy of polished copper and bronze. The tensile medium was pulled tight over a masterpiece of bone structure. Her fingers itched to indulge in a much-neglected pastime and sketch its every detail: the leonine forehead, the patrician nose, the slashing cheekbones, the powerful jaw and cleft chin.

After transferring the framework of his unique face to paper, she'd linger over every hair framing his majestic head, the most robust mass of raven silk she'd ever seen. But among all those wonders, two things transfixed her.

The wide, sculpted lips bowed in a mysterious quirk. And his eyes.

Apart from their amazing shape and startling blueness, it was what they conveyed that sent her heartbeat into disarray. Contrary to the opacity of his smile, his gaze radiated an amalgam of expressions. Amusement and austerity. Curiosity and superiority. Astuteness and calculation. And a dozen other things she couldn't decide on.

Those were the eyes of a scientist. But equally they were the eyes of a conqueror.

Which probably summed him up just right.

As he walked into room, déjà vu struck her.

Among his photos, one in particular had arrested her. A rare shot of him and his partners in Black Castle Enterprises.

They'd been captured as they'd exited their opulent New York headquarters en masse. It was an unrehearsed shot that was far more hard-hitting than any posed shot could have been, and it had earned its photographer instant fame.

The photo had captured their essence in such starkness that when it was published, Black Castle stock prices spiked to unheard-of levels. The men looked like a pantheon of warrior gods who'd descended to earth in the guise of ultramodern businessmen. The array of sheer male power and beauty in that photo was breathtaking. It had clearly robbed the whole world of breath.

Yet even among those gods among men, Antonio had stood out.

Not only had his brand of gorgeousness thrummed the chords of her specific taste, something else had fascinated her on a fundamental level. Though they were all extraordinary, she'd felt he had an edge over the other men. Even in the remoteness of a photo she felt he had the coolest head, the most deliberate mind. Even in her fury, that had appealed to her so fiercely she'd found herself saving the photo for leisurely inspection at a later date, maybe even as material for a future illustration.

And here he was in the impossibly perfect flesh, the epitome of splendor and sangfroid.

She wouldn't be surprised if he belonged to some next-step-in-evolution elite who'd eliminated all human frailties and imperfections and who operated on pure, merciless intellect.

He now stopped at the table and leaned his six-foot-plus frame to flatten his palms on its shining surface.

Seething with renewed resentment at his effect on her, she followed his serene gaze as it swept the room. From the chain reaction she felt going off around her, he seemed to be making eye contact with everyone. Everyone but her. His gaze skipped over her as if she were a blank space.

After the momentary consternation of being passed over, she was relieved. If his mere presence provoked those reactions in her, she didn't want to find out what she'd feel if that all-seeing gaze bored into her.

Once he'd had them holding their breath, he inclined his head. "Thanks for accommodating me at such short notice. I'm glad you could all make it."

Man, that voice. If everything about him weren't too much already, that darkest vocal spell would have been bad enough on its own. Making it even worse was an ephemeral accent that intertwined through its meticulous articulation, deepening its impact.

As murmured responses rustled around the room, he straightened to his towering height.

"I don't want to hold you up, especially those of you whose schedule is nine to five, so I'll get right to the point of my visit." A perfectly timed dramatic pause. "I hope you're as optimistic as I am about the new state of affairs, and will find working under the Balducci umbrella a rewarding experience, scientifically and financially."

He spread a prompting smile around the room and Lili saw everyone grin back at him like hypnotized fools.

Without taking his eyes off the assembly, he gestured to someone she realized had been behind him all along. The shorter man in turn directed four people behind him to come forward. They had piles of folders, which they passed around the room. When it was her turn to receive one, she stared down at the inch-thick glossy volume graced with Balducci's distinctive serpent logo.

"In your hands is comprehensive info on Balducci's operations," he explained. "As well as the mission statement for its new merger with your facility." Merger, huh? Big of him to call his incursion that. "Until you read everything in detail, let me give you a brief summation.

"I founded Balducci R & D to furnish the world with visionary medical solutions. A dynamic, adventurous and fast-paced researching, manufacturing and distribution organization specializing in state-of-the-art products and technologies in a number of leading medical fields. My aim remains to provide the medical community with unparalleled clinical products that set the trend in medicine. For six years, Balducci has been the primary supplier, to hospitals, clinics and research institutions, of advanced medical solutions in a variety of fields. With a constantly growing global team of the best the world has to offer in their disciplines, which I'm proud for you to be a part of now, we provide exceptional value, service and support much above the industry standard. And we achieve the highest customer retention rates in every market we currently dominate. But there are new frontiers I aim to conquer." Yeah, just what she'd figured. "And this is where you come in."

Everyone sat up, taking even closer notice. The man really had masterful timing and delivery.

When he'd made sure everyone was hanging on his

every breath, he went on, "I don't need to tell you that your team is composed of some of the most avant-garde researchers of our time. I have no doubt you're well aware of your individual and collective worth. I certainly am best equipped to know it. I'm still suffering from the very sizable hole in my assets it took to acquire your services."

As chuckles of pleasure spread through the room, Lili's hackles rose higher. What was wrong with her colleagues? They were proud they had a price? Sure, he pretended "acquiring their services" had taken a toll on him, but they all knew this was untrue. The man was worth over a dozen *billion* dollars!

Then he spoke again, dousing her new spurt of irritation.

"The methods and results you've contributed to the medical community working with limited funding and resources is nothing short of astounding. Each and every one of you is exactly the kind of unique-approach, enterprising scientist that Balducci covets. As you'll see from the documents you have in your possession now, each of you has been assigned to a project I believe you're most suited for, where you'll have anything you could possibly want to make progress in it, and hopefully reach a breakthrough. And let me be clear. By anything, I do mean *anything*. My assistants will be available to provide any of your needs. But my own door is always open if what you need is too ambitious, as I hope all your work with me will be."

By the time he finished, she was gaping again.

The man was overpowering. Velvet over steel over an enigma. Not only the most magnificent male she'd ever seen, but the most persuasive, too.

What he'd outlined was every scientist's fairy tale come true. Unlimited resources to be as adventurous as they wished, caring only about the work, while funding and

feasibility were being taken care of by dedicated experts
with access to bottomless pockets and powered by limitless ambition. His.

He'd almost convinced even her. Almost.

But if she had to fight his hypnosis with all she had,
she had no doubt the others were already in his thrall.
A darting glance noted the glassy eyes of those who no
longer questioned that his decreed path was the one to
tread. Even Brian had a budding hero-worship expression on his face.

"That would all be well and good, *if* you were offering
to fund our projects, not yours."

It wasn't until everyone swung to gape at her as if she'd
thrown a grenade on the table that she realized she'd spoken.

And she did it again, without intending to.

"In your R & D career, you've consistently ignored
basic research, what has produced centuries of history-
changing breakthroughs, spawned whole industries and
disciplines in medicine. You've also ignored the kind of
research we do, of untrendy ailments that don't provoke
public or market interest. You've overlooked necessary research for a jumble of popular, feel-good, cash-cow fields
like the cosmetic and weight-loss industries."

The elusive smile that had been hovering on his lips
suddenly froze.

All her blood followed suit.

Her heart thudding, she wished for some cosmic rewind
button so she could erase what she'd just said.

Why had she spoken at all? She'd already found out
her worst-case scenario would come to pass and they'd be
herded wherever he wished. She didn't do posturing con-
frontations. She knew her power, or rather, lack thereof.
So why hadn't she kept her big mouth shut and just tendered her resignation in silence?

Before she could draw another breath into her constricted lungs, he turned his head in her direction and impaled her on the lasers he had for eyes.

And all she could think was...uh-oh.

Two

Lili's heart plummeted as the world emptied of everything but this overwhelming entity who had her in his crosshairs.

Before she obeyed the flight mechanisms that screamed for her to run, tossing a "Don't bother firing me, I quit" over her shoulder, Antonio Balducci started talking, pinning her down even more.

"As my reconstructive surgeries do incorporate an aesthetic element, I do invest in the development and manufacture of all aesthetic disciplines and products."

His voice. That perfectly modulated melody of cultured lethality. A glacial sound of hair-raising beauty. Pouring all over her like a freezing/searing deluge.

Oh, crap. She hadn't thought this through. Hadn't thought at all. That bitter outburst had just...well, burst out of her. What if he got verbally combative?

She'd flay him right back, that was what. Before she ran.

But before she snatched the next breath, still transfixing her with that impossibly blue stare, he went on, serene and far more menacing because of it, "As you'll see from the info I provided, only twenty percent of my operations focus on the 'popular, feel-good, cash-cow' side of my specialty."

Whoa. He was quoting what she'd said. When she'd thought he'd only realized she'd been talking—and criticizing him openly—just before her tirade ended.

But he hadn't only heard her, he'd memorized what she'd said. He'd even *sounded* like her when he'd quoted her. She had a feeling he could recite everything she'd said word for word. Which shouldn't surprise her. It only substantiated her theory of him being some sort of post–human being.

His eyes bored into her, making her feel he'd drilled a hole into her skull and was probing her brain. "The remaining eighty percent of my operations revolve around the more relevant sides of my field of interest, and those of others. Problem is those don't generate media coverage or capture the market's imagination. This is just the state of the world. I didn't invent it."

"No, you just exploit it."

At her volley, he tilted his head, as if plunging deeper into her mind. Then those chiseled lips twitched and her stuttering heart burst into a stumbling gallop.

"The pursuit of luxury products tends to trump necessary ones and 'cash cows' are such for a reason. Alas, human beings will be human beings. I assure you, I have no role in their condition. So what would you have me do? Not provide them with what they wish for? Judge their foibles and let someone else reap the benefits of catering to them? Benefits I eventually put to uses you might deem to approve of?"

Was he teasing her? Nah. He couldn't be.

"And aesthetic concerns are not frivolous luxuries. No matter how *you* view them, they do greatly affect people's psychological and mental health. I don't morally grade what people need or consider worth paying for. Who's to say that products that reverse the signs of aging aren't as important to a substantial percentage of people as depression treatment? And would you view me and my business any kinder if you knew I also research the latter? And am involved in actual aging reversal research, too?"

Okay, he *was* teasing her. Poking fun at her, more like, making her criticism sound misinformed and holier-than-thou, or at the very least naive. And seeming to draw appreciation from everyone in the room while at it, adding to the unhealthy awe he'd already garnered.

He only made her feel like a hedgehog with its bristles standing on end. Mostly because she found her own lips twitching, too.

So, the man had a sense of humor. Had he come complete with it, or had he had it grafted as another weapon in his overflowing arsenal? Or did he realize the benefits of manipulating lesser beings with the illusion of ease and indulgence, and had a subroutine written into his program that he could activate at will?

"Among the commendable-by-your-standards investments I can afford to make with the profits of not-so-commendable ones, there are ones in my own field. Restoring functionality, for instance. Thanks to the money-generating machines, I can invest heavily into integrated prosthetics, microsurgery appliances and research, scar prevention and treatment, and lately, muscle and nerve tissue regeneration. *That* endeavor will be the main focus of this facility in our collaboration. I'm not even putting a limit to the budget for this one. Whatever it takes to reach a breakthrough, I'll provide the resources."

Then just as he'd given her his undiluted attention, he took it away, making her feel as if he'd taken the chair and the ground beneath it right out from under her.

Before she realized she had a response to his rebuttal, she found herself sitting up, her pose confrontational, her tone even more challenging. "Well, it's all quite laudable, I'm sure, that—while not advancing basic science as only someone of your clout and resources can—you invest in advancing your field. But 'this facility' already has its own array of 'commendable' projects under way, and it would be a loss that can't be measured in money if we shelved them to head in the direction where you point us. Just because you acquired our services doesn't mean you can cancel all our efforts, or should dictate which breakthrough is worth benefiting from our expertise backed by your unlimited funds and clout."

This time everyone in the room turned to stab her on the pointy edge of their disapproval. The canny man had already won them over to his side, promising them shiny new projects, not to mention endless means to frolic in the land of scientific possibilities to their hearts' content.

This time, Balducci didn't give her the courtesy of a response. His argument had been designed to win her over, or at least chastise her. From her renewed attack he must have decided further response wouldn't make a difference. As the epitome of pragmatism someone of his success must be, he'd decided she wasn't worth the extra effort. He wouldn't waste more time on a dissenting cog now that he was certain he had the rest of the machine wagging its components awaiting his directives.

Turning his attention to the rest, he directed everyone to read the folder carefully. Everyone's roles and projects for the next year were spelled out to the last detail. Tomorrow would be the first working day under the new management, and he would be available at the provided email or phone number for any questions, concerns or minor adjustments. Any major suggestions would be discussed in the next general meeting. He closed by thanking everyone in such a way as to have them swooning all over again before he dismissed the assembly.

Everyone rose to shuffle around him, waiting their turn to catch his eye or shake his hand. Lili cursed them for the limpets they'd turned into, and cursed him for turning them into such. Still, she was thankful for the milling crowd that gave her the cover under which to escape. Snatching her bag up, leaving the folder behind, she rose. Head down, giving him the widest berth she could, she made a beeline for the door. To her dismay, he was making short work of everyone, and those he'd dismissed were already squeezing out of the room, hindering her escape. She barely curbed the urge to push through them and forced herself to take her turn walking out. Still she bristled at the censure and pity in their oblique gazes, but mostly at *his* disconcerting vibe at her back.

In minutes, she burst out into LA's summer afternoon. She usually hated the transition from the beloved seclusion of her lab and the building's controlled climate to the hot, humid bustle of the sprawling city. But now she was relieved to be out of what had become a place she'd hate to set foot in again. The place that was now Antonio Balducci's.

She'd reached her Mazda in the parking lot when she felt as if an arrow had lodged between her shoulder blades.

It was his voice. Calling her.

What the hell!

Though her hand froze in midair with the remote, her thoughts streaked ahead. Did she dread him so much, like a kid dreads the headmaster singling her out, that she was imagining it? Even if he had called her, he must be here only to get his car, too.

In the next millisecond her analytical mind negated that theory. Antonio Balducci wouldn't use public parking. He wouldn't have driven himself here in the first place.

One of those people who followed in his wake like efficient phantoms must be his chauffeur. He couldn't have just stumbled on her. Which meant he must have pursued her specifically, and very quickly. Which made even less sense than any other theory.

As her mind burned rubber, his voice carried to her on the warm, moist breeze again, the very sound of forbearance.

"Dr. Accardi, I'd appreciate a word."

She swung around, her face scrunching against the declining sun in a scowl. "What for?"

She groaned at how petulant and aggressive she sounded. But this guy tripped all her wires. Watching him approach her like a sleek panther sent them haywire. He was so big he made the parking lot claustrophobic, so unhurried he made her feel cornered, so unearthly gorgeous he made her every nerve ache.

When he stopped two feet away, he siphoned the air from the world. Harsh sunlight struck deepest blue and indigo off his raven hair—which she realized had a smattering of silver at the temples—and threw his every feature in sharp relief, intensifying his beauty. She was sure she looked horrible in such unforgiving lighting, but Dr. Paragon here? He was even more perfect at such total exposure.

As the word *exposure* dragged her mind places it didn't want to go, she yanked it back and squinted way up at him even from her five-foot-eight height. She mentally kicked herself for not having her sunglasses as a barrier to hide behind, as protection against his all-seeing gaze. But since she always went home long after sundown, frequently not at all, she rarely packed them. As if they would have been an extra burden in her mobile home of a tote bag. But that was what she was—always ready for all possibilities in her work, and the personification of unpreparedness in her personal life. Which she now was in such a close encounter with the monolith before her.

Just as she thought he'd stare down at her until he melted her at his feet, he raised his hand, making her notice the folder he'd been holding all the time.

"I brought you this," he said. "You must have forgotten it."

He followed her to give her the folder she'd left behind?

Her mind raced to decipher him and his actions as her senses crackled with his nearness. When she spoke, she sounded exasperated, even if she was more so with herself. "No, I haven't forgotten it."

"So you left it on purpose."

"Apart from omission or commission, are there any other reasons I could have left it behind?"

One corner of his lips lifted in acknowledgment of her chastising logic, intensifying his already staggering effect. She hated to think how he'd look outright smiling or laughing.

"My apologies for the redundant comment. Will asking about the reason you did leave it meet with the same exasperation?"

She exhaled, trying to find the civil, easygoing person inside her who was generally in the driver's seat... and failing. "From what I read about you, and from the evidence of your achievements and power, you possess an unchartable IQ. I'm sure you need none of it to work out the reason I did."

"Indeed. Your motivation is quite clear. It was a material rejection to underscore your verbal one. I had just hoped it was a simple oversight on your part."

"And since you now know it wasn't, if this will be all..."

His forward movement cut off her backward one, along with her air supply again. "Actually, it won't be all. Bringing you the folder was incidental to the main reason I sought you out." He employed another of those pauses he used like weapons, making her bate whatever breath was left in her lungs. "I'd like to further discuss your objections to my policies."

She gaped up at him. That was the last thing she would have thought he'd say, or want. Not that she could actually think with him so near. She could only react.

Not finding any appropriate reaction, the first thing that surfaced in her mind was another accusation. "You said you didn't want to hold us up."

He gave a conceding tilt of his head that made his hair rearrange itself into another pattern of perfection. She could swear she heard the silk swish and sigh.

"I did make it clear I meant those who have a nine-to-five schedule. You're not one of those. In fact, you're the only one who almost makes this place your home."

She stared into his spellbinding eyes as he stared back with the same intentness.

How did he know that?

How? Because the man had a level of intelligence and efficiency she'd never before encountered. It stood to reason he'd researched the staff before he'd acquired them. Though she'd thought they'd be too insignificant for him individually, she had to revise that opinion. To reach his level of success he couldn't be a detached leader who left details to others. He had to be hands-on. Nothing and no one was too trivial or below his notice.

She wouldn't be surprised if he had invasive info on everyone who held or would hold any position in his businesses…and had memorized it, too. Thinking that disconcerted her on a primal level. Even if there wasn't much about her to know, just that he did know it put her at an even bigger disadvantage, if that was even possible.

"Nothing to go back home to?"

His quiet question surprised an unfiltered answer from her. "There never really was."

Her dismay deepened at the contemplative cast that came over his gaze. She'd exposed herself even more, and she held him accountable for it, him with his damned hypnotic power.

But her consternation was swept away by the surge of memories. Memories of growing up with only her mother, who moved her around so much following her medical career she'd never stayed long enough in one place to form real friendships. Only when Lili had entered medical school herself had her mother finally settled in LA, just before she fell prey to early-onset Alzheimer's. Lili had gone back to live with her, before being forced to put her in a home for four years before her death a year ago. Her mother's house remained a place to crash when she wasn't working. Being a workaholic was what saved her from feeling lonely. It was the only other thing she'd inherited from her mother. Hopefully. Home had always been wherever she worked. This lab had been her home for the past three years. Her haven. Until *he* happened.

"There you go again."

"There I go what again?"

His lips spread wider. The ground beneath her tilted. "Using me as target practice for your poison-laced glances."

Choking on the heart that his smile yanked into her throat, she shrugged. "They're just dipped in heavy tranquilizers. Or loaded with fifty thousand volts."

At that, he did something she'd dreaded in theory, but had thought would never come to pass in reality. Not in her presence.

He threw his head back and laughed.

And his laughter was...horrible. It did terrible things

to her insides, had her hormones rushing in torrents in her system.

Great. Just great. Just when she discovered she had those kinds of hormones after all, they had to be activated by him of all men. And in broad daylight. When he was laughing his magnificent head off at her, no less.

To make things worse, one big, elegant hand rose to wipe his left cheek. He'd laughed so hard, it had wrung a tear from his eye. Fantastic.

But what was really worth marveling at was how moisture smeared his hewn flesh. Her thoughts caught fire imagining him drenched in exertion, during or after he'd—

Shaking away the sensual images only lodged them deeper into her brain. Her tongue tingled with until-now unknown urges—the sudden longing to drag him down to her, so she could trace that cheekbone, taste his virility. Only his hand combing back the hair that had fallen over his forehead distracted her from those idiotic impulses. The hand of the virtuoso surgeon he was, powerful, graceful, skillful…in every possible way, no doubt—

For God's sake, stop. *Stop noticing his every detail and getting arrhythmia over each one!*

But in the absence of others, she had no buffer against his sheer charisma and sensual power—both of which she was certain he didn't even mean to exercise on her. A man like him must have them on all the time on auto. She'd never even thought men like him existed outside of legends and fairy tales.

After she'd become a jumbled mess, he sobered, the wattage of his smile dazzling her.

"So you don't want me dead, just incapacitated."

She fidgeted, her tote getting heavier by the second. "Ideally, long enough to remove you from my path. I want you gone from my world, not the one at large."

"That's big of you."

Nerves jangling at the outright teasing she could no longer mistake, she sighed. "When it doesn't come to my lab—yours now—I do recognize that, even if it's to your humongous advantage, you are a formidable force for good."

His eyebrows shot up. "Considering your views of me back there it's unexpected to hear you admit that."

"I'm a surprise a second. To myself most of all today. I sure didn't mean to say any of the things I said back there."

"So you didn't mean them?"

"I said I didn't mean to *say* them."

"So you did mean them."

"Can't mean anything more, in the context of my own concerns." She shot him a defiant glance, this man who'd detained her because he could do anything he wanted and have the world bend over backward to accommodate him. "You're sadly misguided if you think you'll get an apology or a retraction."

"You've given me both when you deigned to recognize my worth to the world."

"Still doesn't change the fact that I wish I had the power to make you disappear."

He shook his head, his grin widening, wreaking more havoc with her already compromised nerves.

"What do you find so funny now?" she mumbled sullenly.

"Not funny, delightful. You're definitely not the first person to wish to eliminate me, but you're the first to tell me so to my face."

"Hey, watch your terminology. You go around using words like *poison-laced* and *eliminate*, and if something ever befalls you, I'm a prime suspect. I only wish to be rid of your disruption. All I want is to go back to work tomorrow to the news that you've withdrawn your bid and let us be."

"And if a way presented itself for you to make this happen?"

"I wouldn't hesitate."

He gave another chuckle. "It doesn't seem you were handed discretion at the cosmic assembly line. Are you this blunt with everyone?"

Noticing the watchfulness that entered his gaze at this question, getting the feeling that he somehow didn't relish the idea, she shrugged a shoulder. "Not since I was a kid. Or at least I thought so, until just before you arrived and Brian told me I'm transparent. I thought it was only my expressions that everyone could read, that I wasn't as incontinent verbally, then you started your hypnotic session and I felt my colleagues being assimilated into your hive mind, and I...well, any tact I thought I cultivated evaporated."

"You don't like this about yourself." It was a statement, not a question. "You should. In fact, you should continue being as outspoken about the grievance you have with me. I have a feeling it goes beyond objecting to the change in course I'm proposing."

She almost snorted. "Proposing? You mean dictating. And you think that's not enough for me to consider you and your takeover the worst thing that could happen to this place?"

"I didn't get the impression anyone else shared that unfavorable opinion."

This time, she did snort. "Of course, you didn't. You must be surprised there was even one dissenting voice." Her blood frothed again at how her colleagues had succumbed to him without even a fight. "You know very well the effect you have on people."

"I only noticed the inflammatory one I had on you."

"Yeah, well, I guess I'm the mad scientist type."

"Aren't you all supposed to be that?"

She exhaled. "I thought so. But the promise of open-ended coddling proved irresistible to my colleagues."

"But not to you."

Her shoulders hunched with futility. "Yeah."

The blue of his eyes seemed to intensify. "Why? What makes you so resistant? Why is the promise of everything you've ever dreamed of at your fingertips not as alluring to you?"

"I told you why in agonizing detail and you already know I hate redundancy. Especially after you took such pleasure in deconstructing my argument and having the last word."

"I don't remember I had the last word."

"You didn't bother to have it. You just ignored mine."

"I chose not to engage you again in front of everyone, decided to do so in private. As I am doing now."

"You shouldn't have. I have nothing more to say."

"So do you only take exception to leaving your own project behind?"

"I take exception to being forced to."

"Your results won't evaporate if you shelve them for a while."

"I see no reason to while I'm making progress."

"There are many reasons, scientific and financial. You'll also gain expertise working on my projects, your own work would eventually benefit."

"If you think I need expertise you shouldn't want me working on your projects."

"I meant added expertise. I wouldn't have paid all that money if I thought you were anything but the best."

She waved his placating response away. "You didn't pay anything for me. That hundred million—"

"*Two* hundred million. Half of which is funding for phase one of all the projects I have planned for you."

She forced her open mouth closed. "What's a hundred million dollars more, huh? But whatever you paid was for our collective services and obedience, probably for the rest of our lives. Now that you've found one troublemaking apple in your bushel, you can always toss it out."

"I have no intention of tossing you out."

"Well, I intend to jump out of the cart myself."

His eyes narrowed. "You're contemplating quitting?"

"I'm done contemplating."

His expression went blank. But though there was nothing to read in it anymore, she felt she was getting the first real glimpse of what he hid beneath the polished exterior of the genius surgeon and suave businessman. Something lurked below his placid surface, something more sharp-edged than his state-of-the-art scalpels. *Someone* utterly ruthless. No, more. Someone lethal.

Which was stupid. Whatever else he was, this man was a healer. He didn't end lives, he saved them. All these feverish thoughts must be the sun frying her brain. Or was it such intense and close exposure to him?

Then he spoke again, sending her every hair standing on end. "It's clear contemplation has nothing to do with your decision. I wouldn't even call such a knee-jerk reaction one."

He again sounded like when he'd been addressing their assembly, making her realize how deliberate and calculated he had been in comparison to how he'd been talking to her now. He had been out to subdue and mesmerize everyone. He was trying to make her bow to his will now.

Well, he should have realized by now that his tried and true methods only backfired with her.

Bent on walking away this time, she stood as tall as she could. "Call it what you like. I quit, Dr. Balducci. I'm sure my loss will be nothing more than a negligible annoyance, since BIL is chock-full of those who will ecstatically do your bidding."

"You can't quit, Dr. Accardi."

"Because the lump sum you paid included my price? Just a sec..." She took the bag off her shoulder, rummaged for her wallet, pulled the money she found and stuck the bills out to him.

"What's that supposed to be?"

Extending her hand as close as she dared get to him, she met his glowering with her own. "I don't know what the going rate per head was, but taking into account the premises and everything else, I'm sure I didn't cost you more than that."

His eyes fell to the notes before he raised them to her, full of mockery. "I assure you, you cost me much more than that."

She refused to lower her hand. "You let me know exactly what I cost you, and I'll pay for my freedom in installments. Consider this the first one."

As he realized she wasn't joking, his gaze clashed with hers as if to make her cower before him. She was sure such a glare had brought many adversaries to their knees. Tough, it was going to let him down this time. Even if she felt he'd set her on fire if she held his stare any longer.

A second before she averted her own eyes, he suddenly looked down at the money. He plucked three hundred-dollar bills from the bunch before he raised his eyes again and almost knocked her flat on her back with the mischief filling them.

"Now you really can't quit."

She gaped at his wicked grin. "What?"

"You just paid me for shares in your facility. Now you have to stay and run the place with me. Or for me."

Before another thought could fire in her stalled brain, he turned and strode away.

Out of nowhere, a sleek black limo slithered soundlessly up to him.

Before he got in, he turned to her with a mock salute and said, "See you tomorrow, partner."

Three

Antonio caught himself grinning again and again all the way back to his mansion in Holmby Hills.

Shaking his head for the umpteenth time since he'd left Liliana Accardi gaping at him as if he'd grown a spiked tail and leather wings and taken flight, he again wondered what the hell had happened in that parking lot. Actually, what the hell had happened since she'd blasted him in that meeting room.

This wasn't what he'd envisioned at all. Not after everything had gone according to plan. At first.

He'd made the bid on the lab, knowing he'd find no resistance. He'd finalized everything in record time before moving to the next phase—conquering his new subordinates. He'd done that, too, with more acceptance than his best projections, thanks to his long-perfected methods of making people do his bidding.

He'd started practicing his influence from childhood when he'd been in the clutches of The Organization, which had taken him and hundreds of children to turn them into lethal mercenaries. Even among his brotherhood, as unyielding as they were, he'd enjoyed a unique position of power. While Phantom—Numair now—had been the leader everyone deferred to, it had been Antonio everyone trusted to have the most levelheaded opinion. When he'd become their medical expert, they'd trusted him with their very lives.

He'd taken that skill into the outside world after they'd escaped The Organization. Normal people had been no match for the sway he'd honed with some of the world's most shrewd and lethal people. He'd plowed through the worlds of medicine and business like a laser, being described by rivals and allies alike as irresistible and unstoppable. Not that he reached his goals through aggression or intimidation. He relied on persuasion and manipulation, so no one had a reason to fight him and every reason to succumb to him.

Among his brothers, he was the one who had an equally close and friction-free relationship with all. Yet he'd allowed not even them beyond the serene facade he'd refined.

They believed it was Wildcard—or Ivan Konstantinov as he now called himself—who knew Antonio fully, as he'd been closest to him since childhood. But Antonio hadn't even let Ivan in on everything he'd been through or everything he was. He hadn't told Ivan anything he was doing or planning now.

While the others had searched for their families, sought reunion with them and/or revenge on those who'd stolen them away, Ivan, who'd come to The Organization old enough to know his family, had elected not to contact his family once he'd been out. Antonio had elected not to bother with either finding his origins or seeking revenge. Or so he'd told his brothers. In reality, he'd found out everything about his family.

What he'd learned had made him think The Organization had done him a favor by abducting him. His Italian aristocracy family put its members through hell for appearances' sake, which they enforced at any expense, even abandoning or destroying any of them who threatened their traditions and standing.

As they had him.

His mother's pregnancy when she was seventeen had threatened their image. Her inappropriate lover had been dealt with, while she'd been taken away to avoid the scandal. The same day she'd given birth to him, he'd been given to an orphanage, from which he'd been culled by The Organization less than four years later. Up until that day he'd lived hoping his "real family" would find him.

It turned out he'd been better off with The Organization than in the Accardis' sterile, cold-blooded environment where relationships were warped and members turned into shells of human beings. At least The Organization had let him pursue his true inclinations, what had made him who he was. It had been there he'd forged stronger-than-blood ties with his brothers, nothing like the pathological ones his family shared.

He'd at first decided to ignore the existence of the family that had wronged him so irretrievably. But after three of his brothers had found their roots and reunited with their own families, he'd begun to feel restless until he'd realized that he was being eaten alive with the need to even the score.

And to do that, he had to destroy the Accardis. Starting with his mother.

Agreeing to or at least accepting her family's crime, she hadn't attempted to search for him, had moved on instead and gotten married three times. She'd had legitimate offspring with each of her husbands as well as adopted children. The oldest was a man five years younger than him, the youngest a girl of twelve, making his crop of half siblings no less than six.

He'd planned to infiltrate the family anonymously, to exact up close and personal retribution on those who'd had a hand in his abandonment.

But the elitist snobs hadn't opened up to him, not even with the bait of vital financial relief. Getting close to this family could be through the only way they allowed.

Through blood. Through a member.

After a thorough analysis of the extended family, he'd zeroed in on one member. Liliana Accardi.

Liliana was the daughter of Alberto Accardi, his mother's third cousin. Her American mother had escaped Italy and the poisonous Accardi family when Liliana was only one and run back to the States. But after her mother's death last year, the only child, family-less Liliana had started to reestablish relations with her father. The man who hadn't bothered to see his daughter after he'd granted her mother a lucrative divorce was now eager to welcome her into his life. Surprisingly, the rest of the Accardis seemed as enthusiastic to invite her into the family. That had added to her potential use to Antonio.

Being a fellow doctor was another thing that had made her his best choice. And the fact that she'd graduated at the top of her class, but had ended up in a minor nonprofit lab battling impossible odds. Her quixotic tendencies had only made him consider her an even easier target. Everything else about her from looks to personal history had made her the most surefire as well as most tolerable vehicle for his needs.

He'd decided to approach her in a professional setting, bait her, snare her, then through her, enter the family, exact punishment from within, then walk away when they'd all paid, each to the exact measure he'd decide they deserved.

As for Liliana, she'd been wronged, too, if on an infinitely smaller scale. Though he'd despised her for seeking the family who'd driven her mother away and made Liliana grow up alone, to court their favor and inclusion, he'd intended to be lenient with her. *If* she provided him with a smooth ride to his life's most anticipated surgery, that of excising the petrified heart of the family who'd thrown him away like so much garbage.

He'd had no doubt she'd fall at his feet like all subordinates, like all women. The plan was simple. He'd make a proposal she'd grab at. After all, it would make a much more convincing entry into her family if she was delirious at her phenomenal luck. Then when he broke it off, if she'd benefited him—and if she didn't turn out to be another soulless Accardi or a greedy female—he'd compensate her handsomely.

Then he'd entered that meeting room, delivered his opening speech, and though he'd had the expected deference and delight from everyone else, he'd gotten none of the usual fluttering anticipation and adulation from her. Instead, she'd left him in no doubt of her reaction to his takeover, nor of her opinion of him.

From then on, everything had gone off the rails.

After his first surprise at her impassioned attack on his methods, history and person, he'd tried to overpower her, herd her back to his scripted pathway. Just as he'd thought he'd put her in the place where he needed her to stay, she'd retaliated with a more incontrovertible accusation.

Everything in him had surged to engage her full-on. But that would have been fodder for gossip and would have put him in a defensive position—something he'd never let himself be in. That had been when he'd realized he'd miscalculated.

The woman he'd thought would fall into his palm like a ripe plum had turned out to be a prickly pear.

A change of strategy had been in order.

But for the first time in memory, he couldn't come up with a course of action but to dismiss her. So he'd let her final words hang there in the conference room without a rebuttal from him. That confrontation had ended with the score of Liliana Accardi one, him nothing.

He had decided to resume her conquest the next day, after he'd upgraded his plan. But he'd itched with impatience, all his senses trained on her, the only one of the staff to avoid him. He'd pretended he hadn't noticed her as she'd kept her distance on her way out, when in truth he'd noticed nothing but her.

At one point, when she'd been closest to him, his resolve to ignore her had almost broken down. But he'd managed to let her walk out without doing something stupid.

Then he'd noticed the folder.

He'd realized adjusting his plan might be for nothing. This contrary woman might not be giving him another day. She'd forced him to pursue her there and then.

He'd still been certain that once he had her one-on-one, he'd bring her back in line. But the more he'd tried, the more she'd forced him to improvise, and the more he had, the further away from his desired results he'd gotten.

Not only hadn't he managed to overwhelm her, she'd taken him by surprise again and again. He'd found himself reacting without the least premeditation, something he never did. Then he'd found himself guffawing like a fool. He hadn't meant to laugh, but her unfiltered responses had been so unexpected and droll, she'd been the one to overpower his control and intent.

Not that his unprecedented spontaneity had earned him any leniency. Her disapproval and resistance had only increased until she'd swung the wrecking ball of her "I quit" right into him.

And she'd meant it. He'd been certain she had.

Just as he'd thought he was down to coercion, she'd

done that most ridiculous thing, offering him the money she had on her. After his initial perplexity, it had been like a light had burst inside him, illuminating the tunnel of dwindling options she'd squeezed him in. How to end this impasse on a high note. His solution, not to mention its effect on her when he'd declared it, had brightened his mood in a way he hadn't felt in...ever.

Suddenly, the grin stretching his lips since he'd left her in that parking lot froze.

He might have decided to change the dynamics of dealing with her, but if he'd learned anything about Liliana Accardi so far, it was that she cared nothing about his power or wealth or what she could gain from them. To her, he was nothing but the invader who'd stormed into and defiled what she considered her home.

His parting shot might have been the worst thing he could have said. That defiant creature could now be working herself into a lather, more determined than ever not to return to the lab.

When the limo stopped, his mood was blacker than it had ever been, even during his worst days in The Organization.

Seething in uncharacteristic exasperation, he heaved out of the car and strode inside his mansion, thunderclouds roiling through his veins.

Damn that Liliana Accardi.

He'd picked her as the easy-to-tame lab rat, and she'd turned out to be an impossible-to-curb hellcat.

He had no time for a struggle with her. She wasn't even his target, just a means to an end. But instead of a solution, she'd turned out to be an insoluble problem.

If she insisted on defying him, he'd let her quit. But he'd make sure she'd find no other job in the country. Hell, on earth. She'd either work for him or she could go flip burgers. He'd put her in her place, doing exactly what he thought her good for. Then he'd search for a more amenable member of the Accardis as his bridge into that accursed family.

It was only an hour later, under the beating needles of a punishing jet shower, when he found himself stroking a painfully hard erection to an explosive climax to the memory of the mutinous passion in Liliana's eyes, that he realized his plan was inapplicable.

Logic said he should consider her a lost cause. But this volcanic lust she'd provoked in him—more inexplicable because it was for her being, not her body, which he hadn't even properly seen—made it impossible for him to walk away from her or let her walk away from him. It was the last thing he'd thought would happen, but he *wanted* that aggravating, uncontrollable rebel.

It no longer mattered to him why he'd wanted to tame and acquire her in the first place. All that mattered to him now was that he did. For his own pleasure.

He'd never done anything for his own pleasure.

High time he did. And Liliana Accardi, that intractable creature, the first one to ever defy and spurn him, was the perfect place to start.

Lili ended the phone call with Brian and pinched the bridge of her nose, hard.

She didn't need this. Not after the night she'd had.

After Antonio Balducci had left her feeling punch-drunk, she'd driven home, garnering way more honks from disgruntled drivers than she usually did. She'd never gotten used to driving in LA. Never gotten used to living in that house. All she could think of was it was time to let it all go. Let her mother's memory and everything she'd built in this city go.

That was all she could think when she could focus on anything but Antonio Balducci. When every word he'd said to her, every look, every inflection of his voice and peal of his laughter hadn't been revolving in her mind like a mini tornado.

She'd arrived at the house exhausted in a way she hadn't been since her mother's final days. But her fatigue hadn't been soaked with despondence, but with jittery restlessness.

Antonio had messed her up but good. And he'd known it. He'd almost skipped away knowing he'd shut her up and had the last word this time.

If she'd surprised him with her resistance, he'd shocked her with his response.

See you tomorrow, partner.

Indeed!

When she'd finally fallen asleep, she'd fallen into a turbulent realm filled with heart-hammering glimpses and whispers and touches. All of him.

She'd woken up burning and wet, sure he'd meant to invade her dreams. She'd never squirmed for release like that, but had drawn the line at seeking it. He could rule her subconscious, but she was damned if she'd consciously give him that power over her, even if only she would know about it.

At least that was what she'd told herself until she'd sought the relief of a hot bath and ended up bringing herself to an unprecedented orgasm to his memory.

Damn him.

She'd been still trembling with aftershocks when Brian had called her. Antonio had asked him to let her know their first management meeting was at two sharp.

At Brian's rabid curiosity, she'd said Antonio was just messing with her, as punishment for daring not to prostrate herself at his feet, like they'd all done. She doubted Brian bought that. Even when she believed it to be the truth.

She'd underestimated Antonio's need for control. He'd

pursued her to lasso her back when she'd dared be the only one who didn't roll over and expose her belly. She'd struggled against his inexorable influence, trying to make him consider her a troublemaker not worth the effort it would take to subjugate her, to maintain his no doubt pristine dominance record. That had only backfired, judging by his parting shot.

Even then, she'd really thought she didn't have to worry about him anymore. He might be obsessive when it came to getting his way, but she was certain he was too busy to bother with his employees again, especially rebellious ones. She'd thought he'd walk away and forget all about her, or remember her only as a weird creature who'd afforded him passing amusement. She'd been secure—and oppressively let down—that she'd never see him again.

Then Brian had called.

Antonio hadn't been joking. Or maybe he had been, and he hadn't finished yanking her chain yet. It appeared she entertained him, and it was equally obvious he hadn't had enough of her diversion yet.

Problem was, she had to oblige him.

He was the one to give her the end-of-service releases, recommendations and payments. As much as she would have loved to not look back, she needed all that to be able to leave and survive until she found a new job.

After dressing in her most funereal outfit, she pulled her unruly hair—which seemed to have more red in its auburn depths to go with her mood—in a severe bun. Forgoing even the little makeup she usually wore, she winced at her reflection.

Now that she was aware how she looked to others, she could see that everything she felt was emblazoned on her face. Aversion, aggression, anticipation and, dammit, arousal.

She shouldn't have given in to the urge to seek release. It

had done nothing but inflame her more. Her body throbbed like an exposed nerve, every movement triggering an avalanche of responses. Now sexual awareness was stamped all over her.

Hoping the drive to the lab would dampen her condition, she cursed herself, Antonio and the whole world and headed there. It felt like she was about to sever a chunk of herself and leave it behind. But she had to do it.

She'd try to continue her work elsewhere. If she couldn't, whatever she decided to do then would be her choice, not his. That it would be a choice he'd forced her into would still be better than being forced to do what he wanted now.

Arriving at the lab, she realized from everyone's unusually zippy behavior that he was there. Probably setting up his boss area for whenever he came to inspect. No doubt he was also expecting her to obey his directive. The rat had gotten to her through her best friend so he'd corner her.

Well, it hadn't worked. It was 4:00 p.m. already, and when he got the confrontation he wished for after she'd gathered her stuff, she'd make sure it would be their last face-off.

As she headed to her lab, she noticed everyone was looking at her differently, with incredulousness and something else…a new kind of courtesy, perhaps? The only explanation was that he'd taken his joke too far, had told everyone what he'd told her yesterday.

Annoyance with all of them, especially with him, mushroomed as she pushed into her lab…and felt as if her brain had hit a brick wall.

Antonio sat at her desk. His gaze collided with hers at once, as if he'd been waiting for her to walk in.

"Is this how late you'll be coming in from now on?"

Every nerve in her body fired at the combo of his jaw-dropping beauty and his teasing remonstration.

Before she could consider a comeback, he uncoiled to his formidable height, approached in that indolent predator's prowl, his lips twisting. "I didn't expect you to change to partner mode that quickly. But then you never do anything I expect. I like it. Immensely."

Forcing herself to move as he came to a stop before her, she unhooked her backpack and circumvented him. Without looking back at him, she started emptying her station, every nerve jangling in alarm as he came closer.

"Are you doing what I think you're doing?" When she didn't answer him, he harrumphed. "I enjoy your unexpectedness up to a point. That point is when you use it to deprive me of it. This, Dr. Accardi, I won't sanction."

Packing her last article, she yanked the zipper closed, then looked up. Though she'd braced herself, she felt gut-punched to behold his gorgeousness up close, now smoldering hotter with disapproving authority. Forcing steadiness into her stance, she pulled an envelope from her backpack's outer pocket, and thrust it out at him.

It was déjà vu when he glowered at it, but when he raised his eyes, there was no questioning. He knew what that was.

"I'm not accepting your resignation, Dr. Accardi." His lips crooked into that smile that had her insides liquefying. "Not to mention it would take far more than a piece of paper now to terminate our partnership."

Grinding her teeth at the throbbing between her legs, she thrust her other hand palm-up at him. This time, he raised a questioning eyebrow, making her want to yank that regal head down and bite that perfect wing of provocation.

"My three hundred dollars, please."

"Buying back your shares?" At her nod, he laughed, and her legs almost gave out. "You think your money spent a whole night with me and remained the same?"

Images bombarded her, of spending a whole night with

him and being changed forever. Even if he hadn't meant for her to think that, she did. The man was sex personified. She had to face the fact that she'd walk out of here, never to see him again, and would forever pleasure herself to his memory.

Gritting her teeth, she kept her hand outstretched. "My money, please. This is no longer remotely funny."

"It's the most fun I've ever had. And I don't have your money on me. I don't walk around with three hundred thousand dollars in my pockets."

Her mouth dropped open. "Not even you can multiply stock by a factor of a thousand overnight!"

"You'd be very impressed by what I can do over the course of one night." Her blood boiled over before he added, "But you're right. I was exaggerating. Your money is now around thirty thousand dollars. Still don't have that much on me."

"Keep it, capital and investment. Consider it my contribution to whatever good science you develop."

She had to get away from him. If she succumbed to him in any way, the damages he'd cause her would be worse than his wiping out three years of her work. This man could end her peace of mind. Could turn her into one of those women who groveled at his feet. It was getting harder with every breath to resist his spell and it wouldn't take him long to cast it fully over her. And while others seemed thrilled to be enthralled, it would destroy her.

But when she tried to walk around him, he blocked her, mischief frolicking in his eyes.

Stopping, she clutched her backpack harder. "Listen, Dr. Balducci. Enough, okay? I don't want to work for you, and I sure as hell am not your partner. Accept my resignation and give me what I ask for in this letter. I only ask for my rights."

"I don't care what you think your rights are." He silenced her protest by stepping closer, until the heat of his body and breath singed her. "I don't need to read this letter to know that you make a habit of shortchanging yourself. I, on the other hand, offer you what you really deserve."

That had her heart stuttering. "I only deserve to be left alone to continue my work. I never asked for anything more."

"And if I consider granting you this?"

And *that* had her heart skipping like a pebble over water. "Y-you would?"

"I would. On the condition that you become my partner."

She coughed a mirthless laugh. "I'm not even partner material for an ice-cream stand. I know nothing about running a business. If you're doing this to stop me from leaving for some reason only you'll ever know, I assure you, you don't need to bribe me with any bogus executive position I have no wish for and would be useless at. I'm probably the only person you'll ever meet who considers such a promotion a terrible fate and not a reward. But I'll gladly stay if you let me continue my work."

"So you're fine with me as your boss? You'd stay in spite of all your vigorous objections to me and my methods?"

"As long as you leave me alone, professionally and personally, I don't care if you're developing immunizations to sunlight for vampires and to silver for werewolves."

His lips split in such an exuberant smile, dazzling her with a flash of white teeth and searing charisma.

She was trying not to hyperventilate when he made it impossible, reaching out and slipping the backpack off her shoulder, his long, strong, capable fingers sliding against her flesh, making her core clench with violent need.

"Until we come to a new agreement," he said, "put your personal effects back where they belong."

She clung to the backpack as if to a life raft. "What new agreement? We didn't have an old one."

"Then we'll make a brand-new one from scratch."

With the utmost gentleness, he insisted on tugging the backpack out of her white-knuckled grip.

Letting it go felt as if she were lowering her last shield against him.

After placing it on her workstation, he faced her with a grin that had her swaying like a building in an earthquake. He leaned his hip on the desk, folded his arms over his expansive chest.

"Now that that's taken care of, there's something else I require."

"What's that?" she croaked.

"You. For dinner."

Four

"You want to have me for dinner?"

Lili hated that she'd squeaked. This man kept yanking at her composure. It was a matter of time before he snapped it.

"I meant I want to take you to dinner."

Her insides tightened more at his forbearing tone. "My IQ might be selective, but even I got that. Don't be—"

"—redundant? Yes, I know how you hate that." His gaze took on a new level of intensity. "But the other meaning is also right. Though I'd rather have you for dessert."

More convinced he'd decided to go all out having fun at her expense, she hissed, "Spare me the clichés, Dr. Balducci. And stop looking at me like that."

"Like what? Like you're the most fascinating thing I've ever seen? How can I, when you are?"

"That's what you tell yourself about the people you toy with? That they had it coming, being who they are?" She shook her head as his smile faltered. "But that's not how you're looking at me. At least, it's not how you're making me feel."

Every trace of levity left his face, avidness replacing it. "How am I making you feel? Tell me."

"You make me feel as if you're probing my every last thought."

His lips quirked, the smile back in his gaze. "Why would I do that when you wallop me over the head with everything that comes to your mind the moment it does?"

"It's what I've been asking myself, too, wondering why you bother. But you probably do it automatically. I think you go around scanning people to their molecular level and archiving your findings for future exploitation."

His eyes sobered. "So you don't think I do it for future reference, but for exploitation."

"Actually, I don't think it's only exploitation you're after, but flat-out mind control. You're not probing my thoughts, but trying to herd them where you want them to go. I can feel your mental tentacles trying to steer my brain."

His laugh was louder and longer this time. "Your unflattering opinion of me is devolving into sinister depths."

"I'm sure you don't care about anyone's opinion of you."

"I care about yours." The way he'd said that, his baritone caressing her inside and out… "Stop thinking it's your obligation to fight me on everything." His voice dipped another octave, making her very marrow vibrate. "Accept my dinner invitation, Dr. Accardi. I promise I won't eat you. No matter how tempted I am to do so."

Truth was, it was she who was tempted. To succumb to his persuasion. All she wanted was to say yes, to everything he was asking of her. Come what may.

She kneaded a throbbing temple, as if to stem her fast-dwindling common sense and willpower. "I don't know what's going on inside that convoluted mind of yours, Dr.

Balducci, and I really don't want to know. But whatever it is, I know one thing. What you're doing here? It's a terrible idea."

His eyebrows shot up in imperious query. "It is? Why?"

Though she was certain he knew, she'd spell it out. She'd give him whatever would make him leave her be, spare her the tumult of his inexplicable interest.

"First, you're you and I'm me. Second, you're my boss, until you accept my resignation. I'm against mixing professional and personal stuff. It always has catastrophic consequences, even when the professional situation is ideal, not as problematic and hostile as ours."

"I have zero problems with you professionally. And the last thing I am is hostile. I'm the very opposite."

"So I'm the hostile party. My bad."

His smile widened. "I like your hostility. A lot."

"Yeah, you find it hilarious."

"Tut-tut. I object to your insinuations that I'm having fun at your expense."

"I'm insinuating nothing. You *are* having a ball."

"That I definitely am. You tickle my humor like no one else. I say that without malice or condescension—just the opposite. Like you, I say only what I mean."

"Really? I doubt that—about as much as I doubt my ability to grow fur in winter." That earned her another heart-palpitating chuckle that she did her best to ignore. "If you said only what you mean, I don't think many in your path would remain alive."

"So you're saying I'm tactful, even merciful?"

"Tactful? Maybe, but for your own ends only. Merciful? Sure. And I'm a flying manta ray."

A guffaw exploded from him, seeming to take him by as much surprise as it did her.

His hand pressed his chest as if laughing hurt him. Which it might, since he must be exercising muscles long petrified from lack of use. She had a feeling not much amused him.

His other hand wiped at his eyes. "How does your mind come up with these things? Wait, don't answer. Mad scientist brain at work. And I thought I was one myself before meeting you. Turns out I'm too unimaginative to be one." When she groaned at his self-deprecation, his hands rose in a placating gesture. Then he leveled his hypnotic gaze on her, his lips still twitching, as if unable to stop smiling. "So if it's dubious I'm tactful, and certain I'm not merciful, what do you think I am?"

"You're inexorably diplomatic and inhumanly charismatic. And you wield both traits like weapons of mass manipulation. Not that I fault you for that. That *is* the best way of dealing with underlings for the best outcome. Why cultivate resentments and enemies among lesser beings when you can as easily foster worship and recruit willing slaves?"

"My diplomacy and charisma aren't getting me any worship or acquiring me any slaves in this room. They seem to work in reverse on you."

"Yeah, contrary to my norm, my reactions to you seem the total opposite of everyone else."

"So it's only me who has that effect on you." His eyes flared with something scalding…and smug?

Really? He craved ego-inflating strokes from her? He didn't get enough from everyone else?

Well, she wasn't contributing to the severity of his self-aggrandizing syndrome. And she wasn't letting him keep on trying to break through her barriers.

"*So* since it's clear you won't give me what I came here for, I'll leave you to your manipulation games with your new horde of worshipping followers. But do take this still. Consider it a souvenir."

Pushing the envelope in his hand, she skirted him to

retrieve her backpack. She rushed to the door, forcing herself not to take a last look at him, praying she'd make it out without stumbling. She was almost out when his rich voice had goose bumps storming all over her.

"What did you mean before when you said, 'You're you and I'm me'? What are we exactly?"

She waited until she was outside the door, safe enough to turn to him. Beholding his majesty for the last time, she suppressed a pang of regret and sighed.

"We're two different species."

Antonio watched Liliana Accardi disappear, battling the urge to hurtle after her, to drag her back, preferably thrown over his shoulder, swearing and scratching.

After he managed to get himself under control, he shook his head.

And he'd thought he'd already been beyond intrigued coming here. Now, after she'd defied him again, lambasted him as no one had ever dared to, then walked out on him like no one had done before, his condition had worsened exponentially.

He was hooked. For the first time in...ever.

All through this latest confrontation, he'd kept seeing himself capturing those lush lips, shoving her back onto that workstation she'd cleared, and having his way with her. All the way. Repeatedly.

He'd gotten hard the moment she'd walked in, and remained painfully so, even now. Even when he hadn't guessed what her body looked like under those drab clothes she wore like a camouflage. For the first time physical attributes didn't count to him. Coveting her essential self—something he'd never thought possible—took his arousal to a level he'd never experienced.

He stared down at the envelope she'd foisted on him.

To think he'd set this up thinking she'd be just a conduit. A means to an end.

But it had taken her only one confrontation to derail his meticulous plan. Not only was she the only to ever outright challenge him, but when he'd added the extra pressure of personal interest, the point when other women would have buckled breathlessly, she'd become even more resistant.

Amazing.

She hadn't even bothered considering his invitation. An invitation he'd never issued before, and that other women would kill for. She'd just scoffed it off and walked away. She would have done so without looking back if he hadn't asked her another question. She'd stopped only long enough to give him her final verdict.

We're two different species.

Shaking his head again, he headed back to her workstation, sat down in her chair. Though it was uncomfortable and creaky, it was the only place he wanted to be right now. It made him feel closer to her somehow. He'd take that comfort until he had the woman herself close once again.

If he even managed it.

That was another first. To be uncertain he could win someone over.

After a moment of grappling with this added complication, he tore open her resignation letter.

The wording was appropriate, yet it revealed her unbending spirit, that indomitable spark that fueled her unique persona. Yet with every letter, something tightened more behind his rib cage.

She was asking for far less than she deserved. Than the least contributor in this lab he'd acquired to be near her deserved.

He'd been right. This woman had no idea of her worth.

How had this happened? Why had she come to think this was her due? Who had made her feel worth so little?

Her life was an open book with very few lines, so there could be only two culprits. Her father was the foremost perpetrator. Knowing he'd let her grow up without caring to establish any relationship with her must have formed the early views of her self-worth. Her mother hadn't been the epitome of parenthood, either. She'd been a severely dysfunctional woman who had no right to limit her daughter to her very questionable care. After Liliana's early childhood, she'd become consumed in her work before falling prey to a debilitating mental disorder, repeating her husband's abandonment, albeit in different ways.

It explained a lot about Liliana. Those abandoned as children grappled with not only trust issues, but with sometimes crippling feelings of worthlessness all their lives. He knew that all too well, having been a discarded child himself.

But he'd been lucky. Unbelievably, The Organization had been a better place for a child to grow up than the biological family Liliana had been unlucky enough to be born to.

That meant his approach today had been another miscalculation. He'd thought if he showed her that his interest had become personal, it would soften her. When it had only made her more adamant, he'd thought she'd been alarmed at how fast he was moving, because of his reputation as an indiscriminating female magnet, which he'd cultivated to serve his purposes.

But it wasn't only this part of his public persona that repelled her. It was how she perceived all of him. And how she perceived herself in comparison.

Like no other woman he'd met, she was actually put off by his wealth and power. To her he was a taker, like her father, someone immersed in his own needs and greeds, who cared nothing about the devastation he left behind.

Then came the part concerning herself.

If she didn't value herself, as was evident from that letter, it stood to reason that she was unable to understand his interest in her. So she'd assigned him the most unsavory motive she could think of. That he was toying with her for his cruel entertainment.

What irony, that she suspected his manipulation when he'd already relinquished it.

He could just hear his brothers saying this turnabout only served him right, in punishment for his initial plan to use her. Not that they hadn't done the same in their day. At least Rafael and Numair. They had both initiated their relationships with the women who'd become their wives with self-serving motives.

Not that he wanted to end up with a wife. He just wanted to experience and satisfy those unprecedented urges this spitfire provoked in him. And he would pursue her to the ends of the earth till he did.

He probed those new motivations more deeply. Was he feeling this way only because she defied him and pulverized his plans and expectations?

The internal interrogation ended before it started.

No. That was what had lured him in initially. But he'd stayed and kept going deeper because of *her*. She was a conundrum. A genius in her field, she was also so insightful she'd sensed things about him that no one had before. And she kept none of her insights to herself. Yet with all her brilliance, she was socially awkward, had reclusive tendencies. But what had him at the mercy of this unknown and unstoppable compulsion was that inside that steel shell of resolve and resistance, he felt such vulnerable, untried softness.

It was *that* that made him want to eat her up.

But his need to break down the insulating walls she'd erected around herself, what she kept raising higher around him, was more than desire. More than his dominance demanding she bow to him like everyone did. It actually… dismayed him, what she thought of him. Because it was unnervingly accurate. She saw him more clearly than anyone, even Ivan.

He was suddenly no longer feeling self-satisfied being who he was. Now he actually felt the urge to change, so he could improve her opinion of him.

If anything had ever disturbed him, it was *that* thought.

Could he be getting soft and stupid like his brothers? Behind the suave front he'd meticulously created, he'd always been the one with steel-enforced nerves and diamond-coated insides. Not even this unpredictable fireball could change that…could she?

Of course she couldn't.

And when he got her to succumb—and he definitely would—not only would he remain unchanged, it would still serve his original cause. There'd at least be that, once his desire for her dissipated.

But then, he couldn't even imagine it doing so. From the aroused condition he remained in just thinking of her, it seemed his need for her wouldn't fade easily or soon.

Which suited him. He had all the time in the world.

He would savor her capture and her devouring, slowly, thoroughly, as he'd never done anything in his life.

Lili woke up very late. It had been another restless night filled with outlandish, feverish dreams starring Antonio Balducci.

She'd woken up with a hammering heart and a cramping core. She'd felt so needy that she'd barely refrained from relieving the throbbing between her legs in the shower.

Getting out in record time before she succumbed to temptation and ended up feeling only worse, she eyed the pajamas she'd decided to spend the day in, shrugged listlessly and headed to the kitchen in her bathrobe instead.

She needed sugar. Lots of it. She'd bought giant triple chocolate chip muffins last night. Two for breakfast sounded
about right. It wouldn't compensate for the loss of her job
and security, but it would make her feel better nonetheless. Hopefully.

Flopping on the couch in front of the TV, she decided
she'd binge-watch every single episode of every sitcom she
liked. If that meant she'd sit there with only kitchen and
bathroom breaks for the next month, so be it.

By the fourth episode of her favorite show, she found
herself actually watching and not replaying her confronta-
tions with Antonio in a never-ending loop. Soon she was
chuckling, then laughing, then reciting the lines that had
become engraved in pop culture. She was singing a jingle
alongside one of her favorite characters at the top of her
lungs when the bell rang.

Her raucousness came to a halt as her eyes darted to the
wall clock. At 1:00 p.m. on a Wednesday, the few neigh-
bors in her gated community who ever came knocking
knew she'd be at work.

It had to be one of them checking out the inexplicable
noises. Or the mailman leaving something she'd forgotten
she'd ordered online, as usual.

Coming to this conclusion, she turned the volume down,
subdued her hair and tightened the belt of the two-sizes-
too-big bathrobe. Failing to locate her slippers, she pat-
tered barefoot to the door.

She pulled it open, eyes down looking for a package.
Instead, they fell on a pair of big shoes. Polished, hand-
made ones.

Her eyes trailed up, over endless legs, a lean abdomen,
a door-wide chest and shoulders, all encased in darkness
that seemed to absorb the sunlight like a black hole.

"You're sitting at home watching sitcoms and causing

a neighborhood-wide alert, when you should be in your lab advancing medical science?"

Lili blinked, for a moment believing the colossus she was staring at was an apparition. Perhaps she'd been thinking of him so obsessively she'd actually conjured him.

Not that even her fevered imagination could replicate him. Antonio Balducci was really on her doorstep, glowing like a gilded god in the afternoon sun, perfect in ways that she hadn't known possible and that should be outlawed.

And there she stood in front of this vision of grandeur, the hair she hadn't combed a riot of tangles, no doubt looking like a freckled porcupine drowning in its parent's garment.

When she continued to gape at him, he folded his arms over his chest, his gaze mock-severe. "May I remind you that you didn't ask permission to take the day off?"

His reprimand finally snapped her out of her stupor. "May I remind you that I tendered my resignation?"

His majestic head jerked up in dismissal, presenting her with an even better view of his formidable jaw and cleft chin. "You may also remember it was categorically rejected."

She tossed her head back, too, attempting to emulate his haughtiness. "I needed you to approve my resignation only so you'd provide me with my end-of-service benefits. Your approval is unneeded if I relinquish them. Which I did. So I can do what I want. And I'm doing exactly that. Sleeping in and watching TV."

He gave such a pout, it was a wonder she didn't jump him to bite those maddening lips. "I hate to burst your bubble, but a rejected resignation only means you still work for me."

"No, it means I give up all the rights that come with an accepted resignation."

"Accepted resignations don't only come with benefits. They come with recommendation letters—"

She cut in. "I'll do without those, too."

He continued as if she hadn't interrupted him. "—endless severance forms to fill and to sign—"

She butted in again. "I'll do that sometime next week."

That made him stop, his gaze merrily roaming her, his lips twitching on the verge of ending his not-so-convincing stern act.

Yeah, tell her about how ridiculous she looked.

"Won't you invite me in?"

"No."

Her immediate answer gained her an equally swift "Why?"

"Because of all of the above."

His eyes twinkled in the sunlight, a more crystalline and intense blue than she'd ever seen. "It's not good for your health to hold a grudge."

"Oh, it's very cathartic to do so, for a limited time. I've allowed myself a week of hurling curses your way."

As his lips lost the fight and broke into a smile, the image burst in her mind of a lightning bolt striking him in that perfect ass. And she burst out laughing.

His eyes narrowed as he examined her. "Are you drunk, Dr. Accardi?"

"What if I am?" she spluttered. "I can't get a ticket riding my couch."

Without warning, he crossed her threshold.

A thousand alarms rang in her head. "Hey, you can't do that. I haven't invited you in."

He walked her back into her foyer, his advance slow, smooth, a sweep of power and seduction, the very opposite of her ungainly stumbling.

"Like a vampire, you mean?"

"I wouldn't be surprised if you were one."

"Then I would have certainly developed that anti-sun vaccine you mentioned before." He took another step closer. "I would have also developed a no-invitation-needed immunization."

Another few steps back had her thudding against something hard. The archway of the great room. Her heart bobbed in her throat as he bent his head closer and inhaled deeply, his eyes watching her intently.

"You smell of...you."

The way he said that, it was as if he were bracing himself against some sharp ache. His velvet groan was the darkest she'd heard his voice.

Trying not to let the shudder that traversed her body rattle it visibly, she smirked. "Thanks for the news flash. And here I always thought I smelled of someone else."

"Do you have any idea how you smell?"

"As long as I don't smell bad, who cares?"

"If you don't know who, I won't tell you. Yet." He lowered his head, closed his eyes and drew another deep inhalation. "I know now that defiance and dry wit and fearlessness have scents. Hot and sweet and bright." Before she decided if she'd swoon or not, he added, "You also smell of ginger and orange." He'd pinpointed the scents in her shampoo and conditioner. His eyes opened, heavy and hooded, filled with so much she couldn't understand but that still seared her to the marrow. "And chocolate."

Gulping, she nodded. "Yeah, I've overdosed on triple chocolate chip muffins."

"Sounds great. Smells better. Offer me some."

"What makes you think I have any left? Should I refresh your memory about the definition of *overdosed*?"

He gave her a perfect Bela Lugosi leer. "Should you be haggling with a hungry vampire who's doing you the courtesy of settling for chocolate instead of blood?"

"The hungry vampire will take the blood anyway, so I'm at least saving the chocolate."

Shaking his head in gesture of surrender, he laughed. Peal after peal of debilitating male amusement. That thick, corded neck jutting from his open black silk shirt was the closest it had been to her lips. It was so tempting, as if inviting her to reach up and sink her teeth—

Dammit. Get away!

Though he wasn't really crowding her, she sucked in her stomach as she squeezed out from between him and the wall. Grabbing the remote, she turned off the TV, then swung back to him. He'd followed her, was facing her across the couch.

"How about we dispense with the comic relief and get to the reason for your home invasion?"

"I came to resolve the issue that made you skip work today."

"For the last time, I skipped nothing. I quit."

"Yes, I got that the first time you said it. I'm here to tell you quitting isn't an option."

"It's my only option. You gave me ultimatums—"

"I offered you alternatives."

"—and I rejected them. So I was back to square one— working on your project and having mine swept aside."

He shook his head. "You keep making assumptions of what I think or what I'll do, and they're consistently inaccurate."

"What's inaccurate in all I said?"

"Only the most relevant part. Your assumption that I wasn't open to compromise. Which I certainly was. You pushed, I countered and our negotiations were just starting when you took off."

"There was nothing more to negotiate."

"There's always more. Nothing is ever final."

"I thought with you everything is."

His gaze swept her from head to toe and back, swathing her in fire. "I thought so, too. But I'm learning that was because I never found a worthy challenger."

"Me? Yeah, right."

"I will cure you of that self-deprecation yet. For now, I'm here to tell you that you can have your project back, with all the logistical support and financial backing I would have offered you to work on mine. I ask for nothing in return."

Her mouth fell open but nothing came out.

It was only on the third attempt that she croaked, "So what's the catch?"

"You're *assuming* again."

"Just spit it out. The one thing I can't handle is surprises. I have to know what I'm walking into while I'm still a thousand miles away."

His eyes gleamed with approval. "A control freak, I see."

"Takes one to know one. But then again, I'm just a wannabe who has nothing to show for my obsessive proclivities. You're the real deal with the billions to prove it."

"Again, you shortchange yourself." He frowned for a moment before he exhaled. "There's no catch, Dr. Accardi. Your pressure tactics worked."

"What pressure tactics?"

His huff was incredulous. "Seems it's not only me who does things on autopilot. You flat-out bulldozed me."

"I was only struggling not to let you bulldoze me."

"And your struggle was so ferocious you upended the tables. It took me a while to realize I was beaten, since it never happened before. But there's a first time for everything. So here I am, coming with a white flag. If there's one thing I ask, it's that you promise you'll separate our professional and personal interactions from now on."

"We have no personal interactions."

"Something I aim to rectify, starting now, over lunch."

"What is it with you and meals?"

"We do have to eat. We'll eat together."

It was her turn to shake her head, disbelief coursing through her. She'd expected him to consider her a pest, to dismiss her and spare her his disconcerting focus. But not only had he come after her again, but the more obnoxious she was, the more patient and persuasive he grew.

But for whatever reason he was doing this, there was only so much temptation she could withstand.

Clinging to the last vestiges of sanity, she exhaled. "You must be in dire need of amusement. But let's say I accept, how about something quick? Coffee? Here?"

He shook his head, unmovable. "Lunch. Out."

"I'll give you a muffin."

His laugh rang out again, and she could swear all of her mother's crystal still distributed around the living area where she'd left them sang in response.

He was still chuckling when he persisted, "Lunch. A leisurely one. So clear your agenda."

"What agenda? I'm unemployed now."

"You're no such thing. We're celebrating your triumphant return to your lab. This is nonnegotiable, Liliana."

Her heart somersaulted. It didn't matter that it was impossible. It did. Then it attempted to burst out of her chest.

At her distressed cough, he covered the distance between them urgently, held her by the arms, solicitous, singeing her even through the thick terry cloth.

"Are you all right?" When she nodded and tried to step away, he followed, hands tightening on her arms. "Liliana..."

"Lili." It was too much hearing him say her full name, making it an overpowering spell. "If you're no longer calling me Dr. Accardi, then call me Lili like everyone else."

An eyebrow rose imperiously. "You're Liliana to me and I will always call you that. That is also nonnegotiable."

Stepping back so she could breathe again, she raised her hands. "Okay, okay, call me whatever you want. I will call you whatever I want, too."

"And what's that?"

"I didn't mean to your face."

His guffaw was more delighted than ever. "And what will you call me outside of your internal rants?"

"I'd rather not call you at all."

He took her arm again, steered her toward the ground-floor bedroom where she slept. "Call me anything you want. I eagerly anticipate whatever you come up with. Now go dress."

"I haven't said I'll go out to lunch with you."

"You will."

"Is this the billionaire's entitlement or the surgeon's god complex, or were you just born an overbearing brat?"

He whooped in laughter again. "You'll get a chance to find out over lunch. Now go put on something nice."

She yanked her arm from his grip. "I don't have something nice. Not by your standards."

"Anything that doesn't smother you in layers of cloth."

"I don't have that, either."

"Anything not hideous. I'm sure you can manage that."

"This bathrobe isn't hideous. Would you settle for that?"

"I would. Would you?"

She should go out with him in her bathrobe and bare feet and see if he'd still take her to lunch.

Her thoughts paused before she huffed in resignation, threw her hands up and headed to her bedroom.

She'd bet he wouldn't bat an eyelid. If she even stripped naked it wouldn't deter him. Or maybe *that* would change his mind about taking her out and he'd—

Oh, shut up. He'd nothing. All this was probably him conducting some experiment, and he considered her the perfect test subject.

After that lunch, and after he was sure she'd go back to work, she doubted she'd see him again. Even had he been interested in her *that* way, Antonio Balducci had perfected the art of the one-night—or the one-outing—stand.

So what would one lunch hurt, anyway? She should actually make the most of it.

It would be her first and last chance with him.

Five

She'd worn something nice.

As nice as she could manage from a wardrobe designed for a life that had no social or romantic components.

Not that she'd thought it was nice when she'd put on the dark green sleeveless above-knee dress with matching three-inch sandals.

That verdict was his.

When she'd come out of her bedroom, flushed because he'd been across from her door when she was totally naked, he was watching the same sitcom episode she had been when he'd arrived.

He'd thrown his head back like a lazy feline, then had said one word. *Nice.*

The word itself was innocuous enough. It had been the way he'd looked at her and the way he'd said it, that lethal gaze and that purr of bone-liquefying seduction, that had swept her in flames of longing.

Not that she thought that was his objective. Seducing

her was too far-fetched a motive behind everything he'd done so far. Her amusement factor remained the most probable reason.

She reeled all over again at the cascade of events that had led her to this point, where she was sitting beside him in his luxurious Lamborghini.

When he'd found her eyeing everything as if she feared touching it, he'd only said that he always bought Italian-made cars, as a nod to his heritage—which she shared. Knowing he was trying to disprove her "different species" comment without tackling it head-on, she'd countered that he found this car appealing not because of its country of origin but its million-dollar price tag. He'd only sighed about her continued gross misjudgments and, with a wiggle of an eyebrow, *under*estimates.

Feeling it would be obnoxious to criticize his personal spending habits, she'd instead questioned the absence of his limo and chauffeur. His response had been yet another blow to her equilibrium. That he hadn't been about to pick her up for their first lunch together with another man around.

Another woman would have been flattered out of her mind, with all sorts of ludicrous hopes soaring. *Her* response had been to stress what self-preservation dictated this should be—their first *and* last lunch together.

He'd given her an enigmatic look and let her statement stand. Either he agreed, or he'd let her say whatever she wanted because he knew he'd get his way in the end anyway.

Now she stole another glance at his sonnet-worthy profile as he negotiated a stretch of unruly traffic in downtown LA. Questions spun faster inside her mind.

What exactly was his way? What could he want with her? It couldn't be her as a woman that he was after. Could it?

Okay, so she was pretty enough, in what people called an unusual way. She'd had lots of interest from good-looking and successful guys. It had been her who'd been uninterested. A romance, or even a hookup, with all promised upsides, hadn't been worth the consequences she'd obsessively calculated.

But in comparison, *any* guy was a straggly tomcat to this majestic lion beside her. Whatever her attractions to men, she couldn't be up to *his* standards, not when he waded among the rare beauties of the world and didn't give even them the time of day.

That brought her back to her one plausible theory. That she entertained him like none had ever done, intrigued him because she hadn't fallen at his feet, and was still challenging him with every breath. Even as she melted inside.

"We're here."

His deep drawl jerked her out of her musings as he brought the car to a smooth stop. He sprang from the low-slung car fluidly, then rushed around to help her out. Her exit from the car was nowhere as seamless as his, his boost compromising her balance more, landing her against his unyielding strength.

He steadied her, that disturbing intimacy flaring in his eyes, and every primal urge in her fiercely wished she could remain engulfed in his heat and dominance and security.

As her ingrained aloofness kicked in and she stepped away from his support, a valet rushed to take the car away. Assorted other men in formal suits—she counted six—descended from two cars and stood at varying distances, clearly his bodyguards.

Following the trajectory of her gaze, Antonio sighed as he guided her over the curb to wide marble stairs. "That's my partner Richard being overprotective. He's Black Castle Enterprises' security specialist, and his men follow us every second, till we die. If it's up to him, we never will."

Something dreadful lurched inside her at the thought of such an indomitable being dying.

His gaze stilled on her face, as if he'd felt the intensity of her reaction and was probing her mind for its cause. "I hope it's not bothering you."

She blinked up at him as they ascended the stairs toward an ornately carved mahogany double door. "Why should it?"

"Because you're out with a man who allegedly needs that much protection. Not a comforting thought, I'm sure."

That was what he'd thought had dismayed her?

Not that she could fault his inaccuracy. She'd given him no reason to think she'd be disturbed at the thought of his death. But she was, jarringly so.

"When we try to make him lay off, Richard tells us we're lucky he posts guards at that distance. It's pointless arguing with him when his only alternative is 24/7 surveillance much closer up."

"He has a good reason for his vigilance," she murmured. "You're too high-profile. You're as recognizable as any Hollywood celebrity, and much more influential. There must be many people whose lives would be easier with you out of the way."

She fought not to clutch his arm in reflex protection as two doormen opened the doors for them. She hoped he'd tell her that she watched too many action movies, that paranoid prophylactic measures were merely part of his partner's job.

As if diagnosing her anxiety right this time, his gaze gentled. "As you so keenly observed before, I never make enemies. I also make sure it's in everyone's best interest to keep me around and healthy. I'm in no danger whatsoever."

"Really?"

His smile broke out again, brightening her mood at once after the sharp dip it had taken. "Really."

Believing him, she exhaled her pent-up breath. "But the valet is *your* man. You wouldn't trust someone you haven't picked and vetted yourself with that car of yours."

His eyes glowed, though with what she couldn't diagnose. Whatever it was, a girl could get addicted to it, could get lost in it, and be lost without it.

"*That's* the mind I wanted working on my projects."

"An hour ago you considered that that mind jumps to rash and unsubstantiated assumptions."

"Only when it comes to my motives. We did agree I invert your thought process. How about you try to keep it upright from now on?"

"I don't do it on purpose, you know. But I'll try for the duration of lunch. Should be easier when I'm busy eating."

He swept an arm forward to usher her inside. "Then by all means, let's eat."

The restaurant he'd chosen turned out to be a place she hadn't known existed in the city she'd lived in for the past eight years. Inside a building she'd passed a hundred times before.

On the outside, it looked like any other upscale building in LA. On the inside, it made any other grand place she'd ever been inside look shabby. It wasn't only the old-world, aristocratic luxury, but the very atmosphere radiated mystery and exclusivity. She kept expecting to see James Bond and his gallery of villains walking through the hyper-real setting.

But then, next to the god who led her deeper into his domain, every other larger-than-life character, real or fictional, would fade to nothing.

As they made their way deeper into what had to be a club of some sort, everyone in their path, each clearly hailing from a world of extreme breeding and wealth, exclaimed reverential greetings. Some actually bowed.

And she'd thought the Italian clan she belonged to by birth, who'd recently burst into her existence, was the epitome of elitism. But Antonio's affluence, not to mention the awe he commanded, far surpassed the Accardis.

Not that wealth or power were of any interest to her. Her family's or his. The only reason she was debating entering her father's world was so she would have the family she'd never had. As for Antonio, the trappings of fame and fortune actually detracted from the far more impressive man cloaked in them.

With a hand on the small of her back, he led her into a ballroom-sized room with only one table for two in the center, exquisitely set in silk, silver and crystal. Her mind boggled at what it took to empty such a place and reserve it exclusively, at such short notice. If he didn't keep it perpetually reserved for himself, that was.

He'd just sat down opposite her when her phone vibrated with a loud buzz in her purse. Still jangling from Antonio's gossamer touches as he'd seated her, she almost jumped.

His hand rose in pure graciousness, permitting her to take the call, but his eyes remained fixed on her, letting her know he'd give her no privacy.

Getting the phone out, she fumbled it in unsteady hands, mumbled her chagrin at him, and herself, under her breath. It came out louder than she'd intended, since it elicited a blinding flash of his teeth.

She reeled in her runaway reactions, groaning as she saw the caller ID. Not the best time to talk to the *other* man who caused her emotional upheavals.

The moment she croaked a hello, her father's voice burst into her ear. "*Mia bella* Lilianissima, how are you, *tesoro*?"

Lili winced. Her father's over-the-top enthusiasm never ceased to jar her. It was weird he'd be so vocally eager after a lifetime of not even acknowledging her existence. It was even more unsettling after her mother's detached treatment, and the fact that Lili had been raised to think her father and the whole Accardi clan had ice water running in their blue-blooded veins. Recently, everything had been one contradiction after the other.

She took a breath and steadied her voice before she spoke. "I'm fine, Alberto. How are you?"

"*Tesoro*, when will you start calling me Padre or Daddy?"

She licked her lips, Antonio's vigilance intensifying her nervousness. "Maybe one day I can manage Father…"

"Then make that day today, *tesoro*. *Per favore!*"

"Uh, listen, Albe… Father…" She paused as her father celebrated her capitulation on the other end with another deluge of endearments. "I'd love to talk, really, but I'm at lunch with…an associate." Antonio's eyes glowed with something that made the electricity surging through her system spike. "I'll call you when I get home. Or tomorrow. With our time difference it must be already very late for you."

"I'm not in Venice, *tesoro*. I'm in New York City. Among the reasons I'm calling you is to tell you all the US-based Accardis are anxious to meet you. They're holding a reception in your honor in our main ancestral home here."

She almost blurted out a refusal. Not that she expected such an event to be unpleasant. So far every Accardi her father had introduced to her had been gracious and welcoming. Either her mother had falsely advertised the family in order to explain why they never had anything to do with them, or they were accommodating her father's fervent desire to include her in their exclusive ranks. Up till now, though, she'd met the Accardis one or two at a time. The idea of meeting them en masse was enough to give her performance anxiety.

"Is this weekend good for you?"

"No." The response came out far sharper than she'd intended. Biting her tongue, she tried again. "I...have work to do."

"On the weekend?"

Her gaze again clashed with Antonio's watchful one, then saw the satisfaction there. Her blood heated to the point where she felt steam rising off her body.

"Our lab has been taken over, and our new taskmaster has turned things upside down. I'm behind in my schedule because of his antics, and I have no idea when I'll get caught up."

Antonio's grin became as wide as she'd ever seen it as he beckoned to a waiter bearing champagne chilling in an ice-filled antique silver bucket.

Narrowing her eyes, she moved to end the call. One turmoil-inducing man at a time was her limit.

"Please let them know I'm unavailable this weekend before they put any plans in motion. When I sort out my stuff here, we'll discuss this further, okay?"

"*Certamente, tesoro.* Call me whenever it's convenient for you. Don't worry about the time difference or any other considerations. Wake me up, interrupt my meetings, anything at all. Talking to you is far more important than anything else. I have a lifetime of unmade calls I need to make up for."

To that she grumbled something vague around the lump that suddenly filled her throat and ended the call.

As she put her phone away, struggling to swallow through the tightness, Antonio poured champagne in her crystal flute and handed it to her.

"Your father?"

She grimaced. "Rhetorical questions fall under my redundancy ban. My father was so loud you must have heard his every word. And you heard me call him Father."

He also no doubt knew everything about her personal life, such as it was. Who her father was and that she'd grown up without him must have been the first things in the dossier he must have on her as he had on everyone in his employ. He probably knew the recent developments, too. He just wanted her to elaborate with her own version of details and updates.

At his unrepentant, probing stare, she sighed. "Yeah. My father. Long-absent and recently very much present. Therefore the extreme enthusiasm. He'll cool off, eventually. But for now I'm the daughter he reconnected with, all grown-up minus the hassle of years of teething, tantrums and teenage angst."

That still, strange expression on his face deepened before he exhaled. "This is another thing that proves we're not two different species at all."

"What? That I happen to have an Italian father, too?"

"And that you grew up without said father."

"You…" Suddenly the lump was back in her throat. It was ridiculous, when she'd never really considered herself unfortunate, but imagining the boy Antonio had been growing up fatherless…hurt.

It was clear *he* wasn't going to elaborate. Which was fine by her. Though curiosity burned inside her, she didn't want to learn anything that would make her stupidly ache more on his behalf.

To assuage the pain she suffered now, she gulped a big mouthful of silky champagne. "That sort of barely puts us in the same genus."

He toasted her with his flute. "At least it's a step up the ladder toward us occupying the same evolutionary status." Taking a sip, he put his glass down. "But we do share far more than that. We're both doctors—"

"Who've trodden diametrically different paths, have opposing approaches, and reached incomparable results."

Undeterred, he continued as if she hadn't interrupted him in this volleying rhythm between them they seem to have perfected. "We're both unyielding—"

"Yeah, that's why I'm sitting here having lunch with you in this top secret hideout for billionaires and spies and not watching my sitcoms as I wanted."

"And that's why you made me bow to your demands without any of my own objectives realized in return."

Her lips twisted. "So you say."

"So it *is*. This round is all yours." He beckoned to the maître d' without taking his gaze off her, a new heat entering his eyes. "But don't think you're going to win every time."

His warning made it sound as if their interactions would continue beyond this lunch, or her going back to work.

A thrill of disbelief, dread and expectation buzzed through her all during their ordering process.

As soon as the maître d' left, Antonio sat forward, his eyes growing somber, worsening her condition. "There's just one thing I'm confused about."

She took another sip to relieve her drying mouth. "You get confused like mortals?"

His smile didn't reach his eyes this time. "No, I don't, actually. But you affect me in unprecedented ways. You confuse the hell out of me. Therefore my inability to understand how you would seek the father who abandoned you. I have firsthand knowledge of how you can do without anything or anyone. Not to mention how unforgiving you are."

"You describe me like *such* a well-rounded sociopath."

"I describe myself, too. More things we have in common."

"Things of which I have a drop while you have an ocean." She fell silent until the waiters placed soup in front of them and left. "But you're right, as usual. I had no intention of seeking him out. I lived my life without him and his family, and I never wished to change that. It took him months of persistence after my mother's death until I finally agreed to see him."

That earlier strangeness returned, deeper now, as if that piece of information disturbed him. Which made no sense.

Suddenly famished, for food or other things, she sought the refuge of the soup and changed the subject.

For the rest of what turned out to be the most incredible meal she'd ever had, they talked about so many other things, never again broaching anything personal.

After lunch he insisted on taking her to another place for coffee. Another place where he was treated like a god, and where she almost felt it was sacrilegious for her to be. And again, the place had only them.

She finally had to comment. "You emptied the restaurant at your exclusive club, and this place, too, for only us, didn't you?" He only nodded. "Why? Do you have something against eating in other people's presence?"

"I ate in yours quite successfully, as I recall." He leaned back in his seat, regarding her with that intentness she'd come to expect but would never get used to. "I wanted you to relax without intrusions or distractions."

"I *am* known for being around human beings without any adverse reactions." She shook her head, picked up her cappuccino cup, the finest china she'd ever touched. "But you're way stronger than I am. Apart from the evident ways."

"Care to explain that statement?"

"You can stomach all this over-the-top luxury and sycophancy. I wouldn't be able to, even on an occasional basis. It's actually one of the reasons I'm so reluctant to get any deeper into my father's life. Like you, he lives in a rarefied world where I can't belong."

* * *

Antonio stared at Liliana and again felt everything spinning even further out of his control.

He'd orchestrated that lunch to give her a taste of what it would be like to be with a man of his caliber. Though his money and power had no effect on her when her research hung in the balance, he'd thought when she was made their beneficiary on a personal level, it would be different.

But the more he immersed her in its benefits, the more repulsed she was by the evidence of his status. She'd made sideway remarks through the past hours, but now she'd come right out and said it. Being in such surroundings, getting the treatment only limitless wealth bought, disturbed, not dazzled, her.

Taking another sip of cappuccino, she shrugged. "To each his own, of course, but I don't see why you need to exercise your power in such ways."

He gritted his teeth on another unknown sensation. Chagrin. "Maybe I was trying to impress you."

A not-too-delicate snort made her put down her cup before she spilled its contents. "You thought this would impress me? Have you met me?" She sat forward, her eyes wide and earnest. "You know what *really* impresses me? It's that if you were stripped of all your financial assets right this second, with that brain of yours, filled with all your knowledge and experience, with those hands that perform miracles on a regular basis, your worth wouldn't be affected. Anything you lost, you'd re-create, bigger and better, because luck and circumstances played no role when you first created it. So no, this—" she swept a hand around "—doesn't impress me. If anything, all this glitter and bustle doesn't become you, actually taints your true value. Without any of those trappings, it's you on your own, your gifts and abilities, that's invaluable."

Something swelled inside his chest until he couldn't

breathe. So he didn't, let himself succumb to those whiskey eyes as they penetrated him to his core with their absolute truthfulness.

No one besides his brothers had ever treated him without artifice. But their candor had been nothing like this. It was indescribable being exposed to hers. Her ruthless bluntness at once slapped him for being a pathetic showoff and bestowed on him the most validating evaluation of his life.

He got adulation wherever he went, but no one had ever told him anything like that. That his intrinsic value remained unchanged without everything he'd achieved or acquired. It was what he'd told himself since he'd escaped The Organization. That his abilities would bring him success, would amass fortune and power, would re-create them if he ever lost them. But only Liliana had ever expressed that exact same belief in him.

And she did so when she still considered him an antagonist. She was fair enough that she'd give even an enemy his full due.

She raised her cup to her lips. "Though I commented because you dragged me to this creepily empty seven-star establishment, I hope you don't always feel the need to flaunt your wealth and impose your worth on the world. I assure you you're the last man on earth who needs to do that."

He finally exhaled his pent-up breath. "I'll be sure to make a note of that."

So not only had he failed to impress her, she'd ended up counseling him.

To make things worse, he'd totally lost track of time. Six hours had passed, when he'd intended to tantalize her for only a couple of hours and leave her wanting more, so next time she'd be more eager, or at least, less resistant.

But he'd been incapable of ending the most enchanting day he'd ever had, the most exhilarating duel he'd ever waged. He'd been swept on the tide of their affinity, the hunger that had been building inside him demanding more of her. It now craved all of her. Now, not later.

She pushed her cappuccino cup away. "Was that leisurely enough for you?"

"Not quite."

"C'mon, you said lunch, and it's now time for dinner."

"Then we have dinner. At a place of your choosing."

"You think it's possible for me to eat anything else? I can barely breathe. But you're a big boy who needs his nutrition, so you go ahead. I'll walk back home." She tapped her slightly curved belly through that dress whose color made her skin glow and her hair and eyes sparkle with red and gold fires. "I can sure use a long, hard walk."

"So we'll walk together. Then I'll drive you home." She started to object and he cut her off. "You don't think I'd let you go back home on your own, do you?"

"Why not? I've been doing it since I was a kid."

"You're not doing it on my watch." Before she could say anything else, he was on his feet, his hand extended to her.

Though she grumbled that he was an entitled chauvinist, she gave him her hand. It was all he could do not to yank her by it, slam her against his aching body and drink her dissension dry.

As they stepped out into the night, the warm, humid ocean breeze was so strong it swept her curls across his face. He groaned, getting another whiff of her scent, which had almost had him pouncing on her back in her house. His hardness had long crossed from painful to agonizing.

Giving in, he reached out to catch those locks. He'd send his plans of taking it slow to hell, would capture her by that lush cascade of silk, push her against the nearest building and devour her.

But she aborted his feverish intentions, pulling her locks away, one from between his lips. And their hands touched.

Jerking hers away as if he'd electrocuted her, she mumbled that her hair came alive in the wind, produced a clip from her purse and secured her rioting hair in an improvised updo.

Triumphantly declaring the problem contained, she starting walking. It took him a moment to get his stiff legs to fall into step with her. His breath had clogged in his chest so hard again he had to force himself to breathe.

That tightness increased all through their two-hour walk down the bustling streets. As did his enjoyment.

They argued, agreed, bickered and shared companionable silences. He even got her to laugh many times, once so hard she shed tears.

Getting her to lower her guard enough with him, then to respond to his wit and teasing so unreservedly, was the most rewarding thing he'd ever done.

Then to his dismay, she said that her feet were starting to hurt, being so unused to heels. He should have considered this, at least realized her discomfort when she'd slowed down. Not only had he been inconsiderate but now their walk had to end.

He offered to carry her so they could go on, and she laughed it off, thinking he was joking, which he wasn't. He called Paolo to deliver his car, and she took her sandals off while they waited, so he did scoop her up. No matter how much she spluttered for him to put her down, he insisted he wasn't letting her stand barefoot in the street.

Once driving, every cell of his body on fire, he kept wondering how he'd prolong the drive and his time with her.

He didn't want this night to end.

Then he felt her looking at him. At the next light he turned to her, found her gaze fixed on him with what looked like distressed embarrassment.

The tightness he was getting used to feeling around her returned in full force. "What's wrong?"

Her lips twisted. "Just that you went to great lengths to show me a good time and I was only a rude jackass in return."

"You only said what you thought without filters."

"Which is the definition of rudeness. I played back our whole outing and I realized you've been nothing but gracious while I've been obnoxious. At first I was so on purpose, but then I decided to stop, and I was still downright offensive."

"You were no such thing. You even paid me the biggest compliment anyone ever has. To everyone I *am* my success and power and money. You're the only one who ever thought I am the one who gives worth to my achievements and assets." Those wide eyes he never wanted to stop staring into grew larger. He gritted his teeth as he had to turn back to the road and drive again. "And even if you've been rude, I would have deserved it, since you consider I've coerced you into this outing."

"You didn't. I know I could have said no. But I did want to come. And I did enjoy everything, because I was with you. You're the best company I've ever had."

His gaze swung to her, caught her expression as she'd said these unbelievable statements.

Had he ever thought her anything less than the most perfect thing he'd ever seen? Was that how she truly felt? Could he be that lucky?

And whatever remained of his premeditation snapped. "I don't want to drive you home, Liliana. Come with me to mine."

The moment the words were out, he wanted to kick himself.

This was the last thing he should have said. He'd barely gotten her to trust him enough to enjoy being with him and to admit it. And he had to go and crash through her limits like an overeager teenager.

Now she wouldn't only refuse, she'd swat him back to persona non grata status. Women usually played demure at this point, so men wouldn't think them easy. But *her* refusal would be the most legitimate response ever.

Amidst the fury of self-disgust, he almost missed her answer. Braking too abruptly at the light, jerking her in her seat, he turned to her, disbelieving.

"What did you say?" he rasped.

Looking up at him without the slightest trace of guile, she repeated what he hadn't believed he'd heard her say.

"I said okay."

Entering Antonio's sprawling mansion a fraught half hour after he'd asked her to go home with him, Lili still wondered if she was having another wish-fulfillment dream. One far more detailed and realistic…and outrageously ambitious. She kept wondering if she'd wake up any moment now.

But the dream continued, tangible, all-encompassing, like his heat at her back, his aura intoxicating her like the champagne had failed to. Everything was way over the top.

Problem was, it was really happening. He'd asked her to come home with him and she'd accepted. In embarrassing speed and eagerness.

"Would you like a drink?"

She swung around at his quiet question, almost losing her balance, and found him watching her with the most unreadable glance he'd leveled on her so far. Every fiber in her body quivered. He'd been almost silent since she'd said okay. Now the way he regarded her… What was he thinking?

To give herself space, to figure out what to feel or do, she nodded. With an even more disturbing glance, he nodded back as his powerful hand loosened his tie and undid a button as if they were suddenly suffocating him. Her dry throat convulsed as she watched him turn away, cross the lavish, ultramasculine great room to a wet bar at its end, his every movement sheer poetry of grace and control.

Her mind raced as he prepared their drinks, every now and then saying something that only necessitated monosyllabic responses from her.

She was now convinced he was interested in her. As a woman. Also known as sexually. While she could tell him he couldn't have picked a worse candidate for such interest, she doubted he'd listen. His intense fixation on her had only grown at her attempts to dissuade him from coming closer.

Maybe because he could talk to her, or she jogged his jaded senses, or she was a type he'd never encountered. Whatever the reason, he was interested.

But *interest* was too mild a word, insultingly so, to describe what he provoked in her.

She *craved* him.

When she'd never wanted anyone. Or anything, for that matter. Besides scientific discovery. Not that she'd ever felt anything this out of control for science.

Still, mere craving didn't describe her feelings now. Every last component of her being was aroused. Her mind, her senses, her body. She was in an uproar. For him. Only ever him.

But while his interest had grown directly proportionate to her resistance, since she'd stopped resisting him back there in his car, something had changed. He'd been almost...subdued.

Had he regretted inviting her here the moment she'd agreed? Had he only done so because, based on her behavior so far, he'd fully expected her to decline? Was he already losing interest now that she'd suddenly stopped providing him with the only things that had attracted him to her, resistance and surprises?

This probably explained the way he was behaving now.

Even if it didn't, she knew if she capitulated and joined his worshipping hordes, he *would* lose interest in her and move on. Sooner would be better than later. The longer she was exposed to him, the more severe the havoc he'd leave in his wake.

That led her to one possible decision. She'd give him what he expected as his right from all mortal beings.

He was sauntering back now with the drinks, as if he were postponing reaching her as much as he could. Stopping two steps away, when he'd always kept only one between them, he brooded down at her as he handed her a glass.

Gulping down agitation and regret, she took it. Then she reached for his glass, too. His eyes widened as he unclasped the glass and let her take it. Trembling in earnest now, she put the glasses down on a nearby coffee table.

His expression was perplexed when she straightened. It became stunned when she covered the space he'd kept between them, then reached up and pulled the tie he'd fully undone right off.

Dropping it to the ground, she lowered her eyes, unable to take the brunt of his blazing eyes this close up, or his disappointment that she'd turned out to be like every other woman he'd ever met. Squeezing her eyes shut, she did what she'd been aching to do since she'd laid eyes on him.

Sliding her hand beneath his shirt, she longingly glided her shaking, prickling hand over his hot, hard flesh.

Six

Antonio felt his mind short-circuiting.

Liliana. She was touching him. Igniting him into an uproar. Shocking him into paralysis.

This wasn't even among the things he'd expected or hoped for. He'd planned to court her, to break down her resistance in stages. But with a single "okay," she'd thrown everything out of whack. He felt like he'd been pushing with all his strength against an immovable object when suddenly all resistance was removed. He found himself hurtling with unstoppable momentum, falling flat on his face.

He'd still been struggling to adjust his thinking, and his actions accordingly as he'd handed her that drink, when she'd thrown him for a loop again by taking his, too, then proceeding to whisk off his tie. As the silk had hissed against his neck, as if relieved to part with his shirt, he'd frozen, his every sense converged on her eyes, trying to fathom from her expression what the hell had been going on.

But they'd been turbid with so many emotions. He *thought* he'd seen shyness, uncertainty, resignation, recklessness...and hunger, before she'd closed them as if to escape his analysis. Not that he could have been certain of anything. His mind had been a tangled mess by then.

And that was before she'd *touched* him.

Now a small, delicate hand slid beneath his shirt, as if searching for his heart. He felt as if she'd found it, taken hold of it. It was the only explanation for why it boomed in erratic thunder, when it had always remained steady in emergencies and under literal fire.

Her touch was like nothing he'd ever felt. It was like *he'd* never been touched before, and her tentative softness was his first exposure to human contact, to sensual stimulation. Sensations he'd never felt before exploded within him, detonating every single barrier inside him. The last dam was his control.

He was no longer in command of his thoughts or reactions, nor did he want to be. Of its own accord, his hand clamped her wrist, stopping the torment of her touch. Her eyes jerked open and up, alarm and mortification spreading in their gold depths. And his last thread of restraint snapped.

A primal rumble surging from his depths, he did what he'd wanted to do every second of the past three days. He yanked her against his body, hard. He growled something incoherent at the music of her cry, enveloping her in his arms and crushing her against him.

For one suspended moment, their gazes merged. Hers was at once stunned and surrendering. His heart felt as if it would explode if he didn't possess those lips that spilled those mind-melting sounds of submission.

"Antonio..."

He swooped down, his open mouth swallowing her gasp as he drove his tongue between her lips and plumbed her depths. The taste and scent of her, both overpowering aphrodisiacs, made him growl again and again as he feasted on her.

Opening to him, letting him all the way inside her, she whimpered, squirmed. He gave her what she was wordlessly begging for, deepening his possession, every glide against her moist silkiness, every thrust inside her fragrant deliciousness pouring fuel on his fire. Mindless with the need to devour her, to invade her, he hauled her up into his arms and strode to his bedroom with her curled up against him.

He flung himself down on the bed, taking her on top of him. She cried out as she impacted him, then again as he reversed their positions, taking her yielding, trembling body underneath him. His hands were almost rough in his haste to push her dress up and open her thighs. He groaned at the feel of her velvet firmness filling his hands. Lodging himself between her splayed smoothness, he rose on his knees to take off his jacket and shirt, tearing the latter in his haste.

Her eyes grew heavier as he exposed himself, her body undulating its plea beneath him, her voice quavering as she gasped his name between fractured breaths.

With pants still on, he slid over her again, undoing her hair's improvised confinement, driving trembling hands into her thick tresses, his gaze feverishly roaming her flushed face. That face, that essence, had taken control of his desires and fantasies from the instant he'd seen her. Now he'd take her body. He'd possess it until she wept with pleasure.

Her eyes glittered with molten gold then overflowed. He jackknifed up, gaping at her as tears spilled down her hectic cheeks in pale tracks. His thought just now had been metaphorical, but she was shedding tears for real.

She was that aroused? As aroused as he was?

Triumph and hunger raged through him like wildfire. He should be shocked at their ferocity. But he reveled in feeling out of control for the first time in his life.

"Antonio, please..."

Her tearful plea, her body buzzing beneath him with a need as brutal as his own, undid whatever sanity he had left.

He fell on her like a starving predator, his lips wrenching at hers, his tongue driving inside her as he ground himself against her.

Suddenly she was heaving beneath him, her moans becoming strangled shrieks.

It was only when her cries in his mouth turned to whimpers and her body melted limply beneath his that realization trickled through his fury of arousal.

Had she...climaxed?

Struggling to stop grinding against her, he raised himself on shaking arms, found her staring at him from slit lids, panting through swollen lips, her body nerveless.

She *had* orgasmed. Before he got her naked, before he took her, just from him emulating the act of possession. She lay beneath him, boneless, the sight and scent of her satisfaction maddening him more. Her eyes told him release had only left her hungrier, readier for his invasion.

But he'd already been jarred out of his fugue. And what he realized he'd been about to do horrified him. He would have taken her without preliminaries. Without protection. He had none here. He'd never had a woman in this house, let alone this bed, had never intended to have one here.

He could pleasure her again, but he was in too precarious a condition. If he'd lost his mind from one touch, if he continued touching her, he'd get her naked, would end up buried inside her, would ride her until she climaxed around him, wouldn't be able to stop until he spilled deep inside her womb. It would be an irretrievable step that would spoil everything.

Among all the inhuman tests he'd been exposed to and had always passed with flying colors, raising himself off her now, ending this, was the hardest thing he'd ever done.

Her hands clung weakly to him, trying to coax him back to her. He'd never resisted anything so overwhelming.

But he managed to. Rising from the bed, keeping his eyes off her so he wouldn't launch himself back at her, he strode to his dressing room and replaced the shirt he'd shredded before he strode back out to her.

His heart almost stopped when he found the bed empty. Exploding into a run, he only slowed down when he found her in the foyer, retrieving the purse she'd left on a table there.

"Liliana…"

His voice sounded as if it issued through gravel, which he felt filled his throat. Slowly, she turned to him, her face for the very first time totally unreadable. She said nothing.

"I'm sorry I pounced on you like that. It wasn't why I invited you here."

"I know. I'm the one who invited it."

Her exoneration was yet another unexpected blow that ratcheted his upheaval.

Feeling that anything he said now would make the situation worse somehow, he exhaled in frustration. "Maybe it's better if I take you home now."

Her eyes the darkest he'd seen them, she shook her head. "It's better if you don't. I'll call a cab."

He needed to argue, to convince her to let him see her home. Maybe he'd find something sane to say on the way to right the course of events that had devolved into this stilted mess. But he knew in his condition he'd only compound his mistakes.

Deciding to let her go, and to stay away from her until he got his act together, he exhaled. "I'll get Paolo to take you home." At her nod of consent, he reached for the intercom. "He lives on the premises, so he'll bring the car to the front door in a couple of minutes."

Without meeting his eyes, she again nodded, turned away and walked to the door. In seconds, she was gone.

He didn't know how long he remained rooted, staring at the door through which she'd disappeared. All he could see was how she'd looked as she'd walked away. Steady yet subdued, the energy and fire he'd always seen and felt in her every step now gone, as if something had been extinguished inside her.

Collapsing on the nearest seat, he pitched forward, burying his face in shaking hands.

What had he done?

"Won't you finally tell me what you did?"

Lili winced as Brian walked into her lab. His mood was so bright, she felt like closing her eyes to avoid its glare.

"I've been letting you get away with not telling me long enough," he said, "but after this morning, I can't wait any longer."

Yeah. Because this morning Antonio had sent a decree down his chain of command that everyone in the lab had their choice of project, whether it was one of his, their original ones or a new endeavor. Not only that, but if anyone saw fit to work on several projects simultaneously, they would be given all logistical and financial support. For scientists, who were always tied up in endless financial red tape, to be given such free rein was a dream.

"For God's sake, Lili, you have to tell me," Brian urged. "The only things I don't tell you are things you certainly don't want to hear."

She returned her eyes to her laptop to escape his merriment and curiosity. But she no longer saw the data she'd just inputted, what she believed was her first breakthrough, which had caused the first lift in her spirit in the last two weeks. The two weeks since she'd last seen Antonio.

"For the last time, Brian," she mumbled. "I didn't do anything. The man just reconsidered."

"*After* you gave him all of your mind, not just a piece of it." Brian perched his hip on her desk. "But I thought that only made him give *you* back your research. Judging from today's developments, you must have done more."

"Unless I've developed some sort of long-distance mind control, I can't see how I could have. I haven't seen the man since the day I came back to work."

The day after her magical time with Antonio came to a disastrous end.

Brian regarded her as if he was deciding whether she was telling the truth. Then his grin widened even more. "Seems you didn't have to do more. That initial dose you gave him worked like a vaccine. Its effect intensified as time went by, until he developed full immunity, or in this case, empathy with your own views."

"Botched scientific metaphor aside, it's so nice to be likened to attenuated or dead microorganisms."

"I'm likening you to the tiny busters who save lives, like you've saved ours."

Slumping back in her chair, she exhaled. "Don't exaggerate. I didn't do anything. And what lives? You were all gung ho about joining his projects."

"I myself would have worked on anything that kept me employed and serving the cause of science. But this? This is what I became a scientist hoping to do one day. This is the beginning of a life I never thought I'd be able to live. And whatever you say, I know I have you to thank for it."

"Fine. Believe whatever you want and leave me in my own version of reality, where everything is the absolute opposite of what you insinuate about my effect on Antonio Balducci."

Brain sobered when he realized she was barely reining in her agitation. "Have I put my foot in it?"

"Down to the knee joint."

Dismay flared in his eyes. "Don't tell me you've…"

"Fallen for him" went unspoken. And "been rebuffed" was also concluded.

"Man, Lili! Granted, the guy is a god, and all the women and half the men around here are swooning over him, but you of all women… I thought you'd be immune."

"Well, you thought wrong."

His gaze switched from disconcerted to solicitous in a heartbeat. "You know the last thing I want to do is step on your toes, but I know how you bottle stuff up, and how you always feel better when you talk to me about it."

"Not this time, Brian, so just drop it, okay?" His persistence had helped her once before, after her mother's death, when he'd finally gotten her to unburden herself. But knowing it wouldn't help this time, she changed the subject. "But since you're so eager to listen to me, do you have an hour? I think I'm onto something big here and I want your opinion."

Her diversion tactic worked, since scientific curiosity was the only thing that could take Brian's mind off just about anything. And for the next two hours she showed him her latest findings and he corroborated her every hope. By the time he left her, they were both certain she'd just broken through to the next level in her research.

Though this was huge, and she was beyond thrilled, that excitement didn't carry to the rest of her being. Most of her remained a prisoner to the memory of that night with Antonio.

That night, after his driver had taken her home, she'd

collapsed in bed, shaking like a leaf with both mortification and arousal.

Instead of dreaming of him, she'd stayed awake all night, her mind filled with memories of the mindless minutes when she'd offered herself to him, when he'd almost taken her. His every touch and look and breath had replayed over and over, burning her with their vividness and her humiliation. She'd been so on fire for him, it had only taken him a few thrusts through their clothes for her to climax.

While it had stunned her, since she'd never reached release so easily, so violently, it had shocked him more. Maybe even alarmed or disgusted him. For what kind of woman would go off like that from just a few kisses and grinds? He must have figured he'd terribly miscalculated, and the iceberg he'd thought he'd enjoy melting had turned out to be a powder keg that would end up blowing up in his face.

She couldn't blame him that he hadn't wanted to be anywhere near her after that. He'd torn his gaze away from her pleading eyes and himself from her clinging arms, rushing to put clothes on to show her there'd be no further intimacies. Not that she'd been about to wait for him to come back to tell her that. She'd tried to run out of his mansion without seeing him again. But he'd caught up with her before she could, and though he'd tried to be considerate, what he'd said, how he'd looked at her, had been an even worse blow. Besides his obvious dismay and regret, it had seemed as if he'd…pitied her.

She hadn't closed her eyes till morning after that night, agonizing over whether to continue her earlier plan of leaving California, or going back to the lab he'd promised she could return to on her terms.

She'd ended up going back to work. A major part of her decision had been the hope that she'd see him again.

She'd kept envisioning scenarios of how he'd come and what she'd say, in apology, or at least in an attempt to excuse or explain her actions. Anything to take them back to where they'd been before she'd touched him and spoiled everything.

That first day back in the lab, she'd kept expecting Antonio to walk in at any moment, kept jumping at any movement or sound, imagining she'd heard his voice or caught a glimpse of him.

But he hadn't come. Not that day, not since.

With each passing day, she'd been torn more among shame, longing and despondency. Antonio had disappeared from her life as she'd known he would, only sooner and under far worse circumstances. She'd been right. All he'd needed was her capitulation. Once he'd had it, and so resoundingly, he'd lost interest. He must have even been horrified by her extreme reaction. He might have even feared he could have set himself up for a *Fatal Attraction* scenario.

It mortified her that she wouldn't be able to tell him he had nothing to worry about from her, or that she would always cherish whatever time she'd had with him. If that sounded pathetic, as it probably was, she didn't care. It was true. Being with him had been the most intense experience of her life. It pained her that what would always be a precious memory to her would be a distasteful one to him.

It also dismayed her that he'd disappeared before she could thank him. For going above and beyond in giving her everything she'd thought she'd never have, and thereby enabling her to reach the next level in her research. And he'd done that even after her accusations and suspicions and nastiness, then her reversal into a sex-starved maniac.

If she let him know through his deputies what she hoped to do, she feared he'd assign her some unsavory motivation.

Even knowing she'd never see him again, the thought of losing his admiration, his respect, hurt the most.

"Are you busy?"

That voice. *His* voice.

In the split second before she looked up, she was certain she'd find nothing there. She'd jumped at too many phantom sounds and images of him before.

But this time, her gaze didn't land on nothingness. It collided with the too-real, too-magnificent sight of Antonio Balducci.

He was really there. Peeking around her lab's door, only his head and part of his shoulders visible. As if he was ready to retreat if she said yes, she was busy.

The world dimmed, and for the first time she knew how it was possible to faint with a brutal surge of emotions. Shock, elation, trepidation and a dozen other contradictory things.

Had he come to see her? Or was he here inspecting the status of her research, thanks to his generosity? Oh, and, by the way, to put things straight with her?

"I can come back later if you prefer."

His baritone reverberated in her very being, shaking her out of her paralysis. She rose unsteadily. "No. Actually you're just the person I wanted to see."

"I am?"

"Yes, yes, I…wanted to tell you a couple of things."

Walking in and closing the door behind him, he straightened to his daunting height, this carefulness of the last time he'd faced her, almost a wariness, still permeating his body language.

Man, she'd really managed to scare him. Was he worried she might jump his bones or something?

Circling him as far away as possible, she linked her hands behind her back. "I was going to make a formal proposal and send it to you up the chain, but since you're here…"

"You don't need to do that when you need more funds or resources for your research."

"It isn't for my research." She inhaled a bolstering breath. "I've taken a comprehensive look at your…folder, and I owe you an apology. The research you wanted me to helm is right up my alley and I find it very ambitious and exciting. If I reorganize my schedule to make a timetable that would have me working on both projects simultaneously, it is completely doable, with your resources and support in place. So if you'd still like me on the project, count me in."

"Actually, I no longer want you on it."

Her heart plummeted yet again with the validation of her worst fears, that her value to him had been negated by that foolish episode. It felt like a physical blow that almost rocked her on her feet.

Struggling not to choke on the lump that expanded in her throat, she waved her hand in dismissal. "Never mind, then. It was just an idea." Then an even worse thought detonated in her mind. "If…if you don't want me here at all, I understand. You still have my resignation, and you can approve it any time you—"

"Stop." His admonition was exasperated, almost pained. "Stop jumping to conclusions about me and what I mean. I don't want you on my project because I don't want your efforts and focus divided. I want them on your own work, where you're making remarkable progress."

He did? And he knew that? How?

"But when you conclude your work successfully, if you're still interested in any of my projects, there's nothing I want more than to have the benefit of your vision and expertise." He paused, exhaled, the searing blue of his eyes suddenly darkening. "But I'm not here to talk about work."

The heart that had been expanding with his every word felt as if it shriveled again. He was here to clear that personal land mine that now existed between him and an employee he wanted to keep.

She nodded. "I understand."

"I doubt you do."

"You must want to talk about that night two weeks ago. That's the other thing I'd hoped to talk to you about. I want you to forget that embarrassing episode ever happened, and be sure nothing like that will ever happen again. Just chalk it up to pathetic inexperience and let it go at that, okay?

As if he hadn't heard a word she'd said, his gaze focused on her eyes with such intensity, she felt them misting.

"Do you know why I've stayed away these two weeks?" he asked quietly.

She forced everything in her to go still, refusing to jump to more conclusions, especially ones laden with false hopes. She'd already accepted that he'd streak through her life like a meteor, affording her a brief blaze of splendor before he disappeared. She should be thankful he'd hurtled on before he'd done more damage. She should cling to the shield of resignation, even if every cell in her body still popped with the electricity of anticipation.

When she said nothing, Antonio answered his own question. "I retreated to give you space, to reassess the damages I caused when I pursued you, besieged you, forced you out of your comfort zone and into what you might come to regret."

That was why he'd stayed away? Not for the horrible, degrading reasons she'd been torturing herself with?

"But there was another reason, too."

Her heart hit Pause, dreading his next words.

"I had to rethink everything I'd intended for this lab, to make decisions that would benefit everyone the most, by letting them resume their work or make their own choices, with my adjustments." He started walking closer, the gaze fixed on her filling with so much she couldn't bring herself to believe. "I had to prove to you, and to myself, that I can do what you can approve of, can be someone you can truly value and admire. You made me reconsider everything I do, professionally and personally."

By the time he was close enough for her to reach out and touch him again, she was ready to collapse at his feet. And that was before he made his closing statement.

"And that's why I'm here now. To tell you I want to hit a restart button with you. At your pace, on your terms."

Antonio had never dreaded anything in his life, a life filled with horrors and dangers and catastrophes. Not really.

But he dreaded Liliana's answer. He didn't know what he'd do if she rejected him.

Could he just walk away? How, when the thought of losing her sent him straight out of his ordered, controlled mind?

For two weeks he'd forced himself to stay away, until he could provide her with tangible proof of what she meant to him, how she'd changed him. That time apart from her had been almost more than he could bear. He'd spent every moment struggling not to charge after her, to carry her back to his bed and keep her there until he'd branded her, made her unable to walk away from him ever again.

But first he had to prove to her he could become a man she could trust and respect for his ability to change, to do the right thing, not only a man she could admire for his abilities or lust after for his body and the unstoppable chemistry they shared.

Waiting for her verdict as if it would decide his fate, believing it would, he struggled to keep his expression from betraying the upheaval inside him. The last thing he needed was to scare her off with the intensity of his need.

"Why?"

After every scenario he'd played out in his head, she managed to surprise him yet again with that one-word question for an answer. She neither jumped on his offer, nor made him grovel some more, nor rejected him outright.

"You'll have to help me here, Liliana. Why what exactly?"

"Why me? Really? Now that the element of my surprise, my novelty, is gone, not to mention my resistance? When I never considered those reasons enough for you to pursue me in the first place?"

His heart contracted with an emotion he'd never bothered with. Shame. But also wonder, that she was so attuned to him she'd sensed his early ulterior motive. This *was* his punishment for harboring those intentions, to have them resonate in her psyche, tainting her view of his motives when they no longer existed. When he now just wanted her.

Those eyes that filled his every waking and sleeping second probed his, filled with the candor and strength and vulnerability he'd become addicted to. "If you don't have specific reasons why you want me, then just tell me. Tell me what you expect from me, what you wish from being with me. I also want to know all the possible outcomes."

His head spinning, he blinked. "Outcomes?"

"Yes, like what to expect when you lose interest, how you intend to handle the eventual end of whatever we start." Her shoulders lifted in a self-conscious shrug. "I told you I can't handle uncertainty or afford upheavals."

Her scientific approach to his offer, insisting on analyzing his motives and charting a probable course for their relationship, was at once endearing and stunning. But what oppressed him was her expectation of worst-case scenarios.

"You mean you'd accept being with me even when you expect it to be a limited and finite liaison?"

She gave him such a look, as if he'd just said the most ridiculous thing, as if it was impossible for her to expect anything else, either from him or for herself.

Then she laughed, the sound mirthless. "I think anyone who enters a liaison without such expectation is just courting disaster. But I do want you so intensely that I'd take whatever is being offered, as long as I know what it is. I just need to go in knowing what to expect. That's all I ask. Total honesty."

His heart twisted with another feeling he'd never suffered from. Guilt. Total honesty was the one thing he couldn't offer her. He couldn't come clean about his initial plot to use her to get close to the Accardi family. He doubted even her pragmatic nature could forgive that. Even if it did, he feared her spontaneity with him wouldn't survive the revelation.

But he couldn't bear that she thought herself his inferior, that she expected nothing but impermanence and limitations as her due.

Itching to shake her out of those beliefs, he took her by the shoulders, groaning with the pleasure of her response, of touching her again.

"I'll say this once more and never again, Liliana. You are not only absolutely wrong in how you value yourself, but you appallingly underestimate my desire for you. I've *never* wanted anything like I want you. As for why I do, let me enlighten you. I want you because of *everything* you are. Every single thing about you fascinates me, elates me, inflames me. I adore your candor, and your wit leaves me with the bends. Your mind delights me and everything else about you, every gesture and breath and inch, makes me want to devour you. I'm the one who worries that once you come closer, it might be you who loses interest."

To say she looked incredulous was as accurate as saying she was reticent. But those eyes he'd been lost without flared with renewed life with his every word. Now their blaze made him almost give up any pretense of control.

But it was she who mattered here, and he had to make her feel secure. "All this doesn't only equalize our positions, Liliana, it makes me the supplicant. As such, I have no expectations. It's you who'll state your terms, set your parameters and every other thing you wish for in our intimacies."

Growing excitement glinted in her eyes. "What if I make outrageous demands?"

"I will welcome anything." His lips twisted as he surveyed the caring and generosity filling her expression, what he knew made up most of her being. "Though I doubt you'd ask for anything. You don't have a selfish or greedy cell in your body."

"I don't know about that, but I'd never make any demands. I want you free of obligations, for they have no place between us. I want you, and if you want me, for me, I'll be with you. Until it no longer makes you and therefore me happy." He started to object, furious that her insecurity about him hadn't been appeased, but she overrode him. "What I want to renegotiate is our professional situation. As my boss…"

He groaned his frustration at her evasion. "Will you please forget that? I'm no longer your boss. I gave you back full control over your work."

"Did you do that only to please me? To remove the obstacle of the boss/employee dynamic between us?"

He shook his head. "I do want to please you, Liliana, and remove all barriers between us, but I would have found another way to do so if I didn't believe your work held more merit than mine, given that you're so much further ahead in your research. I only attempted to force you to relinquish it initially as a demonstration of dominance. But not only am I now giving you absolute autonomy, I'm here to turn the whole lab over to you."

She staggered back. "Holy one-eighty, Antonio."

He caught her closer again, needing to convince her. "That's how you make me feel, Liliana. Like nothing I ever cared about matters anymore. Nothing but you, but us, matters to me now."

"Even so, you don't toss a two hundred-million-dollar lab at me to prove it. I told you I'm not partner material, and you want to make me director?"

"Even if you lack management skills, your scientific knowledge and your insight into your colleagues make you perfect for the job. I'll provide you with support staff who'll deal with the executive and financial issues. But in every other way, you'll make a far better boss than I can be for this place."

"Okay, time-out." She held her hands in the famous gesture. "You're clearly suffering from an extreme case of U-turn. So it's up to me to moderate you until you level out." He reached out to her hands, but she grabbed his instead. "Now listen, Antonio. I'm not taking this carte blanche or any other offer you come up with. And that's final. I only wanted to reach a common ground where both my goals and your interests could be met. I wish nothing more than to realize them both in a way that's the most beneficial for everyone."

As he looked into her earnest eyes, it was at this moment that Antonio realized something monumental.

What he felt for her.

Exactly what his brothers described they felt for their soul mates.

Love.

Seven

Love.

The word echoed in Antonio's mind as he stared at Liliana, who continued to detail how the common professional ground she was suggesting would work.

It had to be love. It *was*. This pure, limitless emotion.

But how? When he'd been in her presence only a handful of times? When he'd lived his life believing he didn't even have a heart?

But as he looked into her eyes and saw clear to her soul, saw what had delighted and spellbound him from the first, he knew.

Time was irrelevant. And he now did have a heart.

Liliana had planted one inside him.

Totally at peace with the discovery of its creation, and ecstatic about its captivity in Liliana's kind hands, he swept her in his arms and silenced her with everything that was bursting in his newly forged heart.

She melted into his kiss, not reciprocating, just yielding to him, letting him do whatever he wanted to her. That communicated how much she wanted him to possess her far more than if she'd gone wild in response.

He tore his lips from hers. "If you don't want me to take you right now, you'd better stop that."

Her long, thick lashes rose languidly, revealing passion-filled eyes that almost made him drag her down on the ground and take her there and then. "I'm not doing anything."

Pushing her back against the nearest wall, he pinned her there with his full weight, needing to imprint her with his body. "Exactly. Your surrender is sending me berserk."

"Yes, please."

"Liliana…" Her name erupted from his chest as he hitched her legs around his hips. His tongue plunged inside her open mouth, swallowing her gasps and eliciting more as he drove his hardness against her core through their clothes. "Will you come for me again?"

"Antonio…" She arched against the wall, making a fuller offer of herself.

Feeling her precious flesh burning in his hands, he quickened his cadence, the need to see her coming apart for him again riding him harder with each thrust.

"Do you know what it did to me when I felt you climaxing under me that night?" Her moans fractured, the flush staining her cheeks deepening before she buried her face in his chest. An incredulous laugh escaped him. "Are you shy?"

Suddenly she wriggled in his arms until she made him put her back on her feet, her eyes downcast. "I thought you were horrified…I thought that was why…"

A deeper wave of color surged over her face and neck. He cupped her jaw, made her look at him. "Why I stopped? I did that only because feeling you heave and tremble beneath me, realizing that I aroused you so much I drove you to orgasm even before taking you, snapped my control for the first time in my life."

She regarded him with a mixture of self-consciousness and disbelief. "You didn't seem out of control at all."

"It must be my surgeon facade. But if I'd remained near you one more minute, I would have taken you. Without protection. And I knew you'd let me."

Her eyes widened in realization and admission, proving he'd been right. She *would* have let him. She wanted him inside her without barriers, branding her with his pleasure. As he would, soon.

"I had to get away from you since I had no more control and your every touch and breath and glance had me at breaking point."

A keen escaped her as she crushed herself to him, silently demanding he stop holding back.

Unable to even contemplate it anymore, he pressed her to the wall again. He was devouring her whimpers, undulating feverishly against her when a one-note buzz jolted through them both.

His phone. The line he kept for his brothers.

Dammit.

Setting her down but unable to stop caressing her, he gestured an apology as he pulled the phone out.

It was an integral part of their brotherhood's pact, to answer a call from a brother at once. They'd depended on one another to survive, then to escape, then to conquer the world. A brother's call trumped everything. They never called one another on those special lines unless it was something serious. As the group's doctor, he'd gotten many of those calls.

Then came the last couple of years. Since then he'd gotten calls that were serious only in his brothers' eyes. After all, they considered any twinge their wives or children suffered the end of the world.

But this was Ivan. He wasn't married and would never be if all remained right with the world. Ivan had never called him on this line. Not once.

His heart thudding in mounting trepidation, he pushed the answer button. "Ivan?"

"Tonio, I'm landing in LA in half an hour. I need you and your best surgical team ready. Code Whiteout."

Code Whiteout meant he needed Antonio's secret surgical facility, where he had a special team on standby and where he treated injuries they needed kept below law enforcement's radar.

He gritted his teeth at the agitation he felt cracking his best friend's usual Siberian composure. "Tell me."

"A…friend and his sister. They were gunned down. I have a team stabilizing them. I need you to put them back together."

"I'll meet you there."

Ivan ended the call without another word. Antonio turned to Liliana, found she'd walked away to give him privacy.

He rushed after her, caught her in a ferocious hug. "I have to go, *mi amore*. Emergency surgery."

She almost jumped at his endearment, her eyes flooding with such exquisite delight. "Of course."

"Do you know how I hate leaving you now?"

"If it's as much as I hate you leaving, I pity you fiercely." Her smile wobbled as she caressed his cheek. "But duty calls. To both of us. I'd better get back to work before the bright ideas I was working on evaporate." He hugged her again as if afraid *she* somehow would. Seeming to read his paranoia right, she grinned. "I'll be right here when you're done."

"From the preliminary report, I don't foresee being done for the next twelve hours. If that."

"Then I'll see you whenever you can see me." She brushed his hair back, her touch soothing and bolstering.

He got out his keys, pressed them into her hand. "I'll text you my security codes and Paolo's number. He'll pick you up from your house after you get what you need. I want you there when I get home."

Her eyes made him this promise, and so many more, all of which he knew she'd keep no matter what. Then she stood on tiptoes and kissed him, giving him a glimpse of the ecstasy they'd share.

Before he grabbed her again, she stepped out of his arms, turned him around and marched him to the door. "The sooner you're gone, the sooner you'll be back to me."

As he stepped outside her lab, his heart lurched. Leaving her felt like leaving behind a vital part of himself.

"I'll be home as soon as I can."

"Oh, no, you're not rushing a surgery on my account. I'll be there no matter how late you are. And if you're not home by tomorrow morning, you know where to find me. Now, shoo."

At her grin, he groaned and turned away, forcing himself not to look back. He'd be late if he did, and Ivan would kill him. He'd do his job then rush home to her.

The anticipation kept him flying high all the way to his secret facility on the fringes of LA. It was only when he was entering it that he realized something.

When he'd given Liliana his keys, he'd been asking her to move in with him. He'd texted her nonstop on the way, but from her answers it was clear she thought he wanted her there only tonight. Even thinking that, she'd taken the keys happily. It pained him all over again that she didn't have any expectations, was truly content with anything he offered.

It made him wonder how such unconditional passion

was possible, and how he of all people was on its receiving end.

But even if he didn't deserve it yet, he would.

He would deserve *her*.

It was 2:00 a.m. by the time he finished the surgeries.

It would have been much longer if he'd had to perform trauma repair and reconstruction on both patients. But by the time he had them on his table, he'd known one of them would not make it. Ivan's friend. The sister was critical but could survive with a liver transplant. Her brother was a tissue match for her and Antonio could harvest his liver, which had been one of the few things remaining intact in him. Ivan, who'd been watching everything in the gallery, had told him to do *anything* to save her. Which he had.

Letting his team take her to the ICU now, he tore his bloody scrubs off and stepped out of the OR. Ivan was right at the door, looking like he'd go on a rampage at any moment.

"Sorry about your...friend." Antonio wouldn't ask for details. Ivan would tell him if he wanted him to know. "I trust you know who did this to them?"

Ivan's usually forbidding face turned positively demonic. "They're already dead."

That was quick, even for Ivan. But then, no one could hide from him. Ivan had always traced the untraceable. But being the lord of the cyber world wasn't where his talents ended. His business rivals called him Ivan the Terrible, unsuspecting that Ivan was literally lethal. He was as accomplished an assassin as any of their other brothers.

"She will be fine, won't she?"

Antonio exhaled, rubbing his stiff neck. Ten hours of operating on Ivan's mystery woman had been extra grueling, mostly because of Ivan's volcanic agitation. Antonio did everything he could for all his patients, but when one of his brothers was involved, the stakes were almost unmanageable. Something he didn't relish while having a human life under his scalpel.

"She will be. But even after I discharge her, it'll be a long road to recovery. Does she have anyone to take care of her?"

"She has me."

Antonio went still. Coming from Ivan, this was major.

It *could* be duty driving him, or a debt he owed his dead friend. But Antonio felt this went far beyond that. Though Ivan had never intimated that he'd ever cared for a woman, Antonio felt this one was important to him. Very important. In a way no woman had ever been.

This was either a relationship Ivan had chosen not to tell him about, or it was a new development, as intense and life-changing as his situation with Liliana.

And if this weren't such a grim occasion, Antonio would have told him about her, would have joked about the brothers falling like dominoes one after the other.

But if Ivan felt about this woman like Antonio did for Liliana, what had happened to her, what was still ahead of her, must be killing him. While he had so much joy to look forward to with Liliana starting tonight, Ivan could only watch the woman he cared about struggle for her life.

Feeling guilty that he was the happiest he'd ever been while Ivan suffered his worst pain, Antonio grabbed him by the shoulders. "She *will* be fine, Ivan. She's strong, and you brought her to me in the best condition possible. I believe her brother was lost at the scene, and it was only your efforts that kept his systems going till you got him here. It's the only reason his organs were viable, making the transplant possible. It was you who saved her."

Ivan avoided his eye, kept his downcast under the blackest frown Antonio had ever seen as he turned away. But not before Antonio saw what felt like a blow to the solar plexus. His iceberg of a friend's eyes filling with tears.

Knowing Ivan wouldn't want him to acknowledge his upheaval, he followed him in silence to the ICU's observation area.

He stood behind him, felt agony radiating off him as he watched his mystery woman being hooked to monitors and drips.

"I'm a phone call away, Ivan."

Back rigid, breathing strident, Ivan only nodded.

Knowing he could do no more for now, Antonio exhaled at the unaccustomed feeling of helplessness and walked away.

An hour later, Antonio entered his mansion. It was dim and quiet. But he knew Liliana was there. She'd texted him, and so had Paolo the moment she'd gone inside safely.

He walked through the foyer into the great room and found her there on the couch, her hair streaming off its edge in a cascade of curls. She was sound asleep.

He approached her soundlessly and looked down at her. With his best friend's ordeal reverberating in his being, seeing her there, whole and irreplaceable, had a storm of emotions raging inside him. He wanted to wake her up, lose himself inside her, hide her within himself. And none of it was about lust. It was about passion and protection. Tenderness and togetherness. And everything he'd never shared with or offered another human being.

Unable to keep away anymore, he bent to pick her up. The moment he touched her, she opened her eyes. They penetrated him to his very recesses with their instant welcome. As she tried to sit up, he scooped her up and pressed her head to his shoulder.

"Shh, *cuore mio*, don't wake up."

She nestled deeper into his hold, her lips moving against

his thundering heart as she spoke. "I was just dreaming of you…as usual."

"Then continue dreaming, *mi amore*."

He carried her to his bed, their bed now, wondering again that he was using Italian.

He'd learned the language in The Organization, perfecting it before he had English. They always taught every child his mother tongue, so they'd use him in missions involving his country or countrymen. But he'd never spoken it outside of those times.

Liliana made him speak it. He wanted to lavish on her the passionate endearments unique to the language he should have grown up speaking. Somehow, only they felt right to express what he felt for her.

Reaching his bed, he placed her lovingly on it before remotely parting the drapes, letting the moonlight in. He started to undress her, and she stirred again. She caught his hands, embarrassment staining her cheeks in the silver light.

He kissed her, pushed her back gently, crooning encouragement and praise to her as his hands roamed her body, and she melted back again, letting him do anything he pleased. And it did please him, beyond words, to get rid of every barrier, to finally see that body that had inflamed his though it had always been obscured.

And she was divine. Smooth and strong and sinuous, in the exact proportions he'd just discovered translated into his personal definition of perfection.

She watched him throughout, hanging on his reactions. He didn't leave it to her deductions. He told her exactly what he thought. Then he started undressing himself, reveling in the awed, voracious look that possessed her face. If there was ever a reward for the years he'd spent training and maintaining his physique, it was *that* look. He was already addicted to it. Then he removed the last of his clothing, letting her see just how hard her beauty and her hunger made him.

At the sight of his erection, she gasped and sank back deeper in the bed, as if she already felt it invading her, pinning her to the mattress. She licked her lips, those lips he wanted nothing more than to feel around his hardness.

But that would come later. Now he needed to reassure himself that she was safe with him. That she was his to cherish, to protect.

Getting into bed beside her, he pulled her into his burning body. He groaned in unison with her long moan, aching and relieved, as their flesh touched without barriers for the first time. Then, gradually, he felt her tension dissipate in the serenity of deep sleep.

He watched her, at peace in his arms, for as long as he could, before he too succumbed. To the first true rest of his life.

He woke up to unknown yet breathtaking sensations. Silk and velvet sweeping all over his body.

Liliana was trailing her hands and hair and lips over him, caressing and kissing and delighting in him.

The light beyond his closed lids said it was around sunset. He'd never slept that long. Nor had he ever slept with anyone present except his brothers. He'd certainly never fallen asleep with a woman in the same bed. Not once in his life.

He kept his eyes closed for as long as he could bear, to savor her worshipping, his heart drumming to a slow, hungry rhythm.

Then he couldn't take it anymore. In the same second he opened his eyes, he reached for her, swept her around and beneath him. This time, there would be no stopping him.

"Antonio."

The way she made his name sound like an aching plea. For him. For everything with him.

He took her lips. A thousand volts crackled between them, unleashing everything inside him in a tidal wave.

Maddened by the immediacy of her surrender, he captured her lower lip in a growling bite, stilling its tremors, attempting to moderate his passion. But she made it impossible when she parted her lips wider for his invasion, and her taste inundated him.

Such unimaginable sweetness. And the perfume of her breath, the sensory overload of her feel. Everything about her was a hallucinogen that pounded through his system, snapping the tethers of his sanity.

Her whimpers urged him to intensify his possession. His hands shook with urgency as he wrapped her legs around his hips, rose to revel in the overpowering sight she made trembling in his arms.

"Tell me, *mi amore*. Tell me you need me to take you."

Her answer was only squeezing her eyes in languorous acquiescence.

"I will take everything you have, Liliana, devour everything you are and give you all of me. Is this what you want? What you need? Now? And from now on?"

Lili heard Antonio as if from the depths of a dream.

Everything that had happened since he'd come to her yesterday making his offer of himself, on her terms, felt like one.

But in her wildest fantasies, she wouldn't have dared hope for Antonio to feel the same sweeping desire for her, or to succumb to it, let alone as quickly as she had.

But he did. He had. And once again he was demanding her confession and consent. He was holding back to make certain she craved his invasion and sanctioned his ferocity.

Oh, how she did. Even if the power of his dominance,

the starkness of his lust, staggered her. She might have come to his mansion, let him take her to his bed, might have been so bold as to wake the sleeping tiger, but now as she lay beneath him, waiting to be devoured, a storm of agitated desire overwhelmed her.

Her heart plunged into arrhythmia and she felt as if her every cell swelled, screamed for his possession.

Almost swooning with need, she gazed up at him as he loomed above her, the fiery palette of the horizon framing his magnificent body, setting his beauty ablaze. His eyes looked filled with tempests, precariously checked. He was giving her one last chance to dictate the terms of her surrender before he devastated her.

Feeling she'd die if he didn't she told him, "Take all of me, give me your all. Do everything to me, Antonio...*everything*. I need it all."

Raking her body in fierce greed, he bared his teeth on a soft snarl as he cupped her breasts in hands that trembled, kneaded them as if they were the most amazing things he'd ever felt. Then he bent and took one nipple in the damp furnace of his mouth, squeezing a shriek out of her. She unraveled with every nip and suck, each with the exact pressure and intensity to extract maximum pleasure. He layered sensation upon sensation until she felt inundated.

She was shaking out of control when he slid down her body, painting her with caresses and licks until he stilled an inch from her core, his breath on her making her feel she'd spontaneously combust.

He lit her fuse when he spoke, his voice a ragged, bass growl. *"Perfetto, bellezza, magnifica."*

As if everything about him weren't overkill already, he had to go speak Italian. It made her writhe.

"Antonio, *please*..."

"Si, amore, I will please you...always and forever."

He pressed his face to her thighs, his lips opening over

her quivering flesh like a starving man who didn't know where to start his feast. Her fingers convulsed in his silky hair, pressed him to her flesh, unable to handle the stimulation, yet needing even more.

He dragged a hand between her thighs, electrifying her as the heel of his thumb brushed open her outer lips. Her undulations became feverish, her pleas a litany till he dipped a finger between her molten lips, stopping at her entrance.

"I dreamed of you like this from that first day, open to me, letting me possess and pleasure you."

He spread her legs, placed them over his shoulders, opening her core to him fully. Her moans became keens, sharpening, gasping.

He inhaled her, rumbling like a lion at the scent of his female in heat, as she was. He blew a gust of sensation over the knot where her nerves gathered. Her hips rose to him, a plea escaping her lips. It became a shriek when he finally, slowly, slid a finger inside her and she came, pleasure slamming through her in desperate surges.

He'd again made her climax with one touch.

Among the aftershocks, she felt his finger inside her, pumping, beckoning at her inner trigger. Her gasp tore through her lungs as his tongue joined in, circling her bud. Each glide and graze and pull and thrust made her need ignite again as if she hadn't just had the most intense orgasm of her life.

Soon she was sobbing, bucking again, opening herself fully to his double assault until he had her quaking and screaming with an even more violent release.

She tumbled from the explosive peak, drained, stupefied.

From the depth of drugged satiation, her heavy gaze sought his in the receding sunset. His eyes glowed azure, heavy with hunger and satisfaction.

"From now on you're on my menu every single day," he whispered. "I'm already addicted to your taste and your pleasure."

Something squeezed inside her until it became almost painful. It flabbergasted her to recognize it as an even fiercer arousal. Her satisfaction had lasted a minute and now she was even hungrier. No, she felt something else she'd never felt before. Empty. As if a void inside her was growing, demanding to be filled. By him. Only ever him.

"Don't indulge your addiction now." She barely recognized her voice, sultry with hunger, hoarse from her cries. "If you don't give me yourself right now, I might implode."

All lightness drained from his eyes as he squeezed her mound possessively, the ferocious conqueror flaring back to life. "And you will have me. I'll ride you to ecstasy until you can't beg for more."

His sensual threat filled her with nervous anticipation. Her heart went haywire as he slid back up over her, sowed kisses over her from her mound to her face, before he withdrew to look down at her.

His exhalation was ragged. "Do you realize how incredible you are?" As she mumbled something between dismissal and embarrassment, he persisted. "Don't you *see* how incredible I find you?"

He rose above her, displaying the full measure of his sculpted perfection. She struggled to her elbows, her mouth watering, her hands stinging, with the need to explore him, revel in him.

But he wasn't inviting her to witness or examine his splendor, but demonstrating her effect on him. Glimpsing his manhood in the semidarkness last night had filled her sleep with sexual torment. It was why she hadn't been able to keep her hands off him when she'd woken up, though she hadn't dared remove the sheet he tented even in sleep.

Now she forced her gaze down…and was again awestruck at the size and beauty of him.

What if she couldn't accommodate him? Please him?

His muscles bunched as he reached down to the floor, picked up the pants he'd discarded and produced a foil packet. He was ready this time. Last time he hadn't been, which meant he didn't have women here. That was such a momentous realization, it made this even more incredible than it already was.

Then holding her eyes in such promise, he tore the packet open.

She almost came again just watching him sheath himself.

"Now I take you, *mi amore*. And you take me."

Though she shook with agitation, she whimpered, "Yes…yes, please."

She received him in trembling arms as he came down over her. She cried out at how her softness cushioned his hardness.

Perfect. No, sublime.

Pushing her legs wider apart, his eyes solicitous, tempestuous, he bathed himself in her readiness in slow strokes from bud to opening, driving her to desperation before he growled and finally sank inside her in one long, fierce thrust.

A red-hot lance of pain had the world flickering out for long moments, squeezing a cry from her very depths, before other sensations surged back in a rush, none she'd ever felt before. Fullness, completion.

Her eyes fluttered open to find him turned to stone on top of her, his eyes wild with worry.

"You're a… You were a… It's your first time!"

Quivering inside and out, the last thing she wanted was to talk, her mind unraveling with the feel of him filling her. But she had to answer his strangled exclamation. "You do remember me saying I was pathetically inexperienced, don't you?"

His distress ebbed, tenderness replacing it. "Oh, yes, I do. *Dio mio*, you're a surprise a second. Make that a shock a second. I didn't think you meant...*that*."

"What else did you think I meant?"

"I didn't think. I basically *can't* think around you."

Then he started withdrawing from her depths, making her feel he was turning her inside out.

"No!" She clung to him with her arms and legs, tried to drag him back inside her. "Don't go. Don't stop."

Throwing his head back, he squeezed his eyes. "I'm only trying not to lose my mind here, *mi amore*, in consideration of your...state of inexperience. Don't make it impossible." He opened his eyes. "I'd only stop if you wanted me to."

Emptiness threatening to engulf her, she thrust her hips upward, impaling herself on his massive girth, uncaring about the chafing pain, even needing it. "I'd die if you stopped."

His groan was pained, as if she'd hurt him, too. "Stopping would probably finish me, as well. For real."

She thrust up again, crying out as he stretched her, the sensation making her delirious.

His hand combed through her hair, dragged her down by its tether to the mattress, pinning her there. Her heart shook her like an earthquake as she crushed herself against him. "Don't hold back. I love the way you feel inside me. I *love* it. Fill me, hurt me until you make it better."

"*Si, amore*, I'll make it so much better." He cupped her hips in both hands, tilted them into a cradle for his own, then slowly thrust inside her to the hilt.

It was beyond overwhelming, being full of him. The reality, the meaning and carnality of it, rocked her essence.

He withdrew again, and she cried out at the unbearable

loss, urged him to sink back into her. He resisted her pleas, taking his time, resting at her entrance before he thrust back inside her. Then again, and again. Slow, measured, making her cry out hot gusts of passion and open herself wider with every plunge.

Holding her gaze, he watched her intently, avidly, adjusting his movements to her every moan and grimace, waiting for pleasure to fully submerge the pain. He kept her at a fever pitch, caressing her all over, sucking her breasts, draining her lips, raining wonder over her. *"Perfetto, amore*, inside and out. Everything about you is perfect."

Her body soon rewarded his patience and expertise. It gushed readiness and pleasure over him, demanding everything he could give her.

"Antonio, I need everything now, please."

"Si, bellezza, everything." His groan reverberated in her mouth as he drove his tongue inside her to his plunging rhythm, quickening both.

Everything within her tightened unbearably, her depths rippling around him, reaching for that elusive something, something way beyond orgasm, nothing she'd ever attained, but that she felt she'd perish if she didn't have now.

No longer coherent, she begged him, over and over. "Please, Antonio, please."

But he understood, knew she couldn't bear the buildup anymore. *"Si, amore, ora*. Now I give you all the pleasure this divine body of yours can withstand."

Tilting her up toward him, he hammered inside her with a force and cadence that rattled the whole world, dismantled her every cell. He breached her to her womb on each plunge until he detonated the coil of desperation in her deepest recess.

Convulsions tore through her, clamping her inner muscles around him as her insides splintered with pleasure too agonizing to register, then to bear, then to bear having it end.

But it didn't end. It went on and on as he gave her more and more, until finally she cried out with his each jarring thrust.

Then came a moment she'd replay in her memory forever. The sight of him as he climaxed inside her.

Her orgasm intensified as he threw his head back to bellow his own pleasure. He fed her convulsions with his, his release so fierce she felt it through the barrier, making her sob with the need to feel its hot surges filling her.

Whimpering as he continued to move within her, completing her pleasure, her domination, she was helpless to do anything but let the enormity of his first possession drag her into oblivion.

Eight

An eternity later, Lili surged back into her body, realizing what had brought her back. Antonio was moving, starting to leave her body.

Unable to bear separation, she clung to him. He pressed soothing kisses to her eyes and lips, murmuring reassurance in that voice that strummed everything in her as he swept her around, careful to remain inside her. Then she was lying on top of him, satiated in ways she couldn't have imagined, reverberating with the magnitude of the experience and in perfect peace for the first time in her life.

When her heart stopped thundering enough to let her breathe, she raised a wobbling head. "Is it…always like that?"

His eyes looked as dazed as she felt, and his lips twitched. "It's never been like that for me. Everything with you is always a first."

"You're telling me that's not why people make such a

fuss about sex? Because it's that…that…" No description could do what had happened between them justice.

"In my experience, 'sex' has absolutely nothing in common with what we just had. This was…magic."

Her body began to throb all over again. "It was for me."

"You have nothing to compare it to, but I do, so I know how magical it was, and what made it so." Before she could infer the meaning of his confession he added, "It's because I love you."

She bolted upright, gaping down at him.

He started withdrawing from her depths carefully as he sat up, too. In spite of her paralysis, her moan echoed his groan at the burn of separation. Her gaze remained meshed with his as he looked at her as if she were the one thing he lived for.

"I realized it yesterday. That all those overwhelming feelings I feel for you are love."

She collapsed on the bed in a daze, could do nothing but watch him as he rose to discard the condom. Then he came back to tower over her, godlike, still fully engorged, a frown of uncertainty creeping over his face.

"I can see this comes as a shock."

Her heart stumbling, eyes stinging, she could only choke, "That's the understatement of our era."

"Is it a good or bad shock?"

He seemed actually worried. Very worried. *Really?*

It was the only thing she could say out loud. "Are you for real? Is that even a question?"

His shoulders rose and fell. "I've learned to never assume anything with you. You never react in any way I expect. I also realize this could seem too quick—"

"You think?" She felt caught in a hurricane of disbelief and jubilation that uprooted her very existence. "It's been less than a week."

"It's been *three* weeks."

"Two of which you didn't even see me."

"Because I was on a mission to be worthy of you and your trust and respect. And I did see you. I was watching you."

Her mouth dropped open. "You were?"

His grin was sheepish. "I practically stalked you. At home, at work. Before you ask how, I…have my ways."

She struggled up to her elbow, incredulousness mushrooming inside her. "I'm sure you have. But even so…"

Lowering himself to the bed, he stretched out beside her, gathering her along his hot, hard body. "I've always made life-and-death decisions in seconds. Taking three weeks to conclude that I love you is a glacial pace for me. I took that long only because the decision to love you for the rest of my life is way more weighty than any life-and-death issue I've ever dealt with."

She shook her head. How could all this be happening?

His large hand cupped her head. "Do you know why I came back to you when I did?"

"Because you completed that quest you thought would make you worthy of me?"

"You think it took me two whole weeks to do that? Everything was in place in two days."

She blinked dazedly. "So why?"

"I was waiting for you."

"To do what? Seek you out?"

"No, to reach your breakthrough. I knew you were close when I first acquired the lab, and that when you used the resources I put at your disposal, you'd no doubt reach it. I didn't want to come back before you did. I wanted you to have this achievement you so deserve, before I distracted the hell out of you."

That was tremendous. Unbelievable. But… "If you came the next day and explained that I didn't put you off and you didn't fear I'd boil your rabbit, I wouldn't have agonized over you with every breath. I might have even reached that breakthrough sooner."

His frown was spectacular. "Dammit. Everything I do because of you or for you backfires right in my face."

She caressed his cheek placatingly. "With an end result that's far better than any plan could have projected. Look at where I am now with my work, how ecstatic everyone is that you bought the lab. Look at me lying here with you, after you've given me absolute pleasure and so much more I never dreamed I'd have, and are now telling me that you... you..." A strangled cry escaped her as she buried her face into his chest, tears pouring from the depths of her soul. "This is...you are...too much. Way more than my heart can withstand or contain."

"You are impossible for my heart to withstand or contain, too. What I feel for you is so intense, I feel I would go mad if you don't reciprocate."

"Oh God, I do, Antonio. I *love* you. I think from the first moment I saw you. But I never thought you could love me back."

"You captured me from that first moment, too. I know myself, and I can promise you one thing—I'll love you more every day. I only hope you never think I love you too much."

She surged into him, shaking, tears flowing, unable to talk or breathe anymore. Her heart was overflowing. He soothed her, caressed her all over, sucking her lips, her nipples, lavishing the most amazing endearments and praise on her until she wrapped herself around him, undulated against him.

"Take me again, Antonio."

His laugh was distressed as he unclasped her thighs from around his waist. "You might think you're ready for another round, but trust me, you're not." He laid her back gently, his gaze scorching her all over before returning to her eyes, filled such sensual indulgence her core cramped with need. "So…never before, eh?"

Feeling free to show him everything in her heart and how wanton he made her, she rubbed her nipples against his rock-hard chest. "Apart from…uh…self-help, no. Why bother, when it wasn't you?"

His gaze went supernova as he crushed her to him, then her lips beneath his.

When he let her breathe again, she felt self-conscious again. "So you're not wondering how I reached this age without having sex? You don't find it…"

"Pathetic?" he repeated her earlier description of her inexperience. "What's pathetic is how ferociously glad I am that you didn't." He pressed into her, his arousal undiminished, his body buzzing with vitality and dominance and lust. "And I don't find it strange at all, now that I know you. You don't do anything unless it satisfies your meticulous, exacting mind, and I am only proud and grateful I'm the one who does. After you made me work my ass off for it, of course."

He understood. And appreciated. Her heart swelled with thankfulness, even as it still quaked with the enormity of knowing he loved her back.

She caressed his hewn cheek, letting him see everything inside her. "I never wanted anyone, never considered anyone worth the trouble. But even when I thought you were unattainable and knew you would be trouble of unimaginable magnitude, I wanted you. I craved you, in any way, for any length of time, no matter the price. Or I thought I craved you. After this…cataclysm, I'm addicted to you."

After another smothering, devouring kiss, he withdrew. "It's merciful you are, since I'm beyond addicted to you. It's also lifesaving for those men you didn't bother with. If you had, I would have gone hunting them."

She burst out laughing. "Now I've got an image emblazoned forever in my mind. You in a loincloth, chasing poor, inferior men, clubbing them over the head and throwing them in a pile."

His smile was predatory. "*Si, amore*, laugh at the caveman your love has made of me."

Arching with an unbearable surge of delight and desire, she opened for his erection, needing him back inside her. "Go caveman all over me, please."

His pupils flared in warning. "I'm barely holding him back, so behave. You're too sore now."

"But I want you to let him loose. Make me almost die of pleasure again, Antonio."

Groaning as if in pain, he thrust against her. "From the first time you cut me up with that tongue of yours, I knew. That under the guise of the prim, contentious scientist there was a woman I wanted desperately. But even I wasn't ambitious enough to hope I'd find this, the most perfect, uninhibited sex goddess. You almost killed me with pleasure, too."

"Then take us to the edge of mortality again, *please*."

"Command me, *amore*. You only have to breathe, to just be, and I would literally die for you."

Before her mind could wrap around those earthshaking words, he rose over her, opened her wide around his hips and slid his hardness between the molten lips of her core. He nudged her nub and the world vanished in a burst of pleasure.

It came so quickly, a boil in her blood, a tightening in depths that now knew exactly how to unfurl and undo her. She opened herself for him, knowing he would only pleasure her this way, undulating faster against him until another orgasm, different yet still magnificent, tore through her.

He pinned her down as she came, gliding his shaft against her quivering flesh in the exact pressure and rhythm to drain her of every spark her body needed to discharge.

After she slumped in quivering fulfillment, he rose between her spread legs and pumped himself to a roaring climax.

Watching him take his pleasure over her trembling body, the body he now owned, was mesmerizing. It was the most flagrantly erotic sight she'd ever witnessed, and the most profoundly fulfilling emotion she'd ever felt.

Pulling her to his body, he mingled their sweat and pleasure and heartbeats, surrounding her in his love and cherishing, dragging her into a realm of safety and contentment.

When next she woke up, it was to Antonio's caresses.

He was wiping her down with something wet and warm. Moaning, she opened her eyes to find him bent over her in dim, golden light, a being out of a fable, cosseting and worshipping her. Joy surged on a tremulous smile as she sought his eyes, only for it to be aborted at the sight of the disturbed expression in their depths.

That had her scrambling up, her heart shedding its languor, starting to drum painfully. "What's wrong, Antonio?"

He exhaled, continued to rub her stomach. "I was watching you sleeping so trustingly in my arms…and I kept wondering how you feel the same for me. Or how you'd continue to."

She stopped his hand. "Where is this coming from?"

Extricating his hand from her grip, he threw the hand towel aside squeezed his eyes shut briefly. "Apart from my…partners, I never had any relationship of any sort with anyone."

This was all? She poked her elbow in his side, inviting him to grin back at her. "Same here."

"You're nowhere near the same, *mi amore*."

"Of course I'm not. You're unique."

He shook his head. "It's you who are. While having more money and power than almost anyone doesn't mean I'm anywhere near your level."

"I already told you I don't factor your money and power in your uniqueness. The man you are beneath the trappings, the force of nature who achieved such success, who saves lives and puts bodies back together like no one else can, who turns everything he touches into the best it can be...that's the man I love."

"*Dio mio, dea mia.* You're far more than I ever imagined anyone could be. You're far better than I deserve."

She scrambled up to her knees, caught his hot face in trembling hands. "Why, my love? Why do you feel that way? When you said you feared I'd be the one to lose interest, I thought you were being gallant. But you meant it, didn't you?"

He nodded. "It scares me like nothing has before, that one day you'll look inside me and hate what you see."

This was more serious than she'd first imagined. And it needed to be resolved, at once.

She sat back on her heels, feeling it was the most natural thing to be naked with him in every sense of the word.

"When you told me you grew up without your father, too, I thought I saw scars beyond your perfect, placid facade and I hoped they'd been long healed. But now I feel this goes far deeper than growing up fatherless like me, that you suffered way more hardships and injustices and abuse than anything I can imagine. And it makes me even more proud of you and in awe of what you attained in spite of it all."

"What if you're right, and there's way more to me that you can dream of in your worst nightmares? What if it's so terrible that if you knew, it would send you away screaming?"

"You're not hypothesizing, are you? You're really afraid I can't handle the truth." His eyes went bleak, overwhelming her with the need to unburden him. She pressed her hands to his heart, needing to absorb his pain. "This damage I feel inside you…it goes beyond a physical or psychological ordeal. You've…done things. Ugly things." His gaze faltered, and it felt as if his last reluctance gave way, letting her plunge deep. And she felt she was reading everything inside him, dragging out every festering darkness. Her voice shook as she put what she saw into words. "You were involved in…violence. You used your skills in cold-blooded and lethal ways. Even to…kill."

She bated her breath as his eyes widened, stunned.

Then all the fire that had ever been there was extinguished and he only said, "Yes."

Ever since Antonio had realized he wanted Liliana, he'd broken out in cold sweat just thinking how it would hurt her if she ever learned she'd initially been a tool in his plan of revenge, even if he hadn't and would never act on it.

Though he couldn't come clean about it, ever, he needed to be honest with her any other way he could. He'd already started by opening up about his feelings. Now he needed to go further, all the way, and open up about himself.

His surface was as perfect and placid as she'd said. But he was anything but inside. Not even his brothers knew of the wreckage inside him. But *she'd* seen it. She'd said it made her proud of him that he'd become what he was in spite of what he'd been through. But though she'd somehow seen what no one else had even guessed at, she still couldn't even guess at the specifics.

What if he told her all the things he'd done as a slave of The Organization, what he'd had to do to gain his freedom, and it horrified her? What if she thought him too damaged, beyond redemption, and ran for her life?

But he owed her the whole truth. He'd keep from her only what might hurt her feelings or damage her trust in him. What didn't apply to them anymore anyway, and never would.

More than anything he wanted to make her promise she'd never leave him no matter what she learned, but he couldn't do that. She'd give him her pledge, and she'd keep it, even if she hated it and him. She was that noble, that kind. No, she had to have total freedom to act in her own best interests. Even if it meant leaving him behind. Even if he couldn't survive without her.

Needing to put some distance between them so he wouldn't weaken, he pulled away from her, rose to fetch his pants.

As he came back to stand over her, she pulled the sheet over herself, as if she feared she couldn't face whatever he'd say in the vulnerability of nakedness. It made him hate himself more for causing her even a moment's uncertainty or anxiety.

Holding her suddenly fragile gaze, praying she wouldn't end up hating him, he said, "Though I'd give anything for you not to know, you need to know. What I am, what I've done. I'll abide by whatever decision you make once you know everything."

And he exposed all the horrors of his past, what not even his brothers knew. The only thing he left out was the identity of the family who'd discarded him.

All through his confession, what most agonized him were the brutal emotions that ravaged her, from shock to horror to denial to desolation. He couldn't stop to analyze each one so he could go on.

When he was done, he stood before her, unable to believe he'd finally unburdened himself, shaking with the discharge of a lifetime of torment and rage that he'd suppressed under layers of steely discipline. But what truly shook him was dreading the reason behind her weeping.

Before he could bring himself to ask, she scrambled off the bed and launched herself at him so explosively, she made him stumble and fall.

He barely caught himself before he crashed flat on the ground, cushioning her on top of him as she rained copious tears and frenzied kisses all over him. She sobbed so hard he was terrified she'd do herself real damage.

He frantically tried to soothe her. "*Mi amore*, please, nothing is worth your tears. I beg you, don't cry."

She shook her head and cried harder, but he finally understood what she was reiterating in her incoherent sobbing.

"My love, my love, I'm sorry, I'm so sorry, so sorry…"

This was all for him.

His one-of-a-kind, magnanimous firecracker was breaking her own heart on his behalf.

He crushed her to him, trying to defuse her upheaval. "*Mi amore*, it's all in the past. I just needed you to know."

She struggled out of his hold and rose above him, her eyes reddened, her lips quaking. "And I'd give anything, *everything*, if I could undo it all, make you un-suffer every single second."

He caught her face, stilled its shuddering. "You have. Just telling you, just that it didn't matter to you, worked like an antidote to the poison I had in my system. I can now leave it all behind where it can't touch me, or us, again. Just loving you erases it all, makes up for it a hundred times over."

Her sobs lessened as he talked, stroked her hair, pressed her to his chest.

With her upheaval fading, she spoke against his flesh. "You know what's driving me insane right now? Besides being unable to go after those who hurt you and making them suffer a far worse hell than the one they put you through? It's that I had such a ridiculously easy life compared to you. I can't even share your ordeals except in my imagination. And I *hate* it!"

He went still beneath her. His heart had expanded until he wondered if it would burst. Not a bad way to go, he thought. If he didn't want to live forever. To be with Liliana.

"*Mi amore, sposami.* Marry me."

His words echoed in absolute silence.

They'd both stopped breathing. The very world stopped turning.

Then both their chests emptied on ragged moans as she raised an unsteady head to look down at him, flabbergasted.

And everything poured out of him. "I never had a heart, but you created one inside me. A heart that was made to love you, that can't survive without you. So if you want me alive, you'll have to say yes."

She burst into tears again. "God, Antonio, yes...*yes.* But..."

"No buts."

"I was just going to say—but I think you should slow down, take more time to think about this. After you do—"

His lips silenced hers. "I can't slow down, and I won't think about it. I want nothing else but you. I now realize everything in my life has been leading up to this. This moment. This union. You." He took her in another compulsive kiss. "So never say 'but' again."

"Even if I say that no word remains after what you said 'but' yes?"

"You can say anything, as long as it ends in yes."

And for the rest of the night, she said almost nothing but yes. She whimpered, whispered and screamed it. She said yes to him, to them, and to everything their future together would bring.

* * *

"You have to tell us, Lili."

Lili turned to the redhead who regarded her with such warm curiosity. Scarlett Kuroshiro, the wife of Raiden, one of Antonio's brothers, was unearthly beautiful. Her husband, who sat beside her, clearly as besotted with her as she appeared to be with him, was Japanese by birth and as gorgeous as she was in his own way. But what truly amazed Lili was their year-old baby daughter, who mixed them both into an incredible mixture. Their adopted children, five of them from four to eight years old, were all playing on the grounds of Antonio's mansion with the other brothers' kids and their nannies.

"Yes, you have to." That was Jenan, another brother's wife, the guy who looked like a genie. Sheikh Numair Al Aswad, the brotherhood's leader. Jenan looked like she'd walked out of *Arabian Nights* herself, and actually *was* a princess. "We must know what you did to Antonio," she said. "What superpowers do you have?"

Lili smirked. "This coming from the pantheon of gods and goddesses Antonio has for brothers and sisters."

Everyone laughed. They'd been laughing every time she'd said anything. It was either that Antonio had given them strict orders to be super delighted with her every word, or that her brand of humor tickled them as much as it did him.

"It's fate." Rafael, the youngest brother, a Brazilian and another juggernaut, hugged his wife, Eliana, into his side tighter. "So our brotherhood would be blessed by the duet of Eliana and Liliana."

Eliana looked adoringly up at her husband before she winked at Lili. "I somehow don't think fate conspired such a perfect match just so your brotherhood would have wives with rhyming names. Besides, I'm Ellie and she's Lili."

"No."

"No."

Both Antonio and Rafael spoke in unison, each vehemently refusing his mate's nickname.

Eliana sighed, giving Lili a we're-in-this-together look. "You're Liliana and never Lili to Antonio, right?"

Lili wiggled one eyebrow at Antonio. "Yeah, and he has exclusive rights to it. So y'all better call me Lili if you want to remain on your doctor's good side."

"It's clear to *me* why Antonio is falling over himself to marry you." That was Richard Graves. Not Antonio's brother, but his partner, the one who smothered them all in security measures, who used to be Rafael's handler. The Brit was the perfect combination of suave and grit, a Bond/Lancelot hybrid. His hand laced with Isabella's, his wife and a surgeon herself, his body touching hers from shoulder to calf, as if he couldn't be away from her. It was weird, since the guy looked as cold as a cobra. "You're a combination I didn't think existed, but exactly what would bowl him over. You must have mowed him down without even trying."

"That she did." Antonio laughed, looking down at her adoringly. "I'm down for the count. For life."

"That's what you guys do. Even those who resist their fate for years." Isabella pinched Richard, who growled and buried a kiss in her neck. She giggled, looking at Lili. "When they give in and give you their hearts, it's yours forever. They'd conquer the world for you, live and die for you. They're a bit scary, but each of them is one-of-a-kind and we can't think how we lived before them."

Richard squeezed his wife tighter as the other women fervently corroborated her statements and their husbands hugged them closer, too.

Lili looked up at Antonio, as usual finding his heart in his eyes, the heart he said he'd grown to love her with.

Pulling him down, she murmured against his lips, "I have no idea at all how."

She surfaced from his drowning kiss to the hoots and claps of the couples, and the disgusted groans of Jakob Wolff, the guy who looked like a Viking marauder, and the only single brother around.

Antonio had just told them about his proposal last night. The ladies had insisted on meeting her at once, and the men had made their wishes come true without delay. They'd all converged on LA from wherever they'd been in the world, arriving at Antonio's mansion one after the other. By the time they'd started arriving, Antonio had told her everything about their previous and current personas, and she'd memorized all the info.

The only one who was missing was Ivan Konstantinov, Antonio's best friend. But he certainly wouldn't have left the side of the woman Antonio had saved that first night she and Antonio were together. Antonio had told her they were missing another brother, but that she wouldn't be seeing him. He'd left their brotherhood six years ago, vowing never to return. It seemed it had been an unspeakable falling-out, since Antonio, who'd so far shared the most horrendous stuff with her, wouldn't say a word about why "Cypher" had left them.

Antonio had wanted their wedding to be three days from now, a whopping week after he'd proposed. But she'd convinced him it was either forgo a wedding completely, or if he wanted an actual party, they needed at least a month. Adamant that there was no way he wasn't giving her a wedding, and reluctant about what he called an unbearable delay, he'd succumbed and set the date.

The evening proceeded in escalating mirth and harmony. Those juggernauts—who between them could rule the world and did to a great degree—and their gorgeous mates promised to be available at all times to help with the wedding preparations. Lili was so delighted with them all, his "family", she kept thanking him for rounding them up for this impromptu engagement party, and thanking them for coming and for being this fantastic.

Everything was so amazing it made her feel she'd plunged into another level of the fairy tale she'd been living with Antonio since that day he'd changed her life. And every now and then one incredulous question floated in her mind.

Could anything in this world be that perfect?

Nine

"My father called again yesterday."

The razor in Antonio's hand stilled over his left cheek. The eyes that had been promising her another session of devastation in the mirror, clean-shaven this time, emptied.

Next second he refocused on shaving, grunting something vague.

Her heart slumped a notch in her chest.

His reaction to the subject of her father and her family was the only thing that marred the perfection they'd been sharing so far.

Her father had been after her to set a date for that reception the Accardis wanted to hold in her honor. When he heard of her engagement, and to whom, his cajoling had become persistence. He couldn't wait to meet her fiancé.

And she couldn't wait for Antonio to meet him, too. Now that she'd been included in Antonio's family, her reluctance to establish a relationship with her father and

the Accardis had evaporated. She now wanted to attend
the party in which she would meet her long-lost family.

But though Antonio was always eager to do everything
with her or for her, joining her for that party wasn't a fore-
gone conclusion. As he'd just proven again.

She tried again. "He's really eager to meet you, and
he's hoping I can give him a final answer about the Accardi reception."

Next moment, her heart lodged in her throat. At the
shocking burst of wrath and revulsion she saw reflected
at her in his eyes.

He suppressed his reaction at once. But she'd seen it.

This was far worse than she'd first thought. It was like
this lethal persona that lived within him had surged to the
surface. And it had been positively murderous.

Feeling close to tears for thoughtlessly causing him this
flare-up, she squeezed her eyes shut and turned to leave
the bathroom. "Please, forget it. I shouldn't have brought
this up."

"No." She heard the razor clatter in the marble sink, and
then the sound of his hurried, powerful footsteps a second
before his hands clamped her shoulders and turned her to
him. "*Dio mio, mi amore*, no. You should always tell me
everything. Everything you want to do, anything on your
mind. Always. I beg your forgiveness if I made you feel
you can't talk to me about this."

A tear trickled down her cheek, inciting a vicious string
of self-abusing expletives from him.

Furious with herself, she wiped it away, pointed at the
moisture. "This is for *you*. I hate that I didn't take a hint,
cornered you into letting your anger surface. I know how
you hate your harsh side, what it takes to curb it so perfectly, to maintain your inner peace. I hate that it's only
on my account that you can fall prey again to such aggressive emotions."

Clad in only low-riding black silk pajama bottoms, he scooped her up in his arms, his erection lodging in her quivering belly. "Well, you'll have to live with the fact that I would give up all the peace in existence for the savage emotions you inspire in me, along with the sublime ones. You'll have to make your peace with the fact that I can happily kill for you, not only die for you."

Melting in his hold as he swept her up and carried her to bed, she wrapped her legs around his waist. "Since I'd rather you live for me, thank you very much, let's forget I brought up my father and my family. You probably think I'm stupid to consider accepting his advances. You must consider they more or less did to me what your family did to you."

He started to speak, then clamped his lips. Because she'd put her finger on the truth and he wasn't about to say she didn't. He always told her the truth.

As he came to half lie over her, she cupped his cheek and reveled in his beauty, this god among men who desired her so completely, who was unbelievably hers. "I understand how your anger toward your family extends to mine, and it's totally justified. I wouldn't have considered being anywhere near my father or any of the Accardis on my own. But he's been trying so hard, I wanted to give him a chance before I decide whether to have him in my life. I didn't want unresolved bitterness lurking anywhere if I could work it out. The best I expected was that my family would be a once-a-year presence in my life, and my father would be a peripheral one.

"But that was before I realized how forcefully you feel about this. *Nothing* is worth making you suffer the least discomfort. You, and our lives together, are the only things that matter to me. I *did* mean it when I said let's just forget about this."

Antonio stared down at his woman, the woman he'd been falling deeper in love with each passing second.

Every time she'd mentioned her father and their joint family, his agitation had built. Though he now considered whatever debt they owed him paid a million times over just for being the reason he'd met Liliana, he abhorred their very existence. He never wanted to see any of them, not to punish them or to have anything to do with them. But the idea that they were trying to enter her life, when they were bound to taint it, made his loathing mount. He'd destroy them all before he let them cause her the least heartache.

But she needed closure and now, because she considered only him and his feelings, she was dismissing that need.

And there was no way he'd deprive her of anything at all. He'd swallow his hatred, hell, he'd swallow molten steel if it provided her with peace. On the off chance that her father and his family brought her a measure of contentment, he'd even tolerate them. He'd be there for her, with her, at every event, honoring her and showing them she had a lethal protector in him. Just in case any of them thought to show their true colors.

He gathered her closer, delighting in her feel, her love. "We'll forget nothing. I'm going to meet your father, and we're going to New York to meet your family." Anxiety flared again in her reddened eyes. He caught her lips in a cherishing kiss, aborting her protest. "We'll do everything that might provide you with even a remote possibility of well-being, always. And that, *mi amore*, is that."

Flying to New York on Antonio's private jet, Lili felt she'd plunged deeper into the parallel universe she'd stumbled into since the day he'd entered her life.

The Accardis had set the reception for the very next weekend, two days after Antonio had insisted they accept their invitation. The haste had to be her father's doing, no doubt. But this meant that the first time Antonio met him would be at the reception.

All the way, Antonio had placated her worries about his aversion to her family. He assured her if she enjoyed knowing them, he'd be lenient and might even consider liking them. After all, she made him so happy he could forgive any past transgressions and afford to be magnanimous like her. That had reassured her, until they entered the Accardi family mansion.

Now she felt something writhing inside him. Something dark and vicious.

Before she told him she would leave if he didn't want to be here after all, her father came rushing toward them as soon as they crossed the mansion's threshold.

In the seconds before he reached them, his smile as wide as humanly possible, Lili noticed something for the first time. Her father and Antonio looked alike. Apart from the size and age difference—Antonio was much bigger, and her father had wrinkles and silver hair—the two men shared the same bone structure and skin tone. If she'd seen them on the streets, she would have thought them relatives. In fact, if someone saw the three of them, with her looking like her mother, people would have thought it was Antonio who was her father's son.

"*Mia bella Lilianissima*, you're here!"

Feeling Antonio going rigid beside her, she stood with a wooden smile, awkwardly letting her father hug her.

Thankfully, he did so more briefly than in the few times she'd seen him. For now he had a distraction in Antonio.

"Dr. Balducci, a hundred welcomes to Casa Accardi."

"One would do, Signore Accardi." Antonio took her father's extended hand after a telling hesitation, as if he loathed touching him. He still managed a courteous nod, for her sake.

Oblivious to Antonio's aversion, her father enfolded Antonio's hand in both of his fervently. "I'm beyond delighted about your and Lili's engagement. Only the best man is worthy of her, and that's what I hear you are. And an Italian, too. It's just perfection. Everything is coming together in the exact perfect way that my incomparable daughter deserves."

As if he'd reached his limit, Antonio withdrew his hand from her father's grip. "Liliana is beyond incomparable, and deserves only the best of everything. Which I'll make sure she gets, now and forever."

Antonio's words sounded like a warning. He was telling her father he'd better be on his best behavior with her, or else.

Her nerves jangled at Antonio's barely veiled threat. Regardless of whether her father deserved it for his past behavior, she'd hoped her fiancé would offer him that leniency he'd talked about. It was clear Antonio wouldn't offer any until her father proved himself. Which she was sure Antonio wouldn't make easy.

Not that her father noticed any subscript in Antonio's words. He now led them to the open doors at the end of the expansive entrance hall, from which the sounds of music and conversation were emanating. "Between us, we're going to make sure of that, Dr. Balducci." Her father looked at him expectantly. "Can I call you Antonio?"

"If you wish." That was said in the tone of "don't you dare." Antonio looked so forbidding it was only thanks to her father's enthusiastic obliviousness that he hadn't turned to stone. Then his voice plunged into the subzero domain. "I understand you had no contact with Liliana as she grew up. Now, in your new eagerness to know her, I keep wondering what could possibly explain the years of absence and silence."

Her father stopped, looking as if Antonio had just handed him the best gift he'd ever had. "I'm *so* glad you asked! I tried to explain to Lili when I contacted her after

Luanne's death. But she always insisted what was past was past."

Yeah. She hadn't wanted to hear his reasons. She could establish some kind of relationship with him not knowing them. But if she knew them and found them pathetic or unacceptable, she wouldn't be able to go forward in any kind of relationship with him.

Her father clamped her and Antonio's arms. "Come, please. This can't be told with dozens of nosy Accardis around."

Her father rushed them to an old-fashioned smoking room filled with burgundy leather chesterfields, Persian rugs and dark wood paneling. Though everything was authentic and antique, it showed the weight of time and clearly hadn't had any recent maintenance. Though the three-hundred-year-old mansion was imposing, it wasn't in the prime condition she'd expected from such an elite family.

After her father sat them down side by side, he stood before them as if to give the performance he'd been waiting for all his life.

Then he began. "Luanne was glorious, very much like you, my beloved Lili, at least in looks and in her brilliant mind. Unorthodox, independent, a trailblazer. I fell in love with her on sight in Saint Mark's Basilica, as I believe she did with me. She told me she was the only child of a single mother who also worked in the medical field, that all she'd known since childhood had been academic endeavor and excellence."

So she'd been living her mother's life. Until Antonio.

"She'd just finished her medical residency and was about to start her fellowship when she discovered she hadn't actually lived yet. So before she plunged into her hospital work she'd decided to take two years to roam the world. Italy was her first stop.

"We spent every minute together for two weeks until she said she was heading north. I was besotted with her, but knew I'd never see her again if she left, so I proposed. She was stunned, refused on the spot, left the next day. So I followed her, all over Europe. My mother and uncles were enraged. I'd just taken my father's place in the family law firm, which I'd trained all my life to do, and I left them in the lurch. Then Luanne finally succumbed and we got married in France, but when we went home, no one was happy. Not only had my desertion caused the firm irredeemable losses, but I was supposed to marry to benefit the family. But I wanted none of that. I told them I wouldn't take my father's place permanently, that I wanted to leave and be with Luanne and the baby we knew by then we'd made. You, my darling girl."

Her throat tightening with every word, she leaned closer into Antonio, who intensified his hold on her as if protecting her from her father's revelations.

Her father went on, his gaze looking backward in time. "My mother told me Luanne wasn't wife material, would make a terrible mother, that I'd destroy my life and yours if I remained with her. Luanne hated my mother, too, hated all the Accardis and their elitism, hated being in Venice, and in what she called a moldy dwelling fit only for monsters and ghosts.

"When our stay in Venice lengthened and Luanne gave birth to you while I took care of the problems my absence caused, she started believing I'd never stand up for myself or for you, that I'd remain under my family's boot forever. To prove that only she and you mattered, I set a date for when I'd leave it all behind and go back with her to the States.

"At first, she was ecstatic. But as your first birthday neared and I was getting ready to leave, she began asking me what I would do there while she worked. Stay home and raise you? I knew nothing but the law, but I wouldn't be able to continue that in the States. My family threatened to disown me if I left them again, which would have left me penniless, but I didn't care. Then on your first birthday, Luanne told me she no longer wanted me, that I was suffocating her, that she wanted me and my family out of her life. Out of yours, too.

"I was convinced she was suffering from prolonged and severe postpartum depression. I told her so and she broke down. She wept and wept and begged me to let her go. My heart broke, but I couldn't reach her. I could only say that whatever happened between us, I would remain your father. I had rights to you, and you had a right to me. Her misery deepened as she asked how I would be your father across continents. What would it do to you, always waiting for a father who'd come only when my family let me go? How many times a year would that be and for how long? I insisted I'd manage something regular, but she thought it would only keep her and you in purgatory forever.

"After I failed to soothe her and her health declined, I was forced to grant her a divorce, but I gave her all the money I had. I wanted her to buy a beautiful house in an upscale neighborhood, to have enough money to bring you up in luxury, so she never had to work too hard and could be with you more. Problem was, only a portion of the money was mine. The rest was family funds. I thought I'd manage paying it back before anyone found out, but they did.

"They went after her for the money and things escalated. I was helpless to stop it from spiraling into an ugly legal fight. During the proceedings, my family even tried to get custody of you, claiming she was unbalanced. That was when she told me she never wanted to see me again, that she'd already told you I didn't want to see you, and that my family were horrible people who wanted to throw you out on the streets. I still came regularly through the years, trying to see you, but she wouldn't let me. She said you were stable and hardworking and the last thing you needed was the upheaval of my erratic presence and the influence of my evil family.

"By the time you became an adult and I could approach you without her consent, you'd had too many years without knowing me. I knew she'd turn it into a fight over you, causing you the upheaval she said she protected you from. I felt I already failed you, so... I gave up.

"When she became ill, I installed a lump sum in a new account in her name, asked her attorney and bank to let you think it was a backup plan she always had, and gave you full control of it, so her care didn't burden you, at least financially. *Dio mio, figlia mia*, my daughter, I wanted to be there for you, but I didn't know what to say. I didn't want to blame her for anything in her condition. But the moment I heard of her death, I had to try again. She wasn't there to be hurt if your opinion of her changed, or for you to be torn between us. And...here we are."

It all added up. Knowing her mother, Lili accepted this as a plausible explanation. It shed a new, understandable light on the Accardis and a favorable one on her father.

Before she could get any words past the vise gripping her throat, her father bent over her, taking her hands in his. "I don't ask that you forgive me for not fighting harder to be your father. I only hope you'll give me the chance to be in your life now, in any way. Like your future groom, I believe you deserve only the best, and I hope you'll give me the privilege of doing my best to provide you with it."

And she found herself in his arms, hugging him and being hugged by him, the father she'd never had, but would now have for as long as life allowed them.

After her father deluged her in apologies, and obtained

her promise to let him into her life, she turned to Antonio. He was on his feet, muscles bunched, gaze pinned on them.

Unable to read his expression, she reached out to him.

He at once claimed her to his side, wincing down at her. "*Mi amore*, your tears kill me, even ones of happiness."

Blubbering a laugh, she wrapped her arms around him. "You'll have to withstand those. It's not every day that I get my father back." She met his turbulent gaze and smiled, asking him silently for his blessing.

As he took her trembling lips, he murmured against them for her ears only. "He can call me Antonio."

Whooping with delight, she invited her father closer, hugging him with her other arm. "You can call him Antonio."

Realizing the significance of that, her father poured jubilation all over them. After getting confirmations that they'd make use of him in their wedding preparations, and anything else, for life, he led them back to where the Accardis awaited them en masse.

Entering the ballroom tucked into Antonio's protection, Lili boggled at the number of polished elites who queued to introduce themselves.

Not that she thought their regard had anything to do with her. They were here at her father's demand, to make a grand gesture in his atonement campaign. But all the awe everyone exhibited was on Antonio's behalf.

The night blurred from then on. The only thing she registered clearly was Antonio's simmering intensity. He might have sanctioned her father's story and had acquitted him of being a cold-blooded deserter, but it was clear the Accardis hadn't passed his test.

Then suddenly, the unease she felt in Antonio spiked to something else. Something darker.

Trying to understand why, she paid extra attention to

the people who'd just come forward, but she found nothing different about them.

Before she could probe the situation further, her father pulled her away while Antonio remained held back by the newcomers.

As she greeted two more of her father's cousins twice removed, her focus remained on Antonio as he frowned at those who thronged around him. Then one of the two men said something to her that made her give him her full attention.

"You'll go down in the annals of our family history as the one who saved us all, Lili." At her incomprehension, he elaborated, "As you may know, our family businesses are intertwined, and over a year ago, some bad stock market decisions led to a domino effect in all our holdings. Dr. Balducci, through his Black Castle division, offered to bail us out, saving us from the impasse—that has since regretfully worsened—in return for acquiring our major ancestral assets."

The other man nodded. "We two were the ones charged with conveying the family's decision to turn down his offer. The damned family rules dictate those assets stay within the family at any cost. I can't tell you how relieved everyone is now that we can finally accept his offer, since he *will* be family shortly."

"*If* his offer is still on the table," said the other man.

The first man winked at her. "If it isn't, we're sure you, dear Lili, can convince him to put it back there."

As her father exclaimed that he'd never heard of this, Lili's gaze sought out Antonio again, her mind spinning.

He'd never mentioned it. So maybe he hadn't been involved and it had been his brokers trolling for acquisitions?

No, there was no way he wouldn't be in charge of every offer issuing from his organization. So why hadn't he told her about this aborted transaction involving her family?

Could it have slipped his mind? That was again something she found impossible to believe. Nothing slipped Antonio's mind.

Could part of his tension around her family be on account of the thwarted deal? And it continued in part because he didn't know yet that it would go through? Did he know their engagement would provide a solution to this deadlock?

Whoa. It seemed she could still slide back into insecurity. She thought she'd stopped wondering why Antonio wanted to marry her, stopped looking for reasons besides that he loved her.

But this deal certainly couldn't be even a contributing reason. The financial benefit would all be her family's in their current bind. At best, the acquisitions could have only minor value to him compared with his other assets.

Dismissing her absurd thoughts, she concluded her side meeting, laughingly promising the two men to put in a good word for them with Antonio.

As she rejoined him, his mind seemed to be elsewhere as he received her, his gaze leaving her whenever anyone came to talk to them to fix on one certain part of the ballroom. She followed it and saw the same relatives who'd first made him tense up.

By the time he asked her if she didn't mind leaving, she'd had enough tension for one night and eagerly agreed.

Her unease lingered until the moment they entered their hotel suite. Then he swept her up in his arms, threw her down on the bed and took her with an even more ferocious hunger than ever before. Flesh on flesh, he melted her disquiet and bound her deeper under his spell.

In the next week, her family members competed to invite them to their homes.

Antonio gave her carte blanche to accept all invitations,

though it meant flying all over the country. His brother-hood family had taken up the slack in the arrangements for their wedding and kept them apprised of all developments, so they could afford the time to get to know hers better.

As the visits started, a new discomfort crept over her. Though he seemed willing to know everyone for her sake, and she was grateful since there were some members she liked and wished to know better, she soon noticed his focus was on one woman. One of those he'd tensed around during the reception. She'd become a common denominator in all the gatherings.

Sofia Accardi.

Sofia, her father's third cousin, was in her late fifties, but looked like a great mid-forties. She oozed charisma and distinction and she seemed intensely interested in Antonio. Her children—her daughters especially—were present on most occasions, flocking around him like moths to the flame.

Then Sofia invited them to her home, despite it being in the midst of a major renovation. When Lili said they'd come later when the work was done, the woman was insistent. It was Antonio who ended the debate, accepting the invitation.

It was insidious—the feeling Lili had that Antonio had consented to every invitation so far only so it wouldn't look strange when they accepted Sofia's. The woman he'd remained stilted around all week.

Now as the day progressed at Sofia's estate, everything Lili felt from Antonio intensified her suspicions.

Sofia *did* provoke something inside him. Something volcanic in intensity. Could it be…attraction? Lust? Worse?

Sofia, though older, was incredibly beautiful and voluptuous, a very sensual woman who was known as a man-eater, having gone through three husbands and uncounted lovers. Lili, in her relative inexperience, felt decidedly lacking compared to the woman who was more on his level than she would ever be.

After dinner, while she was trapped in conversation with Sofia's daughters, Antonio, who'd said almost nothing to her all evening, walked out of the family room. And her agitation boiled over.

She couldn't wait until they left. She had to find him, ask him, now. If he was having second thoughts of any sort, this was the time to come clean.

As she excused herself, she realized it wasn't only Antonio who was unaccounted for. Sofia, too, had disappeared.

Feeling like her whole world was sinking under her feet, she went in search of them through the immense house.

The areas under renovation were barricaded, so that left only the private quarters. The bedrooms. Nowhere a guest like Antonio would be. It couldn't…he *wouldn't*…

Suddenly she heard his voice. An emotion-filled growl. It was followed by a husky, pleading moan. Sofia's.

Her heart almost uprooted itself in her chest and every muscle trembled as she stepped through a door she hadn't noticed was ajar in the dimness of the corridor, one a barricade announced off-limits.

The room inside was pitch-dark, but its French windows opened to a terrace, from which their voices emanated.

Then she saw them.

In the lights coming from the garden, under the canopy of a starlit night, Antonio stood like a monolith with his back almost to her as Sofia hugged him frantically.

Then slowly, as if he couldn't resist anymore, his arms wrapped around her.

Ten

Lili froze.

The sight in front of her... Antonio, with another woman...

There was nothing. No more air. No more heartbeats.

Then the woman's lament pierced her like a bullet. "You have to believe me, Antonio. I never wanted to give you up."

The agony the words contained lodged like an ax in her chest.

They...they had a previous affair? And Antonio still felt that fiercely for her? Still loved her? But he'd said *she* was his first love. He'd said he'd grown a heart to love *her*.

Antonio pushed Sofia away on a butchered groan, as if tearing himself from her arms hurt him, badly. The sound of his torment made Lili shrivel.

Had he been with her only because he'd thought Sofia had abandoned him? Because he couldn't have her? And now that he evidently could, he was fighting his desire for her?

But Lili didn't want him honor-bound or obligated. If he didn't love and desire her as completely as she did him, she only wished him to have what he wanted. If that was no longer her, she had to set him free. Now. *Now.*

Before she could force her numb legs to move, Sofia started sobbing, and what she said robbed Lili of all power, made her sag to her knees.

"I held you only once after my C-section when I was still drowsy from anesthesia. You were the most perfect baby boy."

Sofia was…was…*his mother.*

"When I fully came to, my family had sent you away. I threatened to kill myself if they didn't return you but they told me it was too late, that an undisclosed adopter took you. I went mad. I tried to commit suicide." She extended her hands to him so he could see the scars she still bore. "After I was saved, I knew I'd been stupid, since I couldn't find you if I died. But there seemed no way to find anything about you, and I fell into a deep depression. Three years later I met my first husband, and he promised to help me find you. But his investigations only discovered that my parents and uncle had lied, that they'd put you in an orphanage. When Mark found out which one, I eloped with him and we went to the orphanage. But you were no longer there and we couldn't find your trail. I drove myself insane imagining you'd fallen into the worst of hands."

A vicious huff crackled from Antonio. "You can't even imagine the kind of hands I fell into. They make slave traders look like Good Samaritans."

The sob that tore through Sofia sounded as if it had ripped her apart inside. She reached her hands out to him.

"Don't." He pulled away, as if her touch would burn him. "I don't need your pity or your guilt. As you can see, I far more than survived."

She tried to approach again before her hands fell to her sides, defeated. "You're right. I can't even imagine what you went through, or how you conquered your horrific beginnings and then the world. I can only tell you my side, how I lived with the trauma of your loss, of imagining your fate." A sob choked her, soaked her voice in tears. "But I did always feel you were out there, alive, strong. Then I saw a photo of you in a magazine and felt that I knew you. Then I saw you face-to-face and felt the connection between us. Your half siblings felt it, too, even if they couldn't imagine what drew them to you like that. I thought I was crazy, but the way you looked at me, at them, made me hope you felt it, too. But today, I just *knew* who you are, and that you know who I am. I felt you didn't want me to acknowledge our relationship. But I had to do it. Had to tell you I recognized you, that losing you tore a hole in my soul that nothing has ever mended, not even having more children, or adopting two boys who reminded me of you. My father and uncle died years ago, and my mother is now senile, but I still curse them every day as I did for the past forty years, for what they did to you and to me."

This time, when she reached for him, he let her cling to his arms. She looked up at him, her eyes beseeching. "I know I can never undo what's been done to you. I can't do *anything...*" Another harsh sob escaped her throat. "Nothing but hope that you'll let me know you, and maybe one day, in some way, I'll make it up to you."

Lili was a mess of tremors. Sofia's impassioned confession shook her far more than her father's had. To imagine what some of those Accardis—his family like they were hers—had cost him, was beyond endurance.

Then he finally spoke, his voice darker than the night. "When I discovered what your family did to me, what I thought you agreed to, I planned to exact punishment, on you and on the whole family whose rules dictate throwing away unwanted children. I wanted to buy your ancestral assets, lure you all into a merger with the promise of saving you from bankruptcy, so I'd end up in control of your very lives, before I took my time destroying you, each in the way you deserve. But even in their desperation, the Accardis rejected my life raft because, of all the irony, I wasn't 'family'."

The realization hit Lili so hard she felt her head would burst with it. What she'd always felt but couldn't even guess at. The reason he'd approached her in the first place.

He'd needed an in into the family.

It had been her.

That was why he'd pursued her, why he'd proposed to her.

It all made sense now. He'd never loved her. Never even wanted her. He'd only wanted revenge. She'd been nothing but his means to his lifelong retribution.

The blow of realization was so brutal it interrupted her very heartbeats.

"But now after you told me how—"

Antonio's words were suddenly cut off as he tensed and turned to look in Lili's direction.

There was no way he could see her in the darkness. And she hadn't made a sound. She couldn't move, couldn't even breathe.

"Liliana?"

He did feel her. Or it was her devastation he felt. Now she realized that everything between them had been a lie.

Suffocating, feeling she'd rather die than face him now, she scrambled up, stumbling as she ran back out of the room.

"Liliana!"

His shout punched her between the shoulder blades, intensifying her desperation.

She had to escape him, escape the agony. But she couldn't pass through the others on her way out. She had to find another exit.

Spilling into the next barricaded room, which must open onto the same wraparound veranda leading to the garden, she rushed to open the closed French doors, growing frantic as his thundering footsteps drew closer, his shout begging her to stop another lash propelling her forward, making her more frantic.

Then everything happened at once. Sofia's shrill warning, Antonio roaring, and she was falling.

Pain exploded, sharp and searing, tearing through her midriff. A simultaneous agony splintered through her thigh, almost fracturing her awareness.

Then she was on her back, staring up at the stars as they blurred, the night darkening around her.

The whoosh of blood in her ears receded, only to be replaced by Antonio's frenzy as he begged her not to move.

Not that she could. Even drawing enough oxygen not to pass out was excruciating. She lay there, paralyzed with pain, watching his massive silhouette, an avenging angel jumping down a steep drop to crouch over her.

Vaguely, she realized the veranda she'd tried to escape through wasn't there. She'd fallen through its skeleton, getting stabbed on the way down by protruding concrete-reinforcing steel bars. From the agony now emanating from her left side, she realized she must have damaged some internal organs. Probably her spleen, intestines, maybe a kidney. Her left femur was also fractured. Muscle damage was a given, maybe nerve damage, too.

She couldn't see Antonio's face, could only hear his strident breathing as he swept her in the bright beam of a flashlight.

Then she heard the tremor of dread in his voice as he pressed down on her side. He'd assessed her injuries and was applying pressure to slow the bleeding. "I'm here, *mi amore*, I've got you. Just don't move."

"*Dio mio, dio mio*, is she…?"

Without looking up, he hissed, "Leave *now*, Sofia. Tell no one."

Sofia's gasp at Antonio's harshness carried to Lili's wavering consciousness, but the woman complied, disappearing from Lili's field of vision. Then Antonio started talking, barking sharp, concise orders. To Paolo, to fetch his medical kit from the limo. To his pilot, to get a helicopter. To the medical center, to prepare his OR.

Working at top efficiency, Antonio, the miracle worker who put people back together, had everything ready in minutes to reconstruct her. After he'd broken her, torn her apart.

He bent over her, raining frantic kisses all over her face. "You're going to be okay, *mi amore*, I promise."

She tried to cringe away. "You…shouldn't…"

"Don't talk. Just let me take care of you."

"You shouldn't…" Her teeth clattered, more with desolation than with blood loss or pain. "…have done…this to me…"

A groan escaped him, his shudder transmitting to her trembling body. "Whatever you heard, whatever you understood, whatever you think I did, you're wrong, *mi amore*, I swear."

Tears oozed out of her very soul. "I…loved…you…"

"And I worship you. You're everything to me. *Everything.*"

All light faded, taking his image with it as blackness sucked her under. "I—I think…it's better…this way…"

As she slipped away, she wished it would be forever. So

she wouldn't live knowing she'd never had him, or with the agony that would never go away.

Antonio watched Liliana's eyes flutter closed, felt her bloodied body going limp and still, and went mad.

His roar almost tore out the heart that had been exploding with every beat since he'd watched her plunge into that jagged maw of concrete and steel.

He'd done this to her. This was his fault. All of it.

She was lying here, torn and broken, because he'd lied to her. Because he'd overridden her disinclination and accepted his mother's invitation. Because she must have picked up on his weirdness, because he'd left her behind without explanation, making her follow him, hear what had made her escape him so desperately through the house they shouldn't have been in.

If he lost her...

No. He'd *never* lose her. He *would* save her. He'd pay his very life and far more to restore her, body and heart.

But before he could do anything, he had to suppress the insanity of terror and the violence of self-hatred. He had to go through his perfected motions. Everything he'd ever learned, every skill he'd acquired, every bit of experience he'd accumulated through the long years of slavery and struggle and success, had all been for this moment.

Everything he was had been made for her. Everything he could do, he'd learned to save her.

From the injuries he'd caused her.

Antonio raced against time in a crazed fast-forward, spiraling through all levels of hell.

In what seemed like minutes, he'd flown Liliana to his nearest medical center where he'd had to cut her open, literally this time, so he could mend her. He'd poured all his expertise, all his being, into saving her. It had driven him insane, not only the extent of her injuries and the reason she'd sustained them, but the feeling that she was resisting his efforts. He might have been unhinged with terror and guilt, but he did feel as if she wanted him to fail.

It had been when she'd flatlined, when there'd been no medical reason anymore that she should, that he'd become sure.

She'd wanted to die.

In the horrific lifetime until he'd managed to restart her heart, he'd known. If he'd failed, his heart would have stopped seconds after hers.

Now she lay in the ICU, just like Ivan's mystery woman had three weeks ago. But the latter had fought to survive. He could feel Liliana still fighting to escape. He'd hurt her so much, it was as if she didn't want to wake up to face the agony.

Some of her last words revolved in his mind again, hacking it to pieces. *You shouldn't have done this to me. I loved you.*

He'd been a coward, avoiding a confession that could have caused a passing crisis, a pain he could have healed. He'd been self-deluding, thinking she wouldn't pick up on the turmoil that racked him every time he saw his mother. Liliana had always felt he'd been hiding something, but because of his evasions, when she'd overheard him, she'd concluded the worst. What had once been the truth.

And it had destroyed her.

Sagging to his knees beside her bed, he let the tears he'd never shed before pour out of his very soul.

"You're my life, *mi amore*. I can't and won't live without you. I beg you, don't punish me by harming yourself."

In response, her vitals only grew more erratic.

Exploding to his feet, he rummaged for medications, roaring for his assistants to prepare emergency resuscitation.

Just as he was about to inject the cocktail into her drip, a deep voice broke over him.

"I don't think she needs that."

He swung around to blast whoever was interfering, then rocked on his feet with the aborted aggression when he saw Ivan.

His head nurse was scurrying away. Had she fetched Ivan to deal with him? He sure would have blasted her, as he'd done every member of his medical team all night.

Ivan approached him as if he were approaching a wounded tiger. "I know she doesn't need that because you never second-guess yourself, never up your meds. You get it right the first time. Always."

"But it's *Liliana*. And I doubt I'm even sane anymore."

Ivan's hand clamped his, forced it down. "Come with me, Tonio."

He glared at his friend through his tears. "She needs—"

"She needs you to leave her alone for now." Ivan dragged him away, his pull inexorable in Antonio's shaken state. "You told me...*she* would feel me in her sleep, and it would give her strength, make her fight. When she woke up, she told me it was true. Now your lady feels you, too, and to me it looks like your presence distresses her. You might be the very thing compromising her survival."

It killed Antonio to admit this had to be the explanation. There was no medical reason why Liliana shouldn't be stable.

Letting Ivan tug him to the observation area, he sagged down, his gaze pinned on Liliana's inert figure and inanimate face. He plummeted into a deeper hell of guilt and desperation.

It was only when Ivan's assessment proved right and Liliana's vitals stabilized that he finally choked out, "How did you know? How did you come?"

"Paolo called me, and I called the others. As for how...

she insisted she is stable, can spare me for hours and told me to go to you. If it had been a choice between being by her side or yours…"

"You would have chosen her." Antonio looked back at Liliana. "I'd choose her, too, over anything or anyone. Starting with myself."

Just then, his brothers and their mates began arriving.

It wasn't long before he told them to go away. His sanity was hanging by a thread, and their empathy, their every bolstering word, the very sight of them together, was about to snap it.

Finally, they reluctantly left, with Ivan promising he'd keep them updated. He told Ivan his presence wasn't helping anymore, to leave, too, but the icy Russian just ignored him.

As the last of his brothers disappeared from view, Ivan turned to him. "I take it from your condition, and her unconscious reaction to your presence, this isn't just an accident?"

Suddenly feeling the crushing need to share everything with his oldest and closest friend, Antonio told Ivan everything.

After he fell silent, Ivan's gaze grew contemplative. "This is good for you, you know?" Anger exploded inside Antonio, making him lunge to grab Ivan by the lapels. Ivan crushed his hands in the vise of his, forcing him to listen. "You were always too serene, too untouchable. I always knew this meant what's inside you was even more nightmarish than any of us. And this woman has reached inside you and dragged out your chaos, so she could dispel it. She also released every emotion you never thought yourself capable of."

"She created them. And I am the reason she's lying there. Because I lied to her, because she thinks I never loved her."

Ivan shrugged. "But you'll prove you do, and that you had some stupidly noble reason for hiding what you hid from her. But even if she thinks you don't love her now, I suspect deep down she feels that you do, since she's found the perfect method to brutally punish you."

"I'd take any punishment but this." His eyes burned with more tears.

"But this is what she's choosing, even unconsciously, hurting you by showing you how you hurt her. So you'll take it, until she believes you've had enough, until *you* believe you've atoned. Then if everything the brothers say about her and what she feels for you is true, she'll take you back."

Antonio didn't even dare hope it would be that easy, or that it would come to pass at all. But somehow Ivan's prophecy stopped the spiral of madness. He couldn't have Liliana wake up to find him totally deranged.

And she *would* wake up. He'd transplant his very life into her if that was what it took. He would have her whole again at any price.

For the next two days as Liliana remained asleep, Antonio discovered that hell was bottomless.

He'd forced himself to heed Ivan's theory that her deterioration was directly proportionate to his proximity. Though despondent, he'd watched her from afar, every second he could.

On the third day she woke up while one of his assistants was tending her. He watched every nuance of her return to consciousness, then awareness, feeling as if he were waiting for a verdict of life or death.

Her lashes fluttered open, a hand jerking when she found herself hooked up to drips and monitors. Her whole body tensed before slumping back, realization replacing confusion on her face.

Through the open mike where he'd listened to her every breath, he heard his nurse explaining her condition and reassuring her. Liliana only listened, but as his assistant finished checking her, she said something he couldn't hear in her ear.

A minute later his assistant came out and, with a wide smile, told him he'd pulled off another miracle. Liliana was far better than expected after such an extensive surgery.

And she'd asked to see him.

Afraid to breathe, to hope, he didn't know when he'd moved, but he found himself standing over Liliana.

She spoke without raising her eyes, her voice hoarse from intubation, chafing his every nerve ending. "Thank you for saving my life. Even if you no longer need me."

He must have misheard her. She couldn't have said... "What?"

Her eyes rose to him now, but they were no longer hers, but a stranger's. "Since you've revealed yourself to your mother, I'm sure you can now enter my—your family to destroy it from within on your own."

He didn't know how he remained standing. He'd thought there could be no more pain than what he'd suffered in the past three days. He'd known nothing.

This, what she believed, was true agony.

"*Per Dio*, am I that big a monster in your eyes now?"

"You're a vigilante, and you do what needs to be done to achieve your goal no matter the price. You're also a surgeon and you save patients regardless of their value to you."

"You think I considered you just another patient?" he choked out, unable to believe how horrible it had all become.

"It's a fact you no longer need me."

"I will need you, and only you, till my dying breath."

Her gaze emptied more. "You probably didn't wish it

to end this way. I do realize you must feel bad about my injuries—"

He cut across her mutilating words. "I don't feel bad, Liliana, I feel devastated."

"You shouldn't. I'm responsible for what happened to me. I barged into clearly labeled danger zones, repeatedly."

Both the under-construction site, and his life.

He gritted his teeth against the mounting pain. "What devastates me is that I destroyed your faith in me, in yourself, so completely. And it's why you almost…almost…"

"But I didn't die, thanks to you." She surveyed his agitation with a blank look, as lifeless as her voice. "And I do understand your need for exacting retribution on the family that threw you away. If only you'd told me in the beginning, I'd have helped you, if only for the possibility you'd find a peaceful and just resolution, and you wouldn't have needed to go to these lengths to use me as your stealth weapon."

"You must believe me, *mi amore*. Whatever I intended to do, I abandoned it all after I first saw you. I wanted only you since."

As if she hadn't heard him, she went on, "But now that you discovered you've misjudged your mother even worse than I have my father, I hope you'll reconsider your revenge. The guilty ones are either dead or as good as. And I doubt no one else, no matter their faults, deserves your wrath. I hope you won't destroy everyone indiscriminately for the crimes of some of their own. And that you'll give your mother the chance she hoped for."

It agonized him more that even in her own devastation she was thinking of others.

He dropped to his knees beside her, his hand trembling as he took hers. "I avoided even talking about your family, not only because none of them mattered anymore, but because I was afraid they'd hurt you. I only agreed to meet them when I realized how much you needed to settle their issue, and to be there to protect you from them. It turned out the only one I needed to protect you from was myself. And I failed. I failed you."

"I failed myself. And now I'll have the scars to remind me never to do so again."

Before he took her hand to his lips, she pulled it away with surprising strength, as if she could no longer bear his touch. She turned her head away, closing her eyes. Her dry eyes.

It was as if she had nothing left to say to him. As if she had nothing left inside her.

He remained on his knees beside her as depletion claimed her again, at last learning the meaning of helplessness.

During the next two weeks, as Liliana recuperated, Antonio never left the center, always hovering around, trying again and again to get her to talk to him. But after that time when she'd first woken up, she'd given him nothing but silence. His presence seemed to plunge her into deepening despondency.

Everyone kept telling him to let her bounce back from the trauma, that she was hurt that much because she loved him as fiercely and that he'd eventually heal her with his love. But the days had passed and Liliana seemed to be drawing further into herself.

And today he couldn't bear it anymore. He'd just entered her room, said he would stand there beside her bed, no matter how long it took, until she talked to him again.

Then she finally did, and shattered his heart.

Eyes no longer distant, raw, ravished, she looked up at him, her pain and betrayal skewering him to his vitals. "You lied to me, Antonio, when all I ever asked of you was honesty. Even if you've developed feelings for me, everything that you said or did, everything that happened between us, is tainted by this lie. Now I can't trust or feel again. My emotions, my faith, like the body you've put back together, have been damaged and will remain scarred."

Before he could swear to her that he'd wait forever for her to heal, that he'd erase her scars, she sat up, swung her good leg followed by her casted leg over the side of the bed. "There's no more medical reason for me to remain here. I want you to discharge me."

All he wanted to do was rave and rant and keep her there until she gave him another chance.

But he couldn't press her more in her fragile state.

"I will. But please, Liliana, whatever you think of me or however you feel now, *please*, come back with me to our place, let me take care of you as you recuperate."

She shook her head, and for the first time since her accident tears started to fall. He hated himself more with every track of moisture that stained her pale cheeks.

He wished *she'd* rave and rant. Her subdued misery was so much worse than any passionate display that would have given him hope he could revive her emotions.

All he could do now was stop hurting her more, let her go and hope she'd heal enough one day to let him in again. Pray that she wouldn't shut him out like her mother had her father, for the rest of her life.

The day that should have been their wedding day came and went in total silence from Liliana.

She hadn't gone back to Antonio's mansion. And she hadn't returned to the lab.

He was hailed as the leading expert of mending catastrophic injuries, but he'd injured the one person he needed to live, an injury he was helpless to heal.

It was during one of the surgeries he now buried himself in that he realized the truth.

It didn't matter that he healed her so she'd come back to him. It mattered that she healed for herself, so she could resume her life, her work. He and what he felt were of no consequence.

Only she mattered.

And because only she did, if her emotional health depended on letting her go, he would.

Even if it destroyed him.

Eleven

Three months after the accident, though Lili had fully recovered physically, she hadn't gone back to work.

Among those who regularly came visiting, Brian had been the one who kept persistently trying to convince her to do so. She'd insisted right back that she'd decided to take all her missed vacations at once.

Ever since Antonio had discharged her and sent her back to LA on his private jet, she'd left the house only for follow-ups and the intensive physiotherapy Antonio had scheduled for her, both performed by others under his command.

She hadn't seen or heard from him since.

At times, longing for him made her unable to breathe.

Her father, whom she'd told a severely edited version of the truth, had been adamant it meant she'd healed enough to believe in Antonio's love again. But she knew missing him had nothing to do with being over the trauma. Missing him, with every breath, had always been her default.

As for his love, after being dedicated to her after the accident, he had been silent since he'd discharged her. Whatever he'd felt for her, it seemed she'd pushed him away so hard he'd given up on her.

She couldn't heed her father's fervent advice to contact him. She couldn't impose on him if he'd moved on.

She was indulging in what had become an obsession, driving herself insane again wondering if he'd ever really loved her and if she'd killed his love, or if he'd discovered he didn't feel enough for her after all, when her doorbell rang.

Since everyone called before passing by, the hope that it was Antonio propelled her to the door the fastest she'd moved since the accident.

But it wasn't him on her doorstep. It was Sofia Accardi.

After exchanging a long stare, Lili stunned and disappointed, Sofia discomfited and tentative, Lili invited her in. Questions flooded her mind, all about Antonio. Instead of asking them, she awkwardly offered Sofia something to drink.

Over a cup of tea, Sofia finally started talking. "I would have come earlier, but Antonio said you needed space."

Was that what he thought? Was that why he hadn't attempted to contact her?

"He also said you're healed completely."

"I...am." Physically, at least. "Antonio is a virtuoso. Even my scars are negligible, and fading every day."

An exquisite smile adorned the woman's gorgeous face, which now Lili could see was an older, feminine version of Antonio's. "His scars are fading, too. He's been letting me and his siblings closer, and it's been...indescribable. I always felt my baby had survived, had grown strong and special, but Antonio surpasses my every fantasy."

As he surpassed Lili's. So much so it was why she'd always felt she couldn't possibly deserve his love.

Sofia went on. "He told me you asked him to give me a chance. So I owe you the happiness of having my son back." Her smile faded as she continued. "But he abhors many members of the family for being of the same school of thought that led my parents to deprive me of him, and toss him into the nightmarish fate he still won't tell me about. These people owe you their *lives*, since you're the one who stayed his hand."

She'd had that much influence on him? Or had he just considered none worth the trouble of revenge?

Whatever the reason, she took joy in knowing that he was letting go of his bitterness and rage, letting his family heal him, accepting the love he deserved. If her role in his life had been to get him to this point, it was enough for her. She wanted him happy, even if she'd never be again.

Sofia reached for one of her hands. "But I'm really here to express how sorry I am for everything that happened since I insisted you visit me when my house was such a mess. Antonio explained why overhearing us upset you so much, but he said nothing further. I feel so guilty."

Lili put her other hand on top of hers. "Listen, Sofia, the renovation was barricaded, and I stupidly barged inside it. I was an idiot to overreact and run away in the first place. You have nothing to feel guilty about."

Tears glittered in the woman's eyes. "Even so, I felt terrible, and so helpless watching everything come apart. Your wedding…"

Unable to hear another word about their aborted wedding, she interrupted Sofia. "That's another thing that was all my doing. But I'm only happy that I brought you and Antonio back together."

"If only I could do the same." Sofia hugged her. "I would have loved to have you as a daughter-in-law."

Stunned by the woman's display of affection, distressed that her words meant Sofia thought a reunion with Antonio wasn't in the cards, she numbly hugged her back. "I would have loved to have you as a mother-in-law, too."

From then on and until Sofia left, they diverted the conversation to less stressful areas. When she took her leave Sofia made Lili promise to keep in touch.

As she closed the door behind her, Lili felt a new friend had entered her life. But what would that matter if she'd couldn't bear having her in it, if she only reminded her she'd lost Antonio?

Would her very life matter if she had?

And she could no longer bear not knowing.

She had to let *him* tell her. If there was still a chance, or if she should just surrender to despair.

The decision to approach Antonio was easier made than executed. All morning, fear held her back. Uncertainty, which she'd always been unable to handle, was now what kept her going. Because part of uncertainty was hope. If she killed the hope that she had a chance with Antonio, her life wouldn't be worth living.

But she not only couldn't go on not knowing for sure either way, but something terrible roiled inside her, prodding her to seek him out today. Right *now*. It wasn't the usual longing that gnawed at her. It was something ferocious that demanded action.

Just as she was about to leave the house to go to his medical center where she knew he was every day, her cell phone vibrated.

It was a number she didn't know.

Heart hammering, hoping against hope that it was him, she answered. The deep, dark voice that poured into her ear almost had her pile in a heap on the ground.

Because it wasn't Antonio.

It took her a second to recognize the voice. Jakob Wolff.

"Hello, Lili, it's Jakob. I have Ivan with me and we were wondering if you could see us."

Trembling with worry, she croaked, "Of course. When and where?"

"Right now. We're parked right outside."

"Oh. Oh! Please, come right in."

Tripping in her haste, she rushed to the door, opening it in time to see the two men step out of an imposing Rolls Royce. Breath bated, she watched these two who were an intimate part of Antonio's life walk up to her door.

Inviting them in, leading them where she'd had Sofia just yesterday, Lili and Ivan were soon immersed in their first face-to-face meeting. He seemed as curious about her as she was about him. Until recently, Ivan had been the closest person in the world to Antonio. If they'd gone through with the wedding, Ivan would have been his best man, would have become the brother she never had.

Suddenly Jakob sat forward, making Lili aware of his presence again, and of his impatience. "We're not here for chitchat."

Ivan sighed, nodded, got a dossier out of his briefcase, handed it to her. "Indeed. We're here to give you this."

Confusion deepening, she took it from him, and at his prodding, opened it and read.

With each line, each page, her shock deepened.

These were legal documents. Written in extensive, meticulous terms. Turning over Antonio's R & D empire to her.

When she finally raised flabbergasted eyes to them, Jakob's lips curled in disgusted disapproval. "Antonio believes you're better equipped to benefit the world with what he's built. He also believes you'd probably want to segregate it from Black Castle and become your own independent business, which he believes would be best for you and for your nonprofit policies and pursuits."

"If you're wondering what he'd do instead," Ivan said, watching her closely as if to document her reaction, "he'll turn full-time to what he's best at. Surgery. But he says he'll now emulate you, direct his skills and resources to nonprofit work. But as a surgeon, that would take him into the field of humanitarian work. He's already organized his first mission."

Lili stared from one man to the other, as if they'd suddenly laugh and tell her it was all an elaborate joke.

But from their grimness and their clear dismay at their brother's bequest, and mostly from the wording in those papers, which she knew was Antonio's, this was real.

"Needless to say," Ivan said, "we are extremely disturbed by his decision. We know no one could ever replace him, but since it's you, the others have empowered us to extend you an offer. We will accommodate anything you wish, if you agree to keep the division part of our joint business."

She could only stare at them, totally numb.

Jakob added, "He also said you'd have qualms on account of having no financial or management skills, but he assures you everything will be run by his deputies, while you orchestrate the scientific direction of the organization. He himself will always be available to you as a consultant whenever you wish."

And it was as if a dam burst inside her, making her blurt out, "Is he insane?"

Ivan nodded with another sigh. "Bonkers."

"It gets worse." Jakob produced another file from his own briefcase. "These are the deeds to his mansion in LA, his penthouse in New York City, his best jet, and assorted assets and holdings with a collective net worth I couldn't stomach registering."

She felt as if she'd been caught in an explosion, and the shock waves were widening, tearing down everything.

All she could finally manage was a whisper. "I—I don't get it."

"Don't you?" Jakob tilted his head, a contemptuous edge creeping into his steel-hued gaze, making him look pretty sinister. "From where I'm sitting, you seem to have gotten everything you could have wanted and way more."

She shook her head, shell-shocked. "I only want him."

"Now *that's* priceless." Jakob scoffed. "You dare say that, when you put the man through a hell far worse than all his ordeals combined?"

Ivan frowned. "Jakob's right on this one. According to Antonio you had every right to punish him, but I kept hoping you'd stop your punishment before you finished him. When you went past even that, I wondered what kind of succubus could do that to him. Then I saw you and I don't get it. You're filled with marshmallows and rainbows. How could you do this to him?"

"I didn't do anything," she cried out. "How could I punish him when I thought what he felt for me was…*nothing* like what I felt for him? When he left me alone after he discharged me, and I thought he'd realized he was better off without me, as I always thought he would be?"

Ivan's eyes narrowed before they shot wide. "That's it. That's my answer. You're really *that* insecure, aren't you?"

A shudder of misery shook her. "Only when it comes to him."

Ivan huffed mirthlessly. "Then, boy, are you two even. He's totally, explosively, inventively irrational when it comes to you, too. The man has been punishing himself for hurting you far more brutally than any of our abusers ever did."

"The only thing that hurt me was thinking he didn't… didn't…"

"Didn't love you?" Ivan supplied for her. "If he loved you any more he'd be downright dangerous. As it is, I think he is, very much so, to himself. All this…" Ivan flicked a hand at all the paperwork. "Signing his life away to you? Going to put bodies back together in the most dangerous war zone he could find? He might not be doing it consciously, but I know him. He's given up on you, and he can't face life without you, so like a missile on its last burst of fuel, he's trying to go out with a bang."

The horror of Ivan's analysis and prophecy froze the blood in her arteries.

Then she exploded, pouncing on the two men, shoving the folders at them and dragging them up. "You have to stop him!"

Jakob's gaze became contemptuous. "You think we didn't try? After the number you did on him, he's been like an automaton with no course-correction function left."

Anger broke through her distress. She grabbed Jakob's arm, shaking him "Aren't all of you all-powerful? *Do* something!"

Still probing her, Jakob remained unperturbed by her agitation. "Antonio instructed us to give you all this after he left for his mission."

The world spun, made her stagger back. "He—he already left?"

Jakob steadied her, his gaze no longer accusing. "Not exactly, but that was another instruction. Not to tell you when he left or where he went."

Ivan took her arm, turned her to him. "And that's actually why we're here now. To tell you he's leaving tonight. Because we're not the ones who're all-powerful here. You are. The only one who can stop him is you."

Lili believed Ivan and Jakob would never talk to her again.

Not after she'd blasted them for wasting all that time

testing her and not telling her about Antonio's plans right away.

She'd also drafted them for a ride to his mansion, where they said he'd be, packing and emptying it for her possession. On the way, with Antonio's phone shut off, going mad thinking she'd be too late, she'd piled more and more invective on their sullen, silent heads.

Now they both turned to glare at her as she spilled out of the car at Antonio's door.

Before they drove off in a shower of gravel, Jakob shouted from his window, "You broke him, now you fix him."

Lili rushed to the front door. Climbing steps was still awkward for her, but she took them two at a time.

She entered the mansion to total silence, and dread almost chomped her in half. Was she too late? She'd failed to intercept him before he disappeared out of reach, maybe forever?

Terror mushroomed out of her on a scream. *"Antonio!"*

Footsteps exploded from the direction of the bedroom, which had been theirs once. They thundered before abruptly stopping. And then Antonio appeared across the great room.

He froze, just like she did.

But even across the distance his eyes told her everything, explained everything, put to rest everything that had been driving her insane.

He did share her heartache and misery, felt her same desperation and pain. But his agony seemed to have broken him. Her invulnerable Antonio. She'd done this to him.

Would he leave still because she'd hurt him beyond repair?

Suffocating with dread, all she could say was, "I love you. Please forgive me. Don't go." Then everything turned black.

* * *

"Liliana!"

Antonio exploded into a run and caught her before she hit the ground in a dead faint. After a frenzied exam proved she was physically fine, he rushed her to his bed. The bed he hadn't come near since she'd left him.

Though he knew from his obsessive follow-up of her condition that she was perfectly healed, she looked so spent and fragile. Just like he'd felt...until he'd heard her screaming his name, seen her standing there, her eyes open to him again, showing him into the depths of her soul. Until she'd said she loved him and asked him not to go.

Holding her made him feel as if the heart that had been ripped out of his body was restored. Feeling her warm and whole and *there*, he felt that the life that had oozed out of him every second since he'd lost her was returning. She was here to revive him, to give him another lease on life.

She came to with a gasp, her eyes frantic before she saw him. Then she came apart, clinging to him, a quaking, weeping mass.

Her sobs tore him up inside. "Don't go, please. Don't leave me. Don't leave me anything of yours. I want you, only ever you...please..."

His lips silenced her agony, his tears mingling with hers. "And I want only you. I wanted to leave everything behind when I thought you could no longer want me back."

She wrenched at his neck, his chest with trembling lips, soaking his flesh with her tears, covering it with the worship he'd withered without. "I'll stop wanting you when I stop breathing. Probably not even then."

Before he succumbed to the need to reclaim her, he had to know one thing for sure.

He rose above her, holding her precious face in his trembling hands. "Do you forgive me, *mi amore*? *Really* forgive me, for how I once planned to use you? I don't want the least doubt or bitterness lurking in your heart. That's what you said that day I let you go—that's why I couldn't persist anymore. I felt I could overcome your pain, but I would never erase your mistrust. And I couldn't do that to you. So do you really believe that I loved you from the beginning, and that I did change for you?"

She burst out in another weeping jag, dragging him down to her and deluging him with kisses and tears. "I believe you. I'll always believe you."

After the storm had abated, she drew back to look at him with such earnestness. "But I want you to promise me that if you ever feel any differently, you will tell me. You must never hide anything from me again, whether you're afraid it would hurt me, or know for sure it would."

"I take it this is a two-way street? If you ever stop feeling the same as you do right now, you'll tell me?"

"Since I'll never stop loving you, the only thing I'll confess is that I'm loving you more."

"But if for some unimaginable reason you stop loving me?"

She rose, her eyes telling him everything he needed to breathe again, to live again. "I'll always tell you the whole truth. You know I'm incapable of saying anything else."

"I know." His groan exorcised the last of his tension. Then he let her push him on his back, reveling in her beauty and honesty and openness, all the treasures he'd thought he would never be blessed with again, in the absoluteness of her love, which he'd thought he'd destroyed. "It's why I was in such despair. I knew you would never exaggerate to punish me, so I truly thought I'd lost you forever."

"I would have remained yours forever even if I never found my way back to you."

"And what good would that have done me?" he exclaimed.

She took his lips in a deep, devouring kiss before she pulled back, a grin lighting up her beauty. "I'd already found my way back to you. When your brothers arrived to give me your insane bequest and tell me of your crazy plans, I—"

He heaved up, his whole body tensing. "Those bastards! I'm going to strangle each and every one of them. I told them not to—" Then it hit him. "What am I saying? It's because they disobeyed me that you're here in my arms again."

"Actually, it isn't. That's what I was trying to say. I was coming to you when they came knocking." She looped her arms around his neck. "It seems I felt you were going to do something drastic, and I reached my limit at the same time you did."

"Even if you hadn't, and you decided much later to call me back, I would have come running."

"If I'd missed you, you would have come back to find your brothers roasted." At his incomprehension, she grinned sheepishly. "They put me through their elaborate tests to determine if I'd been manipulating you into giving me what you left me. It almost made me too late to stop you. If it had, I would have turned into a fire-breathing dragon."

A guffaw escaped him, the world suddenly bright and limitless again. "That must have been Jakob and Ivan. No other brother who got his wife's seal of approval on you would have *dared* suspect you of any ulterior motives."

"Yeah, it was Starsky and Hutch." As another laugh burst out of him, she clung to him again, her shudder shaking through him. "Promise me that whatever humanitarian missions you undertake won't be in areas of active conflict. If you don't want to kill me with worry."

Taking her down, he covered her, pressed into her, as

if he wanted to absorb her into his being. "I'd never put myself in harm's way when you need me."

Her fingers convulsed in his hair as she pulled his head up, her eyes fierce with conviction. "The whole world needs you, alive and well and being the irreplaceable force for good that you are. And this brings me to your bequest. All I'll ever need from you is your heart, your trust, your appreciation. But only you can direct everything you've built and achieved."

"You do have a better scientific mind than me."

"My mind and whatever else I have are at your service always. It will be an honor, a privilege and a pleasure to work with you in any capacity. But only you know how to bring everything together, to create and grow the best businesses that are beneficial to the world. You must take everything back." She suddenly chuckled, her golden eyes gleaming. "If you only saw your brothers imagining me filling your shoes, you wouldn't have had the heart to suggest it. Holmes and Watson were having little heart attacks at the very thought."

His laughter rang out with hers, until they were both almost in tears all over again.

Then merriment turned to passion, then to desperation and they were tearing each other's clothes off, competing to give more pleasure, to drag the other deeper into oblivion.

After repeated storms, full domination and surrender, Antonio rose above her and finally touched the places he'd avoided all night. Her faint scars. As he traced them, tears blinded him.

At her gasp, he raised his gaze, found her own eyes streaming again. She realized how he felt.

He still needed to put his feelings into words. "Those moments when your lifeblood bathed my hands as I struggled to stem it, when I was forced to cut into your flesh to save your precious life, when I felt you fighting me so you could let go… I'll never heal from them."

Hers sobs fractured her breath, her words. "I'm sorry, so sorry."

Wiping at his eyes, he smiled with everything in him. "Never be sorry for anything. Just like you made me a new man who has no rage or darkness, who can be ecstatically in love, who can be a son and a brother, you've probably absolved me from every sin I've ever committed. This punishment is enough to take care of all of them. I only wish you didn't have to get hurt so I'd be punished. It's a catch-22 really, since I can only be hurt through you."

Her dawning grin caught on another sob. "I hate being your Achilles' heel."

He hugged her again. "But I love having you as my only vulnerability. I can't live without you being everything to me. My strength and weakness, my joy and agony, my desire and dread."

"You're all that to me and everything else and it's… enormous."

Heart swelling with gratitude, he nodded sagely. "Humongous."

They shared another moment of total communion, before they laughed again. Their mirth caught fire again and they were again surrendering to the power of their bottomless passion and hunger.

Afterward she lay satiated in his arms, wondering what she'd ever done in her life to deserve him.

As if he'd heard her thoughts, he turned her face to him, his words sounding like an irrevocable pledge.

"The heart that grew inside me from the first moment I saw you is yours forever because you gave it life. You changed my perspective and priorities. You made me let go of my anger against my family even before I met them.

It's because of you that I gave them and myself a chance, why I have them back in my life now. You're the reason I *have* a life, not just a race for more achievements and ac-quisitions. You're the reason I want to live forever."

The tears that came so easily to her now flowed again, ones of bliss this time. "Maybe immortality should be my new research, then. I've been eyeing gene therapy for longevity for a while now."

"If anyone could find its secret, it's you." He gathered her tighter, his expression becoming adamant. "And it *is* you who's more qualified scientifically to run the research division, while I want to give back to the world now. And that's another reason I'm yours. Until I met you, I took what I thought life owed me, and I gave back only stra-tegically, to increase my profits. But now that I've found you, now that you love me, the world has given me far more than I can ever deserve. Now I have to create bal-ance, give back everything I can so that I can continue to deserve having the miracle of you and your love."

Drowning in his love, in relief and gratitude, she took hold of the hands that had given her her life back, took them to her lips as she gave him her own pledge.

"And I only want the privilege of sharing your excep-tional journey. You have all of me—the heart that grew to love you, the body you awakened and owned and saved, the soul that became whole only when you healed it, and everything else that I am. They're all yours, my love. Now and forever."

* * * * *

"Still can't resist the sports guys?"

"I'm a slow learner."

She'd been anything but a slow learner the one time they'd had sex. She'd been the sweetest thing he'd ever tasted.

He cursed silently. He had to stop thinking about her. Even though right now the sunlight from a nearby window caught in her hair, creating a halo effect, and illuminated the fascinating flecks in her eyes. But what really drew him was the bow of her mouth. Soft, pink and unadorned—just waiting to be kissed, even now, fifteen years later.

She frowned. "Are you okay?"

"Fine. I'm stalked by schoolteachers all the time." She flushed.

"If you came to get my attention, you've got it."

* * *

Second Chance with the CEO
is part of the The Serenghetti Brothers series—
In business and the bedroom, these
alpha brothers drive a hard bargain!

SECOND CHANCE
WITH THE CEO

BY
ANNA DEPALO

MILLS & BOON

First Published in Great Britain 2016
By Mills & Boon, an imprint of HarperCollins*Publishers*
1 London Bridge Street, London, SE1 9GF

© 2016 Anna DePalo

ISBN: 978-0-263-91877-9

51-0916

Our policy is to use papers that are natural, renewable and recyclable products and made from wood grown in sustainable forests. The logging and manufacturing processes conform to the legal environmental regulations of the country of origin.

Printed and bound in Spain
by CPI, Barcelona

USA TODAY bestselling author **Anna DePalo** is a Harvard graduate and former intellectual-property attorney who lives with her husband, son and daughter in her native New York. She writes sexy, humorous books that have been published in more than twenty countries and has won the RT Reviewers' Choice Award, the Golden Leaf and the Book Buyers Best Award. For the latest news, sign up for her newsletter at www.annadepalo.com.

For Colby, Nicholas & Olivia,
for understanding that I write.

One

"Cole Serenghetti," she muttered, "come out, come out, wherever you are."

She knew she sounded like a corny fairy-tale character, but she'd been short on happy endings lately, and the words couldn't hurt, could they?

Then again, there was always *be careful what you wish for*...

As if she'd conjured him, a tall man appeared under a crossbeam at the construction site.

A feeling of dread curled in her stomach. How many times had she started out thinking she could do this and then her courage had flagged? Three? Four?

Still, the students at Pershing School depended on her bringing Cole Serenghetti to heel—her job could hinge on it, as well.

Marisa lifted her hand from the steering wheel and squeezed it to stop a sudden tremor. Then she raised her field glasses.

Features obscured under his yellow hard hat, the man

strode down the dirt path leading to the opening in the chain-link fence surrounding the construction site, which would soon be a four-story medical office complex. Clad in jeans, a plaid shirt and vest and work boots, he could have been just any other construction worker. But he had an air of command...and his physique showed potential for inclusion in a beefcake calendar.

Marisa's heart pounded hard in her chest.

Cole Serenghetti. Former professional hockey player returned to the family fold as CEO of Serenghetti Construction, high school troublemaker and her disastrous teenage crush.

Could the package be worse?

Marisa slunk lower in the driver's seat, letting the binoculars dangle against her chest from their cord. The last thing she needed was for a police officer to come around and ask why she was stalking a rich bad-boy real estate developer.

Blackmail? Pregnant with his child? Planning to steal his Range Rover, parked oh-so-tantalizingly close and unguarded at the curb of the office building under construction?

Would anyone believe that the truth was much more mundane? Everyone knew her as Miss Danieli, sweet-natured teacher at the Pershing School. Ironic if her new secret life as a millionaire stalker came at the cost of her job and reputation when all she was trying to do was help the high school-aged students at her college-preparatory school.

Tossing aside her field glasses, she popped out of her Ford Focus and darted down the street, her open coat flapping around her, as her quarry reached the sidewalk. There were no pedestrians on this side street at four in the afternoon, though it was nearing evening rush in the city of Springfield. She'd seen construction workers earlier, but there were none on the street now.

As she approached, the dank smells of the construction site hit her. It was dirty, and the air was heavy with particles that she could almost feel, even in the damp cold that clung to western Massachusetts in March.

She heard her stomach grumble. She'd been too nervous about this meeting to eat lunch.

"Cole Serenghetti?"

He turned his head while taking off his hard hat.

Marisa slowed her steps as she was jerked back in time by the sight of the dark, ruffled hair, the hazel eyes and the chiseled lips. A scar now bisected his left cheek, joining the small one on his chin that had been there in high school.

Marisa felt her heart squeeze. His newest scar looked as if it had hurt—*bad*.

But he was still the sexiest man she'd ever crossed.

She tried hard to hold on to her scattered thoughts even as she drank in the changes in him.

He was bigger and broader than he'd been at eighteen, and his face had more hard planes. But the charisma of being a former National Hockey League star—and sex symbol—turned millionaire developer was the biggest change of all. And while he sported the new scar, he showed no signs of the injury that had been serious enough to end his hockey career. He moved fine.

Even though Pershing was located on the outskirts of Welsdale, Massachusetts, the town that the Serenghettis called home, she hadn't been anywhere near Cole since high school.

She didn't miss the once-over he gave her, and then a slow smile lit his face.

Relief swept through her. She'd been dreading this reunion ever since high school, but he seemed willing to put the past behind them.

"Sweetness, even if I wasn't Cole Serenghetti, I'd be saying yes to you." The lazy smile stayed on his face but his gaze traveled downward again, lingering on the cleavage revealed by her long-sleeved dress, and then on her legs, shown off by her favorite wedge-heeled espadrilles.

Oh...crap.

Cole looked up and smiled into her eyes. "You're a welcome ray of sunshine after a muddy construction site."

He didn't even recognize her. Crazy giddiness welled up inside. She'd never forgotten him in the past fifteen years, worrying over her betrayal—and his. And all that time, he'd been sleeping like a baby.

She knew she looked different. Her hair was loose for a change and highlighted, the ends shorter and curling around her shoulders. Her figure was fuller, and her face was no longer hidden behind owlish glasses. But still...she plummeted to Earth like a hang glider that had lost the wind.

She had to get this over with, much as she hated to end the party.

She took a steadying breath. "Marisa Danieli. How are you, Cole?"

The moment hung between them, stretching out.

Then Cole's face closed, his smile dimming.

She curved her lips tentatively. "I'm hoping to hold you to that *yes.*"

"Think again."

Ouch. Well, this was more like the script that had been playing in her head. She forced herself to keep up the polite professionalism without, she hoped, tipping into desperation. "It's been a long time."

"Not long enough." He assessed her. "And I'm guessing it's no accident you're here now—" he quirked a brow "—unless you've developed a weird compulsion to prowl construction sites?"

She'd always been bad at door-to-door solicitation jobs, and now, it seemed, was no exception. *Breathe. Breathe.* "The Pershing School needs your help. We're reaching out to our most important alumni."

"We?"

She nodded. "I teach tenth-grade English there."

Cole twisted his lips. "They're still putting their best foot forward."

"Their only foot. I'm the head of fund-raising."

He narrowed his eyes. "Congratulations and good luck." He stepped around her, and she turned with him.

"If you'll just listen—"

"To your pitch?" He shot her a sideways look. "I'm not as big a sucker for the doe-eyed look as I was fifteen years ago."

She filed away *doe-eyed* for later examination. "Pershing needs a new gym. I'm sure that as a professional hockey player, you can appreciate—"

"*Former* NHL player. Check the yearbook for athletics. You'll come up with other names."

"Yours was at the top of the list." She picked her way over broken sidewalk, trying to keep up with his stride. Her espadrilles had seemed like a good choice for a school day. Now she wished she'd worn something else.

Cole stopped and swung toward her, causing her to nearly run into him. "Still at the top of your list?" He lifted his mouth in a sardonic smile. "I should be flattered."

Marisa felt the heat sting her cheeks. He made it sound as if she was throwing herself at him all over again—and he was rejecting her.

She had an abysmal record with men—wasn't her recent broken engagement further proof?—and her streak had started with Cole in high school. Humiliation burned like fire.

A long time ago she and Cole would have had their heads bent together over a book. She could have shifted in her seat and brushed his leg. In fact, she had brushed his leg, more than once, and he'd touched his lips to hers...

She plunged ahead. "Pershing needs your help. We need a headliner for our fund-raiser in a couple of months to raise money for the new gym."

He looked implacable, except that twin flames danced in

his eyes. "You mean *you* need a headliner. Try your pitch on someone else."

"The fund-raiser would be good for Serenghetti Construction, too," she tried, having rehearsed her bullet points. "It's an excellent opportunity to further community relations."

He turned away again, and she placed a staying hand on his arm.

Immediately, she realized her mistake.

They both looked down at his biceps, and she yanked her hand back.

She'd felt him, strong and vital, his arm flexing. Once, fifteen years ago, she'd run her hands over his arms and moaned his name, and he'd taken her breast in his mouth. *Would she ever stop having a heated response to his every touch, every look and every word?*

She stared into his eyes, which were now hard and indecipherable—as tough as the rocks he blasted for a living.

"You need something from me," he stated flatly.

She nodded, her throat dry, feeling hot despite the weather.

"Too bad I don't forgive or forget a deliberate betrayal easily. Consider it a character flaw that I can't forget the facts."

She flushed. She'd always wondered whether he'd known for certain who'd ratted out his prank to the school administration, earning him a suspension and likely costing Pershing the hockey championship that year. Now it seemed she had her answer.

She'd had her reasons for doing what she'd done, but she doubted they'd have satisfied him—then or now.

"High school was a long time ago, Cole," she said, her voice thin.

"Right, and in the past is where the two of us are going to stay."

His words hurt even though it had been fifteen years. Her chest felt tight, and it was difficult to breathe.

He nodded at the curb. "Yours?"

She hadn't realized it, but they were near her car. "Yes."

He pulled open her door, and she stepped off the curb.

A swimming sensation came over her, and she swayed.

Still, she tried for a dignified exit. A few more steps and she'd put an end to this uncomfortable reunion…

As the edges of her vision faded to black, she had one last thought. *I should have eaten lunch.*

She heard Cole curse and his hard hat hit the ground. He caught her in his arms as she slumped against him.

When she floated to consciousness again, Cole was saying her name.

For a moment she thought she was fantasizing about their sexual encounter in high school…until the smells of the construction site penetrated her brain, and she realized what had happened.

She was cradled against a warm, solid body. Her trench coat was bunched around her like a cocoon.

She opened her eyes, and her gaze connected with Cole's. His golden-green eyes were intense.

She was also up close and personal with the new scar traversing his cheek. It looked painful but not jagged. *Had he taken a skate blade to the face?* She wanted to reach up and trace it.

He frowned. "Are you okay?"

Heat rushed to her cheeks. "Yes, let me down."

"May be a bad idea. Are you sure you can stand?"

Whatever the effects were of his career-ending injury, he seemed to have no problem holding a curvy woman of medium height in his arms. He was all hard muscle and restrained power.

"I'm fine! Really."

Looking as if he still had misgivings, Cole lowered his arm. When her feet hit the ground, he stepped back.

Her humiliation was complete. So total, she couldn't bear to face it right now.

"Just like old times," Cole remarked, his tone tinged with irony.

As if she needed the reminder. She'd fainted during one of their study sessions in high school. It was how she'd first wound up in his arms...

"How long was I out?" she asked, not meeting his eyes.

"Less than a minute." He shoved his hands in his pockets. "Are you all right?"

"Perfectly fine. I haven't been to an emergency room since I was a kid."

"You still have a tendency to faint."

She shook her head, looking anywhere but at him. *Talk about being overwhelmed by seeing him again.* Anticipating and yet dreading this meeting, she'd been too nervous to eat. "No, I haven't fainted in years. The medical term is vasovagal syncope, but my episodes are very infrequent."

Except she had a terrible habit of fainting around him. It was their first meeting in fifteen years, and she'd already managed a replay of high school. She didn't even want to consider what *he* was thinking right now. Probably that she was a consummate schemer with great acting skills.

He suddenly looked bland and aloof. "You couldn't have planned a better Hail Mary pass."

She cringed inwardly. He was suggesting that fainting had allowed her to buy time and get his sympathy. She was too embarrassed to get angry, however. "You play hockey, not football. Hail Mary is football. And why would I want to make a desperate last move with little chance of success?"

He shrugged his shoulders. "Confuse the other side."

"And did I?"

He looked as if he wished he were wearing all the protective gear of a hockey uniform. She was throwing *him* off balance. She was dizzy with momentary power, though her arms and legs still felt rubbery.

"I haven't changed my mind."

She lowered her shoulders and stepped toward her car.

"Are you okay to drive?" he asked, hands still shoved into his pockets.

"Yes. I feel fine now." *Tired, defeated and mortified, but fine.*

"Goodbye, Marisa."

He'd closed the door on her years ago, and now he was doing it again, with a note of finality in his voice.

She pushed aside the unexpectedly forceful emotional pain. As she stepped into her car, she was aware of Cole's brooding gaze on her. And when she pulled away, she glanced in her rearview mirror and saw that he was still watching her from the curb.

She should never have come. And yet, she had to get him to say yes. She hadn't come this far to accept defeat like this.

"You look like a man in need of a punching bag," Jordan Serenghetti remarked, hitting his boxing gloves together. "I'll spring for this round."

"Lucky bastard," Cole responded, moving his head from side to side, loosening up. "You get to work out the kinks by slamming someone on the ice rink."

Jordan still had a high-velocity NHL career with the New England Razors, whereas Cole's own had finished with a career-ending injury.

Still, whenever Jordan was in town, the two of them had a standing appointment in the boxing ring. For Cole, it beat the monotony of working out at the gym. Even as a construction executive, it paid to lead by example and stay in shape.

"Next hockey game isn't for another three days," Jordan responded, approaching with gloves raised. "That's a long time to be holding punches. Anyway, don't you have a babe to work out the kinks with?"

Marisa Danieli was a babe, all right, but Cole would be

damned if he worked out anything with her. Unfortunately, she'd intruded on his thoughts too often since she'd dropped back into his arms last Friday.

Jordan touched a glove to his boxing helmet and then grinned. "Oh yeah, I forgot. Vicki dumped you for the sports agent—what's his name, again?"

"Sal Piazza," Cole said and sidestepped Jordan's first jab.

"Right, Salami Pizza."

Cole grunted. "Vicki didn't dump me. She—"

"Got tired of your inability to commit."

Cole hit Jordan with his right. "She wasn't looking for commitment. It was the perfect fling that way."

"Only because she'd heard of your reputation, so she knew she had to move on."

"As I said, everyone was happy." They danced around the ring, oblivious to the gym noises around them.

Even on a Wednesday evening, Jimmy's Boxing Gym was humming with activity. The facility was kept cold but even the cool air couldn't diminish the smell of sweat and sounds of exertion under the fluorescent lights.

Jordan rolled his neck. "You know, Mom wants you to settle down."

Cole bared his teeth. "She'd also be happy if you quit risking thousands of dollars in orthodontia on the ice rink, but that's not going to happen, either."

"She can pin her hopes on Rick, then," Jordan said, referring to their middle brother, "if anyone knew where he was."

"On a movie set on the Italian Riviera, I've heard."

Their brother was a stuntman, the risk taker among them, which was saying a lot. Their long-suffering mother claimed she'd lived at the emergency room while raising three boys and a girl. It was true they'd all broken bones, at one time or another, but Camilla Serenghetti still wasn't aware of her sons' most hair-raising thrills.

"It figures he's on a paparazzi-riddled set," Jordan grum-

بترس از کسی که مظلومان که هنگام دعا کردن

یاجابت از درِ حق به سر استقبال می آنند

bled. "No doubt there's at least one hot actress in the picture."

"Mom has Mia to fall back on, even if she is in New York." Their youngest sibling was off pursuing a career as a fashion designer, which meant Cole was the only one based in Welsdale full-time.

"It sucks being the oldest, Cole," Jordan said, as if reading his thoughts, "but you've got to admit you're more suited to run Serenghetti Construction than any of the rest of us."

In the aftermath of Cole's career-ending hockey injury, their father, Serg, had suffered a debilitating stroke. Cole had grasped the reins of Serenghetti Construction eight months ago and never let go.

"It doesn't suck," Cole said. "It just needs to be done."

He took the opportunity to hit Jordan with a surprise right. Damn, it felt good to rid himself of some frustration in the ring. He loved his brother, so it stunk to be even a little envious of Jordan's life. It wasn't just that Jordan was still a star with the Razors, because Cole had had a good run with the team himself. His younger brother also enjoyed a freedom missing from Cole's own life these days.

Their father had always hoped one or more of his sons would carry on the family business. And in the casino of life, Cole had drawn the winning card.

Cole had been familiar with the construction business ever since he'd spent summers working on sites as a teenager. He just hadn't anticipated having his hockey dream cut short and needing to pull his family together at the same time. Business had been tight until recently, and with Serg nearly flat on his back, Cole had been doing some scrambling with the hand he'd been dealt.

With any luck, one way or another, Cole could get on with his life again soon. Even if his future wasn't on the ice, he had his own business and investment opportunities to pursue, particularly in the sports field. Coaching, for one thing, was beckoning...

"So why don't you tell me what's got you in a bad mood?" Jordan asked, as if they weren't in a ring trying to knock each other off their feet.

Cole's mind went to his more immediate problem—if she could even be called that instead of...oh yeah, a wrecking ball in heels. He built things, and she destroyed them—dreams being at the top of her list. *Best remember her evil powers.* "Marisa Danieli stopped by the construction site today."

Jordan looked puzzled.

"High school," Cole elaborated and then watched his brother's frown disappear.

He and his brothers had graduated from different high schools, but Jordan knew of Marisa. After her pivotal role in Cole's suspension during senior year, she had for a time become infamous among the Serenghetti brothers and their crowd.

"Luscious Lola Danieli?" Jordan asked, the side of his mouth turning up.

Cole had never liked the nickname—and that was even before he'd started thinking of Marisa Lola Danieli as the high school Lolita who had led him down the path to destruction. She'd earned the tongue-in-cheek nickname in high school because she'd dressed and acted the opposite of sexy.

He hadn't told anyone about his intimate past with Marisa. His brothers would have had a field day with the story of The Geek and The Jock. As far as anyone knew, she was just the girl who'd scored off him—ratting out his prank to the principal like a hockey player slapping the puck into the goal for the game-winning shot.

For years the moment the principal had let slip that Marisa was the person who'd blabbed about him had been seared into his memory. He'd never pulled another prank again.

Still, he wasn't merely dwelling on what had happened

when they'd been about to graduate. The fact that his hockey career had ended in the past year made it bad timing for Marisa to show up and remind him of how close she'd come to derailing it before it had begun. And as he'd told Jordan, he'd accepted his new role as CEO, but it wasn't without its frustrations. He was still on a big learning curve trying to drive Serenghetti Construction forward.

His brother's punch caught him full on the shoulder, sending him staggering. He brought his mind back to what was happening in the ring.

"Come on. Show me what you've got," Jordan jeered, warming up. "I haven't run into Marisa since you two graduated from Pershing."

"Until today, I could say the same thing," Cole replied.

"So, what? She's come back for round two now that you're on your feet again?"

"Hilarious."

"I was always the funny brother."

"Your sense of fraternal loyalty warms my heart," he mocked.

Jordan held up his hands in a gesture of surrender, nearly coming to a stop. "Hey, I'm not defending what she did. It sucked big-time for you to miss the final game and for Pershing to lose the hockey championship. Everyone avoided her wherever she went in town. But people can change."

Cole hit his brother with his left. "She wants me to headline a fund-raiser so Pershing can build a new gym."

Jordan grunted and then gave a low whistle. "Or maybe not. She's still got guts."

Marisa had changed, but Cole wasn't going to elaborate for his brother. These days there'd be nothing tongue-in-cheek about the nickname Luscious Lola, and that was the damn problem.

Before he'd recognized her, his senses had gone on high alert, and his libido had gleefully raced to catch up. The woman was sex in heels. It should be criminal for a school-teacher to look like her.

The eyeglasses that she used to wear in high school were gone, and her hair was longer and loose—the ends curling in fat, bouncy curls against her shoulders. She was no longer hiding her figure under shapeless sweatshirts, and she'd filled out in all the right places. Everything was fuller, curvier and more womanly. He should know—once he'd run his hands over those breasts and thighs.

Before she'd announced who she was, he'd been thinking the gods of TGIF were smiling down at him at the end of a long workweek. Then he'd gotten a reprieve until she'd literally fallen into his arms—a one-two punch.

In those seconds staring down into her face, he'd been swamped by conflicting emotions: surprise, anger, concern and yeah, lust. More or less par for the course for him where Marisa was concerned. He could still feel the imprint of her soft curves. She sent signals that bypassed the thinking part of his brain and went straight to the place that wanted to mate.

Jordan caught him square on the chest this time. "Come on, come on. You're dazed. Woman on your mind?"

Cole lifted his lips in a humorless smile. "She suggested that participating in the fund-raiser for Pershing might be good PR for Serenghetti Construction."

Jordan paused before dancing back a step. "Marisa is a smart cookie. Can't fault her there."

Cole grumbled. Marisa's suggestion made some sense though he'd rather have his front teeth knocked out than admit it. He'd never liked publicity and couldn't have cared less about his image during his professional hockey days, to the everlasting despair of his agent. And since taking over the reins at Serenghetti Construction, he'd been focused on mastering the ropes to keep the business operating smoothly. Community relations had taken a backseat.

Marisa had a brain, all right—in contrast to many of the

women who'd chased after him in his pro days. She'd literally been a book-hugger in high school. The jocks in the locker room hadn't even been able to rate her because it had been hard to do reconnaissance.

He'd eventually had the chance to discover the answer—she'd been a C-cup bra. But the knowledge had ultimately come at a steep price.

These days he'd bet the house that she had an A-plus body. She was primed to set men on their path to crashing and burning, just like old times.

Except this time, her next victim wouldn't be him.

Two

Squash racquet back of hall closet. I'll pick it up.

Marisa hit the button to turn off her cell phone. The message from Sal had come while she was out. She'd been so shaken by talking to Cole for the first time in fifteen years that she hadn't realized she had a text until after she'd gotten back to her apartment.

Annoyance rose up in her. As far as text messages went, it wasn't rude. But it hadn't come from just anybody. It had come from her former fiancé, who'd broken things off three months ago.

During their brief engagement, she'd been sliding into the role of the good little wife, picking up Sal's dry cleaning and making runs to the supermarket for him. From Sal's perspective, asking her to retrieve his squash racquet from her hall closet was unquestionably fair game. No doubt Sal had an appointment to meet a client at the gym, because even sports agents had to establish their athleticism—though

Sal played squash only once in a blue moon when an invitation was issued.

She contemplated heaving the racquet out the window and onto the lawn, and then asking Sal to come find it.

Before she could overrule her scruples, she heard someone turn the lock in the front door. She frowned, nonplussed. *Hadn't she asked Sal to return his key...?*

She yanked the door open, and her cousin Serafina stumbled inside.

Marisa relaxed. "Oh, it's you."

"Of course it's me," Serafina retorted, straightening. "You gave me a key to the apartment, remember?"

"Right." She'd been so lost in thought, she'd momentarily assumed Sal had come back to retrieve the racquet, letting himself in with an extra copy of the key. *And he was uptight enough to do it. The rat.*

She was glad now she'd kept her condo even when her relationship with Sal had started getting serious enough that they'd contemplated moving in together. She'd bought the small two-bedroom five years ago, and at the time, it had been a major step toward independence and security.

She wondered where Cole called home these days. In all likelihood, a sprawling penthouse loft. She wouldn't be surprised if he lived in one of his own constructions.

One thing was for sure. He was still one of Welsdale's hottest tickets while she... Well, shapely was the most forgiving adjective for her curves. She was still a nobody, even if she had a name at the Pershing School these days.

"What's with you?" Serafina asked, taking off her cross-body handbag and letting it slide to the floor.

"I was thinking of a place to bury Sal's squash racquet," she responded and then waved a hand at the back of the apartment. "It's in the hall closet."

"Nice." Serafina smiled. "But with all the dogs in this complex, someone's bound to sniff out the cadaver real quick."

"He needs it back." She'd been hurt when she'd been dumped. But notwithstanding her irritation at Sal at the moment, these days she simply wanted to move on.

Serafina's lips twitched. "The racquet is an innocent by-stander. It's not like you to misdirect anger, especially the vindictive kind."

After a moment Marisa sighed and lowered her shoulders. "You're right. I'll tell him that I'm leaving it on the table in the building foyer downstairs."

Ever since her debacle with Cole in high school, she'd been worried about being thought of as a bitch. She didn't need Cole Serenghetti; she needed a therapist.

"But tell the jerk what he can go do with it!" Serafina added.

She gave her cousin a halfhearted smile. Serafina was a little taller than she was, and her hair was a wavy dirty blond. She'd been spared the curly dark brown locks that were the bane of Marisa's existence. But they both had the amber eyes that were a family trait on their mothers' side, and their facial features bore a resemblance. Anyone looking at them might guess they were related, though they had different last names: Danieli and Perini.

While they were growing up, Marisa had treated Sera as a younger sister. She'd passed along books and toys, and shared advice and clothes. More recently, having had her cousin as a roommate for a few months, until Serafina found a job in her field and an apartment, had been a real lifesaver. Marisa appreciated the company. And with respect to men, her cousin took no prisoners. Marisa figured she could learn a lot there.

"Now for some good news," Serafina announced. "I'm moving out."

"That's great!" Marisa forced herself to sound perky.

"Well, not now, but after my trip to Seattle next week to visit Aunt Filo and Co."

"I didn't mean I'm glad you're leaving, I meant I'm happy

for you." Three weeks ago her cousin had received the news that she'd landed a permanent position. Serafina had also gotten plane tickets to see Aunt Filomena and her cousins before starting her new job.

Serafina laughed. "Oh, Marisa, you're adorable! I know you're happy for me."

"Adorable ceases to exist after age thirty." She was thirty-three, single and holding on to sexy by a fraying thread. *And* she'd recently been dumped by her fiancé.

Of course, Cole had been all sunshine and come-here-honey...until he'd recognized who she was. Then he'd turned dark and stormy.

Serafina searched her face. "What?"

Marisa turned, heading down the hall toward the kitchen. "I asked Cole Serenghetti to do the Pershing Shines Bright fund-raiser for the school."

She hadn't died of mortification when she approached him for a favor after all these years, but she'd come close. She'd fainted in his arms. A hot wave of embarrassment washed over her, stinging her face. *When would the humiliation end?*

Some decadent chocolate cake was in order right now. There should be some left in the fridge. A pity party was always better with dessert.

"And?" Serafina followed behind.

Marisa waved her hand. "It was like I always dreamt it would be. He jumped right on my proposal. Chills and thrills all around."

"Great...?"

"Lovely." She spied the cake container on her old scarred moveable island. "And yummy."

Cole Serenghetti qualified as yummy, too. There were probably women lined up to treat him as dessert. A decade and a half later he was looking better than ever. She'd seen the occasional picture of him in the press during his hockey days, but nothing was like experiencing the man in person.

And tangling with him was just as much a turn-yourself-inside-out experience as it had always been.

"Um, Marisa?"

Marisa set the cake container on the table. "Time for dessert, I think."

The kind in front of her, not the Cole Serenghetti variety, even though he probably thought of her as a man-eater.

Marisa uncovered the chocolate seven-layer cake. She'd been so insecure about her body around Sal—she had too many rounded curves to ever be considered svelte. But now that he was in the past, she felt free to indulge again. Of course, Sal had a new and skinny girlfriend. He'd found the person he was looking for, and she was the size of a runway model.

"So Cole was thrilled to see you?" Serafina probed.

"Ecstatic."

"Now I know you're being sarcastic."

Long after high school Marisa had told Sera about her past with Cole, and how things had heated up between her and the oldest Serenghetti brother during senior year—before they'd gone into a deep freeze. Her cousin knew Marisa had confessed that Cole was responsible for the ultimate school prank, that Cole had been suspended as a result and that Pershing had lost the Independent School League hockey championship soon after.

Getting out two plates and cutlery, Marisa said, "It's not a party unless you join me."

Serafina sat down in one of the kitchen chairs. "I hope this guy is worth five hundred calories. Let me guess, he still blames you for what you did in high school?"

"Bingo."

Marisa relayed snatches of her encounter with Cole, the way she'd been doing in her mind since leaving the construction site earlier. All the while, Cole's words reverberated in her head. *I'm not as big a sucker for the doe-eyed look as I was fifteen years ago.* Oh yes, he still held a grudge. He'd been impossible to sway about the fund-raiser. And yet, damningly, she felt a little frisson of excitement that he had fallen under the spell of her big, brown eyes long ago...

Serafina shook her head. "Men never grow up."

Marisa slid a piece of cake in front of her cousin. "It's complicated."

"Isn't it always? Cut yourself a bigger piece."

"All the cake in the world might not be enough."

"That bad, huh?"

Marisa met her cousin's gaze and nodded. Then she took a bite of cake and got up again. "We need milk and coffee."

A little caffeine would help. She felt so tired in the aftermath of a faint.

She loaded water and coffee grinds into the pot and then plugged the thing into the outlet. She wished she could afford one of those fancy coffeemakers that were popular now, but they weren't in her budget.

Why had she ever agreed to approach Cole Serenghetti? She knew why. She was ambitious enough to want to be assistant principal. It was part of her long climb out of poverty. She credited her academic scholarship to Pershing with helping to turn her life around. And now that she was single and unattached again, she needed something to focus on. Pershing and her teaching job were the thing. *And* she owed it to the kids.

Marisa shook her head. She'd volunteered to be head of fund-raising at Pershing, but she hadn't anticipated that the current principal would be so set on getting Cole Serenghetti for their big event. She should have tried harder to talk Mr. Dobson out of it. But he'd discovered from the school yearbook that Cole and Marisa had been in the same graduating class, so he'd assumed Marisa could make a personal appeal to the hockey star, one former classmate to another. There was no way Marisa was going to explain how her high school romance with Cole had ended disastrously.

"So what are you going to do now?" Serafina asked as Marisa set two coffee mugs on the table.

"I don't know."

"It's not like you to give up so easily."

"You know me well."

"I've known you forever!"

Marisa summoned the determination that had helped her when she'd been the child of a single mother who worked two jobs. "I'll have to give it another try. I can't go back to the board admitting defeat this fast. But I can't lie in wait for Cole again at a construction site, like some crazed stalker."

Serafina wiped her mouth with a napkin. "You may want to give Jimmy's Boxing Gym a go."

"What?"

Serafina gave her an arch look. "It's beefcake central. Also, Cole Serenghetti is known to be a regular."

Marisa's brow puckered. "And you know this, how?"

"The guys down at the Puck & Shoot. The hockey players are regulars." Sera paused and pulled a face. "Jordan Serenghetti stops in from time to time."

Judging from Sera's expression, Marisa concluded her cousin didn't much care for the youngest Serenghetti brother.

"Are you doing more than moonlighting as a waitress there?" Marisa asked with mock severity.

Serafina shrugged. "If you hung out in bars, you wouldn't need the tip." Then she flashed a mischievous grin. "Use it in good health."

Of course Cole Serenghetti would go to a boxing gym. The place was most likely the diametric opposite of the fancy fitness center where Sal played squash. She'd given up her own membership—with guilty relief—when Sal had unsubscribed from their relationship.

She rolled her eyes heavenward. "What do I wear to a boxing gym…?"

"My guess is, the less, the better." Serafina curved her lips. "Everyone will be sweaty and hot, hot, hot…"

One week later…

Cole saw his chance in Jordan's sudden loss of focus and hit him hard, following up with a one-two punch that sent his brother staggering.

Then he paused and wiped his brow while he let Jordan regain his balance, because their purpose was to get some exercise and not to go for a knockout. "I don't want to ruin your pretty face. I'll save that thrill for the guys on the ice."

Jordan grimaced. "Thanks. One of us hasn't had his nose broken yet, and—" he focused over Cole's shoulder "—I need to talk pretty right now."

"What the hell?"

Jordan indicated the doorway with his chin.

When Cole turned around, he cursed.

Marisa was here, and from all the signs, she didn't have any more sense about a boxing gym than she did about showing up at a construction site in heels. She was drawing plenty of attention from the male clientele—and some were going back for a second look. But her gaze settled nowhere as she made her way toward the ring that he and Jordan were using. She looked pure and unaware of her sexuality in a floaty polka-dot dress that skimmed her curves. The heels and bouncy hair were back, too.

She was the perfect picture of an innocent little schoolteacher—except Cole knew better. Still, for all outward appearances, the tableau was Bambi surrounded by wolves.

"Now that," Jordan said from behind him, "is a welcome Wednesday night surprise."

Cole scowled. *Not for him, it wasn't.* He moved toward the ropes, pulling at the lacing of one glove with the other. A staff member for the gym came up to the side of the ring to help him.

"Where are you going?" Jordan called.

"Take a breather!"

"I saw her first," his brother joked, coming up along-side him.

From when they'd hit puberty, the Serenghetti brothers had one rule: whoever saw a woman first got to make a move.

Cole leveled his brother with a withering look as the gym assistant pulled off his gloves. "That is Marisa Danieli."

Jordan's eyes widened, and then a slow grin spread across his face. "Wow, she's changed."

"Not as much as you think. Hands off."

"Hey, I'm not the one who needs a warning. Who yanked off his gloves?" Jordan looked over Cole's shoulder and then raised his eyebrows.

Cole turned. Marisa had pulled the ropes apart and was stepping into the ring, one shapely leg after the other.

"This should be good," Jordan murmured.

"Shut up."

Cole pulled off his padded helmet. The front of his sleeveless shirt was damp with perspiration, and his sweatpants hung low on his hips. It was a far cry from the way he looked in meetings these days—where he often wore a jacket and tie.

He handed off his helmet before turning toward the woman who'd crept into his thoughts too often during the past week. Sweeping aside any need for pleasantries, he demanded, "How did you find me?"

Marisa hesitated, looking as if her bravado was leaving her now that she was facing her opponent in the ring. "A tip at the Puck & Shoot."

Cole figured he shouldn't be surprised she was a patron of the New England Razors' hangout. She could scout for her next victim at a sports bar, and it would be easy pickings.

Marisa took a deep breath, and Cole watched her chest rise and fall.

She smiled, but it didn't reach her eyes. "Let's start again. And how are you, too, Cole?"

"Is that how you start the day in school? Correcting your students' manners?"

"Sometimes," she admitted.

Jordan stepped forward. "Don't mind Cole. Mom sent us to Miss Daisy's School for Manners, but only one of us graduated." Jordan flashed the mega-kilowatt grin that had earned him an underwear advertising campaign. "I'm Jordan Serenghetti, Cole's brother. I'd shake your hand but as you can see—" he held up his gloves, his smile turning rueful "—I've been pounding Cole to a pulp."

Marisa blinked, her gaze moving from Jordan to Cole. "He doesn't look the worse for wear."

Cole's muscles tightened and bunched, and then he frowned. He should be used to compliments… Besides, he knew she had an ulterior motive—she still needed him for her fund-raiser.

"We stay away from faces," Jordan added, "but his nose has been broken and mine hasn't."

"Yes," she said, "I see…"

Cole knew what he looked like. Not bad, but not model-handsome like Jordan. He and his brother shared the same dark hair and tall build, but Jordan's eyes were green while his were hazel. And he'd always been more rough-hewn—not that it mattered at the moment.

Jordan flashed another smile at Marisa. "You may remember me from Cole's high school days."

Cole forced himself to remember the expensive orthodontia as the urge hit to rearrange his brother's teeth. He noticed how Jordan didn't reference the high school fiasco in which Marisa had had a starring role.

"Jordan Serenghetti…I know you from the sports news," Marisa said, sidestepping the whole sticky issue of high school.

Cole had had enough.

"You don't take no for an answer," Cole interrupted, and had the pleasure of seeing Marisa flush.

She turned her big doe eyes on him. "I'm hoping you'll reconsider, if you'll just listen to what I have to say."

"If he won't listen, I will," Jordan joked. "In fact, why don't we make an evening of it? Everything goes down better with a little champagne—unless you prefer wine?"

Cole gave his brother a hard stare, but Jordan kept his gaze on Marisa.

"The Pershing School needs a headliner for its Pershing Shines Bright benefit," Marisa said to Jordan.

"I'll do it," Jordan said.

"You didn't graduate from the Pershing School."

"A minor detail. I was a student for a while."

Marisa took a step and swayed, her heels failing to find firm ground in the ring. Cole reached out to steady her, but she grasped one of the ropes for support, and he let his arm fall back to his side.

Careful. Touching Marisa was a bad idea, as he'd been reminded only last week.

"Cole's the better choice because he graduated from Pershing," Marisa said, looking into his eyes. "I know you have some loyalty to your school. You had a few good hockey seasons there."

"And thanks to you, no championship."

She looked abashed and then recovered. "That has to do with me, not Pershing, and anyway, there's a new school principal."

"But you're the messenger."

"A very pretty one," Jordan volunteered.

Cole froze his brother with a look. He and Marisa had known each other in a carnal sense, which should make her off-limits to Jordan. But he wasn't about to let his brother in on those intimate details—which meant he was in a bind about issuing a warning. Jordan was a player who liked women, making Marisa a perfect target for the charm that he never seemed to turn off.

Jordan shrugged his shoulders. "Maybe it wasn't Marisa's fault."

None of them needed him to elaborate.

"It was me at the principal's office," she admitted.

"But you're sorry…?" Jordan prompted, throwing her a lifeline.

"I regret my role, yes," she said, looking pained.

Cole lowered his shoulders. He'd gotten the closest thing to an apology.

Still, Marisa had another motive for showing up today. And while he may have gotten over high school and his suspension a long time ago, forgiving and forgetting *her* treachery was still a long time coming…

Jordan shot him a speaking glance. "And Cole apologizes for being Cole."

Cole scowled. "Like hell."

They hadn't even touched on intimate levels of betrayal that Jordan knew nothing about.

Jordan gestured with his glove. "Okay, I typically leave the mediation talks to the NHL honchos, but let's give this one more try. Cole regrets messing up with his last prank."

"Right," Cole said tightly but then couldn't resist taking a shot at his brother to dislodge the satisfied look on his face. "Jordan, talk show host is not in your future."

His brother produced a wounded look. "Not even sportscaster?"

"Since we're all coming clean," Cole continued pleasantly, looking at Marisa, "why don't you tell me what's in this for you?"

She blinked. "I told you. I want to help the Pershing School get a new gym."

"No, how does this all help you personally?"

Marisa bit her lip. "Well… I hope I'll be considered for assistant principal someday."

"Now we're getting warmer," he said with satisfaction, cocking his head because this was the Marisa he expected— full of guile and hidden motives. "Funny, I had you pegged for the type who'd be walking up the aisle in a white dress by now and then juggling babies and teaching."

Marisa paled, and Cole's hand curled. She looked as if he'd scored a dead hit.

"I was engaged until a few months ago," she said in a low voice.

"Oh yeah? Anyone I know?" Had Marisa entrapped someone else from high school? Unlikely.

"Maybe. He's a sports agent named Sal Piazza."

Beside them, his brother whistled before Cole could react.

"You might know him," Marisa continued, "because he's now dating your last girlfriend. Or at least you were photographed in the stands at a hockey game with her. Vicki Salazar."

Damn.

"Hey, can this be called *entangled by proxy*?" Jordan interjected, his brow furrowing. "Or how about *engaged by one degree of separation*? Is that an oxymoron?"

Cole felt a muscle in his face working. His brother didn't know the half of it. "Put a lid on it, Jordan."

Cole looked around. They were attracting an audience. The speculative ones were wondering whether this was a lovers' spat and Marisa was his girlfriend—and whether they could intercept her as she made her way out of the gym. "This is ridiculous. The ring isn't the place for this conversation. We're a damn spectacle."

Marisa looked startled.

He fastened his hand on her arm against his better judgment. "Come on." He lifted the rope. "After you."

Marisa cast a glance at Jordan.

"He isn't coming," Cole said shortly.

Marisa stepped between the ropes and Cole followed, taking the wooden steps down to the gym floor.

Ignoring curious looks, he steered Marisa toward the back entrance—the one leading to the parking lot. When they reached the rear door, he turned to face her and said, "So you're engaged to Sal Piazza."

"I was." She lifted her chin. "Not anymore."

"Still can't resist the sports guys?"

"I'm a slow learner."

She'd been anything but a slow learner the one time they'd had sex. She'd been the sweetest thing he'd ever tasted.

He cursed silently. He had to stop thinking about her. Even though right now, the sunlight from a nearby window caught in her hair, creating a halo effect, and illuminated the fascinating flecks in her eyes. But what really drew him was the bow of her mouth. Soft, pink and unadorned—just waiting to be kissed, even now, fifteen years later.

She frowned. "Are you okay?"

"Fine. I'm stalked by schoolteachers all the time."

She flushed.

"If you came to get my attention, you've got it." He jerked his head toward the way they had come. "Along with that of most of the guys in there."

"It's not my problem if they have a fetish for overworked and underpaid educators."

He almost burst out laughing. "Your job of recruiting me makes you overworked and underpaid?"

She pursed her lips.

"Your sports agent fiancé didn't give you any pointers about recruiting athletes?" The dig rolled off his tongue, and then he cocked his head. "Funny, you don't strike me as Sal Piazza's type."

"I'm not." She smiled tightly, looking as if she'd be dangerous with a hockey stick right now. "He left me for Vicki."

"He cheated on you?"

"He denied it had gone as far as…sex. But he said he'd met someone else…and he was attracted to her." Marisa looked as if she couldn't believe what she was telling him.

"So Sal Piazza broke up with you to get Vicki in bed." Cole smiled humorlessly. "I should warn the guy that Vicki prefers anything to a bed."

"Don't be crude."

Hell if he could puzzle out Sal. Vicki and Marisa couldn't even be compared. One was a zero-calorie diet cola—you could guzzle twenty and they wouldn't fill you up—and the other a decadent dessert that could kill you.

He was also still wrapping his head around the fact that Sal and Marisa had been engaged. Sal was a sports nut, center-court wannabe. And in high school at least, Marisa couldn't have cared less about sports—her hookup with the captain of the hockey team aside.

On the other hand, from the few times Cole had run into Sal at some sports-related event or another, he'd struck Cole as an affable, conventional kind of guy. Medium build, average looks—bland and colorless. No surprise if Marisa had thought of him as safe and reliable. Not that the relationship with Sal had worked out the way she'd expected.

"When did the breakup happen?" he asked.

"In January."

Cole and Vicki had last seen each other in November.

"Worried that Vicki might have cheated on you with a mere sports agent?" Marisa asked archly.

"No." His involvement with Vicki had been so casual it had barely qualified as a relationship. Still, he couldn't resist getting another reaction out of Marisa. "Even ex-hockey players rank above sports agents in the pecking order."

She got a spark in her eyes. "So, according to you, I've been on a downward trajectory since high school?"

"Only you can speak to that, sweet pea."

He felt some satisfaction at provoking her. She'd been

working hard to maintain a crumbling wall of polite and professional civility between them.

"Your hubris leaves me breathless."

He smiled mirthlessly. "That's the effect that I often have on women, but it's because of my huge—"

"Stop!"

"—reputation. What did you think I was going to say?"

"You're impossible."

"So you give up?" He glanced around them. "Good match. We both got in some nice jabs. I accept your concession."

"The way you accepted my apology?"

He jerked his head toward the interior of the gym. "Is that what it was?"

She nodded. "Take it or leave it."

"And if I leave it?"

She twitched her lips, her eyes flashing. "Time to go for Plan B. Fortunately, Jordan's already given me one. Now all I need to do is convince the school that he'd be a good substitute."

She started to turn away, and Cole reached out and caught hold of her upper arm.

"Stay away from Jordan," he said. "You've already messed up one Serenghetti. Don't go for another."

He'd gotten first dibs on Marisa more than a decade ago. And given their history, first dibs held even now, whether Jordan knew the details or not.

"I'm flattered you think so highly of my evil powers, but Jordan is a big boy who can take care of himself."

"I'm not kidding."

"Neither am I. I'm running out of time to find a headliner for the Pershing fund-raiser."

"Not Jordan."

She pulled out of his grasp. "We'll see. Goodbye, Cole."

Broodingly, Cole watched her exit the gym.

Their meeting hadn't ended the way she'd wanted, but it wasn't the way he'd envisioned it, either.

Damn it.

He had to keep her away from Jordan, and his script didn't include admitting, *I slept with her.*

Three

Cole had to wait a week to corner his brother because Jordan had three away games. But he figured their parents' house was as good a location as any for a showdown. As he exited his Range Rover, he looked up at the storm clouds. *Yup.* The weather fit his mood.

When he didn't spot Jordan's car on his parents' circular drive, he quelled his impatience. His brother would be here soon enough. Jordan had replied to his text and agreed they would both stop by the house this evening to check on how their parents were doing. So Cole would soon have blessed relief from the irritation that had been dogging him for the past week. Marisa and his brother—*over his cold dead body.*

Cole made his way to the front doors. The Serenghetti house was a Mediterranean villa with a red-tile roof and white walls. In warmer months, a lush garden was his mother's pride and joy, keeping both her and a landscaper busy. As Serg's construction business had grown, Cole's parents had traded up to bigger homes. The move to the Mediterranean villa had been completed when Cole was in middle

school. Serg had built a house big enough to accommodate the Serenghetti brood as well as the occasional visiting relatives.

Cole's jaw tightened. If Jordan had been contacted by
Marisa, then his brother needed to be warned off. His
brother had to understand that Marisa couldn't be trusted.
She may have changed since high school, but Cole wasn't
taking any chances. On the other hand, if Marisa had been
bluffing about asking Jordan to be her second choice, so
much the better. Either way, Cole was going to make damn
sure there wasn't anything going on.

Memories had snuck up on him ever since Marisa had
traipsed back into his life. Yeah, he'd taken a lot for granted
when he'd been at Pershing—his status as top jock, his pop-
ularity with girls and the financial security that allowed
him a ride at a private school. Still, there'd been pressure.
Pressure to perform. Pressure to *outperform himself*—on
and off the ice. He'd set himself up for a fall by trying to
outdo his biggest game, his latest prank, his most recent
sexual experience...

Back in high school, Marisa had been outside his inner
circle but had seemingly been able to look in without judging. At least that was what he'd thought. And then she'd
betrayed him.

Sure, he hadn't liked it one bit when Jordan had turned
his charm on Marisa at the boxing gym. But it was because
he hated to see his brother make the same mistake he'd
made. It had nothing to do with being territorial about a
teenage fling. He didn't do jealousy. Marisa was an attractive woman, but he was old enough to know the pitfalls of
acting on pure lust.

As a professional hockey player, he'd always had easy
access to women. But after a while it had started to lose
meaning. When Jordan had joined the NHL, he'd given his
younger brother *the talk* about the temptations facing professional athletes from money and fame. Of course, Jor-

dan was a seasoned pro these days—but Marisa presented a brand of secret and stealthy allure.

He should know.

Cole tensed as he recalled how ready Jordan had been to succumb to temptation last week. Because his brother had been on the road for away games since then, with any luck he'd been too busy for Marisa to reach him.

Cole opened the unlocked front door and let himself in. The sounds of "We Open in Venice" hit him, and he wondered if his mother was again playing all the songs from Cole Porter's *Kiss Me, Kate*. She loved the musical so much, she had named her firstborn after its legendary composer.

Cole thought his life didn't need a soundtrack—least of all, that of the musical based on Shakespeare's *Taming of the Shrew*. Still, was it a coincidence—or the universe sending him a message? He had about as much chance of taming Marisa as of returning to his professional hockey career right now. Not that he was going to try. He was only going to make sure that he and any other Serenghetti were outside Marisa's ambit.

He made his way to the back of the house, where he found his mother in the oversize kitchen. As usual, the house smelled of flowers, mouthwatering food aromas…and familial obligation.

"Cole," Camilla said, pronouncing the *e* at the end of his name like a short vowel. "A lovely surprise, *caro*."

Although his mother had learned English at a young age, she still had an accent and sprinkled her English with Italian. She'd met and married Serg when he'd been vacationing in Tuscany, and she'd been a twenty-one-year-old hotel front-desk employee. Before Serg had checked out in order to visit extended family in the hockey-mad region north of Venice, the two had struck up a romance.

"Hi, Mom." Cole snagged a fried zucchini from a bowl on the marble-topped kitchen island. "Where's Dad?"

"Resting." She waved a hand. "You know all these visitors make him tired. Today the home-care worker, the nurse and the physical therapy came."

"You mean the physical therapist?"

"I say that, no?"

Cole let it slide. His mother had a late-blossoming career as the host of a local cooking show. Viewers who wrote in liked her accent, and television executives believed it added the spice of authenticity to her show. For Cole, it was just another colorful aspect of his lovable but quirky family.

"You beat me to the food. Did you taste the gnocchi yet?"

Cole turned to see Jordan saunter into the kitchen. Cole figured his brother must have driven up as soon as he'd entered the house. "How do you know she prepared gnocchi?"

Jordan shrugged. "I texted Mom earlier. She's perfecting a recipe for next week's show, and we're the guinea pigs. Gnocchi with prosciutto, escarole and tomato."

Camilla brightened. "I tell you? The name of the show is goin' to change to *Flavors of Italy with Camilla Serenghetti.*"

"That's great!" Jordan leaned in to give his mother a quick peck on the cheek.

Cole nodded. "Congratulations, Mom. You'll be challenging Lidia Bastianich in no time."

Camilla beamed. "My name in the *titolo.* Good, no?"

"Excellent," Cole said.

Camilla frowned. "But I need to schedule more guests."

"Isn't that the job of the program booker at the station?"

"It's my show."

Jordan made a warding-off gesture with his hands. "Remember when you had me on last year, Mom? I made you burn the onions that you were sautéing. And Cole here wasn't much better when he was a guest."

From Cole's perspective, he and Jordan had been worth something in the sex appeal department, but his mother's show would never have mass crossover appeal to the beer-and-chips sports crowd.

Before he could offer to sacrifice himself again on the altar of his mother's show-business career, Camilla started toward the fridge and said, "I need somebody new."

"I'll put in a word with the Razors," Jordan offered. "Marc Bellitti likes to cook. And maybe a member of the team can suggest someone with better skills in the kitchen than on the ice."

Cole turned to his brother. "Speaking of ice, great game for you last night. You would have scored another goal if Peltier hadn't body-checked you at the last second."

Jordan grumbled. "He's been a pain in the rear all season." Then keeping an eye on their mother, as if to make sure he wouldn't be overheard, he added, "Guy needs to get laid."

At the mention of sex, Cole locked his jaw. "Has Marisa Danieli contacted you?"

Jordan cast him an assessing look. "Why do you ask?"

"She still needs a guinea pig for her fund-raiser. As I understand it, you're eager guinea pig material."

Jordan's lips quirked. "Being the test subject isn't half bad sometimes. Anyway, she wanted you."

"I told her no."

"Admirable fortitude. The guys in the locker room would be impressed."

"I'm asking you to tell her no."

"It hasn't come up."

Cole relaxed his shoulders. "She hasn't tried to reach you?"

"Nope. And quit focusing on the decoy. I'm a bad one. There's something else you'll find a lot more interesting."

Camilla set a big bowl of gnocchi on the counter and announced, "I'm goin' to check on your father and be right back."

"Take your time, Mom." Cole knew his mother was worried about his father's rough road to recovery. It had been several months since the stroke, and Serg still had not made a complete recovery—if he ever would.

When their mother left, Cole turned to Jordan and wasted no time in getting to the point. "What is it?"

"Word is that the job for the new gym at the Pershing School is going to JM Construction."

Cole's lips thinned. *She'd done worse than get Jordan on board for her fund-raiser.*

As far as jobs went for a midsize construction company like Serenghetti or JM, the new gym at the Pershing School was small-fry. However, JM would get the attendant publicity and goodwill.

Damn it. They'd been outbid twice in the past few months by JM Construction. Like Serenghetti, JM operated in the New England region, though both sometimes took jobs farther afield. Serenghetti's main offices were in Welsdale—at Serg's insistence—but they kept a business suite in Boston for convenience, as well as a small satellite staff in Portland, Maine.

"You know this how?" Cole demanded of his brother.

"Guys talking down at the Puck & Shoot. If you hung out there, you'd know, too. You should try it."

"A lot happens at the Puck & Shoot." Cole recalled that Marisa had found out how to run him to ground from a tip at the bar.

"The drinks aren't bad, and the female clientele is even better."

"I'm surprised you haven't spotted Marisa there."

Jordan snagged a cold gnocchi from the bowl and popped it into his mouth. "She doesn't look like the type to be a sports bar regular."

"A lot about her may surprise you."

His brother swallowed and grinned. "I'm sure."

"Jordan."

"Anyway, I was killing time. Someone brought up my recent ad campaign, so I mentioned an opportunity to do a little local promo for the Pershing School. I asked if anyone was interested."

"Putting in a good word for Marisa?" Cole asked sardonically.

There was laughter in Jordan's eyes. "Well, I knew you didn't want to volunteer. And you'd have my head on a platter if I did the fund-raiser."

"Good call."

"But I felt bad for her, to be honest. She was even willing to tangle with you in order to find a celebrity."

"She knows what she's doing."

"She seems like a good sort these days. Or at least her cause is a good one."

"Right." *Whose side was his brother on?*

"Anyway, you remember Jenkins? He graduated a couple of years after you did and played in the minors for a while?"

"Yeah?"

"He said the rumor was that JM Construction had the inside track on building the gym. So he thought it was curious I was mentioning the school fund-raiser to the Razors. He indicated it was mighty magnanimous of me to try to find a recruit for JM's cause."

"Oh yeah, it was." Cole resisted a snort. "Still feeling sorry for Marisa?"

The woman had more up her sleeve than a cardsharp.

Jordan shrugged. "She may know nothing about who's getting the construction contract."

"We'll see. Either way, I'm about to find out."

Life was full of firsts—some of them more welcome than others. Cole had been her earliest lover, and now he was giving her another first. Marisa stepped inside Serenghetti Construction's offices, which she'd never done before.

The company occupied the uppermost floors of a red-brick building that had once been a factory, square in the middle of Welsdale's downtown. The website stated that

Serg Serenghetti had renovated the building twenty years ago and turned it into a modern office complex. For years she'd felt as if she would never be welcome inside, but now she'd gotten a personal invite from Cole Serenghetti himself. It showed how life could turn on a dime.

Of course the actual call had come from Cole's assistant. But Marisa had taken it as a sign that Cole might be softening his stance. She was willing to hold on to any thread of hope, no matter how thin. Because as much as she'd bluffed, she had no Plan B. She hadn't tried to contact Jordan Serenghetti because it would be preferable for Pershing to have someone who'd graduated from the school as a headliner. Besides, she was sure Cole would block any attempt to recruit his brother.

In the lobby, Marisa tried not to be intimidated by the sleek glass-and-chrome design—a testament to money and power. And when she reached the top floor, she took a deep breath as she entered Serenghetti's spacious and airy offices. The decor was muted beiges and grays—cool and professional. The receptionist announced her, took her coat and then directed her down the hall to a corner office.

Her heart beat in a staccato rhythm as she reached an open doorway. And then her gaze connected with Cole's. He was standing beside an imposing L-shaped desk.

The air hummed between them, and Marisa steadied herself as she walked forward into his office. She'd dressed professionally in a beige pantsuit, but she was suddenly very aware of her femininity. That was because Cole exuded power in a navy suit and patterned tie. This was a different incarnation than his hockey uniform, or his hardhat and jeans, but no less potent.

"You look wary," Cole said. "Afraid you're in for a third strike?"

"You don't play baseball."

"Lucky you."

"You wouldn't have summoned me if you'd meant to turn me down again."

"Or maybe I'm a sadistic bastard who enjoys making you pay for past transgressions again and again."

Marisa compressed her lips to keep from giving her opinion. His office was devoid of personal items like family photos and as inscrutable as the man himself. She wondered if this room had been Serg's office until recently, or whether Cole had just avoided settling in by bringing mementos.

Cole smiled but it didn't reach his eyes. "So here's the deal, sweet pea. Serenghetti Construction builds the new gym at Pershing, no questions asked. I don't want to hear any garbage about handing off the job to a friend of a board member."

"What?"

"Yeah, surprised?" he asked as he prowled toward her. "So am I. I've been almost dancing with shock ever since I discovered you wanted me to be a poster boy for someone else's construction job. And not just anyone else, but our main competitor. They've underbid us on the last two jobs. But that's quality for you."

"I'm sure the construction would be up to code. We'd have an inspection," she said crossly.

"Being up to code is the least of your worries."

Marisa felt as if she'd shown up in the middle of the second act of a play. There was a context that she was missing here. "I have no idea what you're talking about. What friend of a board member?"

Cole scanned her face for a moment, then two. "It would figure they didn't let the teacher in on the discussion. Have you ever sat on a board of directors?"

She shook her head.

"The meetings might be public, but there's plenty of wheeling and dealing behind the scenes. It's you scratch my back, I'll scratch yours. We'll go with the headliner you want for the fund-raiser, but you'll back my guy for the construction job."

Marisa felt the heat of embarrassment flood her face. She'd thought she'd been so clever in her approach for Pershing Shines Bright. She hadn't even let Mr. Dobson know she'd talked to Cole because she'd thought her chances of success were uncertain at best. She'd wanted the option of persuading Mr. Dobson to go with someone else without the appearance that she'd failed.

Now she felt like a nitwit—one who didn't know what the other hand was doing. Or at least, didn't know what the school board was up to. She wanted to slump into a chair, but it would give Cole an even bigger advantage than he had.

"That kind of horse-trading is corrupt," she managed.

"That's life."

"I didn't have any idea."

"Right."

"You believe me?"

He made an impatient sound. "You're a walking, breathing cliché. In this case, for one, you're a naive and idealistic schoolteacher who's been kept out of the loop."

"Well, at least I've improved in your estimation in the last fifteen years." She dropped her handbag onto a chair. If she couldn't sit, at least she could get rid of some dead weight while she faced Cole. "That's more than you would have said about me in high school."

"At this point I have a good sense of when you're to blame," he shot back, not answering directly.

"Meaning you have plenty of experience?"

Cole gave her a penetrating look and then said, "Here's what you're going to do. You're going to tell the principal—"

"Mr. Dobson."

"—that you've got me on board for the fund-raiser, but there's one condition attached."

"Serenghetti Construction gets the job."

Marisa had been on a roller coaster of emotions since

walking into Cole's office. And right now elation that Cole was agreeing to be her headliner threatened to overwhelm everything else. She tried to appear calm but a part of her wanted to jump up and down with relief.

Cole nodded, seemingly oblivious to her emotional state. "Let Dobson deal with the board of directors. My guess is that the member with ties to JM Construction will have to back down. If Dobson plays his cards right, he'll marshal support even before the next board meeting."

"And if he doesn't?"

"He will, especially if I say Jordan will show up, too, even though he's not a graduate of the school. Pershing isn't a public school that's legally bound to accept the lowest bid on a contract. And giving the contract to Serenghetti Construction makes sense. The money that the school would save not having to pay a big name to appear at their fundraiser tips the balance on the bottom line."

She sighed. "You've thought of everything."

"Not everything. I still have to deal with you, sweet pea."

His words hurt, but she managed to keep her expression even. "Bad luck."

"Bad luck comes in threes. Getting injured, needing to take over a construction firm, you showing up…"

"We're even," she parried. "I've been cheated on, gotten dumped by my fiancé and had to recruit you for the fund-raiser."

He smiled, and she thought she detected a spark of admiration for her willingness to meet him head-on. "Not so diplomatic now that you know you have me hooked."

"Only because you're willing to be ruthless with your competitors."

"Just like your douche bag fiancé?" he asked. "How did you wind up engaged to Sal? Are you hanging out in sports bars these days?"

"You know from personal experience that I visit boxing gyms." She shrugged. "Why not a sports bar?"

His eyes crinkled. "You showed up at Jimmy's only because you were tracking me. You'd probably claim your appearance was under duress."

"I'm not going to argue."

"You're not?" he quipped. "What a change."

"You're welcome."

His expression sobered. "For the record, you don't know what to wear to a gym."

"I came from school dressed like a teacher," she protested.

His eyes swept over her. "Exactly. As I said, you're a walking cliché."

"And you are frustrating and irritating." She spoke lightly, but she sort of meant it, too.

"Talk to my opponents on the ice. They'll tell you all about it."

"I'm sure they would."

"It's nice to know I bother you, sweet pea."

Their gazes caught and held, and awareness coiled through her, threatening to break free. She wet her lips, and Cole's eyes moved to her mouth.

"Are you still pining and crying your eyes out for him?" he asked abruptly.

She blinked, caught off guard. She wasn't going to admit as much to Cole of all people, but she'd done enough pining and crying in high school to last a lifetime. Still, it would be pathetic if she'd met and lost the love of her life at eighteen. Her life couldn't have ended that early.

"For whom?" she asked carefully.

"Piazza."

"Not really."

She'd dated since graduating from Pershing, but nothing had panned out past a few dates until Sal. It was as if she'd needed to lick her wounds for a long time after high school—after Cole.

There'd been initial shock over Sal's betrayal, of course.

But then she'd gotten on with her life. She had a low opinion of Sal, and she was still angry about being cheated on. But she wasn't lying in bed wondering how she was going to go on—or wishing Sal would see the light and come back to her.

She'd been prepared to be hit by the despair that had assailed her after her teenage fling with Cole. So either she'd matured, or her relationship with Sal hadn't been as significant as she'd told herself. She refused to analyze which was the case.

Cole shrugged. "Piazza isn't worth it. He's a cheating a—"

"You've never cheated on a woman?" They were getting into personal territory, but she couldn't stop herself from asking the question.

Cole assumed a set expression. "I've dated plenty, but it's always been serial. And you never answered my question about how you met Piazza."

"Why are you interested?" she shot back before sighing in resignation. "We did meet in a bar, actually. Some teachers met for Friday night drinks, and I was persuaded to go along. He was an acquaintance of an acquaintance…"

Cole arched an eyebrow, as if prompting her for more.

"He was steady, reliable…"

"A bedrock to build a marriage on. But he turned out to be so reliable, he cheated on you."

"What do you suggest constructing a lasting relationship on?" she lobbed back. "A hormone-fueled hookup with a woman as deep as a puddle after a light rain?"

She didn't pose the question as if it was about him in particular, but he could read between the lines.

"I haven't even tried for more. That's the difference."

"As I said, Sal appeared steady and reliable…" And she'd been desperate for the respectably ordinary. All she'd wanted as an adult was to be middle class, with a Cape Cod or a split level in the suburbs and a couple of kids…and *no money worries.*

Sal had grown up in Welsdale, too, but unlike her, he'd attended Welsdale High School, so they hadn't known each other as teenagers. When they'd met, he'd been working for a Springfield-based sports management company, but was often back in his hometown, which was where they had gotten acquainted one night at The Obelisk Lounge. Sal traveled to Boston regularly for business, but he and his firm mainly focused on trolling the waters of professional hockey at the Springfield arena where the New England Razors played.

Cole looked irritated. "Sal is the sports version of a used car salesman—always preparing to pitch you the next deal as if it's the best thing since sliced bread."

"As far as I can tell, a lot of you sports pros believe you are the best thing since sliced bread."

They were skimming the surface of the deep lake of emotion and past history between them. Every encounter with Cole was an emotional wringer. You'd think she'd be used to it by now or at least expecting it.

Cole shrugged. "Hockey is a job."

"So is teaching."

"It's the reason you made your way back to Pershing."

"The school was good to me." She shifted and then picked up her handbag.

Cole didn't move. "I'll bet. How long have you been teaching there?"

"I started right after college, so not quite ten years." She took a step toward the door and then paused. "It took me more than five years and several part-time jobs to get my degree and provisional teaching certificate at U. Mass. Amherst."

She could see she'd surprised him. She'd gone to a state school, where the tuition had been lower and she'd quali- fied for a scholarship. Even then, though, because she'd been more or less self-supporting, it had taken a while to get her degree. She'd worked an odd and endless assortment of jobs: telemarketer, door-to-door sales rep, supermarket checkout clerk and receptionist.

She knew Cole had gone on to Boston College, which was a powerhouse in college hockey. She was sure he hadn't had to hold down two part-time jobs in order to graduate, but she gave him credit if he continued to work in the family construction business, as he'd done at Pershing.

"I remember you didn't have much money in high school," he said.

"I was a scholarship student. I worked summers and sometimes weekends scooping ice cream at the Ben & Jerry's on Sycamore St."

"Yeah, I remember."

She remembered, too. *Oh, did she remember.* Cole and the rest of his jock posse had hardly ever set foot in the store, but it had been a favorite of teenage girls. She'd waited on her classmates, and usually it had worked out okay, but a few stuck-up types had enjoyed queening it over her. Cole had stopped in during the brief time they'd been study buddies...

"And you worked summers at Serenghetti Construction," she said unnecessarily, suddenly nervous because they weren't squabbling anymore.

"All the way through college."

"But you didn't have to do it for the money."

"No, not for the money," he responded, "but there are different shades of *have to*. There's the *have to* that comes with family obligation."

"Is that why you're back and running Serenghetti Construction?"

He nodded curtly. "At least temporarily. I've got other opportunities on the back burner."

She tried to hide her surprise. "You're planning to play hockey again?"

"No, but there are other options. Coaching, for instance."

Her heart fell, but Marisa told herself not to be ridiculous even as she fidgeted with her handbag strap. She didn't care what Cole Serenghetti's plans were, and she shouldn't be surprised they didn't involve staying in Welsdale and heading Serenghetti Construction.

"How is your father doing?" she asked, trying to bring the conversation back to safer ground. News of Serg's stroke was public knowledge around Welsdale.

"He's doing therapy to regain some motor function."

Marisa didn't say anything, sensing that Cole might continue if she remained silent.

"It's doubtful he'll be able to run Serenghetti Construction again."

"That must be tough." If Serg didn't recover more, and Cole had no plans to head the family business on a permanent basis, Marisa wondered what would happen. Would one of Cole's brothers step in to head the company? But Jordan was having an impressive run with the Razors... She contained her curiosity, because Cole had been a closed door to her for fifteen years—and she liked it that way, she told herself.

"Dad's a fighter. We'll see what happens," Cole said, seeming like a man who rarely, if ever, invited sympathy. "He's joked about the lengths he'll go to retire and hand over the reins to one of his kids."

She smiled, and Cole's expression relaxed.

"How's your mother?" he asked, appearing okay with chitchat about their families.

"She recently married a carpenter." Ted Millepied was a good man who adored her mother.

Cole quirked his lips. "Where's he based? I may be able to use him."

"You don't believe in guilt by association?" The words left her mouth before she could stop them, but she was surprised that Cole would even consider hiring someone related to her by marriage.

Cole sobered. "No, despite what my cockamamie brother may have led you to believe about the Serenghettis and the labeling of relationships to the nth degree of separation."

Jordan's words came back to her. *Entangled by proxy? Engaged by one degree of separation?* In fact, there was no connection between her and Cole. She refused to believe in any. There'd only been dead air since high school.

"My mother is still in Welsdale," she elaborated. "She's worked her way up to management at Stanhope Department Store. In fact, she recently got named buyer for housewares."

She was proud of her mother. After many years in retail, earning college credit at night and on weekends, Donna Casale had been rewarded with management-track promotions at Stanhope, which anchored the biggest shopping center in the Welsdale area. The store was where Marisa's wealthier classmates at Pershing had bought many of their clothes—and where Marisa had gotten by with her mother's employee discounts.

Cole was looking at her closely, and she gave herself a mental shake. They had drifted deep into personal stuff. *Stop, stop, stop.* She should get going. "Okay," she said briskly, "if Pershing meets your terms about the construction job, will you do the fund-raiser?"

Cole looked alert. "Yes."

"Wonderful." She stepped forward and held out her hand. "It's a deal."

Cole enveloped Marisa's hand, and sensation swamped her. Their eyes met, and the moment dragged out between them… He was so close, she could see the sprinkling of gold in his irises. She'd also forgotten how tall Cole was, because she'd limited herself to the occasional glimpse of him on television or in print for the past fifteen years.

She swallowed, her lips parting.

Cole dropped his gaze to her mouth. "Did you mean what you said to Jordan?"

"Wh-what?" She cleared her throat and tried again. "What in particular?"

"Was he your Plan B?"

"I don't have a Plan B."

"What about regretting telling on me to Mr. Hayes in high school?"

The world shrank to include only the two of them. "Every day. I wished circumstances had been different."

"Ever wish things had turned out differently between us?"

"Yes."

"Yeah, me too."

A cell phone buzzed, breaking the moment.

Marisa stepped back, and Cole reached into his pocket. "Mr. Serenghetti?"

Marisa glanced toward the door and saw the receptionist.

"I've got it," Cole said. "He phoned my cell."

The receptionist nodded as she retreated. "Your four o'clock is here, too."

Cole held Marisa's gaze as he addressed whoever was on the other end of the line. From what Marisa could tell, the call was about a materials delivery for one of Serenghetti's construction sites.

But it was the message that she read in Cole's expression that captured her attention. *Later. We're not done yet.*

Marisa gave a quick nod before turning and heading for the door.

As she made her way past reception, down in the elevator and out the building, she pondered Cole's words about wishing things had worked out differently between them. What had he meant? And did it matter?

But there was more to puzzle over in his expression. *We're not done.*

It was more than had existed between them in fifteen years—or maybe they were just going to write a different ending.

Four

Marisa gazed up at him with big, wide eyes. "Please, Cole. I want you."

"Yes," he heard himself answer, his voice thick.

They were made to fit together. He'd waited fifteen years to show her how good it could be between them. He wanted to tell her that he would please her. This would be no crazy fumble on a sofa. When it came to sex, their communication had the potential to be flawless and explosive.

He claimed her lips and traced the seam of her mouth. She opened for him, tasting sweet as a ripe berry, and then met his tongue. The kiss deepened and gained urgency. They pressed together, and she moaned.

He felt the pressing need of his arousal as her breasts pushed against his chest. She was sexy and hot, and she wanted him. He'd never felt this deep need for anyone else. It was primitive and basic and...right.

"Oh, Cole." She looked at him, her eyes wide amber pools. "Please. Now."

"Yes," he said hoarsely. "It's going to be so good be-tween us, sweet pea. I promise."

He positioned himself, and then held her gaze as he pushed inside her. She was warm and slick and tight. And he was sliding toward mindless rapture...

Cole awoke with a start.

Glancing around, half-dazed, he realized he was rest-less, aroused—and alone.

He sprawled across his king-size bed, where damp sheets had ridden down his bare chest and tangled around his legs. Most of all, there was the feeling of being irritated and un-fulfilled.

Damn it.

He'd been fantasizing about Marisa Danieli. He'd itched to ride her curves and have her come apart in his arms. He worked hard to slow his pounding pulse and then threw off the sheets. A glance at the bedside clock told him he needed to be at the office in an hour. He hit the alarm before it could go off and then rose and headed to the shower.

The master suite in his Welsdale condo included a large marble bath and a walk-in closet. He'd bought the place—on the top floor of a prewar building in the center of down-town—in order to have a home base during his hockey career. Not to mention that like the rest of the Serenghettis, he was a keen real estate investor.

The condo had been a place where he could retreat dur-ing the off-season without becoming an extended houseg-uest of his parents. His brothers kept places nearby, while his sister preferred to stay at Casa Serenghetti—as the sib-lings sometimes jokingly referred to the family manse—when she was in town.

He opened the glass door to the shower stall and then stood under the lukewarm spray, waiting for it to cool him down before he grabbed a bar of soap and lathered up.

He told himself he'd been dreaming about Marisa only because he wanted to win. Sex was just a metaphor for crashing through her defenses. Then he'd have some relief from this frustrating dance that they were engaged in.

Certainly he didn't want a round two with her. He wasn't even sure he trusted her...

After dressing, he made the quick drive to his office at Serenghetti Construction. He'd just reached his desk when the receptionist announced that she had Mr. Dobson from the Pershing School on the phone.

Interesting. It appeared Marisa had spoken with Pershing's principal, and Mr. Dobson was wasting no time getting the wheels turning on his end.

Through careful questioning of his contacts, Cole had learned that a Pershing board member was golf buddies with the CEO of JM Construction. He didn't have solid evidence that JM Construction had been a shoo-in for building the gym, but it was enough. In the end, proof didn't matter anyway. He needed that job to go to Serenghetti Construction and not JM.

"Mr. Dobson, Cole Serenghetti here. What can I do for you?" Cole made his voice sound detached, even a bit bored.

Dobson engaged in pleasantries for a few minutes, as if he and Cole already knew each other and the call was an ordinary occurrence. Then without missing a beat, the principal thanked him for agreeing to headline Pershing Shines Bright, and invited Serenghetti Construction to submit a proposal for building the gym.

Cole leaned back in his chair. Since coming to his office last week, Marisa must have delivered the message at Pershing that the fund-raiser and the construction job were a package deal. Still, he needed to make sure there was no doubt about this understanding. He expected at least a handshake deal, if not a signed contract, before the school benefit took place.

Drawing on the business savvy that he'd gotten at an early age by observing Serg, Cole said, "I have an architectural partnership that I work with. I suggest setting up a meeting for next week where we can discuss the vision for the new gym as well as talk about costs and the timeline. Afterward, I'll submit contracts for your review."

Dobson paused a beat and then heartily agreed with Cole's suggestion.

"Feel free to invite any of the directors on your board to the meeting next week," Cole continued. "I want each and every one of them to be comfortable with the Serenghetti team."

There was another beat before the principal responded. "I can assure you that the board couldn't have been more pleased to hear the Serenghetti name mentioned in connection with both the fund-raiser and the construction of the gym. They need no reassurance."

Cole smiled, glad that he and Dobson understood each other. Clearly, the principal was savvy himself. He appeared to have done the math and realized that a *free* appearance by a hockey star or two was worth plenty to the school's bottom line. Cole made a mental note to call Jordan and tell him that *both* of them would be showing up for Pershing Shines Bright.

Thinking he needed to do Marisa a favor for keeping her word, Cole went on, "Invite Ms. Danieli to the meeting, too. If she's in charge of the fund-raiser, she'll need to be able to speak knowledgeably to potential donors about the building project."

"Excellent idea," Dobson concurred. "I will let her know."

As soon as his conversation with the principal had ended, Cole called his youngest brother and put him on speakerphone.

"Put the Pershing School benefit on your calendar," he told Jordan without prelude. "I'll email you the date and time when I get them from Marisa. You and I will be making an appearance in our best penguin suits or closest equivalent."

As he spoke, he opened a blank email and began drafting a message to Marisa. Did she have a black-tie event in mind? He hadn't concerned himself with the details up to now. He also needed to tell her that Jordan would be participating, too. He didn't pause now to analyze why he was relishing communicating with her, even if just by email, after the dead air between them since she'd shown up at his office.

Jordan's unmistakable chuckle sounded over the phone line. "First, you told me to stay away from Marisa, now you want me to attend her fund-raiser with you. Which is it? And more important, will you be a good date?"

Cole figured he should have expected Jordan's needling. "You wouldn't be my date for the fund-raiser, numbskull."

"Why, Cole," his brother cooed, "you do know how to break someone's heart. Did I lose out to Marisa, or is there another teacher who's gotten you hot under the collar lately?"

"Later, Jordan." Cole punched the button to end the call.

He finished his email, and then, after finding an address for Marisa on Pershing's website, fired it off.

Leaning back in his chair again, he allowed himself momentary satisfaction at cutting off JM Construction. Now all he needed to do was wait for Marisa to come calling with the details...

The second time wasn't as intimidating, Marisa thought, as she walked through Serenghetti Construction's offices on a Thursday afternoon.

Last week she'd sat in on a meeting between Mr. Dobson and Cole and his architectural firm to discuss the contract to build Pershing's gym. The talk had been about use requirements, building permits and environmental impact. Then there'd been a discussion of hardwood, maple grades, subflooring, HVAC systems and disability access. Marisa had jotted notes to keep up with the onslaught of details. She'd been aware of Cole's gaze on her from time to time as he'd talked, but she'd kept her head down and stayed in the background, asking only a couple of questions.

She was a teacher, not a builder, but she'd known as soon as the meeting was over that she would have to do some serious studying if she hoped one day to be an assistant principal. School administrators like Mr. Dobson had more on their plate than the curriculum. They were also responsible for the physical condition of the school buildings that they oversaw.

In fact, she had done a little online research this past weekend because today she had to deal with Cole all by herself. She was supposed to look at architectural plans and give her input to Mr. Dobson. The principal had asked her to look at the plans for other athletic facilities built by Serenghetti Construction.

She should be happy about her expanded responsibilities because maybe it was a sign that Mr. Dobson would consider her for a promotion. But instead, her thoughts were on Cole. Since their meeting last week, her communication with him had been limited. They'd exchanged brief emails about the time and place of the fund-raiser, and he'd signed off on the use of his bio and photo.

But her active imagination had filled in what had been left unsaid. She'd gone over every look and word that Cole had given her during their meeting with Mr. Dobson and the architect. She'd also replayed their last conversation at his office—especially the part about wishing their relationship had turned out differently.

She was grateful to him for agreeing to do the fundraiser. And *vulnerable* and *attracted*…

Danger, danger, danger… She could never become involved with Cole. *Not with her family history.* She'd lived with the consequences of the past her whole life, even if she hadn't known the details until her twenties.

Bringing herself back to the present, she gave her name

to the receptionist, who directed her toward Cole's office with little fanfare.

When she reached Cole's door, he looked up, as if sensing her there.

"Marisa." He stood and came around his desk.

Her pulse picked up, and she stepped into the room, resisting the urge to hug her light blazer to her instead of leaving it draped over one arm. As usual, she was hit with an overwhelming awareness of him as a man. Today he was dressed in a suit but he had shed his jacket and tie. Still, even though he wasn't in full corporate uniform, he appeared every inch the successful and wealthy business executive.

Marisa shifted. She'd dressed in a striped shirt and navy pants—an appropriate and understated outfit in her opinion. She dared him to take note of her clothing one more time and call her a cliché.

Cole's eyes surveyed her as he approached, but he said nothing.

Did she imagine that he lingered at the V created by her shirt, his gaze flickering with heat for a moment? It was like being touched by a feather—light, and yet packed with sensation.

When he stopped in front of her, he asked without preamble, "What did you think of our meeting with Dobson last week?"

She resisted saying she thought of it as her and Mr. Dobson's meeting with *him*. "It went well."

Cole nodded. "Dobson wants you to see some older plans today. Every job is unique, but I'm guessing he wants to cover his bases and have you do some due diligence."

"In case he needs to account for the way the construction contract with Serenghetti came about?"

Cole gave her a dry look and inclined his head. "You'll be the one doing the explaining since you're here today. You're going to get a sense of what past clients have gone with."

"Okay." She really was in the hot seat. "Do you have plans for other gyms that Serenghetti has built?"

"One or two." Cole arched a brow. "You might as well get acquainted with the nitty-gritty of construction. Nobody plays around here. Least of all me." He pulled his office door open wider and indicated she should precede him out of the room. "You can leave your stuff here. We'll be back in a few minutes."

Marisa dropped her handbag and blazer on a chair and then walked beside Cole down the corridor and around the corner.

Stopping in front of an older-looking door, Cole retrieved keys from his pocket and opened two different dead bolts.

"I guess not everything at Serenghetti Construction is state-of-the-art," she remarked lightly.

Cole quirked his lips. "The new Pershing gym will be, don't worry. This building dates back to the 1930s, and we kept the old-fashioned storage room with concrete walls and dead bolts. It's where we keep confidential files and old documents."

He opened the door and flipped the light switch.

Marisa saw a small room lined with metal cabinets. A walkable strip down the middle extended about seven or eight feet into the room.

Cole moved inside, and Marisa watched as he scanned the cabinets.

"There must be a few decades' worth of files in there."

"Building rehabilitation is a substantial share of our business," Cole answered, glancing back at her. "We refer to these plans when we do renovations or additions to existing structures, either for returning clients or new owners."

"I see."

He looked amused. "Come on in."

Reluctantly, she let go of the door and stepped inside. She let her gaze travel over the cabinets because the alternative was allowing it to settle on Cole. The labels on the metal drawers were a mystery to her. "How do you know where to look?"

Then, hearing a click behind her, she turned to see that the door had creaked shut. Pushing aside a prick of panic, she said, "I'll, uh, step back out to give you more room to search for what you're looking for."

She grasped the door handle and tried to turn it. The door, however, didn't budge. She jiggled the handle again and pushed.

"Now you've done it."

She swung around, her eyes widening. "What do you mean?"

"You've locked us in."

She gave him an accusatory look. "You told me to step inside!"

"But not to let the door close behind you. There's a door-stop outside. Didn't you see it?"

"No!"

"Are you afraid of small spaces?" he asked sardonically.

"Don't be ridiculous." She had a fear of *Cole and small spaces*.

"Breathe."

"I don't want to suck all of the air out of the room."

He looked as if he was stifling a laugh. "You won't. Does this happen often?"

"It comes and goes," she admitted. "I'm not claustropho-bic, but I'm not a big fan of tiny areas, either."

"Relax."

She sent up a prayer because she was in sensory over-load right now, and his nearness in the closet-like space threatened to short-circuit her. "You're finding this amus-ing, aren't you?"

"Vasovagal syncope, claustrophobia… It keeps getting better and better with you."

"Very funny." She'd never put her best foot forward with him. She felt exposed, her vulnerabilities on display.

"You could scream for help," he suggested. "It might suck all the air out of the room, so think about whether you're willing to go for broke..."

"The only reason to scream is because you're making me crazy."

He stepped toward her, bringing them within brushing distance. "There's always your cell phone."

"I left it in your office along with my handbag." She perked up. "What about your phone?"

"Ditto except for the part about the handbag."

She lowered her shoulders. "How could you let this happen?"

"I didn't," he said with exaggerated patience.

She grasped at any topic she could in order to take her mind off her panic. "Did you ever think that Serenghetti Construction might be your second career after hockey someday?"

"No, but I have a construction background, thanks to working summers at Serenghetti Construction to earn money. I majored in management at Boston College, but I also took community college classes in bid estimating, drafting and blueprint reading that helped at the summer jobs."

"Because your father always wanted you to succeed him at Serenghetti Construction."

"Someone had to, but I never committed."

"And then your hockey dreams were cut short."

He gave her a droll look. "For a woman who doesn't like to confront uncomfortable topics, you sure don't mince words."

She frowned. "What topics don't I like to talk about? I'm just wondering whether it may have been hard to come to terms with your new situation."

He folded his arms. "Like you haven't come to grips with the past?"

"What do you mean?" *He was way too close.*

"Us."

"Some of us weren't lucky enough to have a Plan B that involved a job in the family business."

His gaze sharpened. "Oh no, you don't. I'm not letting you avoid the topic. Why did you go to Mr. Hayes with the story that I pulled the prank? Because I came from money and had a Plan B?"

"Please," she scoffed.

He was too close, too much, too everything.

The school assembly during their senior year had been named Pershing Does Good. It was supposed to have been video highlights of the Pershing community doing volunteer work. Instead, it had turned into a joke because Cole had inserted images of Mr. Hayes's head superimposed on a champion wrestler's body, and one of the principal seemingly dressed only in boxers and socks and posing next to a convertible.

It had been a brilliant piece of hacking, but Mr. Hayes had been in no mood to laugh.

Cole moved closer. "Or was it a way to get back at me after we'd had sex and I didn't shower you with pretty phrases?"

She made a sound of disbelief. "You didn't talk to me, either."

He paused, his eyes gleaming. "Ah, now we're getting somewhere."

"Where?" she demanded. "You've written a script about a jilted lover seeking revenge."

"Weren't you one?"

"I was a virgin."

"Okay, so I was the evil seducer who stole your virginity, and hell hath no fury like a woman scorned? That's a good story, too, except my recollection is that you were a willing participant."

She shook her head vehemently. "It had nothing to do

with sex. At least my confession to Mr. Hayes didn't. You were closer when you thought it had to do with money."

Cole's face hardened.

"Mr. Hayes called me into his office. He guessed there were seniors who knew more about the prank than he did." She fought to keep her voice even. "So he pulled in the person he thought he had something to hold over. Namely, me."

Cole scowled.

"You humiliated and embarrassed him in front of the whole student body. He was going to get to the bottom of it, come hell or high water. So he threatened to take away my recommendation for a college scholarship unless I confessed who did it." She swallowed. "I'd overheard you telling one of your teammates near the lockers that you'd managed to sneak into the school offices."

Marisa had known back then in the principal's office that Mr. Hayes's job was at stake. While working her after-school job sweeping hallways, she'd overheard conversations among the staff about the principal's contract maybe not being renewed by Pershing's board because there was debate about Mr. Hayes's performance. Cole's prank would further make it seem as if Mr. Hayes wasn't a good leader who commanded the respect of the school community.

Marisa had looked at Mr. Hayes, and in that instant, she'd read his thoughts. He was worried because his career might be on the line, and he had three kids to support at home. She had been able to relate because her mother had stressed about her job, too, and she'd had only one kid to worry about.

Cole's frown faded, and then his eyes narrowed.

"I was backed into a corner. I had no Plan B. I needed that scholarship money, or there would be no happy ending for me. At least not one involving college in the fall."

Cole's lips thinned. "It's unconscionable that the bastard would have twisted the arm of an eighteen-year-old student."

"I was on scholarship at Pershing. I was there on condition of good grades and better behavior. Unlike some people, I didn't have the luxury of being a prankster."

Cole swore.

"So you were right all along. I did sell you out, and I'm sorry." She felt the wind leave her, her words slowing after spilling in a mad rush. "If it helps, I was ostracized. People saw me go in and out of Mr. Hayes's office, so they guessed who ratted you out. After all, you got confronted by Mr. Hayes right after I was interrogated, so the rumors started immediately. My only defense was that if I hadn't kept my scholarship, I'd probably have struggled to make ends meet like my mother. I knew college was my ticket out."

She ought to stop talking but she couldn't help herself. The words had come out in a torrent and were now down to a trickle, but she couldn't seem to turn off the flow completely.

"Why didn't you tell me back then about Hayes blackmailing you into a confession?" Cole demanded. "He let slip your name when he confronted me, but he never got into details."

"Would you have been ready to listen?" she replied. "All you cared about was the Independent School League championship. My reasons didn't make a difference. You still wouldn't have been able to play the end of the season."

The old hurts from high school came back vividly, and she felt a throbbing pain in the region of her heart. She'd stayed home on the night of the prom. She and Serafina had watched Molly Ringwald flicks from the '80s. The high school angst on the television screen had fit Marisa's mood—because she'd been into self-flagellation. She'd discovered that Cole—his suspension ended—was going to the prom with Kendra Vance, a cheerleader. She'd cried herself to sleep long after Sera's head had hit the pillow, hiding her grief because she didn't want to invite questions from her cousin.

Marisa sucked in a trembling breath while Cole stared at her, his expression inscrutable. She realized she'd hurt him, and now he was still wary. But there was no way to change the past.

"How are we getting out of here?" she asked, reverting to her earlier panic—because, strangely, it seemed safer territory than the one she'd ventured into with Cole.

Flustered, she gestured randomly until Cole captured her hands. He gave her a look of such intensity, it stole her breath.

"Now would be the time to scream, I think," he said.

"Because we're out of options?"

"No. Because if I haven't made you crazy already, this will."

Then he bent his head and captured her mouth, swallowing her gasp.

Cole folded her into his arms. He kissed her with a self-assurance that sent chills of awareness chasing through her. She felt his hard muscles pressed against her soft curves. Her breasts tingled. *Everything* tingled.

He savored her mouth, stroking her lips until they were wet and plump and prickling with need. His tongue darted to the seam of her lips, and she opened for him. He moved his hands up to cup her head and thread his fingers in her hair. Then he stroked inside her mouth, deepening the kiss, and she met him instinctively. She sighed, and he made a sound of satisfaction.

She wanted him. She'd developed a crush on him in high school, and she still felt an attraction for him that would not be denied. Longing, nervousness and defenselessness mixed in a heady concoction.

Slowly, Cole eased back and then broke off the kiss.

Marisa opened her eyes and met Cole's glittering look.

"That did it."

"Wh-what?" she responded, her voice husky.

"You forgot about being panicked."

He was only partly right. She'd forgotten about the small space they were stuck in, all right. But she'd replaced that anxiety with a sexual awareness of him.

She took a small step back and felt the cabinets press up against her. Frowning, and seeking composure, she asked, "How can you kiss a woman you don't even like?"

"You needed a kiss right then."

She flushed. "What I need is to get out of here."

He moved past her and she tensed. One little push and she'd be back in his arms.

She turned and watched him grasp the door handle and turn it hard. At the same time, he shoved his shoulder against the door—once, twice... The door swung open.

Turning back, he smiled faintly. "After you."

She stepped into the hallway with no small relief. Still, she found herself tossing him an accusatory look. "You knew all along that it would open, didn't you?"

"I knew there was nothing stopping it, except maybe a little stickiness from age. Simple deductive logic. It would have occurred to you, too, if you hadn't been panicked and babbling."

"When I think I'm about to suffocate to death, the words flow." Now the only threat to her life was death by embarrassment. What had she confessed? And she'd melted into his arms... "I've got to go. I—I'm sorry. We'll need to reschedule."

"Marisa..."

She backed up a few steps and then turned and walked rapidly down the hall, not waiting for him to lock the storage room. She stopped only to grab her jacket and handbag from Cole's office as she made her way out the building and to her car.

She'd already consoled herself with chocolate cake—what was left?

Five

Cole perused the job site from where he was standing on a muddy rise. His mind was only half on the discussion that he needed to have with his foreman. The other half was on what he had to do about Marisa.

Unlike the construction project in Springfield where Marisa had waylaid him, this one was already at the stage where drywall and electrical had gone in. But he needed to get updates from his crew and hammer out remaining issues so they could come in under budget and on time. The five-story office complex outside Northampton was another one of their big projects.

"Sam is coming down now!" one of his construction crew called.

Cole gave him a brief nod before his thoughts were set adrift again.

He'd put in a call to Pershing's principal soon after Marisa had fled his offices several days ago. He'd covered for her by taking the heat for their meeting falling through. Hell, it was the least he could do after finding out the truth about fifteen years ago. And, he was willing to humor Pershing's principal to get the job done. Never mind that he thought reviewing the plans for prior construction jobs was a waste of time. Every job was unique; everybody knew as much.

Still, he hadn't been able to stop thinking about Marisa. All these years he'd hated her. *No, that wasn't right.* He'd built up a wall and sealed her off from the rest of his life.

Now he understood the choice that Marisa had faced in the principal's office. And yeah, she'd been right on target about the way he'd been in high school. He wouldn't have wanted to hear her confession. Because he'd been a callow eighteen-year-old to whom a high school championship had meant more than it should.

In contrast, Marisa had been an insightful teen. She'd shown that understanding when it had come to Mr. Hayes, and Cole had spurned her for it. But the truth was, Cole had fallen for her back then precisely because she'd seemed self-possessed and different. She'd stood outside the usual shallow preoccupations of their classmates. The truth was she'd been more mature—no doubt because she'd had to grow up fast.

Cole cursed silently.

Marisa had been wrong about one thing, though. *All you cared about was the hockey championship.* He'd cared about her, too...until he'd felt betrayed.

In the storage room, she'd looked at him with her limpid big brown eyes, and he'd stopped himself from touching her face to reassure her. He was sure that if he'd reached for her pulse right then, it would have jumped under his touch.

Then she'd rocked him with her explanation about being called to the mat by Mr. Hayes, and he'd kissed her. The lip-lock had been as good as he'd fantasized, and even better than his memory of high school. She had a way of slipping under his skin and making him hunger...

His pulse started to hum at the thought…and at the anticipation of seeing her again. He just needed to make it happen.

He took out his phone and started typing a text message. She'd called from her cell phone when she'd needed to set up the meeting at Serenghetti's offices to review construction plans, and he'd made note of the number.

Told Dobson our meeting cut short b/c I had other business. Let's reschedule. Dinner Friday @6. LMK.

As soon as he hit Send, he felt his spirits lift.

Spotting his foreman coming toward him, he slipped the phone into the back pocket of his jeans and adjusted his hard hat. There was unfinished business today, and there would be unfinished business on Friday. But first he had a meeting today that was a long time coming.

As soon as his consultation with the foreman was over, Cole drove to his parents' house. He made his way to the back garden, where he knew he'd find his parents, based on what his mother had told him during his call to her earlier.

Serg was ensconced in a wrought-iron chair. Bundled in a jacket and blanket against the nippy air, he looked as if he was dressed for an Alaskan sledding event. Because if there was one thing that Camilla Serenghetti feared, it was someone dear to her *catching a chilly*, as she liked to say. It came second only to the fear that her husband or one of her kids might go hungry. She hovered near a small round patio table littered with a display of fruit, bread, water and tea.

Cole took a seat and began with easy chitchat. Fortunately, the stroke had not affected his father's speech. The conversation touched on Serg's health before veering toward other mundane topics. All the while, however, his father appeared grumpy and tense—as if he sensed there was another purpose to this visit.

Holding back a grimace, Cole took his chance when the talk reached a lull. "I'm looking for buyers for the business."

Serg hit the table with his fist. "Over my dead body."

Cole resisted the urge to point out that it might well come to that—another stroke and Serg was finished. "We're a midsize construction company. Our best bet is a buyout by one of the big players."

Then Cole could get on with his life. Nothing had panned out yet, but there were coaching positions available, and he wanted to grow the business investment portfolio he'd begun to put together thanks to his NHL earnings.

"Never."

"It's not good for you to get upset in your condition, Dad." He'd thought he could have a rational discussion with his father about the future of Serenghetti Construction, because Serg was never going to make a one-hundred-percent recovery. So unless Serenghetti Construction was sold, Cole wouldn't just be a temporary caretaker of the company, but a permanent fixture.

"You know what's not good for me? My son talking about selling the company that I broke my back to build."

Camilla rushed forward. "Lie back against the pillows. Don't upset yourself."

"Dad, be reasonable." Cole fought to keep his frustration at bay. He'd waited months to have this conversation with his father. But now everyone had to face reality. Serg was not going to show more significant improvement. Maybe he could enjoy a productive retirement, but the chances that he'd be fit to head a demanding business again were slim. The discussion about the future had to start now.

"What's wrong with the company that you want to sell it?"

"It needs to grow or die."

"And you're not interested in growing it?"

Cole let silence be his answer.

"I heard you outmaneuvered JM to get the contract to build a new gym at the Pershing School."

Cole figured Serg had been informed about the gym

contract on one of his occasional phone calls to Serenghetti Construction's head offices. His father liked to speak to senior employees and stay clued in on what was going on beyond what Cole had time to tell him. Cole had told no one at the office about his bargain with Marisa beyond the fact that Serenghetti Construction had managed to stay a step ahead of its competitor JM Construction.

"Grow or die!" Serg gestured as if there was an audience aside from Camilla. "This company paid for your college degree and your hockey training. There's nothing wrong with it."

"Serenghetti Construction is not the little train that could, Dad." The company needed fresh blood at the helm in order to steer it into the future. Serg, like many founders, had taken it as far as he could. And if Cole wasn't careful, he himself would be captaining the ship for decades ahead.

"So what are you going to do instead that's more important?" Serg groused, shifting in his chair and nearly knocking over his cane. "Go be a hockey coach?"

Cole wasn't surprised his father guessed the direction of his thoughts. He'd interviewed for a coaching job with the Madison Rockets last fall, but having heard nothing further, he'd kept the news to himself. If a position materialized, there was no question that his time at the helm of Serenghetti Construction would need to come to an end because he couldn't keep jobs in different states—not to mention the travel involved in a coaching position.

Serg snapped his brows together. "Coaching is a hard lifestyle if you have a family and a couple of kids." He glowered. "Or is that something else you're planning to do differently from the old man? Another part of your heritage that you're planning to reject?"

"Getting married and having kids is hardly part of my heritage, Dad." More like a lifestyle choice, but Serg had jumped ahead several steps.

"Well, we damn sure don't speak the same language anymore! How's that for losing your heritage?"

"Serg, calm down," Camilla said, looking worried. "You know what the *dottore* said."

Camilla had always been the one to run interference between her husband and children. Cole also had a hunch that his mother had more empathy than his father about lifelong dreams and their postponement. His mother had her own second career as a television chef.

"The blood thinners will take care of me—" Serg harrumphed before shooting Cole a pointed look "—even if my children won't."

"I'll take care of you," Camilla said firmly.

Cole looked at his parents. "Well, this is a turnaround."

Serg frowned. "What? Stop speaking in riddles."

Cole wasn't sure his pronouncement would be welcome. "Suddenly Mom is the one with a career, and she's promising to support you."

"You always were a smart aleck," his father grumbled. "Maybe even a bigger one than your brother."

"Which one?" Cole quipped—because both Jordan and Rick qualified—and then stood up. "I'm going to let you continue to rest. I have a couple of calls to return for work."

"Rest! That's all anyone wants me to do around here."

Cole figured if he could rest, he'd be ahead of the game right now. But he had demands on his time, not the least of which was a certain wild-tressed schoolteacher who'd come crashing back into his life...

"Hi, Mom."

"Honey!" Donna Casale rushed forward, delight stamped on her face as she left her front door wide open behind her.

For Marisa, it was like looking at an older version of herself. Fortunately, the future in that regard didn't look too shabby. Her mother appeared younger than fifty-four. Donna Casale had maintained the shapely figure that had attracted male interest all her life—leaving her alone and pregnant at twenty-three, but also permitting her to attract a second admiring glance even after age fifty. And years in the retail trade meant she always looked polished and presentable: hair colored, makeup on and smile beaming. Of course, marriage might also have something to do with it these days. Her mother seemed *happy*.

Marisa felt a pang at the contrast to her own circumstances as she let herself be enveloped in a hug. Her mother and Ted had bought a tidy three-bedroom wood-frame house at the time of their wedding. Marisa and Sal had begun talking about buying a home themselves during their brief engagement, but those plans had gone nowhere.

When her mother pulled back from their embrace, she said, "Come on in. You're early, but I couldn't be happier to see you. You're so busy these days!"

Marisa *tried* to keep occupied. She'd plunged back into work after her breakup with Sal, taking on additional roles at Pershing in order to advance her career and keep her mind off depressing thoughts.

Donna closed the front door, and Marisa followed her toward the back of the house.

"I'm so glad you're staying for dinner," Donna said over her shoulder, leading the way down the hall.

"It's a welcome break, Mom, and you spoil me." Still, Marisa wanted to give her mother and Ted their space so they could enjoy their relatively new married life.

"Well, you're just in time to help me assemble the lasagna," her mother said with a laugh, "so you'll be working for your supper. Ted will be home soon."

When they reached a small but recently remodeled kitchen, Marisa draped her things on a chair, and her mother went to the counter crowded with ingredients and bowls.

Marisa's gaze settled on a framed photo of Donna and Ted on their low-key wedding day. Donna and Ted were all smiles in the picture, her mother clutching a small sprig of flowers that complemented a cream satin tea-length dress. Marisa had been their sole attendant, and one of their witnesses, because Ted had been childless before his marriage.

Marisa bit back a wistful sigh. She and her mother had always been each other's confidantes—the two of them against the world—but now her mom had someone else. Marisa couldn't have been happier for her.

It was just… It was just… An image of Cole rose to mind. What had she been thinking? What had he? He'd kissed her in the storage room last week—and she'd kissed him back. And the memory of that kiss had lingered…replayed before she went to sleep at night, while driving to work and during breaks in the school day.

The teenage Cole had nothing on Cole the man. He'd made her come apart in his arms, and it had both shocked and thrilled her. She'd been under the influence at the time, of course. Panic and proximity—mixed with the confession of long-held secrets had made a heady brew while they'd been locked in together.

Her mother glanced at her, her brows drawing together in concern. "You seem worried. Are you taking care of yourself?"

The question was one that Marisa was used to. Ever since she'd been born a preemie, her mother had worried about her health. She gave a practiced smile. "I'm fine."

"Well, you were a fighter from day one."

Marisa continued smiling, and as she usually did whenever her mother's worries came to the fore, she tried to move the conversation in a different direction. "Serafina found an apartment and is moving out tomorrow."

"I heard."

"I'll have my apartment to myself." Even before her cousin had moved in, she'd hardly felt as if she lived alone. She and Sal had been serious enough that he'd often been at her place or he'd been at hers.

"You should get married."

Marisa bit back another sigh. She hadn't succeeded in steering the talk to safer waters. "I was engaged. It didn't work out."

Ever since her mother had met and then married Ted, she'd viewed marriage in a different light.

"So?" Donna persisted. "He wasn't the right man. You'll meet someone else."

Marisa parted her lips as Cole sprung to mind. *No.* He was her past, not her future, even if he occupied her present. *Get a grip.* "Mom, I know you're still a bit of a newlywed, so you're looking at the world through rose-colored glasses, but—"

Her mother sobered. "Honey, how can you say so? I may be newly married, but I haven't forgotten the years of struggle…"

Donna's amber eyes—so like Marisa's own—clouded, as if recollections of the past were flashing by. Marisa wondered what those memories were. Was her mother recalling the same things she was? The years of juggling bill payments—staying one short step away from having the electricity turned off? The credit card balances that were rolled over because Donna was too proud to ask relatives for a loan?

"I know, Mom," Marisa said quietly. "I was there."

Donna sighed. "And that's part of my guilt."

"What?"

"I didn't shield you enough. Your childhood wasn't as secure as I would have liked it to be."

"You did your best." Wasn't she always telling her students to try their best? "I always felt loved. I graduated from a great school, got a college degree and have a great job."

"Still, I wish you had someone to lean on. I'm not going to be around forever."

"Mom, you're only fifty-four!" In that moment, however, Marisa understood. While she'd worried about her mother, her mother had reciprocated with concern about her.

"I wish I'd left you with siblings," her mother said wistfully.

"You could barely handle me!" Besides, she had cousins. Serafina for one.

"You were a good girl. Mr. Hayes at the Pershing School even came up to me on graduation day to tell me so, and that I'd done a great job raising you."

Marisa smothered a wince and then walked over to the kitchen sink to wash and dry her hands. Naturally, Mr. Hayes had thought she was one of the good guys. She'd ratted out Cole… Marisa had kept her mother in the dark about that part of her life. She hadn't wanted her mother burdened any more than she was.

"How is your job at Pershing, by the way?" Donna asked. "Are the kids taking a lot out of you?"

It wasn't the kids who were responsible for her current turmoil, but a certain six-foot-plus former hockey player. "I'm in charge of the big Pershing Shines Bright benefit in May."

"Ted and I will be there, of course. We want to support you."

"Thanks." Marisa eyed the pasta machine. "You've been busy."

"One of the benefits of having the day off from work. I made the pasta sheets for the lasagna from scratch."

Marisa picked up one of the sheets and set it down in a pan that her mother had already coated with tomato sauce.

"Is the planning going well?" Donna probed.

"It's fine." Marisa shrugged. "Cole Serenghetti of the New England Razors has agreed to headline."

Donna brought her hands together. "Wonderful. He's so popular around here."

Tell me about it. "He's not playing professional hockey anymore. He got hurt."

"Oh yes, I had heard that." Donna frowned. "He was such

a good player in high school… Well, until the incident that earned him a suspension."

Marisa kept her expression neutral. "He's running the family construction business these days, though I'm not sure how happy he is about it. His father had a stroke."

Donna's gaze was searching. "You do seem to know a lot about Cole."

"Don't worry, Mom," Marisa responded, setting down more sheets of pasta for the lasagna. "I also knew a lot about Sal before he dumped me. Once burned, twice shy."

"*Dumped* is such an ugly word," Donna said lightly. "*Fortuitously disengaged* is the way I put it for members of my book club."

"Are you doing ad copy for the department store circular these days?" Marisa quipped.

"No, but I did suggest to the book club that we read *Dump the Dude, Buy the Shoes*."

They shared a laugh before Marisa said, "You did not!"

Actually she thought the title might not be a bad one for the autobiography of her mother's life.

"No, I was joking. But I did tell everyone that I got promoted to buyer for housewares." Donna spooned a thin layer of ricotta cheese mixture on top of the layer of pasta that Marisa had created.

"They must have been thrilled for you." Before Marisa could say any more, she heard her cell phone buzz. Wiping her hands on a dish towel, she walked over to get the phone out of her handbag. When she saw the message on the screen, her heart began to pound.

Told Dobson our meeting cut short b/c I had other business. Let's reschedule. Dinner Friday @6. LMK.

"Is everything okay?" Donna asked, studying her.

"Speak of the devil," Marisa said, trying for some lame humor. "No, not Sal. The other devil. Cole Serenghetti."

Donna's eyebrows rose. "He's texting you? So you do know each other well!"

"First time. He must have a record of my cell number—" she paused to consider for a moment, thinking back "—because I had to call him to discuss something related to the fund-raiser and new gym." She was *not* going to mention to her mother that she'd visited Cole's offices. Because that might lead to mention of the incident in the storage room. And she was *so* not discussing that mishap. Especially with her mother. Even if she was thirty-three and an adult.

"Well?"

"He's invited me to dinner." As her mother's eyebrows shot higher, she added, "A business dinner."

She should go. She was grateful that he'd covered for her with Mr. Dobson. She was also relieved he was willing to keep dealing with her about the fund-raiser and construction project. It wouldn't look good if Cole announced he needed a different contact person at Pershing. And she had twenty questions about what he had to say—who wouldn't?

Dinner? Really?

Still, it wasn't as if they were having an assignation. As she'd told her mother, it was a business meeting. Pure business. The kiss last time notwithstanding. A blip on the radar never, ever to be repeated.

And now that Cole had agreed to the fund-raiser, she'd begun flirting with another idea—that is, until the storage room incident...

Donna continued to regard her. "Honey, trust me, I'm acquainted with the attractiveness of professional athletes."

Marisa knew they were no longer talking only about Cole. They'd both been burned long ago by another man chasing sports fame, except he'd been a baseball player. "This is purely business, believe me."

Marisa wished she could wholeheartedly believe it herself. So she and Cole had shared a kiss. Given the unusual circumstances—her panic and his need to reassure and, uh, comfort—they had an excuse. One that her mother didn't need to hear.

As her mother searched her expression, Marisa stuck to her best Girl Scout face and walked back to the kitchen counter.

Finally, seemingly satisfied—or not—Donna sighed. "We should find time to write that dude book together. Meanwhile, let's finish this lasagna, and I'll open a bottle of wine."

"What's this about, Cole?"

"Dinner. What else?" He looked bemusedly at the woman sitting to his left—the one who had bedeviled more of his nights and days than he cared to count. He'd chosen Welsdale's chicest restaurant, Bayart's on Creek Road, and she'd proposed meeting him there—much to his chagrin. He'd gone along with her suggestion, even though he saw through it as the defensive move it was, because he knew he was still treading on fragile ground with Marisa. He'd ordered a bottle of Merlot, and the waiter had already poured their wine.

Tonight she was in a geometric-print wrap dress that left no curve untouched. *My God, the woman is set on torturing me.*

"I mean the subtext."

He raised his gaze to her eyes. "Subtext? You were always a stellar student in English."

"And you spent your time in the last row, goofing around."

"Charlotte Brontë wasn't my thing."

"She was about the only female who wasn't."

"She was dead."

"Don't let that stop you."

He grinned. "That's what I discovered I liked about you, Danieli. You're able to serve it up straight when you want to. Back then, and now."

"I'm a teacher. It's a survival skill."

"I liked you better than you think, you know."

"Well, that's something, I suppose. Right up there with being someone's sixth favorite teacher."

He laughed because he liked this more uninhibited Marisa—one who felt free to speak her mind. "Still feeling the effect of your confession last time? You're letting it rip. It's—" he let his voice dip "—enticing."

She got an adorable little pucker in her brow and toyed with the stem of her wineglass. "It wasn't intended to be, but why am I not surprised you took it that way?"

"I really did like you," he insisted.

"You're just saying that," she demurred.

"Are you ready to talk about what happened in the storage room?" It was safer than focusing on the wineglass in her hand and imagining her fingers on him.

They could have been on a date, from outward appearances, because Bayart's candlelit interior invited intimacy. In keeping with the restaurant's formality, Cole was still in the navy suit that he'd worn to the office. And Marisa was probably expecting tonight to be all business…

"Wow, you're direct." Marisa blew out a breath. "Isn't it obvious? We're destined for close encounters in small spaces."

He smiled at her attempt at humor and deflection. "Try again." When she still said nothing, he continued, "I'll go first. I wonder what you saw in me while we were in high school. I was a jock and a jerk."

She joined him in smiling, and it was like the sun coming out. "That's an easy one. I admired you. You were willing to take risks. On the ice, you took chances in order to win. And off the ice, you skated on the edge with your pranks. I was meek, and you were confident. I was quiet, and you were popular."

"I was a jerk, and you weren't."

She blinked, and the curve of her lips wobbled.

"Fat lot of good it did me, too. I ultimately wound up

crashing and burning, on the ice and off." It was his offer of a mea culpa—accepting guilt and responsibility. Fifteen years ago she'd called a halt to his pranks. And if he'd been a jerk in the aftermath, it had been for nothing. He'd still gotten a professional career on the ice, and when it had ended, it had had nothing to do with Marisa.

"You know what they say. Better to have tried and failed than never to have tried at all…"

"You've never taken risks?" he probed.

"Well, I did recruit you for the Pershing benefit. I guess you bring out the daredevil in me."

"Yeah," he drawled. "The same way I tempted you to test out the theater department's prop during senior year."

Marisa looked embarrassed.

Before he could say more, the waiter came up to take their order. Marisa waffled on what to have, but settled on the Cobb salad.

"You can't choose a salad," Cole said with dry humor. "It's a sin in a place like this."

"It's not," she responded lightly. "I'm sure everything is delicious here."

Including her. He could tell she'd contemplated ordering a richer entrée, and he wanted to say he appreciated every inch of her lush curves, but he let it go. Maybe a salad was Marisa's go-to choice on a date—not that she thought of this as a date, but certainly dinner with a man. *Him.*

When the waiter had departed, the conversation turned to casual topics, but Cole was determined to shift gears back to what they had been discussing.

At a lull, he said, "It must have given you some satisfaction to see me taken down a peg or two in high school. After all, we did have sex, and then I avoided you."

"It hurt."

"I wasn't prepared to deal with what had happened between us. You were a virgin, and you caught me off guard. I might not have hurt you when we fumbled our way through sex, but I did in other ways."

She lowered her lashes. "We were both young and stupid."

"Teenagers make mistakes," he concurred.

She toyed some more with the wineglass, making him crazy. "It must have been an unwelcome surprise when we were first paired up to make a PowerPoint presentation in economics class."

"Not unwelcome," he replied, shifting. "You were an unknown quantity."

"A nonentity at school, especially among the jocks."

He shook his head. "Sweet pea, you may be a teacher, but you still have no idea how most teenage boys think. The only reason the jocks didn't know how big your breasts were is because you were always hiding them behind a bunch of books."

She stared at him. "You were looking at my chest?"

He smiled wolfishly. "On the sly. And I wasn't just looking. Do you think that whenever I brushed by you during our study sessions it was an accident?"

Her eyes widened, and her hand fell away from the wineglass.

"Definitely a C cup."

"I'm not a simple bra size!"

He reached out and covered her hand on the table, smoothing his thumb over the back of her palm. *Anything to avoid further arousal by her fingertips on a damn glass.* "You're right. I got to know the person beyond the teenage boy's fantasy, and you scared the hell out of me."

"I did?"

The look in her eyes was so earnest, it was all he could do not to lean in and capture her lips.

Instead, he nodded. "I started out a little intrigued and a whole lot bored when I was assigned as your partner in economics. But then I got near you, and the hormones kicked in. A few study sessions staring into your eyes, and I was toast. You were nice, smart and interesting."

"I had a crush on you even before we were paired up to do an assignment," she admitted. "All it took was some casual contact, and I was hooked."

"I didn't need a whole lot of convincing to ditch the books in favor of getting closer to you." They had progressed from kissing to more the next time they were together. And then after a few encounters, they'd really gotten intimate…

"But I bet I'm the first girl who got you involved with a theater department prop."

"I'll never forget that velvet sofa." As a scholarship student, Marisa had had a part-time job helping the custodial department clean the school, so she'd had access to a very convenient set of keys.

"They still have it."

He raised his brows. "Then you'll have to give me a tour when I'm at the school."

She parted her lips, but didn't take the bait, so he slid back his hand.

He angled his head, contemplating her. "You wanted me as badly as I wanted you, so I was surprised when it turned out to be your first time. Why did you do it?"

She shrugged. "I was hungry for affection and attention. I wanted to fit in."

"You were a virgin. You'd gotten under my skin and seen beyond the prankster and the jock. It was too heavy for me, so I did the only logical thing for an eighteen-year-old guy. I avoided you."

"Right, I recall," she said drily.

"You were the first woman to proposition me."

"But not the last."

"For professional athletes, propositioning usually goes with the territory."

"So women like Vicki the Vixen are always throwing themselves at you in bars?"

He bit back a smile at the moniker he was sure Vicki wouldn't appreciate. "I'm not a hockey player anymore. These days I'm a CEO…and Pershing School's knight in shining armor."

The waiter arrived with their food, and they dropped their conversation while plates were set before them and they exchanged polite niceties with their server. Then Marisa tucked daintily into her Cobb salad while Cole mentally shrugged and dug into his filet mignon and potatoes au gratin.

After several moments Marisa took a sip of her wine. "You called yourself Pershing's knight in shining armor." She paused. "And I, uh, have another way for you to shine."

He searched her face, and she cleared her throat.

"I have students who would enjoy a field trip to the Razors' arena as part of Career Week."

He sat back in his chair, his lips twisting with amusement. "It's one request after another with you."

"Since you seem to be more approachable these days, I figured I had nothing to lose."

"I don't come cheap."

"I know. Last time you got a construction contract out of the bargain."

He inclined his head in acknowledgment. Ever since their encounter in the storage room, he'd thought about how it would feel to cup her face in his hands again and thread his fingers in her hair. He'd bet her long curly locks fanned across his pillow would be spectacular—and erotic.

"So what's it going to be this time?" she asked.

He could think of a lot of things he'd like to bargain for. "An answer to a question. I'm curious."

She looked surprised and then wary. "That's it?"

He felt a smile tug at his lips. "You haven't heard the question yet."

She shifted in her seat. "Okay…"

"Why Sal? There are a lot of seemingly reliable, boring guys out there."

She stared at him a moment, eyes wide, and then took a deep breath. "Timing."

"I can appreciate the importance. Timing is everything, on the ice and off."

"Yes, and ours has never been great."

He had to agree with her there. "And Sal's was?"

"It was part of it."

"Which part?"

"My mother had just gotten married…"

"And Sal was available when you were vulnerable?"

"Something like that," she admitted.

"I can understand family responsibility, Marisa. Your mother getting married set you free and maybe even adrift."

She looked surprised by his insight. Hell, he was surprised himself. Where had that bit of pop psychology come from? Too much latent baggage from his own family floating to the surface?

Marisa wet her lips. "I guess I didn't want my mother to worry about me anymore once she was married."

"So Sal had it on timing?" *As opposed to a former hockey player?*

"He can also be quite charming when he wants to be."

"So is a used car salesman," Cole quipped. "So Sal laid on the charm…?"

"He was there, and the type I was looking for."

Cole quirked his lips. "You have a type? I thought your type was high school prankster."

She shook her head. "My goal was to marry someone not like my father."

"You knew him?" He didn't recall Marisa ever mentioning her father in high school except to say he'd died a long time ago.

"No, he passed away before I was born. But I'd always

thought my parents had meant to get married. In my twenties, I found out that wasn't the case..."

Cole said nothing, waiting for her to go on.

"My mother finally revealed my father had broken up with her even before he died in a car accident. He was out of the picture before she gave birth."

"So your father's side of the family was never involved in your life?"

Marisa nodded. "My father's only surviving relative was my grandfather, who lived on the West Coast. As for my father, he was pursuing a minor league baseball career, and a wife and baby didn't fit with his plans. He had big dreams and wanderlust."

"So you believed Sal was the guy for you because he wasn't bitten by the same bug."

"I thought he was the right man. I was wrong."

Cole suddenly understood. Marisa had thought Sal would never leave her. He wasn't a professional athlete whose career came first. In other words, Sal was unlike her father... and unlike Cole, who'd left Welsdale at the first opportunity for hockey.

Marisa had discovered the truth about her father long after she'd finished high school at Pershing. So if Cole's reaction after missing out on a potential hockey championship at Pershing hadn't soured her on athletes, then the truth she learned about her father in her twenties certainly would have.

As Marisa steered the conversation back to scheduling a student field trip to the Razors' arena, as well as setting up another time for her to review Serenghetti Construction's old architectural plans, Cole realized one thing.

He'd had his chance with Marisa at eighteen, but these days she was looking for something—someone—different.

Six

Marisa had never been inside the New England Razors arena, which was located outside Springfield, Massachusetts. The closeness to the state border allowed the team to attract a sizable crowd from nearby Connecticut as well as from their home base, Massachusetts.

Marisa had just never counted herself among those fans. She'd always felt that going to a game would be a painful blast from the past where Cole was concerned. The Razors' games were televised, but she could handle Cole Serenghetti's power over her memories—sort of—when it was limited to a glimpse of a screen in a restaurant or other public place.

Right now, however, she was getting the full Cole Serenghetti effect as he stood a few feet away addressing a group of Pershing high school students. He was dressed in faded blue jeans and a long-sleeved black tee. His clothing was casual, but no less potent on her senses. She was sensitive to his every move, and was having a hard time denying what it was: sexual awareness.

"Look," Cole said to the kids arrayed before him in a

semicircle inside the front entrance, "since it's a Saturday and this is a half-day field trip, we'll do a tour of the arena first and then some ice-skating. How does that sound?"

Some kids smiled, and others nodded their heads.

"And how many of you want to be professional hockey players?"

A few hands shot up. Marisa was glad to see those of three girls among them. Pershing fielded both boys' and girls' hockey teams, but the girls tended to drop out at a higher rate than the boys once they hit high school.

One of the students raised his hand. "Does your injury still bother you?"

Marisa sucked in a breath.

"It's important to wear protective equipment," Cole said. "Injuries do happen, but they're unusual, especially the serious ones."

The kids remained silent, as if they expected him to go on.

"In my case, I tore up my knee twice. I had surgery and therapy both times. After the second, I could walk without a problem, but playing professional hockey wasn't in the cards." Cole's tone was even and matter-of-fact, and he betrayed no hint that the subject was a touchy one for him. "I was past thirty, and I'd already had several great seasons with the New England Razors. I had another career calling me."

"So now you do construction?" a student piped up from the back row.

Cole gave a self-deprecating laugh. "Yup. But as CEO, I spend more time in the office than on a job site. I make sure we stay within our budget and that resources are allocated correctly among projects." He cast Marisa a sidelong look. "I also go out and drum up more business."

Marisa felt heat flood her cheeks even though she was the only one who could guess what Cole was alluding to.

A few days ago she and Cole had finally had their intended meeting at his offices to go over architectural plans for past projects. When she'd shown up this time, Cole had had the plans ready for review in a conference room. She must have appeared relieved that she wouldn't have to step back inside Serenghetti Construction's storage room, because Cole had shot her an amused and knowing look. Still, she'd gotten enough information to go back to Mr. Dobson with no surprises but some valuable input.

Fortunately, they hadn't had the opportunity to discuss their encounter in the storage room. Every time Cole had looked as if he was about to bring it up, they'd been interrupted by a phone call or by an employee with a question.

Cole scanned the small crowd assembled before him. "Today I'm going to show you career fields connected to hockey that you might not have thought of. Sure there are the players on the ice that everyone sees during the game. Their names make the news. But behind them is a whole other team of people who make professional hockey what it is."

"Like who?" a couple of kids asked, speaking over each other.

"Well, I'm going to take you to the broadcast booth, in case anyone is interested in sports journalism. We'll walk through the management offices to talk to marketing. And then we'll go down to the locker rooms, where the sports medicine people do their stuff. Sound good?"

The kids nodded.

"I'll stop before I show you the construction stuff," Cole quipped.

"Is that how you stayed involved with your old sport?" a ninth grader asked.

"Yup." Cole flashed a smile. "We repaved the ground outside the arena."

From her position a little removed from the crowd, Marisa sighed because Cole had a natural ability to connect with kids. He was effortlessly cool, and she was...not. Some things never changed.

Cole winked at her, shaking her out of her musings. "And if you're all good, there might also be an appearance by Jordan Serenghetti—"

The kids let out whoops.

"—who is having a great season with the Razors. But more important, in my opinion, he's having an even better life as my younger brother."

Everyone laughed.

Marisa thought Jordan would dispute Cole's assessment if he were there.

After Cole gave the kids a tour of the parts of the arena that he had referred to, he led the group to the ice rink.

As everyone laced up their skates, Marisa overheard a couple of the kids talking about her with Cole. When they mentioned to him that she was a fantastic cook, she felt heat rush to her face.

She hung back and skated onto the ice after everyone else. She was wearing tights and a tunic-length sweater so her movements weren't restricted, but she hadn't been on skates in a long time. She became aware of Cole watching her, hands in pockets, as the others glided around.

"I wasn't sure what to expect," he said.

She continued to skate at a leisurely pace, now only a few feet away from him. "I've had ice-skating lessons."

He arched a brow.

"It's New England. Everyone assumes you know how to stay upright on the ice."

To underscore her words, she did several swizzles, her legs swerving in and out.

"Looks like you did more than learn how to stay upright," Cole commented. "Where did you learn?"

"At the rec center outside Welsdale," she admitted, slowing. "It opened when we were kids, and they gave free lessons."

"I know. My father built it."

She stared at him and then gave an unsurprised laugh. "I should have guessed."

She thought a moment, concentrated and then gaining speed, did a scratch spin. Glancing back at Cole, now meters away, she shrugged and added, "I picked up a few moves."

She wasn't sure how many moves she could still do, but it seemed that as with riding a bike, some skills she'd never lose.

"So when did you change course from budding skating star to top-notch teacher?" Cole asked as he skated toward her.

She shrugged again. "We didn't have the money for me to pursue the sport seriously. It would have meant lessons, costumes and travel expenses. When I was accepted to Pershing, I had to concentrate on getting good grades in order to keep my scholarship."

She tensed as soon as the word *scholarship* was out of her mouth because they were close to the big bugaboo topic between them. Still, the truth was that Cole had gotten to play in the NHL while she'd received her coveted scholarship and moved on to teaching—a nice, stable profession rather than glitz and glory. He'd been able to afford his dreams while she hadn't.

"I was signed up for figure skating and ice dancing lessons as a kid—"

She laughed because she couldn't envision Cole doing the waltz—on the ice or off. He was too big...too male.

"—but they didn't take," he finished drily.

She bit the inside of her cheek, trying to school her expression. She was a lot better at keeping a straight face in the classroom.

"My mother was determined to make her sons into little gentlemen."

Marisa willed herself to appear earnest. *Instead Mrs. Serenghetti had gotten a bunch of pranksters.*

"You think this is funny."

She nodded, not trusting herself to speak.

"Here, I'll demonstrate," he said, approaching. "I remember a thing or two."

She blinked. "What?"

"We're here to show these kids careers related to hockey."

"Like ice dancing? I thought that branching out usually went the other way."

"Like if you sucked at ice dancing as a kid, you took up hockey instead?"

She raised her eyebrows.

"So now I'm a failed figure skater? Someone who couldn't hack it?" He rubbed his chin. "I have something to prove."

She didn't like the sound of that. But before she could respond, he reached for her hand and then slid his other around her waist, so that they were facing each other in dance position.

"What are you doing?" she asked in a high voice, caught between surprise and breathlessness at his nearness.

"Like I said, I have something to prove. I hope you remember your figure skating moves, sweet pea."

The arm around her was a band of pure muscle. He worked out, and it showed. The power he exuded made her nervous, so she didn't raise her gaze above his mouth—though *that* had potency enough to wreak havoc on her heart.

She and Cole skated over the ice, doing a fair facsimile of dancing together. His hands on her were warm imprints, heating her against the cold of the ice.

When she stole a peek at him, she quickly concluded he was still devastatingly gorgeous. His hair was thick and ruffled, inviting a woman to run her fingers through it. His jaw was firm and square but shadowed, promising a hint of roughness. His lips were firm but sensual. And the scar—oh, the scar. The one on his cheek gave character and invited tenderness. He was a catalog of sexy contrasts—a magnet for women in a much blunter way than Jordan. She lowered her lashes. *But not for me.*

"Are you ready for a throw jump?"

Her gaze shot to his. "What?" She sounded like a parrot but she couldn't have heard him right. "I thought we were just dancing! What about your knee?"

He shrugged. "It couldn't take repeated hits from a defenseman who weighs over two hundred pounds, but I'm guessing you don't weigh nearly as much."

"I'm not telling you how much I weigh!"

"Naturally." Cole's eyes crinkled. "Here we go, Ice Princess. Think you can land a throw waltz jump?"

In the next moment they were spinning around and Cole was lifting her off the ice.

"Ready?" he murmured.

She felt herself moving through the air. It was a gentle throw, so she didn't go very high or far. She brought down the toe of her right foot and landed her blade before extending her left leg back.

Cole grinned, and the kids around them on the ice laughed and clapped while a few chortled.

"A one-footed landing," Cole said, skating toward her. "I'm impressed. You've still got game, sweet pea."

She laughed. "Still, can you see me competing in the Olympics?" she asked, gesturing at her ample chest. "I'd have had to bind myself."

Cole gave her a half-lidded look as he stopped in front of her. "Now that would be a shame."

She'd walked into that one. Students glided by around them, and there were a few gasps as Jordan appeared. This was hardly the place for Cole and her to be having a sexually tinged moment.

"Relax," Cole said in a low voice. "Nobody is paying attention to us anymore."

Easy for you to say. She tingled with the urge to touch him again. "Cole Serenghetti, too cool for school."

"If you were the teacher, I'd have had my butt glued to my seat in the front row."

"You say that now," she teased, even as his nearness continued to affect her like a drug.

"I was a callow teenager who couldn't appreciate what you were going through."

"Callow?" she queried, still trying to keep it light. "Are you trying to impress the teacher with your vocabulary?"

He bent his head until his lips were inches from hers. "How am I doing?"

Oh wow. "Great," she said a bit breathlessly. "Keep at it, and you might even get an A."

It was the pep talk that she usually gave her students. *Keep trying, work hard and the reward will come...* The moral of her own life story, really. Well, except for her *love* life...

Cole's eyes gleamed as he straightened and murmured, "I've never cared about grades."

She didn't want to ask what he did care about. She'd guess his currency of choice was kisses—and more... Troublingly, she could seriously envision getting tangled up with Cole again even though she should know better...

Cole swiveled on his bar stool and looked at the entrance again.

This time he was finally rewarded with the sight of Marisa coming toward him. She was wearing jeans—ones that hugged her curves—and a mint-colored sweater. She had on light makeup, but it was a toss-up whether her curls or her chest was bouncier.

Cole felt his groin tighten.

He hadn't been sure she would show. His text had been vague.

Meet me at the Puck & Shoot. I have a plan u need to hear.

Ever since he'd upheld his end of the bargain by giving her students a tour of the Razors' arena, he'd been desperate to come up with another excuse to see her.

She stopped in front of him. "I heard women proposition you in bars these days."

"Care to make one?"

"How about a drink instead?"

"That's a start." He stood, closing the distance between them even further. "What'll you have?"

"A light beer."

Cole fought a smile. "Lightweight, are you?"

"Only in bars, not in the boxing ring."

"Yeah, I know." At the gym, she could pack a wallop in a simple dress that brought grown men to a standstill. But she wasn't too shabby in bars, either. She could still make him stand up and take notice. Without the baggage of her seeming betrayal in high school, he could acknowledge without reservation what a beautiful woman she was.

He signaled the bartender and placed an order.

She glanced around, as if uncertain. "This is my first visit to the Puck & Shoot."

"I thought you said this is where you got a tip about how to run me to ground at Jimmy's Boxing Gym."

"I wouldn't call it *running to ground*," she said pertly. "You were still standing when I left the boxing ring. Also, I didn't say I got the tip personally. My cousin Serafina has been moonlighting as a waitress here. She overheard some of the Razors talking."

"Like those at the other end of the bar?" Cole indicated with his chin. "The ones wondering what the status of our relationship is?"

Marisa tossed a glance over her shoulder. "Probably, but we don't have a relationship with a status."

He brought his finger to his lips. "Shh, don't tell. I like having them wonder why a gorgeous woman passed them over and made a beeline in my direction instead."

"You asked me to come here!"

He laughed at her with his eyes. "They don't know that, sweet pea." He reached out to smooth a strand of hair away from her face and remembered all over again how soft her skin was.

His body tightened another notch and she stilled, like a deer in headlights.

"I don't think Serafina likes the Razors very much…"

He settled his gaze on her mouth. "They can be a randy bunch."

"You included?"

"I'll let you be the judge," he responded lazily.

He wanted her. *Right now.* He'd dreamed about her again last night, and it had been his hottest fantasy ever.

"Jordan isn't the only joker in the family."

He handed her the beer that had just been set down on the bar and then watched as Marisa placed her lips on the bottle's long neck and took a swill. The woman was killing him with her sexual tone deafness.

"So where's Serafina?" he asked.

Marisa lowered the bottle. "She isn't working tonight. Wednesday isn't on her regular schedule, and she's about to quit for a better position."

"If this had been her shift, would you have met me here?"

"Maybe."

He smiled. "Or maybe not."

He took it as a good sign that Marisa wanted to keep their meetings on the down-low. It meant she cared what people thought about the two of them. *Like maybe there was something going on.* Which there was, whether Marisa would admit it or not. Still, she was skittish about the sexual attraction that still existed between them, and he needed to proceed carefully.

They were both adults, and he was itching to explore what had gotten cut short in high school. As long as he was indefinitely parked in Welsdale, there was no reason not to enjoy himself...

He let his gaze sweep over her. Besides the jeans and sweater, she wore black high-heeled Mary-Janes that showed off her shapely legs. She'd subverted the most school-marmish of shoes and made them sexy and hot...

Marisa raised her eyebrows as if she'd read his thoughts. "Why did you want to meet?"

Because he wasn't ready to share his sexy thoughts, he leaned against the bar stool behind him and gestured to the empty one next to him. "Have a seat."

"Thank you, but I'm fine."

Definitely skittish. Even leaning back, he still had a height advantage on her, but he had to admire her unwill-ingness to give an additional inch. Time to show some of his cards. "I noticed some of the kids on the field trip were interested in hockey. I'd like to give them a few pointers."

His offer, of course, was a pretext for getting her to meet with him again.

Marisa took her time answering, her face reflecting flit-ting emotions until it settled into an expression of determi-nation. "I don't just want you to give them a few pointers. I want you to run a hockey clinic."

Right back at you. He'd underestimated her. "That's a tall order. Giving a few pointers is one thing, and setting up a sports clinic is another. Let me clarify in case you don't understand—"

"Never having been a jock."

"—but training sessions involve drawing up practice plans and small area games—"

"So the kids will have others to play against."

"—and it's a big investment of time."

"You're up to the challenge," she ended encouragingly.

What he was up for was getting her into bed. "I'll tell you what. I'll start with informal coaching for a small group."

She nodded and smiled. "Now that that's settled, let's discuss the remarks you'll be giving at the fund-raiser."

The woman didn't miss a beat. But now it was his turn to hit the puck back at her. "If you search online, you'll come up with my past speeches. My talk to the sports group in Boston on working hard and realizing your dreams. My humorous anecdotes about my rookie year in the NHL—"

"You'll want to say something flattering about the Pershing School." She looked earnest as she said it.

"And my time there?" he queried. "How do I work in my suspension—" he leaned forward confidentially "—or the episode on the theater department's casting couch?"

She shifted. "I thought we'd established I didn't land you a suspension out of retaliation."

"No, but I still think of it as a...highlight of my high school career. How do I discuss my time at Pershing without mentioning it?"

"Stick to sports and academics," she sidestepped. "And it wasn't a casting couch. You're not a Hollywood starlet who had to put out for the sake of her career."

He grinned. "Yeah, but you were definitely auditioning me for the role of study buddy with benefits. How did I do?"

"Could have been better," she harrumphed.

"I am now, sweet pea. Don't you want to find out how much better?" He liked teasing her, and what's more, he couldn't help it.

Her gaze skittered away from his and then stopped in the distance, her eyes widening.

She looked back at him and flushed.

Before he could react, she leaned forward, cupped his face with both her hands and pressed her lips to his.

What the...? It was Cole's last thought before he went motionless.

Her lips felt soft and full, and she tasted sweet. Her floral scent wafted to him. He was surprised by the fact that she'd made the first move, but he was more than happy to oblige...

He parted his lips and pulled her forward.

She slipped into the gap between his legs, her arms encircling his neck.

He caressed her lips with his and then deepened the kiss. He stroked her tongue, tangling with her and swallowing her moan.

The sounds of the bar receded, and he brought a laser focus to the woman in his arms. He silently urged Marisa even closer so that her breasts pressed into him.

Come on. More...

"Talk about a surprise."

The words sounded from behind him, and Marisa pulled away.

Cole caught her startled, guilty look before he turned and straightened, and saw Sal Piazza's too-jovial expression. Vicki clung to Sal's arm, her face betraying shock.

Glancing at Marisa, Cole suddenly understood everything. He settled his face into a bland expression and forced himself back from their heated kiss.

Sal held out his hand. "I didn't expect to see you here, Cole."

"Piazza," he acknowledged.

Vicki's expression subsided from shock to surprise.

Sal dropped his hand as his gaze moved from Marisa to Cole. "You two are together."

It was a simple statement, but there was a wealth of curiosity behind it.

Cole felt Marisa go tense beside him and knew there was only one thing to do. He slid an arm around her waist before responding, "Yup. Not many people know."

Actually, it had been a party of two until seconds ago. And even then, *he* hadn't been sure what was up. That kiss had come out of nowhere and packed a punch even bigger than the one in the storage room.

Sal cleared his throat. "Marisa and I haven't been in touch since the break—"

"Lots of things can happen around a breakup." Cole made it a flat statement—and deliberately left the implication that he and Marisa had started getting acquainted at the same time that she and Sal had broken up.

Sal looked affronted, and Cole tightened his arm around Marisa as she shifted.

Sal twisted his lips in a sardonic smile. "Well, I—"

"Congratulations, I suppose," Vicki piped in with an edge to her voice.

Marisa smiled at the other woman. "Thanks, but we really haven't told many people about our relationship yet."

Cole kept his bland expression. Oh yeah, Marisa was with him. After this was over, though, he'd be quizzing her about their supposed liaison, including that kiss... Had she only planted one on him because she'd spotted Sal and Vicki?

Sal gave a forced laugh. "I guess a little partner swapping is going on."

Cole fixed him with a hard look.

Glancing at Marisa, Vicki narrowed her eyes and thrust her chin forward. "Be careful, sweetie. He's not one to commit."

"Which one?" Marisa quipped.

As Vicki's mouth dropped open, Cole found himself caught between laughing and wincing. They were a train wreck waiting to happen—or a hockey brawl.

"We're here for a corner booth and some dinner," Sal said grimly, his gaze moving between Marisa and Cole, "so we'll cede the bar to you two. Nice running into you."

Without a backward glance, Sal and Vicki headed toward the rear room of the crowded bar.

Cole figured that with any luck, he wouldn't catch a glimpse of the other couple again, which left Marisa and him to their own private reckoning...

Marisa slipped away from the arm around her waist, and her gaze collided with his.

"I'd hate to meet you in the ring," he remarked drily.

She sighed. "You already have."

"Yeah," he said with a touch of humor, "but that time Jordan was there to protect me."

Marisa compressed her lips.

"Well, this is an interesting turn of events," he drawled.

She seemed flustered and shrugged. "Who knew that Sal would show up with Vicki?"

"Since this is a sports bar, and he's a sports agent, not so far-fetched. Besides, it's not what I'm talking about, hot lips."

"I like *sweet pea* better," she responded distractedly. "Anyway, it seemed like a good idea at the time."

"I doubt thinking entered into it. Reacting is more like it."

"Well, making it seem as if we were involved was an easy shortcut answer to what we were doing in a bar together."

"How about the truth, instead?"

"Not nearly as satisfying."

"You got me there," he conceded.

They continued to stare at each other. She was inches away, emanating a palpable feminine energy.

"You know they're going to tell people," he remarked. "The news is too good not to share."

She looked worried. "I know."

He tilted his head, contemplating her.

"We'll have to let people wonder, and the gossip will fizzle out in time."

He shook his head. "Not nearly as satisfying."

She gazed at him quizzically. "As what?"

"As making it seem as if we really are a couple."

"What?"

Her voice came out as a high-pitched squeak, and he had to smile.

"Now that the cat is out of the bag, we'll need to keep up the ruse for a while in order to keep the fallout from hurting both our reputations."

"But I just explained it'll fizz—"

"Not fast enough. People are going to conclude we were trying to get back at our exes."

She looked stung, but then her expression became resolute. "All right, but we keep up the charade only until the fund-raiser. That should be enough time for this to pass out of public conversation."

He thought she was deluding herself about that last part, but he let it go. "Sal must really mean something for you to have pulled that stunt."

He wasn't jealous, just curious, he told himself.

She shook her head. "No, it's more about being dumped for someone who looked like a better bet."

"Vicki?"

"I can't believe you dated her," she huffed.

"Hey, you're the one who went so far as to get engaged—" he jerked his thumb to indicate the back of the bar "—to *that*."

"The correct pronoun is *him*. *To him*," she responded.

"Maybe for school, but not in hockey."

"Why do men—athletes—date women like Vicki?"

He flashed his teeth. "Because we can."

"Sal thinks he can, too."

He picked up his beer bottle and saluted her with it before taking a swig. "After that kiss, I'd say our relationship now qualifies as having a *status*."

Her eyes widened as the truth of his words sank in.

She was an intriguing mix, with the power to blindside him more than any offensive player on the ice. Back in high school and now.

And things were only going to get more interesting since she'd just handed him a plum excuse for continuing to see her...

Seven

He was in heaven.

A beautiful woman had just opened the door to her apartment. And delicious aromas wafted toward him.

Marisa, however, looked shocked to see him.

"What are you doing here?" she demanded.

She was wearing a white tee and a red-and-black apron with an abundance of frills. She had bare legs, and a ridiculous pair of mule slippers with feathers on them showed off her red pedicure.

His body tightened.

Hey, if she wanted to role-play, he was all for it. She could be a sexy domestic goddess, and he could be the guy who knocked on the door and…obliged her.

She was still staring at him. Devoid of any makeup, she looked fresh-faced and casual.

"What are you doing here?" she asked again.

He thought fast. "Is that any way to greet your newest—" What was the status of their relationship anyway? "Love interest?"

"We both know it isn't real!"

"It's real," he countered, "but temporary."

She looked unconvinced.

Ever since their encounter at the Puck & Shoot late last week, he'd been searching for another way to see her again. He'd decided the direct approach was the only and best option this time.

"People will expect me to drop in on my girlfriend." He arched an eyebrow and added pointedly, "And at least know what her place looks like."

She leaned against the door. "Our relationship isn't genuine."

"Everyone seems to think it is."

"We're the only two people that matter."

"How real did that kiss in the bar feel to you?" He wasn't sure how far the news had traveled—he hadn't gotten any inquisitive phone calls from his family *yet*—but sooner or later there was bound to be gossip. Sal and Vicki weren't the only witnesses to the kiss at the Puck & Shoot.

Marisa's brows drew together. "Shouldn't you be insulted that I used you for an ulterior motive?"

He shrugged. "I don't feel objectified. If a beautiful woman wants to jump my bones, she'll get no argument from me."

She tilted her head. "Why am I not surprised you wouldn't put up a fight?"

He gave a lazy smile, but he didn't miss the quick once-over she gave him from under lowered lashes. Her gaze lingered on the faded jeans he wore under a rust-colored tee and light jacket. Apparently, he wasn't the only one fascinated by clothing's ability to hide— and reveal.

"You're persistent."

"Is it working?"

Sighing, she stepped aside, and he made it over the threshold.

She locked the door behind him, and then touched her

hair, which was pulled willy-nilly into a messy knot at the back of her head. Strands escaped, including one that trailed along her nape.

He wanted to loosen the band that prevented her riotous curls from cascading down. There was a large mirror in a yellow scroll frame behind Marisa, so he got a great 360-degree view of her. Underneath the apron, she was wearing a pair of black exercise shorts that hugged a well-rounded rear end.

He needed divine assistance. "You look like you worked out or are about to."

He'd gone out on an early-morning run, but Marisa seemed to prefer to exercise after her school day was finished.

She looked uncomfortable. "I'm trying to get in shape."

She had a fabulous body as far as he was concerned. Her shape was more than fine. Still, if she wanted to exercise, he knew how they could get a workout in bed...

She wet her lips and turned. "Come on in."

He followed her from the foyer and down the hallway, deeper into the apartment.

"It's a prewar building, so this condo has a traditional layout. No open floor plan, like those renovated old factory buildings that you might be used to."

"Something smells delicious." *And someone looked delectable, too.* It was only four-thirty, but maybe Marisa liked to eat early. There was a living room off the hall, done in a flower motif—from plum-colored drapes to a damask armchair covered by a rose throw.

"Parent-teacher conferences are tomorrow night. The school usually has catered fare for the staff, but I got a request to bring my eggplant parmigiana."

They passed two bedrooms, but only the second looked occupied. It had aqua walls offset by white wicker furniture and a white counterpane. There was a mirrored dresser, and a vanity framed by floor-length window treatments.

At the end of the hall, they reached a bright but dated kitchen. The aromas stimulated his taste buds. If she'd been set on seducing him, she couldn't have planned it better.

"I didn't know you were going to show up," she said, as if addressing his private thoughts. "I was mixing the ingredients for cupcakes."

He was going down...but he adopted a solemn expression. "I understand. You're cooking for others."

She gave him a sidelong look. "Well, I did make an extra pan of the eggplant parmigiana to keep around. Would you like some? I just removed it from the oven."

"I'd love some," he said with heartfelt fervor.

Eggplant parmigiana was one of his favorite dishes, but ever since he'd moved out of his parents' house, he didn't often get a home-cooked meal. His specialty was grilling, not frying vegetables and creating elaborate baked dishes. His pasta came prepared from the gourmet market these days.

As Marisa retrieved a spatula, he spied an ancient-looking KitchenAid mixer on her countertop, right next to the fixings for cupcakes.

"Your mixer looks like it's seen better days."

"You mean Kathy?"

"You named your mixer." He was careful to keep his tone neutral.

She adjusted a baking pan on the range with an oven mitt and then glanced at him over her shoulder. "It belonged to my grandmother. It's an heirloom, so it gets a name. In fact, *Nonna* let me name it when I was six. Kathy KitchenAid."

He watched her cut a piece of the eggplant parmigiana for him. Then he hooked his jacket over the back of a chair and took a seat at the well-worn kitchen table. Moments later Marisa set a steaming plate before him and handed him a fork.

The mozzarella was still oozing, and the breaded eggplant peeked out in thin layers—like a delicate *mille fiori* pastry.

He swallowed.

"Would you like a drink?" she asked.

He doubted she had beer on hand. "Water would be fine, thanks."

As Marisa walked to the fridge, he dug in with his fork and took his first bite. Her eggplant parmigiana went down smooth, hot and savory. *Fantastic.*

Apparently, Marisa could cook in the same way that Wayne Gretzky could play hockey.

Cole was four bites in and well on his way to demolishing her baked confection when she returned with a glass of water.

"Not sparkling water," she said apologetically, setting down a tumbler, "but filtered from the tap."

He filched a napkin from the stack on the table, wiped his mouth and then took a swallow.

He was here to seduce her, but she was enthralling him with her culinary skills. Her dish was sublime, and he'd do anything for a repeat of that kiss in the bar. "Marisa, you make an eggplant parmigiana that can reduce grown men to a drool and whimper."

She lowered her shoulders, and her mouth curved. "Don't the Serenghettis have a family recipe?"

"This may be even better, but don't tell my mother."

"I'm sure it's been decades since your mother tried to bring men to their knees. But I'm also certain she wouldn't mind if it was her eggplant parmigiana that did the trick."

"Yeah, she takes pride in her cooking." The truth was that while Camilla Serenghetti used food to lure her sons home, she was a force to be reckoned with in other ways, as well.

Marisa touched her hair. "I'll let you finish your food. I'll, um, be back in a few minutes."

"Sure." Moments later he heard a door click.

Cole finished the food before him, savoring every bite.

When he was done, he got up and deposited his plate and glass in the sink—because if there was one thing Camilla Serenghetti had drilled into her sons, it was how to be polite and pick up after yourself.

Then he looked around and surveyed Marisa's place. It was unsporting of him, but he was willing to use any advantage to get to know more of her. Besides, he was curious about how she lived.

Walking out of the kitchen, he retraced his steps in the hallway. Marisa's bedroom door was closed. Beyond it, he entered the large living room. One corner held a desk, a bookcase and a screen that could be used to shield the nook from the rest of the room. A rolled-arm sofa upholstered in a cream-and-light-green stripe served as a counterpoint to the dominant flower motif. There were also several small tables that looked as if they could be hand-me-down family pieces—sturdy but with decades under their scarred chestnut tops.

From a builder's perspective, Marisa had done a good job sprucing up her prewar apartment without undertaking a major renovation. It was neat, cozy and feminine.

He walked over to a built-in bookshelf dotted with framed photos and found himself staring at a picture of Marisa the way she had looked in her high school days. She was laughing as she leaned against the railing of a pier. Wearing jeans and a sweatshirt, she appeared more relaxed and carefree than she'd been while roaming the halls at Pershing. With a sudden clenching of the gut, Cole wondered whether the photo had been snapped before or after the debacle of their senior year...

He glanced down at the books lining a shelf below eye level. Crouching, he tilted his head to read the titles. *Pleasing Your Man, Losing the Last 5 Lbs., The Infidelity Recovery Plan,* and last but not least, *Bad Boys and the Women Who Shouldn't Need Them*.

It didn't take a genius to make sense of the titles, especially since the final one seemed to be addressed to him personally.

Cole straightened. He'd never have guessed everything going on behind the facade of the normally reserved and occasionally fiery Marisa Danieli. He also couldn't believe his high school Lolita—edible as a sugared doughnut—saw herself as insufficiently sexy. Had ordering the Cobb salad at their dinner been about being thinner and more attractive? What about her exercise routine?

And what kind of jerk had she been engaged to? For sure, she'd had her ego bruised by Sal Piazza's horn-dog behavior. But if she thought Sal had strayed because she wasn't sexy enough, she was marching her feathered mules down the wrong school corridor. If Marisa could glimpse *his* fantasies lately, Cole was sure she'd overheat rather than doubt her sex appeal. He could happily lose his mind exploring her lush curves.

Hearing a sound behind him, he straightened and turned in time to see Marisa walk into the room, hair down and brushing her shoulders. "You've got an interesting collection of books."

Marisa's gaze moved from him to the bookcase, and she looked embarrassed.

"Sal wants to imitate the athletes that he represents," he said without preamble. "Sure he'd like to get his clients what they wish for, but he also wants to be them. That's why he wanted to bag Vicki. It wasn't about you."

"So don't take it personally?" she quipped.

"Those who can, do, and those who can't become sports agents instead," he responded without answering her directly.

"Like that saying about those who can, do, and those who can't, teach?" she parried. "Teaching is one of the hardest—"

"—jobs in the world," he finished for her. "I know. I was

one of those problem students who got himself suspended, remember?"

After a moment, she sighed. "Those who can't become sports agents, and those who can't become teachers. So I guess Sal and I were perfectly matched."

He sauntered toward her, shaking his head. "I'm going to have to detox you."

"Oh no, you don't." She sidestepped him. "You come in and eat my food and read my books, and I still don't know why you're here."

"Don't you?"

"No, I don't!"

"You're a great cook," he said, trying a more subtle maneuver. "I got a sample today, and a couple of your students at the rink last week mentioned it. The kids also said you've brought your homemade dishes to school functions in the past."

She looked surprised and then embarrassed. "And now you have a burning desire for eggplant parmigiana?"

He let the word *desire* hang there between them.

"Everything I know I learned from my mother," she added after a moment.

"Great. My mother has a cooking show on a local cable channel. She's always looking for guests."

Marisa held up her hands. "I don't like where this is heading."

He flashed his teeth. "Oh yes, you do." He was becoming a pro at the tit-for-tat game that they had going on between them. "If I'm going to do the rooster strut at Pershing's big party, then you can cluck your way through a televised cooking show. Fair is fair."

"We already struck our bargain," she countered. "You want to renegotiate now? You're already getting the construction job for the gym, no questions asked."

"I'm prepared to offer something in return for your appearance under bright studio lights," he said nobly.

"And that would be?"

"I'll expand my offer from informal coaching to running that hockey clinic that you want."

She looked astonished. As if he could never tempt her to appear on TV—but he had.

He was willing to coach the kids without receiving anything in return, but he wasn't going to tell her that. He'd created another opportunity to interact with Marisa, and she was going to find it hard to say no. He was brilliant.

"It's a big investment of time. I'd need a good recipe, and then I'd have to prep for the show. The hair and makeup alone will take two or three hours..."

His lips inched upward. "You're starting to sound like I did about the hockey clinic."

"My mother is the real cook in the family," she protested.

"Great. We'll get her involved, too. It'll take the pressure off you."

"No!" She shook her head. "How did we get here? I haven't even agreed to be a part of this crazy plan."

"We'll do a giveaway." He warmed to his subject. "A set of Stanhope Department Store's own stainless-steel cookware that retails for hundreds of dollars. You said your mother was the new housewares buyer, right? It'll be great promo. Move over, Oprah."

He was beyond brilliant.

"I'm busy right now. Parent-teacher conferences. The fund-raiser. The end of the school year... And I'm painting my kitchen cabinets before the weather gets hot because I don't have central air in this condo."

He glanced around them. "Yeah, you've got a retro vibe going."

"I like to call it modern vintage."

He wasn't familiar with the style but he was appreciating Marisa's '50s-style apron, and he had another great idea. "I'll help with the painting."

"You don't need to help. We're not dating."

He shrugged. "This isn't dating. This is an exchange of favors."

"Is that what you called your involvement with Vicki?" she parried. "An exchange of favors?"

He gave a semblance of a smile. "Oh, sweet pea, you're asking for it. Detox, it is."

"And you're going to provide the cure?" she scoffed. "It's pretty clear you're a womanizer."

"I enjoy women, yes. Therapy may be needed later, but right now I'm hung up on teachers with attitude."

"I know a great therapist," she said, her voice all sugar.

"And I've got a better idea for how to deal with our hang-ups."

She parted her lips, but before she could answer him, he pulled her into his arms and captured her mouth.

Marisa stilled, and then she kissed Cole back. She slid her arms around his neck, and her fingers threaded into his hair. He tasted of her baking, but underneath was the unmistakable scent of pure male.

One second she'd been fighting her attraction to him, and the next she'd been overwhelmed by it.

He held her firmly as his tongue stroked around hers. She pressed into him, her breasts yielding, and she felt the hard bulge of his arousal. Her mind clouded, waves of sensation washing over her.

Cole ended the kiss, and she moaned. But he trailed his lips down the side of her throat and then moved back up to suck on her earlobe. His breath next to her ear sent shivers chasing through her. Her breasts, and the most sensitive spot between her legs, felt heavy with need.

She tugged Cole back for another searing kiss. She felt the arm of the sofa behind her and realized that with one small tip, they could fall onto it.

He lifted his mouth from hers. "Tell me to leave now. Otherwise, this is going to end up where I want."

"And where would that be?"

He looked down at her clothes. "I'll be the guy who satisfies your inner domestic goddess."

Wow. His words served to arouse her further.

He gave a slow-burn smile and nodded at her ruffly apron. "I couldn't have dreamed of a sexier get-up if I tried."

"It's meant for cooking," she protested.

"Among other things." His hands settled on her waist, and he rocked against her as he bent and nuzzled her neck. "You didn't tell me to leave."

She couldn't. She tried to force the words, but they wouldn't come.

"You're beautiful and sexy and alluring. I want to be inside you, pleasing us both until you're calling out my name again and again…"

Oh. My. Sweet. Heaven. His words set her on fire. With Sal, sex had always been perfunctory. He'd never given her words…

Cole cupped her buttocks and lifted her, pressing her against him.

She cradled his face and kissed him again.

"Bed," he said thickly, "though the sofa would work, too."

"Mmm," she mumbled.

He must have taken her response for a yes because the next thing she knew, she perched on the back edge of the sofa.

Cole covered one of her breasts with his hand. He shaped and molded the sensitized mound and its taut peak. Then he trailed moist kisses down her throat and along her collarbone.

Releasing her breast, he tugged at the hem of her tee. She helped him, and then they both worked to slide the top over her head.

Cole's gaze settled on her chest, and she tried not to squirm. She'd always been self-conscious about her size.

"You're even more beautiful than I remembered," he breathed.

Then he bent his head and drew one tight bud into his mouth, bra and all, sucking her as if enraptured.

Oh. Oh. Oh. She didn't think she was going to last. She needed Cole now. She ached for him, already halfway to release even though he'd only put his mouth on her.

When he lifted his head, he blew against her breast, and if possible, her nipple grew tighter against its thin and wet covering. Marisa nearly came out of her skin.

Cole unclasped her bra and pulled it off her. He ducked his head and took her breast deep into his mouth, laving her with his tongue and then swirling it around her nipple.

Marisa pulled his head close. Sal had never given her body this level of attentiveness while Cole acted as if he had all the time in the world. Fifteen years ago she'd held Cole to her breast like this. But now he was all man—strong, capable and sure of himself. The scar across his cheek was pulled taught, and the stubble on his face was a gentle abrasion against her skin.

She gripped his head as he transferred his attention to her other breast. Her head fell back, and her eyes fluttered closed. With the world shut out, only Cole and his touch existed, with an even greater intensity than before.

Cole lifted his head, and his breath hissed out. "What do you want, Marisa?"

She opened her eyes to meet his. "You know."

"I want to hear you say it."

"You. I want you."

A look of satisfaction crossed his face. "Some things don't change, sweet pea. I can't keep my hands off you, either."

In response, she guided his hands back to her breasts, where they could both feel her racing heart.

"Marisa, Marisa," he muttered.

He was all appreciation, and it was like a salve to her

soul. She'd never felt like a goddess before, domestic or otherwise.

He gave her a gentle nudge, and she slid off the back edge of the sofa and onto the seat cushions, her legs dangling off one arm. Her mules hit the carpet with one muffled thud after another.

Cole pushed up her apron and then pulled off her biker shorts with one fluid movement. He stroked up her thigh, his calluses a shivery roughness against her skin—reminding her that he had a physical job as well as an office one.

"Ah, Marisa." Pushing aside her underwear, he pressed his thumb against her most sensitive spot while his finger probed and then slipped inside her.

She gasped. "What are you doing?"

"What does it seem like I'm doing?" he murmured, his thumb sweeping and pressing in a rhythm that made her tighten unbearably. "I'm going to make you breathless, sweet pea."

"Make me?"

It was the last thing she said before she gave herself up to sensation. Within moments she convulsed around him, her hips bucking. It was an orgasm born of a forbidden longing that had been brewing for fifteen years.

When she subsided, she realized Cole had satisfied her, but not himself. Her gaze connected with his, and she took in the intense expression stamped there.

"Yes," he said huskily. "It's going to be even better than before."

Better than before.

Marisa heard a knock at the front door, but in her sexual haze, it took her a moment to react. Then she froze.

Cole stilled, as well, apparently having heard the same thing.

There was the distinct sound of a key being slipped into the front door and the lock turning.

Marisa's eyes widened and fixed on Cole's.

In the next instant she was scrambling off the sofa—swinging her legs down and around and bolting to her feet.

Cole tossed her the biker shorts, but she had no time to do anything but stuff them under a pillow as she brushed down her apron.

"Marisa?" Serafina called. "Hello?"

Her cousin appeared in the entrance to the living room, and Marisa thought the whole situation could take the prize for *Most Awkward Situation in One's Own Home*.

Serafina blinked. "Oh...hello."

Marisa prayed her face didn't betray her. "Um, hi, Sera. I didn't know you were going to stop by."

"I overlooked a couple of small things when I moved out." Sera shrugged. "Since I still had the emergency key to the apartment, I thought it would be no problem if I showed up on my way to work. I did knock."

It was as if they were both pretending there wasn't a six-foot-plus sexy guy standing in the corner of her living room.

Marisa glanced at Cole, who was shielded by the high back of an armchair. She had no such cover. She hoped her apron was enough to disguise the fact that she was wearing only underwear. "Sera, you know Cole Serenghetti, don't you?"

Her cousin's gaze moved to Cole. "I thought I recognized you."

"Nice to meet one of Marisa's relatives."

Sera nodded. "I'm going to...go search the kitchen for my small blender."

"Sure, go right ahead," Marisa chirped. "I thought I saw it in there."

When her cousin turned and left, Marisa breathed a sigh of relief. Cole tossed the biker shorts at her, and she slipped into them while avoiding his eyes.

"I'll let myself out," he announced wryly.

"We shouldn't have done this," she blurted. *Nothing had*

changed. She was as easy a conquest for him as she'd always been. Willing to stop, drop and roll anytime, anywhere.

Cole ran a hand through his hair. "Get rid of the books on the shelf. You don't need them."

Marisa stared at him. It was a typical understated and sardonic Cole Serenghetti compliment. She wasn't sure whether to hug it close, or run for cover.

"I'll let you know the timing for the television show." Giving her one last significant look, Cole strode from the room.

Moments later Marisa heard her front door open and close for the second time. Taking a deep breath, she walked toward the back of the apartment. She found Serafina in the kitchen, opening and closing cabinets.

"I know that little handheld blender and juicer is in here somewhere…"

"Have you tried the cabinet above the stove?"

Serafina turned and gave her a once-over. "Well, you look fit for company again. At least the nonmale version."

"Cole came over because we had things to…discuss about the fund-raiser. And because he's looking for a couple of guests for his mother's cooking show, and I'm trying to get him to run a hockey clinic for the kids." *And I kissed him at the Puck & Shoot, and I hope the news doesn't spread…or hasn't already to you.* Fortunately, since she'd never been to the Puck & Shoot before last week, there was no reason for anyone to recognize her as Sera's cousin and make a connection.

Her cousin tilted her head. "And those, uh, discussions happened with your pants off?"

Marisa flushed. *Busted.*

Serafina lifted her eyebrows. "He's hot, for sure. And at least he doesn't have his brother's reputation for going through women as if he needs to spread the love."

"I—"

"You need a bodyguard. You obviously can't be trusted,

or he can't—or the both of you. I'm not sure which it is. It looks like he's forgiven you for high school and then some."

"It's not what you think." *It was pretend—or some of it was.* Sera seemingly hadn't gotten the bulletin yet that Marisa had kissed Cole at the Puck & Shoot, or her cousin would have mentioned it already.

"Wow, and we've descended into cliché, too. Give me a sec—I need to wrap my mind around this one. Maybe a bodyguard and a therapist? I can hunt up recommendations for you."

Marisa sighed. "C'mon, Sera."

"Well, you two have definitely got a thing for one another."

"We don't, really." The denial sounded weak, even to her own ears. *Ugh.*

"He wants you to appear on his mother's cooking show? That's serious."

"It's not as if I'm showing up as a member of the family."

"Just be careful. You two have a complicated past."

"I know."

"Great. Then that's settled." Sera gave an exaggerated sigh of relief. "Phew!"

"There's one tiny wrinkle."

Her cousin stilled. "Oh?"

"We're pretending to be a couple."

Sera's eyes widened. "That's not a wrinkle. That's a—"

"Really. We're faking it."

Sera jerked her thumb in the direction of the living room. "So you two were pretending to go at it in there?"

"No, yes…I mean, our relationship is fake!"

She filled in her cousin on what had happened at the Puck & Shoot, ending with her pact with Cole not to correct the perception that they were an item, at least until the Pershing Shines Bright benefit. Even as she told her story to Sera, Marisa admitted to herself that she had to try harder not to blur the line between reality and make-believe.

When she finished, Sera regarded her for an instant, head tilted to the side. "I wouldn't want to see you get hurt again."

"I'm not in high school anymore."

"No, but you still work there, and Cole has had another fifteen years to hone his lady-killer skills. Plus, he's admitted he wished things had turned out differently between you at Pershing."

"I told him I couldn't get involved. He knows the Danieli family history with professional athletes."

"If that's the reason you're hiding behind, go better. Cole is retired from pro hockey."

"Yes, but running the family construction business is a temporary sideline for him." She didn't want anything to do with someone who still had his hand in pro sports. She's made a good life for herself, right here in Welsdale.

"Well, you could become a temporary sideline to the temporary sideline. There's your reason to be wary."

Marisa threw up her hands. "You and Jordan should try Scrabble. Word play is your thing."

"What?"

"Never mind."

Eight

Marisa had done hard things in her life. Growing up, she'd sometimes been two short steps from foraging in a trash bin for food. But meeting Cole's family on the set of his mother's show, amid swirling rumors of their new status as a couple, trumped stealing away with a supermarket's barely expired eggs, in her opinion.

She hoped Cole had a good story to tell everybody about how they'd started dating.

"Relax," Cole said, giving her a quick peck on the cheek as she stepped onto the set. "It's fine."

"Then why is Jordan giving me a knowing look?" she responded sotto voce, nodding to where Jordan occupied an empty seat where the audience normally sat.

Cole caught his brother's bemused expression. "This situation is rife for humor, and he knows it." He frowned at Jordan, who gave a jaunty little wave in response. "Don't worry, I'll pound the jokes out of him in the ring next week."

Marisa turned away. "I'm going home. I can't do this."

Cole took hold of her arm. "Oh yes, you can."

"Cole, introduce me, please!"

Marisa swung back in time to see Camilla Serenghetti approaching them.

Too late.

Anyone could have guessed this was Cole's mother. Mother and son shared similar coloring and had the same eyes. Marisa had never had an opportunity to meet Cole's parents while she'd been at Pershing, but she'd glimpsed them in the stands at hockey games.

"Either she's the forgive-and-forget kind," she murmured to Cole, "or she's so thankful to see you in a relationship, she's willing to overlook anything."

Cole grinned. "Draw your own conclusions, sweet pea."

"Let's see, Italian mother, no grandkids..." Marisa was too familiar with the dynamics from her own family. "I choose the latter."

"She doesn't know about your part in my suspension," Cole replied in a low voice. "I did a good job of keeping her in the dark about my inner life as a teenager."

Marisa cast him a sidelong look. "So she doesn't know we—"

"—tested out the therapeutic properties of the theater department's couch?"

Cole arched a brow, and she flushed.

Cole shook his head. "No."

"Still," Marisa whispered back, "I know, and it's enough."

Cole's poor mother. First, Marisa had gotten her son suspended. And now she'd drafted him to star in a faux relationship. She could barely keep herself from cringing.

"Watch this," Cole said.

Marisa looked at him questioningly as he bestowed a broad smile on his mother.

"Mom, meet Marisa. She makes an eggplant parmigiana that rivals yours."

Marisa took a deep breath. *Well.* "I learned everything from my mother."

Camilla clapped. "Wonderful. I'm so glad she's comin' on my program, too."

"She should be here any minute. And my mother has seen your show, Mrs. Serenghetti. In fact, both she and I have watched numerous episodes."

She was a glutton for punishment. She avoided Cole's eyes, but heat stained her cheeks. She was a pushover for cooking shows. The fact that the host of this one was Cole Serenghetti's mother was beside the point. At least that was her story, and she was sticking to it. She purposely hadn't sought out news of Cole over the years, but when she'd stumbled upon an episode of *Flavors of Italy* more than a year ago, she'd been hooked.

"Please, call me Camilla. I've been trying to get Cole and Jordan to come back on the show for a long time."

Marisa looked inquiringly at Cole. "You don't want to be on your mother's show again?"

He'd been on the program at least once—how had she missed that episode? It must have been one of the early ones. She should be glad she missed it, so why did she feel disappointed?

Cole raised an eyebrow. "I can only work on saving one parent at a time."

Oh right—the construction company. Marisa could relate—how often had she worried about her mother? Family ties could bind, but they also had the potential to choke.

"You live in Welsdale, Marisa?" Camilla asked.

"Yes, I have my own condo on Chestnut Street."

Camilla looked perplexed. "You live alone?"

"My cousin Serafina was my roommate until recently."

Cole's mother appeared slightly mollified. "Well, is something."

"My mother thinks living alone is wrong," Cole said drolly. "We had lots of relatives on extended stays with us when I was growing up. You could say my mother never got out of the hotel business, even after marriage."

"Cole, don't be fresh."

"What? I'm wrong?"

"Your cousin Allegra is coming to visit with her family this fall."

"And I rest my case," Cole said.

Camilla adopted a slightly wounded look. "My children moved out. There's room."

Marisa was saved from saying anything, however, by the arrival of her own mother.

The family party was just getting started... Jordan Serenghetti, for one, had graduated from looking entertained to outright amused.

Donna Casale glanced around the set and then walked to where Marisa was standing with Cole and Camilla Serenghetti. Scanning the empty audience chairs, she said, "I must be early. There's hardly anyone here. Oh well, at least we can nab the best seats!"

Marisa stepped forward. "Actually, Mom, there isn't going to be an audience." Unless you counted Jordan's avid spectating. "This isn't a taping."

Donna looked confused.

"We're not going to be part of the audience, we're going to be guests on the show." She added weakly, "Surprise!"

Jordan guffawed.

Marisa fixed a smile on her face, willing her mother to go along. She hadn't said anything about their guest appearance because she'd wanted to avoid too many questions. Plus, she figured the element of surprise would work to her advantage because her mother wouldn't have a chance to get intimidated and say no.

Donna's eyes widened. "We're going to be on TV?"

Marisa grabbed her hand. "Yes! Isn't it great?" She needed all the enthusiasm she could muster in order to keep nerves at bay. "Let me introduce you to Camilla Serenghetti...and her sons."

Introductions were made, and Marisa was relieved that

everyone seemed to relax a little. Her mother actually started to appear happy at the prospect of making an appearance on a program that she watched.

Marisa cleared her throat. "And Cole has this great idea that we can do a giveaway on air as an advertisement for Stanhope Department Stores. What do you think, Mom?"

Her mother looked at her speculatively and then smiled. "I'll bring it up with management at work, but I'm sure they'll be thrilled."

Marisa lowered her shoulders, but Cole seemed bemused.

"You didn't tell your mother that she was about to become a star?" he murmured.

"Stop it," she responded in a low voice.

"Mmm, interesting. The first time you've asked me to stop." The sexual suggestion in his voice was unmistakable. "The words never crossed your lips in the storage room, or at the bar…or in your apartment, come to think of it."

"St—" She caught herself and compressed her mouth. "You're enjoying this."

"There are a lot of things I enjoy…doing with you."

Marisa felt a wave of awareness swamp her. Fortunately, their mothers appeared to be deep in their own conversation, because she could barely look at Cole. She grew hot at the memory of what they had done on her couch, which she'd now taken to referring to as Couch #2—never to be confused with the chintzy Couch #1 that still resided at the Pershing School. Whenever the student theater group had used #1 in a play over the years, Marisa could hardly keep her mind on the performance.

And right now Cole looked primed and ready for another round. Except she wasn't about to defile his mother's TV set sofa, no matter how hungry and frustrated Cole was.

She suppressed a giggle that welled up from nowhere and forced her mind back to the topic at hand. Camilla and her mother were engaged in a brisk discussion about whether to make a *tiella* or a *calzone di cipolla* on the air. The potato-

and-mussel casserole and the onion pie were both dishes of Puglia, the Italian region of Marisa's ancestors.

"The calzone is a traditional Christmas recipe," Donna said. "Like plum pudding in England. And since this show is going to air in the spring, I think the *tiella* would be better."

Marisa had told her mother to bring a couple of recipes along today, and had discussed them with her in advance. Her little white lie had been that the show planned to enter audience members in a raffle giveaway if they brought along a recipe.

"Donna, *cara, siamo d'accordo!*"

Cole's mother's enthusiasm and agreement were apparent no matter what the language spoken. Still... *Donna, cara*? When had her mother and Cole's progressed to being bosom buddies?

"You will be *perfetto* on the show, Donna. You and the *bellissima* Marisa."

Marisa felt Cole lean close.

"I'm surprised she isn't suggesting you become a bottle blonde," he murmured sardonically, "like the rest of the hostesses on Italian television."

"This is not an Italian show, Cole!" His mother fixed him with a look that said she'd overheard. "My hair is brown, and I speak English."

"Some people would debate the second part."

"Uh-oh," Jordan singsonged from his seat in the front row. "Cole's gonna be barred from the lasagna dinners."

"Exactly what is your role here?" Cole shot back.

Jordan grinned. "Comic relief. And Mom invited me." He looked around. "Hey, where's the popcorn? The drama's been good up to now, but the concessions leave something to be desired."

Cole ignored his brother and turned toward Marisa and her mother. "What my mother means is that she thinks Mrs. Casale has the personality for television. It's important to engage the audience on the small screen."

"Yes," Camilla agreed. "And dress in bold *colori* but not too much zigzag or *fiori*."

"Chill on the patterns," Jordan piped up.

"Makeup—more is better."

"I'm so glad we're doing this," Donna remarked with enthusiasm. "Marisa has loved to cook and bake since she was a little girl."

"Cole loved to eat," Camilla confided.

"Marisa was born a preemie, so I spent the first few months making sure she put on weight!"

Marisa bit her lip. "Oh, Mom, not that story again." Her mother had a terrifying habit of bringing it up in public situations.

"Scrappy, that's what I've always called her."

"Cole was nine pounds. Was a long labor," Camilla put in.

"Why doesn't anyone think of sharing those types of details on a date?" Cole quipped to Marisa.

"Maybe because you're too busy admiring your date's inner domestic goddess?" she shot back in a low voice before she could stop herself.

Cole gave her a half-lidded look. "Yeah…there's that distraction."

"Your mother is hilarious," she sidestepped.

"Larger than life. It makes her perfect for television."

As if on cue, his mother interjected, "Marisa, *bella*, you will come to the party in two weeks, *si*?"

What? What party?

"Ah…yes." She gave the only answer she could with three pairs of Serenghetti eyes on her.

"I ask your mother already, but she's going to a wedding tha' day."

"Ted's cousin's daughter is getting married," Donna explained in response to Marisa's inquiring look.

"Right." How could she forget? And now it seemed as if she was going to be flying solo with the Serenghettis.

"*Grazie per l'invito*, Camilla," Donna said. "Another time."

"Your mother speaks Italian?" Cole asked.

"She grew up in an Italian-speaking household," Marisa responded distractedly because she was still dwelling on the invite to the Serenghettis' domain.

Camilla perked up. "Cole knows Italian. We did *vacanze in Italia* when he was young."

Marisa figured that explained why Cole hadn't been in her Italian classes at Pershing.

"You speak *italiano*, Marisa?"

"*Abbastanza.*"

Camilla clasped her hands together, and shot a glance at her eldest son. "Enough. Wonderful."

Marisa could swear her expression said *she's perfetto*, but Cole just looked droll.

Fortunately for her, the show's producers interrupted at that point, and the conversation veered in another direction. But once the details of their guest appearance had been hammered out—and the appropriate forms and releases signed for the show's producers—Marisa moved toward the exit.

Unfortunately, Cole stood between her and the door.

"What are you doing this weekend?" he asked without preamble.

"Why do you ask?" she hedged, even though they weren't within earshot of Jordan or their mothers, who remained engrossed in conversation on the studio's stage.

"This weekend I'm having the first meeting of that hockey clinic that we talked about," he said. "But I prefer the rest of my time not be spent with a bunch of teenagers."

"You'd never make it as a teacher."

"I think we've established that," he responded drily. "But I pegged you for one who'd be teaching economics."

"After high school, I knew I'd never really understand economics."

"You seemed to be doing okay to me."

"Right. As if you were in a good position to judge."

He smiled. "We were both distracted back then, but I'm not going to apologize for being a major diversion for you. Speaking of which, how about dinner at Agosto at seven this Saturday?"

"I'm painting my kitchen cabinets."

"You're kidding."

She shook her head.

"I've been turned down for dates before—"

She feigned astonishment.

"—but never because someone needed to paint the kitchen cabinets."

"This relationship has been a land of firsts." She could have bitten her tongue. Of all the firsts, him being her *first* lover was at the top of the list. And from his expression, the thought had hit him, too.

"You, me, a can of paint. I can't think of a kinkier combination."

She rolled her eyes even as she tingled at his words. He'd switched gears smoothly from suggesting dinner at a fine restaurant…to making painting seem adventurous.

"I hope you chose a red-hot shade. Make Me Magenta. Or Kiss & Cuddle Coral."

"You know, I'd never thought of the building business as sexy, but now I see how wrong I've been. Just buying paint must leave you breathless!"

A slow smile spread across his face. "If you invite me over, you can find out what else leaves me breathless."

"I was planning on painting the cabinets by myself."

He looked her over. "Why bother when you have a sexy construction guy to do it with?"

She was starting to feel hot again—and very, very breathless. Damn him. He knew what he was doing, but he was also keeping a straight face. "I don't have the money to hire someone. That's why I was planning to do it alone."

"For you, sweet pea, I come free."

"The kitchen cabinets are a little dreary," she said unnecessarily, trying to cool things down.

"Add color to your life."

She'd paint *him* red—he was definitely a red. "The cabinets are going to be yellow. Unblemished Sapphire Yellow."

He cut off a laugh. "I guess I shouldn't be surprised."

"I've already bought the paint supplies."

"Great. When do we start?"

"I start on Saturday morning." She hoped she sounded repressive enough.

"I'll be there at eight."

When Marisa opened the door to her apartment on Saturday morning, Cole was holding a container with coffee cups and assorted add-ins. He grasped a brown paper bag with his other hand.

"Doughnuts," he announced. "A construction industry morning tradition."

"Thank you," she said, taking the bag from him.

She stepped back so he could enter the apartment, and her heartbeat picked up. He was strong, solid and masculine. And yummy. *Forbidden, but yummy.* He looked great in paint-stained jeans, work boots and an open flannel shirt over a white tee.

By contrast, she'd dressed in a green tee and an old pair of gray sweats. She'd used a scrunchie to pull her hair back in a ponytail. With no makeup or jewelry, she hardly felt sexy—though she still itched with need at the sight of him.

"I'd show you to the kitchen, but we'll be working in there, not…eating." A sudden image flashed through her mind of Cole slipping his hands under her tee and up her midriff, moving ever closer to her breasts…

Wow, it was hot in here.

She led the way into the living room and then turned back toward him.

"Let me take the coffee from you," she said, intending to set the coffee carrier down on the wood tray that covered a rectangular ottoman.

Their fingers brushed, and her eyes flew up to meet his. They both stilled, and then he leaned in and touched her lips with his.

"You're welcome," he said in a low voice as he straightened.

"I thought we'd keep up the pretense about painting at least until nine." She set down the coffee and faced him again.

"Sex first thing in the morning is great," he responded, "and I've been saving it all for you."

"I thought sports guys abstained from sex before a big game in order to keep their edge." If he was going to expend a lot of effort today on painting, wasn't it a similar situation?

"Sweet pea, I don't play professionally anymore, and you'll never see a better painter after this," he responded with heartfelt enthusiasm.

She gave a nervous laugh—because he did make her tense. And aroused. And crazy. It was hard not to be thrilled with a guy who lusted after her even when she looked as if she was going to haul out the garbage. Even if her mind told her she shouldn't.

He stepped forward and cupped her face, his fingers threading into her hair and loosening her ponytail. Gazing at her mouth, he muttered, "You know, I used to steal glances at you when we were working on that presentation for economics class. Just for the sheer pleasure of looking at you."

"Really?" she breathed.

He nodded, and then gave her another light kiss.

When he straightened, she swallowed. "I could tell you were staring at me sometimes…I thought I had a food smudge or a blemish, or you were wondering why my face wasn't completely symmetrical—"

His eyes crinkled. "Marisa?"

"Yes?"

"Adolescent boys think about one thing, and it's not about looking in the bathroom mirror for hours and searching for flaws."

"Oh, and what do you think about?" she asked, even though she had a good idea.

"This."

He claimed her lips for a deeper kiss. He traced the seam of her mouth and then slipped inside. She breathed in his warm, male scent and then met his tongue, leaning into him. The power of the kiss seeped into her.

She followed his lead, meeting him again and again, until she was in a pleasant languor, her head swimming. When they broke apart, she bent her head, her forehead coming to rest against his lips.

He settled his hands on her waist and then slipped them under the bottom of her sweatshirt. He kneaded her flesh, caressing her back and rubbing up to her shoulder blades. With a deft move, he unclasped her bra and she spilled against him.

Raising his mouth a fraction from her forehead, he muttered, "Marisa."

"What?" she asked dreamily.

"I've fantasized about your breasts."

"Now?"

"Now. High school. Forever."

"Mmm."

He pulled the sweatshirt over her head, and she took out the scrunchie holding her hair, shaking her head to loosen the strands.

Gazing down at her, he said, "You still have the prettiest breasts I've ever seen."

"And on a schoolteacher, no less. Go figure," she joked.

"Luscious Lola. You live up to your nickname."

"What?"

He raised his eyes. "You didn't know? It's what the guys

in the locker room called you. But we couldn't agree on how big your breasts were because you had a habit of hugging books to your chest."

Her eyes widened. "You're kidding."

He gave her a teasing smile. "Nope. The nickname Luscious Lola was sort of tongue-in-cheek. The imaginations of teenage boys can outstrip reality." His look turned appreciative. "Not in this case, however."

"I didn't even know I existed in the jocks' locker room!"

"Oh, you existed, all right."

"You gave out nicknames?" She still couldn't believe it. She'd thought she'd been invisible in high school—well, at least until the end.

Cole shrugged.

"Well, you eventually found out how big my breasts were. But I couldn't figure out why you didn't broadcast the news…"

He sobered. "By that point, it was too heavy to share. I'd started thinking of you as my personal Lolita. The girl who slew me and led to my destruction."

"And now?" she asked, curious and a little wary, even as she adopted a tone of mock reproach. "Am I still just a sex object with big breasts?"

He looked into her eyes. "And now you're the woman I've been fantasizing about. *Ti voglio.* I want to make love to you, Marisa."

When he held out his hand, she went weak and then put her hand in his. If she was honest with herself, she'd admit this moment had been inevitable ever since Cole had announced he'd help her paint. The last time he'd been in her apartment, they'd ended up tangled together on her living room couch until Sera's unexpected arrival. She could have done more to avert this moment if she'd wanted to, but in the secret recesses of her heart, she knew she'd always wanted to deal with the unfinished business between her and Cole.

Cole threw some pillows on the floor and tugged her

down to their makeshift bed, where they both kneeled and faced each other. He gently pulled her into his embrace, and then he kissed her, one arm anchored around her waist, the other caressing her breast.

Marisa moaned, her scruples evaporating. Cole's thumb toyed with her nipple, causing sensation to shoot through her and pool between her legs.

"Cole," she gasped, her fingers threading through his hair, "please."

"Please, what?" he asked gutturally.

"Now, more…"

"Yes."

She lay back against the pillows, and he pulled off his shirt and then tugged the white tee over his head.

Marisa sucked in a breath. He was *built*. Bigger and broader than in high school, but solid muscle nonetheless. He might have left the ice, but he seemed as toned and ready for action as ever. He had flat abs, and sculpted muscles outlined his upper arms. She'd gotten a partial look at Jimmy's Boxing Gym, but unclothed, he was even more spectacular.

He gazed at her with glittering promise. Then he grasped the waistband of her sweatpants and pulled them off, taking her panties, socks and canvas lace-ups with them.

Tossing her clothes aside, he moved back to her and stroked a hand down her thigh. He raised her leg, flexed her foot and placed a kiss on the delicate skin behind her knee. "You've got a fantastic figure, sweet pea. Made for loving."

She'd dreamed about this moment in the past. She'd wondered what would have happened if things had turned out differently—if her relationship with Cole had survived to become a real adult one.

For his part, Cole looked like a man who'd reached an oasis and wasn't going to hold back. He stood and pulled off his shoes and then stripped off the rest of his clothes. When she held out her arms, he came down beside her.

He claimed her mouth again, and she ran her hands over

his arms, feeling his muscles move and flex beneath her fingertips. His erection pressed against her, cradled between her thighs.

How many times after high school had she replayed their one time together? The truth was she'd never completely put him behind her.

When the kiss broke off, she touched his cheek. "You explained the knee injury that stopped your career with the Razors. But you never said how you got the scar."

Cole's look turned sardonic. "Simple. Another player's blade connected with my mug."

She frowned and then traced the long, white line bisecting the side of his face. "Have you ever thought of getting it fixed?"

"Nah...and have my good looks marred by cosmetic surgery?"

Impulsively leaning up, she trailed featherlight kisses along his scar. When she was finished, Cole looked as if he'd been undone.

"Ah, Marisa," he said gruffly. "That was...sweet."

"Women would die to have your nonchalant attitude about their physical appearance." She paused. "Women would die to have you, come to think of it."

He gave her a lopsided grin. "After our first time in high school, I used to think about ways to make the experience better the next time."

"You did?"

He nodded. "Yup. I still have a game plan filed away that I never got to use."

She sighed dreamily.

He stroked her arms. "Close your eyes, Marisa. Just feel."

When her eyes had fluttered closed, Cole began to massage her back, loosening her muscles and making her relax. Slowly, she came away from the edge of nervous arousal to something deeper and more soul-stirring.

Cole kissed her and then trailed his mouth down the column of her neck. He paused, blew on her nipples and then laved one with his tongue. When she jerked, he shushed her, gentling her with his hands. Then he drew her other breast into his mouth.

Awash in pleasure, Marisa threaded her hands in his hair, holding him. She felt fantasy merge with reality. Cole was here, making love to her. How many times had she dreamed about it? It was like her fantasies, but better in many ways… He was sure of himself, confident in his ability to please her. The full adult version of the teenager she had known.

"We'll never use a real bed," she murmured.

Cole stifled a laugh. "All in good time, including the kitchen, eventually."

She opened her eyes. "I cook in the kitchen."

"Me, too."

"Not that type of cooking."

"Ah, Marisa." He moved downward and kissed one inner thigh and then the other. Then he pressed his lips against her moist core. He found her with his mouth and caressed and swirled her with his tongue.

She moaned, and her hips rose, but Cole held her to him, his hands under her rear end.

She turned her head to muffle her moans against a pillow as sensation swamped her. But it was too much. Panting, she gave in, and let the world explode as she bucked against Cole's mouth.

Seconds later, spent, she collapsed back against their makeshift bed.

Cole came back up to face her. "It's not over until you're completely sexually satisfied."

Oh. "I need a moment." Her heart was racing, and she could still feel his arousal against her. "You have incredible staying power."

"In hockey and in business, it's about self-control. Like life, generally." He smiled, smoothing her hair. "But don't sell yourself short. You have wonderful stamina yourself."

"You've always had a lot of self-control around me." She knew she sounded wistful, but he'd been able to turn away from her so easily fifteen years ago...

"No, I don't," he corrected on a growl. "Let me show you."

Standing up, Cole withdrew a foil packet from the pocket of his jeans and sheathed himself. Tossing her a rueful grin, he said, "Wishful thinking, but I came prepared."

Marisa licked dry lips. With Sal, it had always been plain-vanilla sex—on a bed, at night and over quickly. She was unprepared for Cole's lustiness, though she'd be lying to herself if she said she didn't like it.

In the next moment Cole flipped her on her stomach and grasped her legs, spreading them as he pulled her to the edge of the pillows. He leaned forward, bracing himself over her, and his erection probed her entrance.

"You are so hot and slick," he breathed beside her ear. "So ready for me."

She felt him slide into her without any resistance and cried out at his possession, while Cole gave a labored groan behind her. He thrust into her once, twice, three times, and she called his name.

He set up a rhythm for them, pumping into her. "Marisa."

She could feel him tightening, and could tell he was close to finding his climax. She clamped down around him, and he cursed. Then they were both spiraling, the air filled with the sounds of their release.

She cried out as she crested on a wave of sensation so pure and beautiful—its power building for fifteen years— that tears stung her eyes.

After a moment, Cole slumped on top of her. Then he kissed her ear and rolled to his side, bringing her with him into the shelter of his body.

Marisa waited for her heart to slow down. Cole had given her one of the most spectacular experiences of her life. She was caught between joy at the wonder of it and embarrassment at her uninhibited response.

"Was that the game plan that you had filed away for fifteen years?" she asked.

He gave a helpless laugh. "Part of it."

There was more? Still, she managed, "It was so much better than on a regular bed."

He smiled against her hair. "I told you it would be better with a sexy construction guy."

Nine

If Marisa had any doubt that she and Cole had grown up in very different circumstances, they were erased when she entered his parents' house—a Mediterranean villa set amidst beautiful landscaping with a stone fountain at the center of a circular drive. She could almost believe she was in Tuscany, which she'd backpacked through one summer.

Still, she'd been nervous about this party ever since Camilla had issued her invite. She'd debated what to wear and had settled on a shirt and short skirt. Cole had driven to her apartment building, and she'd met him downstairs in the entry, not trusting the two of them in her condo alone even for a few minutes. Seeing him in a shirt and khakis, she'd been reassured that she'd at least dressed appropriately.

Thanks to Cole, her kitchen had gotten a wonderful face-lift. After their romantic interlude, they had gotten on with the job of painting, and she'd discovered Cole knew much more about the intricacies of stripping old paint and dealing with molding than she did. Her kitchen looked great—and he'd worked magic on her, too.

Marisa followed Cole through gleaming rooms decorated with a bow to the Serenghettis' Italian heritage to the back of the villa. When they reached his parents' backyard, she took in the impressive outdoor kitchen, blue-stone patio under a striped awning and wrought-iron furniture. It was an unseasonably warm day in May, and the Serenghetti party was mostly an outdoor affair. People milled about, glasses in hand, and platters of food had been set out on most flat surfaces.

Marisa looked over at her construction guy. Though when she'd started thinking of Cole as hers, she couldn't quite say. It was a telling slip that was *dangerous*. They'd had spectacular sex that had transported her from her comfort zone to an area where she was vulnerable, exposed and swamped with emotion and sensation. But still, she couldn't—shouldn't—attach too much importance to it. She had once in high school, and she'd fallen flat on her face. She also hoped it wasn't obvious to everyone that they'd recently become lovers for the first—no, second—time.

Cole placed his hand at the small of her back, and Marisa glanced at him. He wasn't trying to be subtle about their connection—though which of the two of them was a fraud was hard to tell. Weren't they supposed to pretend to be a couple? It was getting so confusing...

Cole bent for a quick kiss. "I'm glad you're here."

"There are more of you Serenghettis than I've ever seen in one place," Marisa responded, wondering how many people had seen that peck on the lips.

Cole laughed. "Don't worry, they don't bite—" he bent to murmur in her ear "—unlike me."

On her quick intake of breath, he straightened, his eyes gleaming.

Quelling the sudden hot-and-bothered feeling, Marisa scanned the crowd. She had known in high school that Cole had three younger siblings, but she hadn't been friends with any of them. She'd heard a bit about Jordan over the years because his hockey career and endorsement deals had kept him in the public eye. And before they'd arrived at the party, Cole had mentioned that his sister, Mia, the youngest, was a designer based in New York, and his middle brother, Rick, traveled the world as a stuntman on movie sets.

"Come on," Cole said. "I'll introduce you."

Marisa bit her lip. "Uh…sure."

The Serenghettis had been a colorful lot so far. She took a deep breath and followed Cole as he made his way toward a lithe and attractive woman who obviously possessed the Serenghetti genes.

"Mia, this is Marisa Danieli."

Cole's sister was beautiful. Her hair was longer than Marisa's, and wavy, not curly. Her almond-shaped eyes tilted slightly upward at the corners, hinting at Slavic or Germanic ancestors—not an uncommon story for those with roots in Italy's north.

"I remember you," Mia said, stepping away from the serving table next to her.

Yikes. In her case and Cole's, recollections of the past couldn't be a good thing. Still, Marisa couldn't fault Mia if the other woman wanted to size up Cole's newest girlfriend and be protective of her brother. Mia hadn't yet reached high school when she and Cole had been seniors, so Marisa placed her at close to Serafina's age.

Mia tilted her head. "You were the smart girl who brought down the high-and-mighty hockey team captain. Come to finish him off?"

Marisa felt heat flood her cheeks. Still, Mia's tone was surprisingly neutral, joking even. Cole's sister had faulted her brother for his arrogance in high school and called Marisa smart.

"Mia—"

Before Cole could say more, Marisa found her voice. "No, I need him too much to polish him off. He's the headliner for the Pershing fund-raiser." She cast a quick glance at Cole. "Besides, he's shaped up to be a decent guy."

Mia's shoulders relaxed a little. "That's what I think." She smiled. "And you're not his typical fashion-model type."

"Thanks for the endorsement, sis," Cole said drily.

"You could be a model yourself, Mia," Marisa interjected, knowing it wasn't just flattery to get into Mia's good graces, it also happened to be true—Cole's sister was a knockout.

"I was a leg model for a while," Cole's sister admitted, her tone rueful as she pushed one of her chestnut locks over her shoulder. "I didn't like it, but I thought that if I wanted to be a designer, it would help to know the fashion industry from the leg up, if you know what I mean. I did a lot of hosiery ads."

"Yeah," Cole cracked, "I tried to get her to insure her legs."

His tone was jesting but there was also an element of brotherly pride. And Marisa felt a sudden pang at Cole's easy bond with his siblings. She had her cousin Serafina, but they'd always lived in different homes, though sleepovers had made up for some of that distance.

"Hmm," Mia said, considering. "Well, don't count me out on the insurance. I may need to continue to model my own clothes, and from the leg up if it comes to it. Designers starting out have to make do with what they have."

"I've got some helpful advice for you," Cole teased. "Put Jordan in drag. If he's a hit with underwear, he'll rock a strapless dress."

While Marisa smiled at the image, Mia laughed. "Jordan is going to throttle you for suggesting it."

"Don't worry, you've got plenty to hold over him. He'll come cheap."

Marisa warmed to Cole's sister, who obviously had a self-deprecating charm. She could also identify with a woman who was trying to get a career off the ground and running.

Cole looked down at her. "Can I get you a drink?"

"Yes, please," she said, realizing a glass would be a good prop to help disguise her nervousness. "A diet soda would be great."

"I think you need something stronger," Cole teased. "You still haven't met all the Serenghettis."

"I'm going to check in with Mom in the kitchen," Mia announced, stepping back. "Knowing her, she's in a frenzy of activity."

When Cole and Mia had moved off, Marisa found herself alone and looked around. The crowd had thinned—some people heading indoors—and she spotted Serg Serenghetti sitting in a chair near the outdoor kitchen. The family resemblance was unmistakable—she'd have recognized him even if she hadn't seen pictures in the local paper from time to time over the years.

He beckoned to her, and she had no choice but to walk toward him.

Serg's hair was steel-gray mixed with white at the sideburns, and he shared some of his eldest son's features—not to mention Cole's imposing presence, even though he was seated.

When she'd neared, Serg waved a hand to indicate their surroundings. "You're a teacher, Marisa. Based right here in beautiful Welsdale, my wife says. Not like those model types…"

How much had Serg been told about her? "Yes, I've been teaching at the Pershing School since I received my teaching degree. Cole has been generous enough to help with our fund-raiser."

"Pstcha," Serg retorted. "It's not generosity. Cole wants you to keep seeing him."

Marisa had stopped listening at *Cole wants you…*

Serg tilted his head in imitation of his daughter. "Smart guy." Then he adjusted the blanket covering his lap and frowned. "My wife likes to keep me bundled up like an Eskimo facing a blizzard even though spring has come early this year."

Cole returned, drinks in hand. "I see you've met the *pater familias*." Handing Marisa a wineglass, he added, "He's curmudgeonly in a teddy bear sort of way. I trot him out to make a good impression on the girlfriends."

"Ha!" Serg replied. "I give thanks every day that your fancy schools at least taught you some Latin."

Cole quirked an eyebrow. *"Acta est fabula, plaudita."*

The drama has been acted out, applaud. Marisa hid a smile. She'd studied Latin, too.

"At least I know how to entertain," Serg grumbled. "Smart-ass."

"Chip off the old block."

Serg made some more grousing noises before glancing at Marisa again. "Beautiful woman based right here in Welsdale. Perfect."

"You'd think so," Cole remarked drily.

"Get Marisa to take you on, and you're set. Then you can stay put and run Serenghetti Construction."

"Right."

What? Cole's mocking tone was undeniable but Serg surely couldn't be serious. Marisa felt as if she'd landed in the middle of a family drama that she didn't totally understand.

Serg shook his head. "I had a stroke but I can still understand sarcasm."

"I'm the best you've got. Jordan and Rick are worse."

Camilla appeared and came forward to fuss over her husband, and both Marisa and Cole stepped back.

Serg looked up from under lowered brows. *"Vade in pace.* Go in peace. Latin was required in my day, too, you know."

As she moved aside, Marisa bumped up against something—or rather, someone—and turned around.

A tall, good-looking man smiled down at her. "Hi."

Cole sighed resignedly. "Marisa, this is my brother Rick.

The prodigal son back from a film set at the edge of the Earth."

"Don't listen to him," Rick said with a lazy grin. "I'm the movie star. But I've been trying to get Cole here to play one of the bad guys for a long time. With the scars and all, don't you think he looks menacing?"

What Marisa was thinking was that Cole made her heart go pitter-patter...

"You're a stuntman and you've been a body double for Hollywood's A-list," Cole replied. "Still doesn't make you a movie star."

"A fine distinction."

Marisa had to concede that Rick had movie-star looks. Closest in age to Cole, he was also rough-hewn. But he'd been a wrestler, not a hockey player, in high school. That much she knew.

"So word is you two are an item." Rick looked at Cole, his expression droll. "Hot for the teacher?"

Marisa heated to the roots of her hair. She took a sip of wine to fortify herself.

"You can always count on a brother to embarrass you for no reason," Cole said drily, though he didn't look greatly perturbed.

"Your taste in women is improving. What's to be embarrassed about?"

"You."

"Payback." Rick grinned. "So what happened? Marisa clobbered you in high school, and now you're moonstruck?"

Marisa observed the back-and-forth between the brothers, a nervous and self-conscious smile on her lips. Still, it seemed as if Rick was willing to be open-minded about her relationship with his older brother—whatever it was.

Cole, on the other hand, looked as if he was praying for patience. "Mr. Hayes made her 'fess up about who doctored the PowerPoint presentation, smart-ass. She was going to lose recommendations for a college scholarship."

"No, really," she interjected, "I think that explains my behavior but doesn't excuse it."

"You had a good enough reason for doing what you did," Cole replied.

"I shouldn't have cared about Mr. Hayes's embarrassment." She shrugged. "Chances were good he'd keep his job regardless. You paid a big price."

"I had it coming. Everything worked out eventually."

Marisa wanted to argue further, but then she caught Rick's amused expression.

"What a love-fest," Rick remarked, looking back and forth between them. "I should get out of the way while you two fall all over yourselves making excuses for each other."

Marisa clamped her mouth shut. Something had been changing between her and Cole. She felt as if there were silken ties—a lingerie robe sash came to mind—binding her to him. For his part, Cole seemed as if he couldn't wait to be alone with her again…

Cole linked his hand with hers. "Come on, there are other people I want to introduce you to."

Rick stepped back. "Have fun. I have my hands full avoiding Mom. She wants to capitalize on my rare family appearance."

Murmuring a nice-to-meet-you to Rick, Marisa allowed herself to be led away. Cole introduced her to one group after another until Marisa found it hard to keep track of so many family members, friends and associates. In between, she ate Camilla's delicious food, and Cole had a burger and hot dog while taking his turn grilling.

When they finally reached a lull, Marisa checked her phone and realized they'd already been at the party for three hours.

Cole glanced down at her. "Let's get out of here."

She looked around. "But the party isn't winding down yet."

He gave her a heavy-lidded look. "Right. It's the perfect

time to go. People will understand we want to be alone. It'll keep up the appearance that we're a couple."

Nervous anticipation spiraled through her. "Where are we going?"

Taking her hand, Cole raised it to his lips. "My place is closer."

She sucked in a breath. "Okay."

She'd never been in Cole's apartment, and it occurred to her that they were crossing another threshold…

The drive to Cole's was quick. They made their way through the understated lobby and ascended in the elevator to the top floor.

When he let them into his loft, Marisa glanced around. The penthouse was like the home version of Cole's office. Masculine and conveying muted power. Everything looked state-of-the-art—from the electronics that she glimpsed in the living area to the appliances visible in the kitchen.

In the next moment Cole backed her against the exposed brick wall for a searing kiss.

When they broke apart, she said breathlessly, "We have to stop this. We're in a pretend relationship."

"This is helping us pretend better."

"I don't follow your logic."

"Then don't. Just go with the flow."

He was making her feel too much. She was afraid…and yet she couldn't resist taking the plunge.

He touched her face. "I want to take you on a bed this time. I want you to cry out my name as I come inside you."

She placed unsteady fingers on the top button of her shirt, and Cole zeroed in on the action.

"I've been glimpsing your lacy bra all night. The peekaboo effect has been driving me crazy."

"You've been staring at my breasts?" How many guests had noticed? And how had she not been aware of it? Probably because she'd been too nervous and overwhelmed by her surroundings.

"Yeah," Cole said thickly, "and Rick caught me at it, too. I haven't bumbled so much since high school."

A girlfriend would have told her that her bra was showing so she could fix the problem. *Not Cole.*

"Think of it as foreplay." He braced a hand on the wall next to her and leaned in to trail kisses from her lips to the hollow behind her ear.

She shivered, and her fingers fumbled with the buttons of her shirt. When she finally finished, she tugged her top out of the waistband of her skirt and opened it wide. The cool air hit her skin, raising goose bumps.

"So pretty," Cole murmured, trailing a finger from her jaw, down her neck and to the swell of her breast.

Marisa lowered her eyes as the back of Cole's hand grazed over the top of her breast...again and again. Her breath hitched. She couldn't wait to experience what Cole wanted to show her—and do with her—this time.

He slid one hand up her thigh and under her skirt, and she leaned against the wall for support. He nuzzled her neck, and then found her with his hand, delving inside her welcoming moistness.

She tangled her hands in his hair. "Cole."

"Yeah?" he said thickly.

"Tell me this isn't in the playbook."

"No, but this is." He crouched and moments later used his tongue at her most sensitive spot.

Her knees nearly buckled, and she sank her fingers into his hair, anchoring herself in a world flooded with sensation. "Cole, please."

"Please, what?" he muttered. "Keep going?"

She was so aroused that she couldn't breathe right. "Oh..."

"My pleasure."

Minutes later her world splintered, coming apart like a kaleidoscope exploding, and she sagged against the wall.

Cole straightened, bracing himself with a hand against the wall near her face, his eyes glittering.

"You're going to ride me," he said huskily. "You're breasts are going to bounce and drive me crazy…and then after you scream for me, I'm going to come inside you in one long rush."

Marisa parted her lips. She'd never been so turned on in her life.

"Bed. Now," she gasped.

"The magic words," he responded, grinning.

He swung her into his arms and strode down the hall. The bedroom was at the end, on the right.

It was an enormous room, with skylights and glass doors opening onto a terrace.

When he set her feet down, they both stripped, their fingers working quickly on more buttons. He beat her to the finish naked when she still had on a bra and panties.

He prowled toward her with purpose. *He was perfect.* All muscle and sculpted maleness. Not an ounce of softness, but still, she was prepared to be cosseted.

He cupped her breasts, kissed the top of each one and then claimed her mouth. With a deft move, he undid her bra and she spilled against him.

He pushed down her panties until they pooled at her feet. And then he was laying her down on the bed and stretching over her. He fanned her hair out across the pillow.

"What are you doing?"

He gave her a crooked smile. "This is the way I've fantasized about you. Your hair spread across my bed…entangling me."

"I thought I was going to be on top."

"You will be," he promised before he kissed his way down her body.

When he was ready, he flipped her on top of him.

She straddled him, and then sank onto him until they were joined. They both groaned, and he helped her set up a rhythm that they enjoyed.

When she finally crested on a wave that was pure and beautiful, she heard her own gasps of pleasure as if from a distant place. Cole's face was contorted with effort until he found his own release and spilled inside her in one long thrust.

Marisa sagged forward against him, and he caught her, their hearts racing.

"I don't think I can survive much more of you, Marisa."

"You don't need to," she murmured. "I've given you all I have."

It was true—and also what she was afraid of. Cole had her body and soul. She only hoped she wasn't just another score…

"Cole, come on up and taste Marisa's cooking."

Cole smiled for the camera. Which producer had come up with this stunt? Or had it been his mother's idea? His mother was looking excited and decidedly innocent. Never mind that the dish to be sampled had more accurately been a joint production of Marisa *and* both their mothers.

If Marisa hadn't been looking so horrified—but how many of her students tuned in to local television in the middle of the afternoon?—he might have suspected her of having a hand in the making of this made-for-TV moment. As it was, he wanted to laugh. He hadn't expected to be an extra in this episode of his mother's show.

When he reached the stage, he said gamely, "I'm sure it's delicious, but I'm not a connoisseur."

Camilla gave Marisa a spoon with a sampling of *tiella* on it—bits of rice, onion, potato and mussels mixed together—and nodded expectantly.

When Marisa turned, she made to hand off the spoon to him.

"No, no, Marisa," Camilla said laughingly. "I always raise the spoon to the *bocca* when I ask my family for an *opinione*."

The audience laughed along gamely, and even Donna smiled at Camilla's exuberant admonishment.

Cole could read the defeat in Marisa's eyes as she realized there was no way out. Unlike him, she wasn't used to being on camera. But they both knew everyone—the audience, their mothers and the producers—was waiting for her to feed him.

Slowly, she raised the spoon, cupping her other hand under it to prevent spills. He locked his gaze on her face, and at the last second, took hold of her wrist in order to guide it. She gasped softly, the moment between them becoming molten even before the food touched his mouth.

The seafood dish was delicious. She was delicious. He wanted to start with the *tiella* and then have his fill of her until he was satisfied—though he had no idea when that would be. He'd always thought she was edible, but a taste wasn't enough. Their two trysts had just whetted his appetite. He wished he could say he was sorry for roping her into an appearance on his mother's show, but the truth was he looked forward to any opportunity to be around her these days.

Marisa finally pulled away, lowering the spoon and looking flustered.

Camilla clapped, her expression expectant. "So?"

Cole swallowed and cleared his throat, raising his gaze from Marisa. "Mmm…fantastic. You could tell it was prepared with love."

He didn't know where he was dredging up the words. He figured he was having an out-of-body experience since he couldn't ever remember being this turned on without having a blatant physical sign of arousal—which would have been an inconvenient turn of events right now, to say the least, even with a kitchen counter providing camouflage from the cameras.

His mother turned to address the audience, saving him from the spotlight. "And now for another special surprise. We are giving away a set of Stanhope Department Store's own brand of stainless-steel cookware today, thanks to our guest, Donna Casale. You can try yourself today's recipe with your own new cookware!"

To much applause, a producer lifted the top of a big, white box to reveal a ten-piece set of gleaming stainless-steel pots and pans.

"Please look under your seats!" Camilla announced. "The person with the red dot is the winner!"

After a few moments, a middle-aged woman stood up excitedly and waved a disc.

"Auguri!" Camilla called, clapping. "Come down to look at your gift."

When the audience member arrived to inspect her prize, Camilla put an arm around her and turned to the camera. "If you like the Danieli family recipe, please go to our website."

She paused for what Cole knew would be a voice-over, and the appearance onscreen of the recipe and web address when the episode aired. Then Camilla thanked her guests and the audience members for coming. "Until next time. *Alla salute!"*

When the camera lights turned off, signaling the end of filming, Marisa visibly relaxed.

"Good job, Mom," Cole said.

Camilla gave him a beatific smile. "Thank you for *l'assistenza.*"

If he wasn't saving one parent, he was saving another. Though he doubted his father would think Cole was saving anything when he heard there was finally a buyer interested in Serenghetti Construction. He'd received an offer earlier in the week but hadn't shared the news yet with anyone.

At the moment, though, he had more pressing concerns.

As the audience began to rise and disperse, he cupped Marisa's elbow.

"Are you okay?" he asked in a low voice. "You looked as if you were about to have a swoon-worthy moment back there."

"Only for your legion of female fans," she replied, blowing a stray hair away from her face.

He suppressed a laugh. *That'a girl.*

His mother and Donna were approached by a couple of audience members, so he and Marisa had relative privacy.

"Looks as if you might have gained some admirers today, too," he remarked.

She eyed him. "Including you?"

"I've always been a fan."

"Of my cooking?"

"Of everything, sweet pea."

Marisa waved a hand in front of her face. "You do know how to turn up the heat."

He gave her an intimate smile. "We haven't done it in the kitchen yet."

At her wide-eyed look, he bit back a grin. He admitted it—he loved flustering Marisa.

"There are other people here," she replied in a low, urgent voice.

He leaned over to whisper in her ear. "Your kitchen or mine?"

She sucked in a breath. "I—I have to show out my mom."

He gave her a lingering look, but nodded. Sooner or later, he'd have another chance to fan the flames with Marisa. He figured he'd survived the last fifteen years only because he hadn't known what he'd been missing...

As Marisa walked out of the television studio with her mother toward the exit that led to the parking lot, she kept her thoughts to herself.

"So what am I not supposed to know?" Donna asked lightly.

Marisa threw her a sidelong look. "I don't know what you mean."

"Hmm…it looks like it's more than just business between you and Cole Serenghetti."

Marisa felt a telltale wave of heat rise to her face. "Just doing a favor to thank him for participating in the fundraiser," she mumbled. "Besides, I thought it would be fun. You love cooking shows. Didn't you have fun?"

"Yes, I did," Donna agreed, "and part of it was the enjoyment of watching you and Cole interact. He looked as if he couldn't wait to be alone with you."

"Mom!"

Donna turned to face her. "You're a beautiful, desirable woman, Marisa. I know what a prize my daughter is. Cole would be foolish not to be interested in you."

There was the problem in a nutshell. She wasn't sure where she and Cole stood—where pretending left off and reality began. And whether they were just hooking up with no possibility of a future together.

"Camilla Serenghetti, for one, believes something is going on, and she couldn't be happier about it. She said she's heard rumors around town…" Donna sighed and then gave her a long-suffering look. "The mothers are always the last to know."

Marisa sighed herself, not having the heart for further denials. "Cole and I have a complicated past."

"All relationships are complicated, honey. But what I saw in there was Cole eating you up with his eyes."

"Mom, please!" she protested, because she wasn't used to such frank talk from her mother.

Donna laughed. "Honey, I'm acquainted with the attractiveness of pro athletes."

"Of course you are."

Her mother looked at her probingly. "I hope your hesitancy about Cole doesn't have anything to do with what happened between me and your father."

They stopped at the closed door leading out of the building.

When Marisa didn't say anything, Donna added, "Oh, honey, if baseball hadn't broken us up, something else would have. We were too young."

Yup, Marisa could identify with the tragedy of young love. She and Cole had been there themselves.

Still, she was surprised by her mother's toned-down reaction. Ever since Marisa had discovered the truth in her twenties about her parents' relationship—that her biological father was out of the picture even before an accident had claimed his life—she'd assumed her mother would be averse to professional athletes and their lifestyle.

Sure, her mother had been matter-of-fact when she'd finally detailed the circumstances around her pregnancy, but Marisa had assumed her mother had adopted that attitude for her daughter's sake. Marisa had vivid memories of exactly what sacrifices had been involved in her upbringing, and she figured her mother did, too, and despite hiding it well, couldn't help but be infected with some bitterness.

It appeared she was wrong—at least these days.

"You know, Mom," Marisa said jokingly, "marriage really has changed your outlook on life."

"Older and wiser, honey," Donna replied. "But the events in my life that you're referring to also happened a long time ago. I had time to move past them and get on with it. And I have never, ever regretted having you. You were a gift."

Tears sprung to Marisa's eyes. "Oh, Mom, stop."

Donna gave her a quick squeeze and then laughed lightly. "Enough about Cole Serenghetti, you mean? Well, let me know what happens there. Sometimes mothers would like to move up from last on the totem pole!"

Ten

Marisa looked around the glittering ballroom where the Pershing Shines Bright fund-raiser was being held. The Briarcliff was a popular event venue on the outskirts of Welsdale. It was also one of the locations she'd scouted for her wedding to Sal.

That last thought made her realize how much had changed—how much *she'd* changed—in the past several months. The man uppermost in her mind was Cole, not Sal.

Because tonight was bittersweet. She was relieved the fund-raiser had come together as a nice event. Thanks to Cole, they'd sold more tickets than she'd ever hoped for, and Jordan was a hit, as well. But even though she and Cole had not talked further about it, after this evening they were scheduled to drop their charade about being a couple.

She looked across the room at where Cole stood talking to Mr. Dobson, and her heart squeezed.

Cole looked beyond handsome in a tux. She knew he'd have no trouble attracting female interest again once people no longer thought that he was dating her. In fact, more than one woman tonight had thrown him an appreciative look or had hung on his words and giggled at something he'd said.

Marisa sighed. She should be focused on other things. Her mother and stepfather were here to support her. And after this evening, she might have proved herself enough to become assistant principal at Pershing. Mr. Dobson had asked her last week to submit her résumé.

The principal had given no indication that he was aware of her relationship with Cole—and she certainly hadn't broadcast it at school. In fairness, however, she'd casually mentioned that she and Cole had begun to see each other, having become reacquainted over preparations for Pershing Shines Bright. Marisa figured it was best the principal got the news from her first. And if Mr. Dobson had been a fan of *Flavors of Italy with Camilla Serenghetti*, he would have seen the episode with her and Cole that had aired two weeks ago, a few days after taping.

Cole glanced her way, and their gazes locked, his look appreciative.

He made her feel beautiful. She wore a green satin dress with a black lace overlay covering the sweetheart neckline, and chandelier earrings. She'd chosen her outfit with him in mind.

In the past couple of weeks, she'd seen more of Cole than she would ever have imagined. They'd attended a Razors game together to cheer on Jordan, where they were even nabbed on the Jumbotron sharing a quick kiss. She'd attended his second hockey clinic for Pershing students, and she'd teased him about making a teacher out of him yet. They'd also bonded in the kitchen, where he'd helped her make some of her signature Italian dishes.

She heated at the thought of what else they'd recently done in the kitchen…

Marisa had known then, if she hadn't before, that she'd fallen in love with him. Because heartbreak was her middle name.

"My God, he only has eyes for you."

Marisa jumped, yanked from her reverie, and turned to see Serafina behind her. "You sound like a bad advertisement for a women's hair-care product."

Serafina shook her head. "It's not your hair that I'm talking about."

"Ladies."

She and Serafina swung in unison to see Cole's youngest brother.

Jordan's eyes came to rest on Serafina, and his smile was enough to melt ice. "Marisa didn't tell me she had an even more perfect relative."

"Oh?" Serafina responded and then glanced behind her. "Where is she?"

Cole's brother grinned. "I'm looking at her, angel. I'm—"

Serafina scowled. "My name is not Angel, and I know who you are."

"Cole's brother," Jordan supplied, still unperturbed.

"The New England Razors' right wingman and leading scorer."

Jordan's smile remained in place. "You watch hockey."

"Leading scorer on and off the field," Serafina elaborated, her voice cool. "I read the news, too. And I've been moonlighting as a waitress at the Puck & Shoot."

"I know, and yet somehow we've never been introduced."

"Fortunately."

Marisa cleared her throat. She was happy she was no longer the focus of Sera's attention, but it was time to step in. "Jordan, this is my cousin Serafina."

"Named for the angels," Jordan murmured. "I was right. Must be divine kismet."

"In your dreams."

"It's where you'll be tonight...unless you also want to join me at the bar later?"

"My God, don't you stop?"

Marisa knew Serafina didn't like players, but she'd never known her cousin to be rude.

Sera's scowl deepened. "How did you know Marisa and I were related?"

For the first time, Jordan's gaze left Serafina for a moment. "Same delicate bone structure, and smooth cocoa butter skin. What's to mistake?"

"Unfortunately nothing, I suppose," Serafina allowed reluctantly.

"You're lovely."

"You're persistent."

"Part of my charm."

"Debatable."

Jordan grinned again and then shrugged. "The offer still stands. The bar, later."

"You're going to be lonely," Serafina replied. "At least for my company."

Jordan kept his easy expression as he stepped away. "Nice to meet you… Angel."

Serafina waited until Jordan was out of earshot and then fixed Marisa with a look. "A professional player."

"Cole is one, too."

"He's retired from the game. At least the one on the ice."

And then with a huff, her cousin turned and marched off, leaving Marisa speechless.

Cole appeared next to her. "What happened?"

She shook her head. "Actually, I don't know, except your brother and my cousin did not hit it off."

Cole frowned. "Surprising. Jordan is usually able to charm the—"

"—panties off any woman?" she finished bluntly for him.

Cole smiled ruefully.

"I think that's Serafina's issue with him."

Cole leaned in close, nuzzling Marisa's hairline. "The only woman I want to use my charm on is you."

Marisa's pulse sped up. "We can't here."

"We're supposed to be a couple."

One that would soon be *uncoupled*. "We're supposed to be professional, too."

She looked away, and then froze as she spotted a familiar figure across the room.

Cole's brows drew together. "What's wrong?"

He followed her gaze, and then he stilled, too.

Mr. Hayes. The former principal had been invited tonight because he usually was for major school events. She just hadn't thought of apprising Cole of the fact. And she'd sort of ducked the issue by not checking with the administrative staff about whether Mr. Hayes had said he would be attending.

She hoped a meeting fifteen years in the making wouldn't spell disaster…

"Cole Serenghetti and Marisa Danieli," Mr. Hayes hailed them.

Cole looked at Marisa but she was avoiding his eyes.

"Mr. Hayes," she greeted the other man. "How nice to see you. You look wonderful. Retirement agrees with you."

Retirement would have agreed with the sour Mr. Hayes fifteen years ago, Cole thought sardonically. Of course, the old codger would be here tonight. He was grayer and less imposing than when he'd held Cole's fate in his hands, but he still had the same ponderous personality from the looks of it.

Cole gazed at Marisa, and she implored him with her eyes to make nice. Tonight was important to her, so he was willing to go along. He gave her a slow smile. *You owe me, and I'll collect later, in a mutually pleasurable way…*

Mr. Hayes glanced from Cole to Marisa. "I understand you two are a couple these days. Congratulations."

Marisa smiled. "Thank you."

"I bet you're surprised," Cole put in.

Marisa appeared as if she wanted to give him a sharp elbow.

"Not really," Mr. Hayes replied.

Cole arched an eyebrow. "I turned out better than you expected."

"Well, naturally—"

"I understand there'll be a video retrospective tonight. Might want to withhold judgment until then."

Marisa widened her eyes at him, and Cole smiled insouciantly back at her. He was willing to play along, but he could still tweak Mr. Hayes's nose and have some fun in the process.

Mr. Hayes cleared his throat. "Speaking of video presentations, I would like to set the record straight on one issue. When Marisa was called to my office that day, and I asked—"

"Interrogated, you mean?"

"—her about the prank, I could tell she cared about you."

Cole tamped down his surprise.

"At first, she was very reluctant to say anything. And then when she revealed your connection to the stunt, she was worried about what would happen to you."

Cole felt Marisa's touch on his arm.

She'd cared about him in high school, and even Mr. Hayes had been able to see it. Cole wondered why he himself hadn't, and realized it was because he'd been blind to anything but his sense of betrayal.

Cole met and held Mr. Hayes's gaze. "I learned a lot from that episode in high school. It was the last school prank I ever pulled." He covered Marisa's hand with his. "But everything ended well. More than fine. I'm lucky."

Marisa went still, and Cole figured she was wondering whether he was playacting for Mr. Hayes's benefit. She probably thought he was highlighting their relationship in order to rub the former principal's nose in it.

But he wasn't acting. He was dead serious. The realization hit him like a body check on the ice.

He wanted Marisa in his life. He *needed her* in his life.

Sooner or later, he was going to make her see she needed him, too.

Two days after the fund-raiser Marisa opened her door to the last person she expected to catch on her threshold again. Sal.

Since Pershing Shines Bright, she hadn't had a chance to see Cole again, though he'd congratulated her by text on a job well done. She'd been on duty the night of the fund-raiser, so she'd departed after everyone but Pershing staff had left. After a quick peck on the lips, Cole had regretfully excused himself because he had an early-morning work meeting.

She was left in a crazy-making limbo about where she and Cole stood, wondering whether the meeting was an excuse because he remembered, too, that the clock on their relationship was due to strike midnight at the end of the fund-raiser.

Still, the morning—or two—after, she hadn't expected Sal.

She reluctantly stepped aside so he could make it over the threshold. "Sal."

"Marisa, I need to talk to you."

Closing the door, she turned to face her former fiancé.

"Vicki left me," Sal said without preamble.

"I'm sorry."

Well, this was an interesting turn of events. Marisa wrapped her arms around herself. In some ways, she should have predicted Sal and Vicki's breakup. They appeared to have little in common, except perhaps for their joint affinity for sports stars.

Still, what did Sal want from her? A shoulder to cry on? She needed consoling herself about Cole.

Sal grimaced. "It was for the best that Vicki made for the door. I've been acting like an idiot."

Marisa couldn't disagree, but she said nothing, not wanting to hit someone when he was down.

Sal suddenly looked at her pleadingly. "I'm done with the high-flying lifestyle of pro athletes, Marisa. I thought I wanted it for myself, but I've tendered my resignation at the sports agency. I'm taking a job with a foundation that brings sports and athletics to underprivileged kids. I want to make a difference."

She couldn't argue with the admirable impulse to help kids. She worked with children every day. It was exhausting but exhilarating work. Still, while she was happy Sal appeared to be in a better place, she wondered about the road he'd taken to get there. "And Vicki leaving you led to this epiphany?"

He had the grace to look sheepish. "She wasn't you, Marisa."

"Of course not. Wasn't that why you were attracted to her?"

"I was an idiot," Sal repeated. "But I've done a lot of thinking in the past few days."

She waited.

"Marisa, I still have feelings for you."

She blinked and dropped her arms to her sides.

Sal held up his hand. "Wait, let me finish. I know it'll be hard to regain your trust. But I hope it won't be impossible. I'm asking you to give me another chance." He reached for her hand. "Marisa, I love you. I'm willing to do anything, whatever it takes, to have you back."

She didn't know where to begin. "Sal—"

"You don't need to say anything." Sal gave a half laugh. "There's nothing you can say that I haven't already thought of. I've called myself every name in the book."

She snapped her mouth closed.

"The thing is, I got cold feet with our engagement." He shrugged. "You could say it took Vicki to make me realize the person I really want. You, Marisa."

As a heartfelt declaration, it wasn't half-bad. But she was no longer sure he was the right man for her.

Sal had made a mistake, by his own admission. But otherwise he was safe and predictable and what she'd thought she always wanted—until Cole had come back into her life.

Still, Cole had never shown any indication of settling down. And while she'd been falling in love with him, he hadn't given any sign that he returned her feelings.

She cleared her throat. "Sal, I—"

"No," he interrupted. "Don't say anything. Think about it. I know I've laid a lot on you."

"Really—"

He gave her a quick kiss, startling her. It was as if he was determined to prevent a knee-jerk rejection. "I'm going to check in with you again soon."

With those words, Sal turned and was out the door as quickly as he had come.

Cole had just gotten off a conference call at work when his assistant put through a call from Steve Fryer, an acquaintance from his days on the ice.

Cole looked at the papers strewn across his desk. He was already pressed for time, his morning occupied with meetings, but Steve had no way of knowing that.

Cole also itched to be with Marisa. He hadn't seen her since the fund-raiser a few days ago. He'd had a busy schedule with a couple of work emergencies, and today was looking no better.

"Cole, I've got good news," Steve announced. "The coach for the Madison Rockets has decided to take the job in Canada after all because the sports advertising agency there agreed to meet his contract terms." Pause. "We'd like to offer you the coaching position."

Cole leaned back in his chair, his world coming to a screeching halt. This was the opportunity he'd been waiting months for. The Rockets were one of the best minor league teams in the American Hockey League. The job would be a good launching pad for an NHL coaching position. Rather than starting as an assistant coach in the NHL, he could prove himself as the head of his own team.

"Great news, Steve. I think the Rockets made the right decision."

Steve laughed.

"I'll get back to you," Cole said, eyeing the jumble of papers on his desk. "As you can imagine, there are things to sort out at this end." He expected Steve would assume he needed to contact his agent—or former agent, to be more accurate—to begin the process of negotiating a suitable employment contract.

Only Cole knew his complications were bigger. He needed to disentangle himself from Serenghetti Construction, for one. He thought again of the offer to purchase the company—it was now or never. And then there was his relationship with Marisa…

"Take your time," Steve responded. "We'll talk next week."

"You'll be hearing from me." Cole gave the assurance before ending the call, his mind buzzing.

The wheels were moving in the direction he wanted, but in the past year he'd become more encumbered than ever in Welsdale. Marisa was chief among those ties…

He'd suggest she move to Madison with him.

A weight lifted as his mind sped up. There would be plenty of teaching jobs there for her. If she had the potential to advance at Pershing, then she certainly had the qualifications to be an attractive hire at other schools. She might even decide that moving someplace else was the better bet—she hadn't yet gotten a promotion at Pershing, and one might never materialize. Another school might start her out in administration from the beginning.

He could make this situation work—for the both of them. He *would* make it work.

But first he needed to tackle a dicier situation. It was time to tell Serg about the offer to buy Serenghetti Construction.

Cole picked up his jacket off the back of the chair and told the receptionist he'd be out and reachable on his cell. After texting his mother, he made the quick drive over to Casa Serenghetti, where he figured he'd find Serg in one of two moods: grumpy or grumpier.

When he stepped inside the house, he greeted his mother with a peck on the cheek and then followed her to the oversize family room, where his father was ensconced in a club chair.

Cole sat in a leather chair and braced his elbows on his knees, his hands clasped between them. Camilla took a seat on the sofa, and there was small talk about the weather and how Serg was feeling. But Cole could tell his father was suspicious about this unexpected visit. Serg regarded him from under his customary lowered brows.

Cole took the bull by the horns. "Someone's offered to buy the company."

"Offered?" Serg shot back in his rumbling voice. "Like someone came banging on your door? Or you solicited a buyer?"

"Does it matter? It's a good offer from a bigger outfit with operations in the Northeast." Cole knew they couldn't expect better.

Serg grumbled, his eyes piercing. "I'm going to have another stroke." Then he bent his head and grimaced.

Camilla shot to her feet. "Madonna. Serg! Where does it hurt?"

But Cole had a better question. "Right now?"

Serg cracked one eye open. "Does it matter when? You've killed me, either way."

"Serg, please," Camilla exclaimed, throwing Cole an exasperated look.

Cole was used to drama from his family. He'd had a lifetime of it.

"You fought hard to get the contract to build the Pershing gym, and now you're planning to sell the company?" Serg asked accusingly. "I was starting to think you had my competitive business instincts."

Cole was ready. "I do, and that's why I believe selling the company is the best thing."

"Camilla, bring me my meds," Serg instructed at the same time that he waved Cole away. "I need to rest."

"The offer is a good one," Cole said again, and then stood because he'd known before he'd arrived that he needed to let Serg get used to the idea. "Let me know when you're ready to hear more of the particulars."

One meeting down, one to go. On the way out the door, Cole texted Marisa to meet him at the Puck & Shoot after work…

Eleven

When Marisa walked into the Puck & Shoot, she was nervous. Cole had asked her to meet him, and she knew she needed to mention Sal's visit.

She slipped into the booth and sat opposite from Cole, not giving him a chance to rise at her entrance. A waitress appeared, and at Cole's inquiring look, she ordered a light beer.

Cole's cell phone buzzed, and she was saved from having to say anything more. Apologizing for having to take a work call, he stood up and walked a few feet away.

The last time she and Cole had been at the Puck & Shoot, she'd thrown herself at him when Sal and Vicki had appeared, and their charade as a couple had started. How fitting would it be if they buried their faux relationship here, as well?

When the waitress returned and set her drink before her, Marisa took a swallow. She was nervous, and she sensed something was up with Cole, too.

Cole slipped back into the booth, pocketing his phone.

Marisa felt her pulse pick up. She wanted to slide into the

booth beside him, sit in his lap, twine her arms around his neck and brush his lips with hers. But she no longer knew whether she was allowed to. She didn't know where they stood. Neither of them had talked about anything substantial since the end of the fund-raiser days ago.

As if reading her mind, Cole stared at her intently. "We've done a good job pretending to be a couple."

"Yes." It was the pretend part that she'd had trouble with.

"I've been offered a coaching job with a hockey team in Madison, Wisconsin."

Marisa's heart plummeted.

Cole, however, looked pleased. Could their relationship—okay, their pretending—have meant so little to him? She wondered why he'd brought up the coaching job right after mentioning their charade. It seemed like a non sequitur...unless this was Cole's way of breaking things off? *It's been good, but now I'm moving on, sweet pea?*

"Sal wants to get back together," she blurted.

She knew it was a defensive move, but she couldn't help herself. Cole hadn't said he was taking the job in Wisconsin, but...he seemed happy. And he knew she was tied to Welsdale and her job at Pershing School—not that he'd said anything about having her move with him.

Her mind was racing, but she just couldn't bear to hear the words *it's over, baby*. She'd been dumped by Sal and had survived, but she wasn't sure she could pick up the pieces after Cole. He meant too much. Still, she couldn't blame Cole for leaving. The fund-raiser was finished, and she'd been the one to insist their pretend relationship would end with it.

Cole blinked, and then his face tightened. "Don't tell me you're considering giving that jerk a second chance."

No, but right now she needed her walls up where Cole was concerned. She had to keep him at a distance. She'd fallen in love with him, but he'd never given any indication that he felt the same way about her. In fact, he was leaving.

Cole nodded curtly. "If you go back to Sal, you'll be playing it safe."

"I'm a teacher. It's a nice, safe profession."

He leaned forward. "If you think you're not passionate and daring, you're wrong, sweet pea. I can tell after our time together."

She wasn't passionate, she was greedy. She wanted it all, including Cole's unwavering love and attention. But Cole had never shown any inclination of settling down, and as far as she could tell, he wasn't starting now. "You're passionate about hockey. You should pursue the dream."

It hurt to say the words. She felt a heavy weight lodge in her heart. But if there was one thing she'd learned from the past, it was that it was futile to stand in the way of dreams.

Cole said nothing, but his hand tightened on his beer.

"Sure your parents would love to have you in Welsdale," she continued. "That's why they liked that we were a couple. But we both know it was pretend." Just saying those words made her ill.

Cole's mouth thinned. "Are you forgetting how we got into a fake relationship?"

Yes, it was her fault. She heated but stood her ground. "And now we're uncoupled."

He gave a brief nod. "There's nothing else to say then. A bargain is a bargain."

Marisa wanted to say a lot of things. *I love you. Don't leave. Stay with me.*

Instead, she nodded in agreement and reached for her handbag beside her. She fumbled for bills to pay her tab.

"Leave it," Cole said, his voice and face impassive. "I've got it."

She nodded and slid out of the booth without looking at him. "I've got to go. I squeezed in a detour to the Puck & Shoot when you texted, but I've got papers to grade tonight."

She would not meet Cole's gaze. It would be her undoing. "Thanks for the beer."

She headed toward the door on autopilot. *Please don't let me faint. Please let me survive this.*

The next night Cole found himself at the Puck & Shoot again. Anyone with a morbid sense of humor would say he enjoyed wallowing in misery by returning to the scene of the crime.

He still knew which way was up, but he hoped to correct the situation soon, starting with the drink before him. He'd never been turned this inside out by a breakup with a woman, and it took some getting used to.

On top of it, he was questioning his plans for Serenghetti Construction. If that wasn't evidence that he needed his head examined, he didn't know what was. Without his knowing it, the family company had grown on him in a sneaky way. It didn't seem right to sell it.

He grimaced. He could handle only one breakup at a time.

"What are you doing? Drinking yourself silly?"

Cole turned, surprised at his brother's voice. "Your powers of observation are impressive, Jordan."

Cole figured he should have chosen a bar other than the Puck & Shoot if he'd wanted to be left alone. At least Marisa's cousin Serafina wasn't working tonight. Unfortunately, however, Jordan had decided to show up for a drink.

"Well? Where's Marisa?" Jordan looked around the bar. "It's Saturday night. I thought you two lovebirds were joined at the beak these days."

"She decided she prefers another guy."

Jordan raised his eyebrows. "Sal?"

Cole didn't answer.

"And you're conceding the field?"

"She made her choice," he responded.

Jordan shook his head. "Man, you are pathetic—"

Cole grabbed a fistful of his brother's shirt and got in Jordan's face. "Leave it alone." Then he thrust his brother away and took another swallow of his scotch. He needed something stronger than a beer tonight.

"You can't see what's in front of your eyes."

Cole propped a hand up in front of him on the bar and spread his fingers. "I'm not that far gone. Yet."

"You want her bad."

"There are other women."

"Vicki."

"Hell, no. We're through."

"So you aren't willing to settle for any—"

"She is." He didn't need to elaborate who the *she* was. *Marisa.* She'd been in his thoughts nonstop. "She's willing to take the horn-dog back."

"Has she said so?"

"She's considering it."

Jordan looked around. "I thought she'd be here."

"Why the hell would she be here?"

"She texted me earlier. She's looking for you. She said she had something of yours to return—"

Probably his heart.

"—and I told her I had no idea where you were, but the Puck & Shoot was worth a try."

Great. There was no way he wanted his brother—and who knew how many others—to witness his final denouement. "She knows how to break up with a guy."

"Too public?" Jordan guessed. "Why don't you go to her apartment then and beat her to it?"

Brilliant idea. The last thing he needed was for Marisa to find him at the Puck & Shoot, nursing a drink like a lonely lovesick puppy. If he seemed pathetic to Jordan, he didn't want to think how he'd appear to Marisa.

If she was looking for him, best to get this over with. He'd save her the hassle of finding him. At least that was what he told himself. He ignored the way his pulse picked up at the thought of seeing her again.

Cole straightened off the bar stool and tossed some bills on the counter for the waiter.

"I'll get you a cab," Jordan offered.

Cole twisted his lips. "Because I'm not fit to drive?"

"Because you're not fit for public consumption. You look like hell, and something tells me you were that way even before you got to the Puck & Shoot."

The ride to Marisa's apartment was swift.

When Cole reached Marisa's door, it was open a crack. He heard voices and pushed his way inside without invitation.

The scene that greeted him made his blood boil. At the entrance to the living room, Sal and Marisa were locked in a tight embrace, Sal's lips diving for hers. It would have been an arresting tableau even without his appearance as the spurned ex-lover, Cole thought, but his unexpected arrival had turned this into a spectator sport.

"Sal, no!" Marisa tried to shrug out of Piazza's grasp.

The scene before him took on an entirely new cast. Cole sprang forward and yanked Sal away, shoving him up against the wall. He put his face in the sports agent's surprised one.

"She said no," he said between clenched teeth.

"Hey, man…"

Cole gave Piazza a rough shake. "Understand?"

"We were just—"

He slammed the other guy back against the wall. "You were just leaving."

Sal struggled. "Get off me. I have every right to visit my girlfriend."

"Your former girlfriend," Cole corrected.

"Same goes," Sal retorted. "You sports guys think you can have whatever you like whenever you want it. How does it feel to be dumped for a change?"

Cole glanced over at Marisa. He was at a disadvantage

because he didn't know what she had said to Sal and what she hadn't.

She looked at him mutely for an instant, as if dumb-founded, and then stepped closer. "Cole, don't hurt him."

Cole turned back to Sal, staring down the red-faced sports agent.

"I'll sue you," Sal said.

"That's what it's always been about," Cole said. "You hankered for the money and the women, and the other baggage that comes with a pro athlete's life. Is that why you want Marisa back, too?"

Marisa gasped.

Sal gave a disbelieving laugh. "I've wised up. You're on an ego trip, Serenghetti."

"Not as big as the one you're on, Piazza."

Marisa came closer. "Cole, let him go. Sal, you need to leave now."

The threat of violence hung in the air even as Cole dropped his hold and stepped back.

Sal shrugged and straightened his collar. Then he ran his hand through his hair before settling his gaze on Marisa. "You know where to reach me, honey. I'll leave you to give Serenghetti his walking papers. He must have had trouble reading them the first time."

Cole tightened his hand into a fist, but he let the sports agent make his exit without further incident.

When the door to the apartment clicked shut, Marisa turned toward Cole. It was quiet, and they both seemed to realize at the same time that they were now alone to face the charged emotions between them.

"What are you doing here?" Marisa asked.

"Thank you, Cole, for saving me," he replied in a fal-setto voice.

"I can take care of myself."

"Right." He still wanted to break Sal in two. "Here's the

better question. What was Sal doing here, and if he wants you to take him back, why were you resisting?"

"Sal and I aren't back together."

Despite himself, Cole felt better. She hadn't taken Sal back *yet*, and from the looks of things, Sal may just have ruined his chances.

"But I told him the reason wasn't because you and I are still together."

"So he saw his opportunity to press his case?"

Marisa sucked in a breath. "Next question. Why did you show up? You couldn't have known Sal was here."

"Jordan said you were trying to track me down."

She shook her head. "No."

Cole clenched his fist. Either his brother was misinformed, or Jordan had duped him into going to Marisa's apartment. If he hadn't agreed to go, would Jordan have tried to lure Marisa down to the Puck & Shoot instead? One thing was for sure—he was going to do physical violence to his brother, upcoming hockey playoffs or no.

First, though, he needed to get one thing straight. "Fine, you weren't trying to track me down. I've still got something to say."

Marisa stared at him without saying a word.

"You're a beautiful woman. You're ambitious and passionate and worthy of whatever life throws at you. The two of us might be finished, but don't settle for Sal."

He wanted to grab her and kiss her, but that would put him in Piazza's league. Instead, he forced himself to turn and walk out the door.

Marisa expected the senior play to be the last big event on the school calendar at Pershing. She didn't think, though, that the seniors' swan song would also be the place she ran into Cole again—maybe for the last time before he left Welsdale.

Ever since he'd left her apartment last week, she'd been

thinking about him. She wasn't about to take Sal back just because Cole intended to leave town for a coaching job in another state. Sal had only been a convenient smokescreen when Cole had announced he was moving to Wisconsin—and yet the realization that Cole may have been misled had done nothing to ease her heartache...

She also had no idea why Jordan would have told Cole that she was looking for him. Maybe Jordan had been misinformed—or maybe he was trying to get the two of them back together. No, the latter was wishful thinking.

She stole a look at Cole, who was sitting across the aisle in a different section of the auditorium. Would she ever stop yearning where he was concerned? She assumed Cole had been invited to the play by Mr. Dobson because he was a famous alumnus intertwined with the school's plans for the future.

Even with the space separating her and Cole, however, she had trouble concentrating. Even more depressingly, Pershing's seniors were staging *Death of a Salesman*. And as the scene opened, her heart rose to her throat. Because there it was...

The sofa where she had lost her virginity to Cole. Right there on stage. She burned to the roots of her hair. She stared ahead, not daring a glance at Cole. Out of the periphery of her eye, however, she thought she detected a movement of his head in her direction...

Marisa didn't know how she made it through the rest of the play. The sofa...the memories... Cole. She longed to race up the aisle, through the doors to the auditorium and all the way home...where she could console herself in private.

She loved Cole, and he didn't love her in return. It was a replay of high school. And like her mother, she was getting burned by a pro athlete who wanted to pursue his dreams.

Somehow she made it through the whole play. She breathed a sigh of relief when the curtain came down and the student actors took their final bow. Any moment now, she could duck out.

But when the audience finished clapping, Mr. Dobson headed to the stage.

After complimenting the students' efforts, the principal cleared his throat. "I'd like to make some final remarks, if I may. It's been a wonderful year for Pershing School. Our fund-raiser was a huge success, and we are constructing a new school gym." Mr. Dobson paused at the round of applause and cheers. "Great thanks go to Cole Serenghetti and his company for donating construction services. I'm also extremely pleased to announce the new gym will be called The Serg Serenghetti Athletic Building."

Marisa's gaze shot to Cole, but he was looking at Mr. Dobson, clapping like everyone else.

No one got a campus building named after them without making a major monetary donation. In all likelihood, Cole had made a significant cash pledge in addition to donating construction services.

But why?

She'd worked so hard to overcome his resistance to helping with Pershing Shines Bright. The only reason he'd agreed to participate was because of the lucrative construction contract. But now even that profit had evaporated because Cole was making a hefty donation to the school.

Mr. Dobson waited for the audience to settle down. "I'd also like to take this opportunity to welcome our new assistant principal starting next year, Ms. Marisa Danieli."

Marisa blinked, shocked. She hadn't expected that announcement tonight. Caught by surprise, she felt flustered, her heart beginning to pound. Most of all, she felt Cole's eyes on her.

"Ms. Danieli earned her undergraduate and master's degrees from the University of Massachusetts at Amherst. She has been a beloved teacher at Pershing for almost ten years, and a tireless and invaluable member of the school community. Marisa, please come up here, and everyone, join me in congratulating her."

Marisa felt a squeeze on her arm as one of her fellow teachers congratulated her, and then she got up and walked to the stage on rubbery legs. The audience applauded, and there were hoots and hollers from the student body.

The minute Marisa was on stage, she sought out Cole with her eyes, but he was inscrutable, clapping along with everyone else. Had he played a role in her promotion? Had he put in a good word for her, as the school's current and likely most valuable benefactor?

She felt the prickle of tears.

Mr. Dobson was looking at her expectantly, so she cleared her throat and forced herself to speak. "Thank you. I'm thrilled to be Pershing School's new assistant principal. Almost twenty years ago, I walked through the front doors here for the first time. I was a scholarship student, and Pershing changed my life." She paused. "You could say I've gone from being called to the principal's office to having the room next to the principal's office. The distance is short, but the road's been long!"

There was a smattering of laughter and a lot of applause.

"I'm looking forward to my new role." Marisa smiled and then shook hands with Mr. Dobson.

As she stepped off the stage and made her way back to her seat, the principal wished everyone a good night, and the audience began to stand and gather their things.

Marisa hoped she could make a quick escape. She needed to get her emotions under control and to take time to process everything that had happened. But she was waylaid by congratulations, and by the time she was finished, Cole stood at the end of her aisle.

Cole's expression gave nothing away. She, on the other hand, was crumbling.

She pasted a smile on her face and took the initiative— she was the new assistant principal, after all. "Congratulations. You must be thrilled about the new building being named for your father."

"He's excited about the honor."

They stared at each other.

She clasped her hands together to keep from fidgeting. It was either that or give in to the urge to touch him. "So you're ready to embrace your alma mater?"

"That's one way to interpret a large donation."

"Thank you."

Cole still looked indecipherable. "Are you speaking in your role as the new assistant principal?"

"Yes. *And as the woman who loves you.*

He nodded curtly.

"Did you put in a good word for me?" she asked impulsively, knowing she might not get another chance. "Did you pull strings?"

"Does it matter?"

"Did you?" she persisted against all reason.

Cole shrugged. "It turns out my endorsement wasn't needed. You were the overwhelming favorite for the job."

She swallowed. "Thank you."

"You worked hard. You got what you wanted."

Not quite. She didn't have him. She'd never have him.

Just then, a Pershing board member came up to them. "Cole, there's someone I'd like to introduce you to."

Marisa was thankful to be saved from any additional awkwardness with Cole. Murmuring her goodbyes, she turned and fled down the aisle, head bent. She was sure anyone who saw her face would be able to read the raw emotion on it.

Tears welled again, and she made for the exit nearest the stage. Everyone else was streaming toward the doors at the back of the auditorium, which led to the street and parking lot. But she needed a moment alone before reaching her car. She didn't know if she could manage even a small blithe lie to explain away why she was crying.

In the hall beyond the exit, she made a beeline for the closest door, and found herself in the theater department's dimly lit prop room. Furniture was stacked everywhere, some of it covered by drop cloths.

Hearing footsteps outside, she reached behind her and turned the lock on the door and then leaned against the frame.

Someone tried the knob. "Marisa?"

Cole. She said nothing—hoping he'd go away.

"Marisa?" Cole knocked. "Are you okay?"

No, she wasn't. He didn't love her. He was leaving. Nothing was okay.

"You looked upset when you said goodbye. Let me in, sweet pea."

Why? So he could leave her again? She didn't think she could stand it. She strangled a sob and hoped he didn't hear it.

She heard Cole move away from the door, and irrational disappointment hit. Moments later, however, she heard the click of a lock, and then the door was creaking open.

She stepped back and turned to face Cole. "Underhanded and sneaky."

He pocketed a Swiss Army knife. "I learned to pick locks in the Boy Scouts." Then he looked around the room. "We have to stop meeting this way."

"We're safe. The sofa is still onstage."

Cole searched her face and then quirked his lips. "Depends on how you define safe."

Marisa's heart clenched. No, she wasn't safe…and yet she felt like she was home whenever she was near him. "Is there anything you do that doesn't involve bulldozing?"

"Not if I'm going to continue to be the CEO of Serenghetti Construction."

Her eyes went wide. "Is that what you want?"

He gazed at her and then slowly stepped forward, his

look tender. He lifted her chin and brushed a thumb across her cheek. "I want you. Marisa, I love you."

She parted her lips and sucked in a tremulous breath, her world tilting.

"I've never said those words to a woman before." He glanced around the storage room before his gaze came back to hers. "And this isn't the way I was envisioning things, but the word at the Puck & Shoot is that you told Sal you wouldn't take him back. Give me a chance, sweet pea."

"You're leaving," she said in a wobbly voice.

"No, I'm not. I'm not taking the job in Wisconsin. I'm staying here to run Serenghetti Construction."

She rested her hand on his arm. "You were angry at me in high school because I interfered with your hockey dreams. I'm not going to make the same mistake twice."

"You're not," he said affectionately. "I'll be coaching here in Welsdale. I'll be teaching teenagers who want to improve their game for a shot at a college scholarship or even the NHL." He paused. "Because I know how life-changing those college scholarships can be."

Her heart swelled. She adored this man.

"The more time I had to think about selling Serenghetti Construction, the more it didn't seem right. I had to acknowledge that construction is in my blood." He tilted his head. "Besides, I've got some ideas, including growing the business into a real estate development firm."

Marisa smiled. "Face it, Serenghetti Construction is just another arena for you to be competitive. That's why you were so set on winning over JM Construction. And who knows? The kids you're coaching may give you another chance at a hockey championship."

"Sometimes, Marisa, I swear you know me better than I know myself." He brushed her lips with his.

"Hang on to that thought because I plan to be around a lot." Cole was good, strong and hardworking. He also happened to be able to make her feel like the sexiest woman alive. He was the person she'd always been looking for.

"You're marrying a construction guy."

"Are you proposing?"

He twined his fingers with hers and raised her hand to his lips. "Damn right."

"I'm ratting you out, Cole, and this time I don't care who finds out." Her voice grew husky with emotion. "I'm telling everyone that you confessed your undying love for me. That you proposed!"

He kissed her. "You forgot *he can't keep his hands off me*, *he talks dirty to me*, and *he gets hard just thinking about me*."

"That's right."

"I'm in love with you."

"Good to know. I love you, too."

She sighed, and he kissed her again.

Epilogue

If they pulled this off, it would be Cole's biggest prank ever.

Leave it to her soon-to-be husband to involve her in the ultimate practical joke. Around her, guests mingled while waitstaff circulated with hors d'oeuvres. Everyone was unaware of what was to come next.

Marisa rubbed nervous palms on her column dress and then brushed aside the curls of hair that caressed her naked shoulders. As she did so, the diamond ring on her finger caught and reflected the light of the chandelier in the main ballroom of the Welsdale Golf & Tennis Club.

At the dais, Cole cleared his throat and called for attention, wineglass in hand. When everyone quieted, he said, "Thank you for joining us tonight. Marisa and I wanted to throw a big party to celebrate our engagement, so there are over two hundred of you here. Big love, big party—"

There was a smattering of laughter and applause.

Cole straightened his tie. "As some of you know, Marisa and I have had more excitement on the way to the altar than most people witness in an NHL game."

Their guests grinned and laughed.

"I had a crush on her in high school." He paused. "And I know what you all are thinking. Pershing's super jock and practical joker thought he had a chance with the beautiful, smart girl who sat in front of him in economics class? She had a mind and a body that turned him into brainless teenage mush."

Marisa swallowed against the sudden lump in her throat.

Cole shrugged. "So I did the only logical thing. I hid how I felt and told no one. Flash forward fifteen years. I got lucky when my fantasy woman skated onto my rink again. This time I knew I wasn't going to let her get away. I asked her to marry me."

Marisa blinked rapidly. Everything Cole had said was true, and yet, he'd cast it in a light that she'd never seen before.

Cole extended his arm. "Marisa, I love you."

A path opened for Marisa as people stepped aside. On shaky legs, she walked toward Cole, who gazed at her with love in his eyes. She placed her hand in his, and raising the skirt of her dress with the other she stepped up onto the dais.

Their friends and family hooted and clapped.

"That was quite a speech," she murmured for Cole's ears only. "I nearly ruined my makeup."

He grinned. "You would have looked gorgeous for the photos anyway."

"You're blinded by love."

"I wouldn't have it any other way, sweet pea." He gave her a quick peck on the lips before turning back to their audience, keeping his hand linked with hers.

"Save the PDA for the honeymoon," Jordan called from the side of the room, to much laughter.

"Thanks for the great lead-in," Cole answered. "Because Marisa and I are getting married. Tonight. Right now."

There were audible gasps, and people looked at each other.

The officiant she and Cole had chosen stepped forward from the side of the room.

"Surprise," Cole announced, and then he pulled Marisa into his embrace for another kiss.

When Cole had first suggested the idea of a surprise wedding, Marisa had thought he was kidding, but she couldn't have asked for anything more. She felt like a bride in every sense. She'd paired an embroidered lace-and-ivory gown with high-heeled gold sandals. And of course, she'd marry Cole anytime, anywhere.

There was a flurry of activity as their guests allowed themselves to be shepherded out of the ballroom and into one that had been secretly set up for a wedding ceremony. A photographer would be documenting the festivities, and a florist waited nearby to hand Marisa a tightly packed bouquet of white roses.

Marisa felt her heart swell, and then caught Cole's grin. Suddenly struck with an idea, she bit back a mischievous smile.

"Oh, Cole, this has been so overwhelming. I think…I think…" She closed her eyes and pretended to swoon melodramatically.

Cole wrapped strong arms around her. "Marisa?"

She opened her eyes and said teasingly, "I'll be falling into your embrace for the rest of our lives."

Cole grinned. "I'll always be here to catch you."

And they sealed their bargain with a kiss.

* * * * *

MILLS & BOON®

Desire™

PASSIONATE AND DRAMATIC LOVE STORIES

A sneak peek at next month's titles...

In stores from 8th September 2016:

- **The Rancher Returns** – Brenda Jackson *and*
  The Black Sheep's Secret Child – Cat Schield

- **The Pregnancy Proposition** – Andrea Laurence *and*
  His Secret Baby Bombshell – Jules Bennett

- **His Illegitimate Heir** – Sarah M. Anderson *and*
  Convenient Cowgirl Bride – Silver James

Just can't wait?
Buy our books online a month before they hit the shops!
www.millsandboon.co.uk

Also available as eBooks.

MILLS & BOON®

18 bundles of joy from your favourite authors!

Get 2 books free when you buy the complete collection only at
www.millsandboon.co.uk/greatoffers